The Last of the Great Romantics

Claudia Carroll

BANTAM BOOKS

LONDON • TORONTO • SYDNEY • AUCKLAND • JOHANNESBURG

THE LAST OF THE GREAT ROMANTICS
A BANTAM BOOK: 0553816659
9780553816655

Originally published in Great Britain by Bantam Press,
a division of Transworld Publishers

PRINTING HISTORY
Bantam Press edition published 2005
Bantam edition published 2006

3 5 7 9 10 8 6 4 2

Set in 12.25/15.5pt Bembo by
Falcon Oast Graphic Art Ltd.

Bantam Books are published by Transworld Publishers,
61–63 Uxbridge Road, London W5 5SA,
a division of The Random House Group Ltd,
in Australia by Random House Australia (Pty) Ltd,
20 Alfred Street, Milsons Point, Sydney, NSW 2061, Australia,
in New Zealand by Random House New Zealand Ltd,
18 Poland Road, Glenfield, Auckland 10, New Zealand
and in South Africa by Random House (Pty) Ltd, Isle of Houghton,
Corner of Boundary Road & Carse O'Gowrie, Houghton 2198, South Africa.

Printed and bound in Great Britain by
Cox & Wyman Ltd, Reading, Berkshire.

Papers used by Transworld Publishers are natural, recyclable products
made from wood grown in sustainable forests. The manufacturing
processes conform to the environmental regulations of the
country of origin.

For all the hopeless romantics out there.
You are not alone.

ACKNOWLEDGEMENTS

Thanks to Marianne Gunn O'Connor, for her calm wisdom and for everything she's done for me in the last year. I really couldn't be happier, luckier or more grateful.

Thanks to Pat Lynch, for his patience and encouragement (not to mention all the great nights out on the town).

Thanks to everyone at Transworld, especially Francesca Liversidge for her brilliant editing (and shopping tips!), Nicky Jeanes and Laura Sherlock. Roll on your next trip to Dublin!

Thanks to Declan Heeney for organizing such an amazing launch party for *He loves me not . . . he loves me.* (I swear, this man could run the country, with one hand tied behind his back. Easy.)

Thanks to Gill and Simon Hess for all their hard work.

Thanks to Vicki Satlow for everything she's done.

Thanks to Anne and Claude, my wonderful parents,

and all the family, especially my aunt Mai in Scotland, a great mentor and a great friend.

Thanks to Patricia Scanlan, Kate Thompson, Maureen McGlynn and Eleanor Minihan for all their support.

On a personal note, thanks to all my amazing friends for all the encouragement you gave me in the last year. Special thanks to Clelia Murphy (for coming with me on the book signings and generally putting up with me), Anita Notaro, wonderful neighbour and friend (or the Champagne Sheilas, as we're in danger of becoming known!), Susan McHugh, Sean Murphy, Karen Nolan, Larry Finnegan, Madge MacLaverty, Lise-Ann McLaughlin, Marion O'Dwyer, Pat Kinevane, Alison McKenna, Frank Mackey, Sharon Hogan, Karen Hastings, Kevin Reynolds, the Gunn family, Kevin Murnane, Ailsa Doyle, Hilary Reynolds and Fiona Lalor.

Special thanks to Maeve McGrath for all her help when I was researching this (otherwise I'd never have known what it's like inside the players' box at a soccer match!).

Thanks to everyone at RTE, especially all in *Fair City*.

Finally, thanks to everyone who gave me such support and said such kind words about *He loves me not . . . he loves me*. It really meant the world to me.

Prologue

' "A HANDBAG?" '

' "Yes, Lady Bracknell, I was in a handbag – a somewhat large, black leather handbag, with handles to it – an ordinary handbag in fact." '

' "In what locality did this Mr James, or Thomas, Cardew come across this ordinary handbag?" '

' "In the cloakroom at Victoria station. It was given to him in mistake for his own." '

' "The cloakroom at Victoria station?" '

' "Yes. The Brighton line." '

'CUT!' snarled a voice from the bowels of the pitch-black auditorium.

'Oh bugger,' Lady Bracknell whispered. 'We're for it.'

'Just out of curiosity,' came the voice from the shadows, dripping with dry sarcasm, 'have either of you talentless travesties bothered doing even the slightest bit of work on your English accents? Bonecrusher Barnes, with a performance like that, if you're not careful you'll end up in a soap opera. Jordan or, God help us, even Jade Goody could do a more upper-class accent than you any day. And you're a thundering disgrace in that corset; you're walking like a drag queen. Lady Bracknell is one of the greatest parts ever written for a woman and you should be honoured to be playing it. Even if you're a man.'

Lady Bracknell hung his shaved head in shame and muttered an apology under his breath.

'He's very tough, isn't he?' whispered one prison warder to another from the back of the auditorium.

'Shhh!' urged his colleague, panicking like a schoolboy afraid of the headmaster's wrath. 'No talking during rehearsals. Mad Jasper nearly killed a warder last year for chatting in the middle of the *West Side Story* dress rehearsal. Said he was putting the cast off. He'll separate us in a minute if we're not careful.'

They were interrupted by the door to the rear of the auditorium opening and another officer joined them, panting and out of breath.

'Howaya, Mick,' the second warder mouthed silently at him, indicating for him to sit down and shut up.

'Lads, I've awful news. You won't believe what the

Governor just told me. What's the mood like this morning?'

'*Quiet at the back of the hall!*' roared Mad Jasper. 'Or I will personally rip your philistine heads off. You're a waste of organs, the lot of you.'

'Judge for yourself,' whispered the first prison officer. 'And stop talking or you'll get us all into trouble.'

Mad Jasper then turned the full force of his venom back to his trembling cast.

'Now, I have directed three prison drama shows and I have had three nervous breakdowns. That's the level of commitment I'm bringing to this play so excuse the hell out of me for expecting no less from you lazy shower of artistically challenged gobshites. Back to Lady Bracknell and Gwendolen's first entrance and this time I want to see a bit of respect for Oscar Wilde and the majesty of the text, if that's not asking too much.'

Unseen by Mad Jasper, there was a flurried, whispered conversation going on at the back, all three prison officers taking advantage of his attention being momentarily elsewhere.

'You're joking, Mick,' said one, his face suddenly ashen with shock.

'Not a word of a lie. The Governor is in bits. God love the poor man, he's the one who's going to have to break it to him.'

'I don't bloody believe it,' said the other, stunned. 'Mad

Jasper finally makes parole in the middle of production week, with three days to the opening night? Jesus Christ, we'll be lucky if he doesn't kill us.'

Chapter One

Portia yawned, stretched and wondered why the bed beside her felt so cold. In her half-asleep state, she'd instinctively reached out to snuggle up against her husband and was startled not to feel his warm, naked body beside her. Odd. She strained to listen for a moment, just in case he was moving around their tiny kitchen downstairs, making steaming mugs of tea for them both and slathering wedges of butter on to fresh toast, just the way she liked it. Serving his wife breakfast in bed was a ritual which Andrew religiously observed, no matter how late they'd been out the previous night. And boy had last night been a late one, Portia thought, pulling the duvet over her head in a futile attempt to try and keep warm.

Yesterday had been Valentine's Day and even though

they could ill afford it, Andrew had insisted on whisking her off to dinner in the Lemon Tree, Kildare's newest, trendiest and most expensive restaurant. 'I know tomorrow's a big day,' he'd said, not brooking no for an answer, 'but we've both worked like Trojans and we bloody well deserve a night off. Besides, the world and its sick dog are going to be at the grand opening tomorrow night, how will I even get a chance to talk to my sexy, gorgeous wife?'

So, smiling, Portia had shoehorned herself into the only weight-minimizing little black dress she possessed and happily allowed her husband to escort her to dinner.

The Lemon Tree was clearly the hippest place to be that night, she thought as the maître d' led them to their table, weaving his way through the roomful of well-dressed diners who thronged the restaurant, filling it to capacity. Although it was mainly lovey-dovey couples eating out that night, Portia was still aware of every female eye in the room silently clocking her husband as they were escorted to their window table which overlooked the minimalist, Japanese-style gardens beneath. A tiny, familiar, momentary pang of insecurity struck her, which she immediately brushed aside. For God's sake, look at him, she thought as the maître d' held out her chair for her; how could you blame any normal heterosexual woman in her right mind for staring at him? And with a flood of love which brought a flush to her cheeks she looked across the table to her husband of almost eighteen months.

At thirty-seven, he was just a few months older than her, although he'd never quite lost that boyish, Robert-Redford-circa-1975-before-he-started-to-turn-into-a-dried-sultana look he always had about him. Tall and fair-haired, he was dressed in a navy suit which brought out his twinkly deep blue eyes and a sexy, crumpled white linen shirt. In short, he looked like a movie star. Not for the first time, she silently marvelled that someone like her could have had the sheer good fortune to land a man like Andrew de Courcey. And what he'd given up for her!

When they'd first met, Portia was struggling to maintain her family's ancestral home, Davenport Hall, a vast, crumbling, eighteenth-century manor house set in over two thousand acres of prime Kildare farmland. Struggling being the operative word. In fact, so run-down, rotting and neglected was the Hall back then, it had become a sort of joke amongst the locals in the neighbouring town of Ballyroan. Alcatraz, they used to call it. Dachau-sur-mer. Or Wuthering Depths, if they were feeling particularly vicious. Portia's long-cherished dream had been to restore the Hall to its former glory and then run it as a luxury five-star hotel. However, she was continually hampered by the family's total lack of funds, exacerbated by the fact that her father, the ninth Lord Davenport, had pretty much gambled away anything they possessed which was of any value. So, in true Cinderella-style, she had fully resigned herself to a life of genteel destitution – poverty behind lace curtains – along with her mother, Lucasta, and younger sister Daisy. Until Andrew came along.

They'd fallen in love and married a disgracefully short length of time after they'd first met, as her mother-in-law never ceased to remind them. He'd spent years working as a successful corporate lawyer in New York and, like most lawyers at the top of their game, had made a fortune there. However, instead of setting up his own practice and scaling the corporate heights to amass even greater wealth, he suddenly decided to jack in the whole rat race. In a career U-turn of which Ronald Reagan or even Arnold Schwarzenegger would have been proud, he came to a decision he'd yet to regret. If Portia wanted to restore Davenport Hall to what it once was, then he was determined to help her realize that dream. He'd slowly come to love the Hall almost as much as she did and the idea of transforming it into one of the most salubrious, classically elegant country house hotels in Ireland was a challenge he couldn't resist.

'Just don't ask me to get involved in the day-to-day running of it, honey,' he'd said to her at the time. 'That is, unless you actually want Basil Fawlty in charge of the place.'

It was an overwhelming gesture. Never having had

money of her own, Portia found it difficult to spend someone else's and Andrew certainly wasn't one to cut corners. His mantra was: 'Penny wise, pound foolish. If this is worth doing, then it's worth doing it properly.' His one and only condition, it turned out, was that he and Portia first renovate the nearby gate lodge and live there while the building work on the Hall proper was under way. It was an arrangement which suited everybody; they were only two miles from the Hall, although still on the Davenport land, and Portia got to decorate the tiny lodge in the simple, fresh style which she loved: all wooden floors and pristine white walls, so utterly different to the high ceilings and opulent Georgian splendour of the Hall. Andrew, moreover, got to begin life as a married man without the added pressure of living under the same roof as his mother-in-law, Lucasta. Not that he didn't adore her; he was one of the few people who got a great kick out of her oddities and eccentricities. One of the very few. Even Portia had to admit that her mother would try the patience of a pontiff.

They were barely three months into the restoration project when the foreman on the job handed in his notice. 'I'm responsible for two dozen men on this site,' he'd explained to Portia, 'and your ma keeps plying them with drink from lunchtime on. Happy hour, she calls it, and that's one thing, but by three o'clock my lads are too plastered to plaster. I can handle her doing their bleedin' star charts for them, I can even handle her telling us that we all worked on the pyramids in a past life – says she remembers cos she used to be Cleopatra – but this, I cannot take. I'm a professional, you know. Suppose one of them fell down off the scaffolding? They'd be rightly tequila slammed then.'

The final straw came when he discovered one of Lucasta's army of cats had done its business right inside his hard hat. He was gone in a matter of moments.

'Just as well,' Andrew had said as his white van drove away. 'If I had to listen to him say: "Now I can't even touch that till Tuesday," once more, I'd have screamed.'

'And have you noticed the way a lot of the coving on the ceiling in the Ballroom is completely offline?' Lucasta had asked him innocently as they walked back inside the Hall. 'Wouldn't surprise me in the least if that gobshite had a glass eye. I won't say what I really think of him, though, because you know how I like to be nice about people. So let's just say it rhymes with trucking tanker.'

There were no two ways about it, Andrew had been the driving force behind the whole project, entrusting only the best and most expensive restoration team with the mammoth job of gutting, reroofing and completely renovating the Hall from top to bottom. Only Christopher Johnson, the country's top architect, was deemed experienced enough by Andrew to handle the enormity of the task. And so, together, he and Portia ploughed every penny of his hard-earned cash back into the Hall – but the substantial savings he'd made from his annual six-figure salary were not even enough to cover the initial estimate. As with all building jobs, they'd gone way over budget within a matter of months and were left with no choice but to remortgage the Hall, on the assumption that once it was up and running as a successful country house hotel, their ship would well and truly have come in.

It didn't stop Portia from worrying though. From worrying herself sick. If there was a tiny blight on the happiness she'd known since her marriage, it was her awareness of the full extent of the debt she'd plunged her husband into. If it weren't for her, he could be enjoying his money and living the high life, she used to think, instead of fretting about how in God's name they were ever going to ask their interior designer for further credit. She was only too well aware of the fact that her esteemed mother-in-law never lost an opportunity to raise this subject.

'So, Portia Davenport has finally got what she wanted. She's frittered away every last penny of Andrew's on that God-awful monstrosity, and now he's as destitute as she ever was. All the Davenports are the very same, you know, never happy till they're bankrupt. Well, she's certainly dragged him into the mire with her and I just hope she's happy, that's all I can say.'

Susan de Courcey was nothing if not a lady, though. She only ever said this behind Portia's back.

As ever, Andrew seemed to be reading her thoughts. Reaching across the table, he lifted the unopened menu from her and gently cupped his hand over hers, his wedding ring glinting under the candlelight. 'Don't spoil tomorrow by worrying, darling. The Davenport Hotel is going to be the biggest success story of the decade, I can feel it. Best investment I ever made. In two years' time, we'll have trebled our money. There'll be a six-month waiting list to get into the restaurant and every A-list celebrity in the world is going to want to have their wedding there. Trust me.'

She looked him square in the eye and smiled, blushing prettily as she always did when it was just the two of them, alone. Andrew was brimming over with confidence and was so full of enthusiasm that it was virtually impossible not to get swept up in the maelstrom of all that positive energy.

'What's so funny, my lady?'

'Nothing. You make me feel like a young girl of thirty-six all over again.'

Portia sat up in the bed, straining to hear sounds of life downstairs. Nothing. Not a peep. She'd half expected Andrew to walk through the bedroom door, breakfast tray in hand and hop back into bed beside her, as he normally would, but there was no sign of him. Hauling herself up on to one elbow she stretched over to the alarm clock on his side of the bed. Jesus Christ, she thought, suddenly wide awake, eleven a.m.! No wonder the lodge is so quiet; he must have let me sleep on and gone up to the Hall by himself. In one movement, she'd leapt out of bed, shivering, and thrown on the first thing that came to hand: a pair of grey tracksuit bottoms and an oversized fleece jumper to match. She paused briefly to glance at herself in the gilt mirror on her dressing table and then wished she hadn't. She'd had way too much to drink in the Lemon Tree last night and boy, did it show. Her eyes were bloodshot and puffy and her normally pale, white skin now looked grey and saggy.

That was the trouble with being thirty-six, she thought, one night on the tear and I look like I need a blood transfusion. She scraped her light-brown shoulder-length hair back into a ponytail to conceal how greasy it was and hastily pulled on a pair of runners. Plenty of time for glamour later, she thought, seeing the stunning new evening dress Andrew had bought her to wear at the grand opening tonight peeping out from behind the open wardrobe door. It was a snug-fitting cocktail dress, pillar-box red and deeply unforgiving, considering the extra few pounds she'd gained since she'd got married.

Portia had always been one of those lucky, naturally slim people who measured their weight gain in ounces rather than pounds, but ever since she'd met Andrew, her whole metabolism seemed to have drastically slowed down to a snail's pace. She wasn't exactly overweight but certainly had ballooned from a small size ten to a large size fourteen. They ate out a lot, she reasoned, which she'd never done before she got married, and anyhow Andrew always said he liked her the size she was now. 'Happiness fat' he used to tease her. So when it came to the tight red dress, he'd categorically refused to take no for an answer. 'It looks stunning on you,' he'd said as she shyly emerged from the fitting room of Khan, one of Kildare's swankiest and most expensive boutiques. 'And I don't care what it costs. Half the county's going to be at the opening and I want my wife looking the part.'

Personally, the only part she thought it made her look was that of an overweight dancer at the Moulin Rouge, and it seemed like such an unnecessary extravagance when she'd plenty of other more suitable outfits at home, but as long as Andrew was happy . . .

Racing downstairs, she grabbed her car keys and was about to dash out of the front door when a flickering red light on the answering machine by the hall table suddenly halted her in her tracks. She hurriedly pressed the replay button, silently praying that it wasn't some catastrophe which would delay her even more. Between florists arriving and last-minute changes to the guest list, never mind somehow trying to squeeze in a hair appointment for herself, she'd quite enough on her plate without any other hassles. The first message was from her younger sister Daisy, politely enquiring whether she could borrow a particular evening dress for the night's festivities, one she'd had her eye on for ages.

'Hi fat arse, it's me.' Daisy was nothing if not direct. 'Let's face it, unless you have surgery the black Donna Karan ain't never getting over your thunder thighs ever again, so *pleeease*, pretty *pleeease* with knobs on, can I have a borrow? I swear I won't sweat into it or puke on it or hand it back to you in a Tesco's bag like the last time . . .'

Portia rolled her eyes to heaven, obediently hoofing back upstairs to get the dress for her. Daisy was one of those people it was just impossible to say no to. Not that her sister needed expensive, designer clothes to make her look well. At just twenty-two, Daisy was unquestionably the beauty of the family, tall like all the Davenports, but rake-thin, with ice-blue eyes and a mane of cascading blonde curls. She was often told that she could make a fortune as a model but Daisy had absolutely no interest in either clothes or fashion, preferring instead to muck around in jodhpurs and woolly jumpers and simply borrow from her big sister when the need arose.

She was to be the Davenport Hotel's new equestrian manager, with sole responsibility for over a dozen stabled horses, a job which didn't exactly call for ball gowns and tiaras. Her voice was still resonating all over the tiny hallway as Portia rushed back downstairs again. Daisy didn't believe in leaving a message on the answering machine when a three-act radio play would do instead.

'And, by the way, don't bother with brekkie, you wouldn't believe the *yummy-licious* fry-up Tim's made, totally organic you know, and there's a pile left over so . . .'

Portia pressed the fast forward button on the machine, knowing full well that she'd have driven to the Hall in the time it would take for Daisy to shut up rabbiting.

The second message was from Andrew, sounding crackly and miles away, as though he was calling from a mobile in his car.

'Hey, sleeping beauty, hope you're not feeling too hung over after last night. Perfect way to spend Valentine's night, if you ask me, getting drunk and doing it twice.'

Portia smiled, glad there was no one else around to overhear.

'Look, darling, I've had to come to Dublin for a meeting. It was urgent; I couldn't get out of it. All very last minute, but don't worry, I'll be back at the Hall by three at the latest and I'll explain then.'

She did an involuntary double-take; who on earth could he be meeting in Dublin? And what could be so important that he'd drop everything to drive almost forty miles for it? And today of all days too, when she was up to her eyes and totally reliant on his being there . . . Her train of thought was interrupted, however, by Daisy's voice leaving yet another message. 'Oh, for God's sake, I'm bringing the bloody dress,' Portia shouted in exasperation at the machine, grabbing her house keys and opening the door.

But there was something in the tone of her sister's voice which made her stop dead in her tracks.

'Portia, it's me. Get here at once, will you? It's urgent.'

It was a magnificent, cloudless day as Portia stepped out into the watery winter sunshine and hopped into her car, foot to the floor for the two-mile drive up to the Hall. It's just Daisy being theatrical, as usual, she thought. Her sister was prone to exaggerating somewhat; she'd never have a mild headache, when a brain tumour would do. Probably just another slanging match between Tim and Mrs Flanagan which needed refereeing, as if she didn't have enough to get on with.

Tim Philips was the new head chef at the Hall, headhunted by Andrew from L'Hôtel de Paris, one of only three Michelin-starred restaurants in Dublin.

'If this venture is going to work, then the Davenport hotel has to become famous for its restaurant,' Andrew had said, justifying the huge salary he was offering Tim to relocate. 'I want it to be easier to win the Nobel Peace Prize than it is to get a table here. That's the way all the top restaurants in New York are run now, honey,' he'd gone on, seeing the worried look on her face. 'The more difficult it's perceived to get a table, the more people will pay. Build it and they will come.'

So Tim had arrived some weeks ago and proceeded to make himself at home in the newly refurbished state-of-the-art kitchen. He was nothing like what Portia had expected: he was in his early forties, small and wiry with an oversized bald head like a scrubbed potato and a comb-over hairstyle which only attracted attention to his shiny, greasy pate. Within days, he'd proved his mettle though, designing a mouth-watering menu and helping Portia whittle down to a manageable few the dozens of applicants who were practically queuing up to work as sous-chefs for him.

There was only one fly in the ointment, though. The Davenports' original housekeeper and old family retainer, Mrs Flanagan.

'She's been here ever since I was in nappies,' Portia had patiently tried to explain to Andrew. 'It's hard for her to be unceremoniously turfed out of the kitchen she's worked in all these years.'

But turfed out she was. Poor Mrs Flanagan was already feeling a bit miffed at having been made redundant by a hotshot like Tim Philips, when, on top of ruthlessly throwing out every knackered kitchen appliance she'd held on to for years, he also removed her TV from the kitchen, along with the tatty armchair she used to sit in for hours watching daytime TV. (Mrs Flanagan's idea of a hard day's work was one where she managed to fit in *Ricki Lake* and *Oprah* on top of all her beloved soaps.)

'Bad baldy aul' bastard with yer electronic fucking juicer!' Mrs Flanagan had roared at him. 'Be careful now ya don't juice one of yer testicles by accident, won't ya?' The final straw had been when he put a blanket ban on smoking outside in the kitchen garden.

'It's far too close to the food-preparation area,' he had explained to Portia in his snivelly, nasal voice, 'and it's playing havoc with my sinuses.'

'I'm within me rights to smoke outside!' Mrs Flanagan had ranted. 'Forty years I'm working here and all of a sudden I can't have a fag? I get through sixty a day and no one's ever complained before.'

'That's because they're all too poisoned by her Dublin coddle to speak,' Andrew had remarked to Portia later. 'You've really got to toughen up and stop being so bloody sentimental here. She is without doubt the most useless housekeeper I've ever seen. And anyway, at her age shouldn't she be thinking about retiring?'

In eighteen months, it was the only thing they'd rowed about. Portia had resolutely stuck to her guns though, insisting that Mrs Flanagan was as good as family and that letting her go was out of the question, not to mention the fact that she had nowhere else to go. They eventually reached a compromise of sorts by giving her the job and title of 'Housekeeping Supervisor', with full responsibility for the small army of chambermaids now employed at the Hall. The job came with a smart black uniform and a nametag, which shut Mrs Flanagan up for the time being, although violent flare-ups still regularly broke out between her and Tim.

'Hand on heart, I've honestly never met anyone like her,' Andrew used to gripe. 'She is quite capable of having a feud with someone and carrying it well into the next generation – over a single oven chip.'

Portia had arrived at the main entrance to the Hall by now and, once again, felt her spirits soar at how impressive it looked. Having spent a year and a half looking at filthy scaffolding and the cracks of builders' arses, as Daisy so poetically put it, it never failed to make her soul sing to see the finished result. The outside stone walls had been sandblasted and were now gleaming white in the watery winter sunshine. Some of the sash windows at ground level were thrown open and she could see Molly, one of the new chambermaids, vigorously polishing the insides of them till they shone. The restoration work had extended to the grounds as well and a whole team of landscape gardeners had collectively bust a gut to have the front lawn looking as elegantly manicured as it did now. A huge surge of pride filled her as she took it all in and, for a moment, she felt all Andrew's confidence was completely justified. The Davenport Hotel was going to work, she could feel it. They'd all worked so hard and the place was looking its pristine best, better than it had done since it was built, over two centuries ago. What could go wrong?

Snapping out of her reverie, she noticed that the van of Fitzpatrick's, the local florist, was parked in the forecourt. Brilliant, she needed to talk to them about the centrepiece arrangement in the main hallway. She'd requested a colossal, towering display of white lilies dotted with long-stemmed red roses, like you saw in all the posh magazines. Hopping out of her car, she was purposefully striding across the gravel when the main door was thrown open and Daisy came bolting out, white as a ghost. Something about the expression on her face sent a sharp stab of worry right to Portia's heart.

'Thank God you're here,' she said, out of breath, 'I've been watching out for you . . . Oh Portia, there's been some awful news.'

'Darling, tell me,' said Portia, starting to feel sick.

'We've just had a phone call from the Irish consulate in the States. It's Daddy.' Daisy was starting to sob by now. 'He's dead.'

Chapter Two

'So sad to think that the last words I ever spoke to my husband in this life were: "Is that smell you, you dirty bollocks?"' Lucasta, Lady Davenport, was nothing if not a gifted actress and now slotted into the anguished role of grief-stricken widow with comparative ease. 'And you know, darling, I had a premonition that something awful like this was going to happen. My toenails didn't grow at all yesterday.'

It was past midday, but she was still tucked up in her enormous four-poster bed, wearing a green wax jacket over her nightie and chain-smoking as she cradled Edward and Mrs Simpson, two of her favourite cats, close to her. Daisy was sitting on the edge of the bed beside her, clutching a snotty Kleenex and red-eyed from crying, when Portia finally came back into the bedroom.

'Did you manage to get him?' asked Daisy, dully.

'Mobile's switched off.'

She'd spent the past half-hour trying to contact Andrew to tell him the news, but couldn't get through to him. Suddenly a searing flush of anger came over her. 'I mean, where in God's name is he? What could be more important to him than being here and today of all days? And now, on top of everything else, I get this news and he doesn't even have his bloody phone switched on.' Hot, stinging tears of frustration started to roll down Portia's face.

'Shh, darling, shhh,' said Daisy soothingly, rising to hug her tightly. 'It's very common to feel anger at first when you get news of bereavement. Just let it out. It's OK.'

'There's bugger all about this that's OK if you ask me,' said Lucasta from the bed, lighting one cigarette from another. 'Of all the rotten days for the bastard to die on. Never in all my past lives have I come across anyone as inconsiderate as your gobshite of a father. The word wanker is bandied about so freely these days but, by Christ, it's the only way you can describe Blackjack Davenport. Even from beyond the grave, he's still pissing me off.'

It was one of the rare occasions when Portia actually found herself in agreement with her mother. Lord Davenport, known far and wide as 'Blackjack' because of his addiction to the game, was never going to be eligible for a father of the year award, certainly as far as his elder daughter was concerned. He'd casually walked out on his wife and family a couple of years back, with his nineteen-year-old girlfriend in tow, made it as far as Las Vegas, Nevada, and stayed put. His family had only seen him once since then, but from what Portia could gather, he'd lived out the rest of his days in a suite at the five-star Bellagio Hotel, dating a string of younger women who worked in what's euphemistically known as 'the entertainment industry', boozing heavily by day and gambling by night, almost like a caricature of a lord from days gone by. In short, it was a lifestyle even George Best would have envied. He'd died of a massive heart attack at his beloved blackjack table, clutching a winning hand close to his chest. The barman had gone looking for him, twigging that something must be amiss when Blackjack went for a whole half-hour without demanding that his whisky and soda be freshened up.

'Not exactly a beautiful death, but at least it's the way he would have wanted to go,' Daisy had said through fresh bouts of tears. Unlike Portia, she had adored her father; helped by the fact that she'd only seen him once in the last couple of years, they only kept in touch by phone, and also by virtue of being a full fourteen years younger than Portia. She had been in nappies when Blackjack's excesses were at their worst and consequently too young to have seen him for what he really was.

The show, however, had to go on. Close to four hundred people had been invited to the grand opening that night so whether the Davenport ladies liked it or not, they had no choice but to put a brave face on things. Lucasta, once she finally got out of bed, was revelling in the role of widowed martyr and anyone who overheard her could easily have been forgiven for thinking that she'd been happily married to a devoted husband. She swanned down the great oak staircase, still in her nightie and wax jacket, with waist-length grey hair streeling down her back, accepting condolences from the staff as though her husband had died in her loving arms a mere ten minutes ago.

'The only proven way to heal the deep grief I'm feeling,' she said to Molly, who was frantically giving the marble floor in the main entrance hall a final going-over, 'is to bathe naked under moonlight in the sweat of ten virgins, so you can see the obvious difficulty involved there.'

'Ehh, yes, I think so, your ladyship,' replied Molly, patiently mopping up the drops of gin and tonic Lucasta was freely sloshing all over the place.

'Yes. Three whole weeks till the next full moon' – Lucasta went on gazing into space – 'which means I'm stuck in mourning until then.'

Daisy did what she always did at times of crisis; she went straight to the stables, saddled up her favourite mare and galloped off towards the low-lying hills which edged the Davenport land. Be a miracle if she's even back in time for the opening, Portia thought, watching her slim outline disappear over the horizon at a rate of knots. Even though she was totally reliant on Daisy's help that afternoon and now had been well and truly landed in it, she found it hard to feel any resentment. Daisy had always been something of a Daddy's girl and was genuinely devastated at the news. She'll be back when she's good and ready, Portia decided, grudgingly thanking Andrew for forcing her to hire the services of a publicist.

Julia Belshaw was exactly the kind of tornado of efficiency they needed to get through the opening tonight. The human equivalent of eight strong cups of espresso coffee, she'd arrived at the Hall about a month previously, instantly impressing both Portia and Andrew with all of the amazing ideas she was brimming over with for the big night.

'Oh, it's just got to be the event of the season,' she'd enthused to them over a coffee meeting in the Library, pushing her Gucci sunglasses into her sleek blonde bobbed hair and wrapping one long, toned, suntanned leg over another. (How did she manage to get a tan in January? Portia had innocently wondered.)

Julia was the epitome of fabulousness, instantly demanding that they both guess her age and then

34

gleefully telling them that she was, in fact, forty-five.

'Wow, I thought you'd have difficulty getting served in pubs, you look so young,' Andrew had gushed, barely able to take his eyes off the permatan.

'Oh, that is just the *sweetest* thing to say,' she replied, playfully touching his arm, addressing Andrew and Andrew only. 'Now, why aren't there more guys like you out there? If a single man said something like that to me, I can tell you right now he'd be on a one-way ticket to panty land.'

Had Julia gone the whole hog and come out with: 'I could just spread you on a cracker, right this minute, you big hunk of gorgeousness,' she couldn't have flirted any more outrageously. Andrew, who had been provoking this reaction in women ever since secondary school (the only boy in his class who never got a single spot), was completely oblivious but Portia bloody wasn't. She knew in her soul that her husband didn't have a wandering eye and that they'd most likely have a good laugh about Julia afterwards, but it still bugged her when other women flirted with him. Particularly with his wife sitting right beside him. Rude, she thought. Really rude . . .

Julia's fee was exorbitant too, but, reluctantly, Portia had to admit that she was worth every red cent. Firstly, she'd tackled the guest list, whittling it down to a mere four hundred. 'It's got to be a hot ticket,' she'd explained to Portia. 'If we want the press to cover this then I'm sorry but neighbours and red-necked farmers have to go. Beautiful people only. And we need to coax celebrities down here, so you'll have to offer them goodie bags or they just won't show. If there's one thing celebs love more than publicity, it's freebies. Expensive perfumes, watches, vouchers for beauty treatments, that sort of thing.'

Portia almost fell off her chair. 'You mean as well as inviting them here, we've got to buy them presents?' She also felt a bit shifty about not inviting old friends and neighbours from Ballyroan, people she'd known for years, some of whom had already begun asking her quite pointedly when the opening was to be. It was beginning to get embarrassing.

'We only get one chance to put the Davenport Hotel on the map,' Julia calmly replied, 'in fact, to put County Kildare on the map. The countryside just isn't hot at the moment, in spite of Madonna going around dressed in tweeds and wellingtons. Wall to wall A list, that's what we need. Of course, I'll invite a few minor B-list people too, just to flesh the party out a little. Soap stars and wannabe actors, that type. They won't be needing goodie bags either; they'd turn up to the opening of a fridge.'

Julia had also worked closely with Tim on the menu for the party, insisting on finger food only and tiny amounts at that. 'We're going to blow the budget on champagne,' she'd explained. 'The less food you serve, the more guests will drink and the more they drink, the better the party. Trust me. If you feed them, you'll get no thanks for it; they'll only fall asleep on you. We want guests to wake up the next morning with royal hangovers, as though they'd been drinking paint-stripper. That's how people judge how much they enjoyed a night out, you know. In direct proportion to how wretched they feel the next day. The worse they feel, the better the night.'

'I did that once you know,' Lucasta had chipped in, wafting through the Library carrying a bowl of cat food, 'drank paint-stripper.' Portia, Andrew and Julia all turned to look at her in surprise. 'It was when the decorators were here and I'd completely run out of booze. First morning in years I woke up without a hangover.'

'And that's another thing,' Julia said under her breath as soon as Lucasta was out of earshot. 'The cats have to go.'

Portia was outside with Mick Feeney, their head gardener, when a bright red BMW convertible sports car came scrunching up the driveway, Julia at the wheel, with her blonde hair blowing in the breeze. Portia had been helping Mick laboriously pour lighter fuel into the bases of three dozen long wooden torches which lined the driveway and was now well and truly freezing, saturated in methane and stinking to high heaven. A torchlit drive-way would look stunning later as guests arrived, she knew, but for now she was glad of the chance to welcome Julia and thaw out indoors.

'I'll be back later to help you, Mick,' she said as she strode over to the car, silently marvelling that even though Julia had driven all the way from Dublin with the top down, her hair still managed to remain shiny and immaculate.

'I've been frantically trying to call you from my mobile, you know,' was Julia's greeting as she stepped elegantly out of the car. 'Why in God's name is there no signal down here? You look terrible, Portia. It's three p.m., you should be having your hair done by now. Didn't you read your itinerary?'

Julia had handed each member of staff, Portia and Daisy included, a detailed agenda for the big day. It was worked out to the tiniest, minutest detail such as: 'Portia. 8 a.m. Get up. Shower. Toilet break in gate lodge. Do not use bathrooms in the Hall; they must be kept pristine and are for guest use only. Do not wear anything that needs to be pulled over your head as this will play havoc with your hairstyle later.' She even handed Mrs Flanagan a cleaning schedule, and was promptly told to shove it up her bony arse.

'Look, Julia, I'm afraid your itinerary's gone out of the window. We've just had some bad news. My father died suddenly this morning.'

'I'm sorry,' Julia replied curtly, clearly looking on this as a minor inconvenience she hadn't allowed for, 'but you have now missed your hair appointment in

Kildare. Greasy hair isn't going to help anyone, you know.'

Before Portia knew where she was, it was seven-thirty and guests had already started to arrive. She had spent the whole afternoon working with Julia to make sure every last-minute hitch was ironed out and that the Hall was looking its sparkling best. In fairness to Julia, she wasn't afraid to get down and dirty; Portia even found her standing on a tapestry chair in the Long Gallery, frantically polishing the mirror behind the bar till it gleamed under the Waterford crystal chandelier above.

And still no word from Andrew. She was really starting to worry by now and was on the verge of calling the police when Julia bossily insisted that she go back to the gate lodge and change. Realizing that she was now in a race against the clock, Portia obediently legged it down the stairs, racking her brains to remember whether or not she'd even switched on the immersion before she left the lodge that morning. Well, if I didn't, a cold shower will just have to do, she thought, bounding down all eight flights of stairs two at a time. She'd made it as far as the upstairs landing when she heard the sound of cars pulling to a halt in the gravelled driveway outside. Peering in a panic out of the stained-glass window that overlooked the main entrance, she realized there was now a long line of flashy cars drawing up outside the Hall, punctually on the dot of seven-thirty, just as their invitations had decreed. Julia had inveigled no less a personage than Robert Armstrong, President of Ireland, to officiate at the grand opening and as it was considered the height of bad etiquette to arrive after the President, there was virtual limo gridlock the entire length of the driveway. 'Oh please, dear Jesus, just give me time to get changed,' she was praying out loud, when running up the stairs came Andrew.

'Darling, Julia's just told me the news about your father,' he said breathlessly, putting his arms around her. 'I'm so, so sorry,' he whispered, holding her tight and racking his brains to think of a few good words he could say about Blackjack. 'He was . . . well, he was quite a character, wasn't he? I'm so sorry I wasn't here for you.'

'Where on earth were you?' she asked, detecting a strong smell of whisky and stale cigarette smoke on him. 'I've been like a lunatic trying to contact you all day and your bloody phone was switched off.'

'Plenty of time for that later,' he said, slurring a bit. 'Now, I know you've had a rough day, honey, but we really have to get you out of that tracksuit before the VIPs get here.' It was tiny, barely perceptible, but there was just the faintest whiff of his trying to avoid the subject, which immediately set an alarm bell ringing in Portia's head.

'No. Tell me now.'

'Portia, do you really want to meet and greet the President dressed like that? Now is not the time. Go. Change.'

She sat on a stair and eyeballed him.

'OK, OK,' he said, realizing that there was no budging her until he came clean. 'Ken Courtney phoned me this morning and asked me to meet him at the airport hotel in Dublin. He was on his way to Frankfurt and didn't have time to drive all the way down here. He said it was urgent, I couldn't get out of it . . .'

'And?' Portia tried hard to keep the impatience out of her voice. Ken Courtney was Andrew's best friend; they'd worked together in the States for years. Portia had never liked him. He was married and openly cheated on his wife with anyone who was willing and didn't particularly care who knew.

'Well, the thing is . . .' Andrew was smiling sheepishly now, as though he were about to launch into a risqué after-dinner anecdote. 'Globex Pharmaceuticals are being investigated by the SEC in New York at the moment and they've hired my old firm to handle the case. Ken and I spent all afternoon going over the notes. But, emm, well, you see, there's a condition.'

'Go on.' Portia's head was starting to pound.

'They want me to represent them. The MD of Globex specifically wants me, or else there's no deal. They're offering huge money, my old apartment on Park Avenue back – it's only for three months, I'd be back in the game—'

'Three months? Just as we're trying to get the hotel up and running? It doesn't matter if they're offering you a king's ransom, Andrew, it's out of the question. I presume you told Ken you weren't available?'

'No,' he replied, looking a bit hangdog. 'As a matter of fact, I didn't.'

Chapter Three

By eight o'clock, the party really was in full swing. The entrance hall was wall-to-wall A list, just as Julia had insisted, all of them looking their fabulous best and competing to be photographed by the society magazines who'd shown up in droves to cover the event. Davenport Hall was thronged with flashbulbs and whirring cameras clicking furiously as actors, politicians, film directors, even one or two movie stars paraded designer-clad toned bodies in front of the assembled media hordes. The great and the good had shown up, all of them in their glittering, dazzling prime.

Even Josh Hamilton had turned up, Ireland's latest twenty-something hotshot export to Hollywood, managing to look scruffy, red-eyed, hung over and yet sexy all at the same time. He was accompanied by Tiffany

Richardson, American teen pop sensation, whose debut album *Get a Load of Me* had recently spent a record thirty weeks at the top of the charts. The joint arrival sent the press into a frenzy and all you could hear were catcalls of: 'Tiffany! Over here, Tiffany! Would you care to comment on your recent twenty-four-hour marriage to Karl Hughes? And the rumours that you and Josh are an item?'

Tiffany beamed, then twirled around in her diamanté-studded hot pants for all to see, before snuggling up to Josh and saying in her husky, rasping, lick-my-underwear smoker's voice, 'I wanna tell you folks that this is the guy for me. I know we only met last Tuesday, but Josh really, really, *really* is the one. It's gonna be a long engagement, but we hope to be married by the end of next week.'

You couldn't have bought publicity like it. No wonder Julia looked pleased.

Tim and his team of galley slaves in the kitchen had pulled out all the stops too, and now waiters dressed in elegant black tie swiftly circulated around the packed reception rooms, loaded down with trays of goodies. Guests were happily nibbling away on confections of shallow-fried sage and anchovy fritters, grilled rabbit tartlets with aubergine caviar and partridge canapés served with artichoke purée, all fish and game courtesy of the Davenport estate.

But the star of the night was unquestionably the Hall

itself. The restoration team really had worked miracles; guests were hard pressed to think of another mansion house in the country which could rival it either for grandeur or for style. There were eight reception rooms in all, including a Billiard Room, a Ballroom, a Library, the Long Gallery, the Red Dining Room (which could comfortably seat eighty) and three interconnecting Drawing Rooms, each lovingly renovated to the highest standards and now looking in their magnificent prime. The Georgian wooden floors in each room were covered with only the best and most expensive hand-crafted Persian rugs, antique furnishings which had rotted away for years were now French polished to within an inch of their lives and stunning tapestries and canvas paintings now graced the walls looking as though they'd been hanging there elegantly for centuries.

They hadn't, of course. The original Davenport art collection had been gambled away by Blackjack over the years, leaving huge, gaping holes on the walls. So Andrew and Portia had duly trooped over to Sotheby's in London and started a new collection from scratch.

'For the amount of money you spent,' Lucasta had moaned at the time, 'I'd have expected a candlelit dinner for two with Joshua Reynolds himself. I don't give a tuppenny bit if he's dead. And if I see one more piece of Victorian shit in the house, I'll train my cats to piddle on it.'

Exactly forty minutes behind schedule, thereby throwing Julia's itinerary right out the window, a string quartet in the entrance hall struck up the national anthem, heralding the arrival of the President. A hush descended on the crowds in the hall as a black, chauffeur-driven limousine pulled up at the bottom of the stone flight of steps which led to the main entrance. All eyes were on the great oak door, which was wide open so everyone could get a glimpse of the guest of honour stepping out on to the red carpet.

Robert Armstrong was a handsome, patrician man of about sixty, although he looked much younger, thanks to a gruelling fitness regime which included daily ten-mile jogs around the perimeter of the Phoenix Park in Dublin and games of tennis which regularly went to five sets. Tall and silver-haired with a charm that was legendary, he was a modern-day example of a true Renaissance man.

As a young man, he'd served with the UN peace-keeping force in Cyprus and had been decorated for his trouble; he'd then gone into business, made a vast fortune from his financial services company and ploughed most of it back into the cancer charity he'd set up in memory of his late wife. After a few years, he was appointed Ireland's ambassador to Washington, where he penned an autobiography based on his experiences there. Not only was his book shortlisted for the Whitbread prize, it also stayed on *The New York Times* bestseller list for a record-breaking forty weeks. On chat shows and in interviews, he was unfailingly warm, funny, self-deprecating and wise. In short, he was easily the most popular president Ireland had ever produced, a national treasure, one of those rare people about whom absolutely nobody had a bad word to say.

He was accompanied by his daughter Eleanor, an only child, who often stepped into the breach at state dos and occasions such as this. Ireland may not have had a first lady, but at least had a first daughter who, at twenty-five, was drop-dead gorgeous. Not in an obvious way, though, no diamanté hot pants for her. She wore a simple black cocktail dress enhanced with a single strand of pearls which had been her mother's. Her waist-length straight auburn hair was tied into a chignon and, pulled back from her face, perfectly accentuated her long, swan-like neck and white, white skin. Well used to dealing with the press on these occasions, she waved demurely in the direction of the cameras before linking her father's arm and gracefully ascending the stone steps.

A line-up of sorts had formed inside the hall door, and guests parted like the Red Sea as the President and his daughter entered. A ripple of applause broke out as Julia guided the guests of honour down the line, as though taking on the role of lady-in-waiting to crowned heads of state. By now, she'd changed into a tight-fitting black bodice worn with a sexy pair of bootleg-cut satin pants, blonde hair tightly gelled back to show off diamond ear-rings so long they practically dusted her shoulders. She looked so sensational that even Tiffany Richardson's star was temporarily eclipsed. Both father and daughter greeted her warmly like an old friend; clearly their paths had crossed somewhere before.

As it happened, the first person the President stopped to speak a few words to was Mrs Flanagan. She was sporting her crisp, new black uniform, but it was her nametag, 'Housekeeping Supervisor', which caught the President's eye.

'You must work here then, I think?' he asked politely, making direct eye contact and smiling. There was nothing insincere about his question though, it was as though there was nothing else on earth he'd rather be doing than discussing a housekeeper's duties with this total stranger. It's a gift from God to be able to walk into a roomful of strangers and immediately launch into the inconsequential patter of small talk, a gift Robert Armstrong had in spades.

'Ehh, yeah . . . I mean, yes, I do,' she answered, staggered that he'd chosen to speak to her and aware of the spotlight that was shining on her. 'Your . . . ehh, President,' she added, unsure how to address the Head of State.

'In that case, I'm sure you must have your work cut out for you, in a house this size,' replied the President.

There was a sycophantic roar of laughter from all around him, led by Julia. Anyone would have thought that he'd just re-enacted the Monty Python parrot sketch all by himself and done all the voices, such was the level of appreciation for this mundane comment. He nodded and smiled and made to move on to the next person, but Mrs Flanagan was having none of it.

'I voted for ya in the Presidential election, ya know,' she said, a bit more confident now.

'Thank you very much. Most kind,' he answered, turning back.

'Yeah. Sure, you were miles better looking than the other fella.'

Next in the line-up was Daisy, red-eyed and sniffling, but still looking beautiful in the Donna Karan dress she'd managed to filch from Portia earlier.

'May I introduce the Honourable Daisy Davenport, your excellency,' said Julia, anxiously looking over her shoulder for Portia and Andrew. No sign.

'Oh, you're a Davenport,' said the President, shaking her hand and smiling warmly. 'You've had the builders in then.' Another roar of laughter from the throng, at which Julia whispered something discreetly in the President's ear.

'I'm very sorry to hear about your father's passing. It must have been an awful shock for all of you,' he added, really looking as though he meant it.

'Thank you,' was all Daisy could mutter in response as fresh tears started to well up, choking her.

'You must introduce me to Lady Davenport too. I'd very much like to offer my personal condolences.'

'Where in God's name have you been? The President is about to make his speech and you're not even dressed!' Julia was snarling by now, well and truly pissed off with lackadaisical clients like these. These people confirmed what she'd always suspected: the aristocracy really were a law unto themselves; the type of people who fell off their horses after a long day's hunting and into their ball gowns without even bothering to shower. Too posh to wash, the lot of them. They'd be herding a flock of sheep through the Long Gallery next.

'We'd run out of champagne, I had to stock up,' Portia replied, indicating to George, the head barman, which crates were to stay in the cellar and which were to be brought upstairs to serve. 'Not very glamorous, I know, but someone's got to do it.'

Ever since Andrew had dropped the bombshell on her, Portia was finding it increasingly hard to stay calm. Particularly with Julia, who, for no other reason than that she looked fabulous, was really getting on her nerves. Just get through tonight, she promised herself, and I'll deal with everything else in the morning.

She had tried her best to make it back to the gate

lodge to shower and change, but guests had already begun to pour through the main entrance and she didn't want to be seen looking like a dirty big knacker who smelt of methane fuel. So she'd sneaked down the back stairs and out through the back door which led on to the kitchen garden but, to her horror, she realized that her car was completely hemmed in by the hordes of newly arrived Mercedeses and BMWs, not to mention the Presidential state limousine. As it was a full two-mile trek to the gate lodge and two miles back again, walking was out of the question. Bitterly upset, she was left with no choice but to stay behind the scenes for the time being, overseeing all the last-minute stuff which somehow always gets overlooked at parties.

'Isn't there something here that you could borrow to wear?' Julia's tone was impatient.

'Unless you want me to appear in one of my mother's Goddess of Samhradh robes, no there isn't anyone I can borrow from. Do you think I hadn't thought of that?' Portia hadn't meant to sound so snappy; it had just been a long day.

'What about your sister? Surely she must have something suitable?'

Portia had to fight really hard to resist the temptation to say, 'Daisy wears a size eight and, compared with her, I'm the size of a carpet warehouse, just in case you hadn't noticed.'

'Come on, Portia, you cannot miss the President's speech. That's out of the question. We've no choice, it seems. You'll just have to go as you are.'

'What some of you may not realize is that the Davenport family has lived in this house for over two hundred years. Now, if only I could stay in office that long.'

Gales of laughter greeted Robert Armstrong's speech and every face in the packed Long Gallery was gazing at him in googly-eyed adoration.

'Of course the Hall was designed by James Gandon back in 1770, who also designed Government Buildings in Dublin. But I think the Davenports might be hoping to attract a somewhat different type of clientele than mere politicians.'

Another howl of laughter. The President could easily have been forgiven for thinking that a new career as a Perrier-award-winning stand-up comedian beckoned.

'And so nothing else remains but for me to declare the Davenport Country House Hotel officially open for business. May God bless her and all who sail in her.'

There was a huge round of applause and Portia could feel people glancing in her direction. She'd slipped up the back stairs and was now trying to wedge herself up against one of the long, shadowy window shutters at the back of the Ballroom in the hope that no one would see her, but she wasn't nearly as invisible as she'd have liked.

There was one thing going for her though: thanks to Julia's dogged insistence on only A-list celebrities being invited, she hardly knew a sinner there. Be hell to pay the next time I bump into any of the neighbours in Ballyroan, she thought. They were entitled to be rightly peeved at not being invited. Mind you, that was the least of her worries tonight.

Across the packed Ballroom, she spotted her mother-in-law, Susan, deep in conversation with one of Ireland's best-loved actresses, Celia Moore, whom Portia recognized from her role in the TV drama series *Affair City*. Susan never failed to look anything less than immaculate and had really outdone herself in the style stakes tonight. She wore a pale blue silk evening jacket with a matching floor-length skirt, nipped tight at the waist to show off her girlish waistline. She'd obviously spent half the day in the hairdresser's too, Portia thought. Susan wore her silver hair in a severe Margaret Thatcher, helmet-style 'do', with enough lacquer to cause another rip in the ozone layer. Andrew regularly teased her about it. 'Are you waiting for that hairstyle to come back into fashion or what, Mum?' he'd say to her. It was the kind of comment that only an adored only child could get away with.

From the corner of her eagle eye, Susan spotted Portia and waved imperiously for her to come and join them. Portia had no choice but to run the gamut of the crowded room, fully aware of the picture she cut in her slobby tracksuit, filthy hair scraped back and not a screed of make-up. But there was nothing else for it but to be polite, she thought, smiling wanly and moving over to her mother-in-law.

'Bloody Julia Belshaw never gave *me* a goodie bag,' she could hear Celia Moore moan as Susan greeted her Mediterranean style, with one careful kiss on each cheek. Then followed an all-too-familiar routine where Susan eyed Portia up and down, taking in her appearance and, what was worse, saying nothing, as though Portia lived, ate, drank and slept in the same stinking tracksuit. Putting her daughter-in-law down was almost a blood sport with Susan, although, in fairness, Portia showed Olympian levels of patience in never rising to take the bait. Andrew's her only child, she used to reason with herself; if he'd married Marie of Romania it still wouldn't be good enough for Susan de Courcey.

'I was very sorry to hear about your father,' was her opener. Portia waited patiently for the put-down, which never failed to follow any sympathetic comment from Susan. 'Although I know you were never close to him.'

There it was, right on the nail and straight to the jugular, as ever. She was saved from having to answer by the appearance of Andrew, who greeted his mother warmly.

'Darling!' Susan cooed at him, standing on tiptoe to

kiss him. 'Why on earth didn't you change?' she asked, noticing that he was still in day clothes.

'Arrived late, I'm afraid, Mum,' he answered, slipping his arm around Portia's waist. He still looked effortlessly gorgeous though, in a floppy-haired, Hugh Grant-ish, country-squire, I-couldn't-really-care-less-what-people-think sort of way. Then, taking Portia aside so they wouldn't be overheard, he said, 'I've been looking every-where for you. Where have you been? Eleanor Armstrong wants a guided tour of the whole house, so I suppose one of us had better oblige.'

'You go. I need to help Tim downstairs.'

From the corner of her eye, Portia could see Julia working the room and making her way over to them. Last thing I need right now, she thought. The sight of Julia looking amazing and flirting with her fella was something she could do without.

'Look, honey,' said Andrew, a bit more softly, 'I know you've had a really shit day and I'm sorry I wasn't here for you. Only another few hours of this and then, I promise, we'll slip off.'

'Great. Look forward to hearing all about your job offer. Big day for me, huh? My father dies and my husband decides to take up some job offer Ken Courtney dangles at him in New York. Without even telling me.'

Andrew looked at her, a bit stung by her narky tone.

So unusual for her. He was about to answer but Julia interrupted, wafting over on a cloud of Chanel No. 5.

'There you are,' she said breathlessly. 'Eleanor is ready for the guided tour now, so shall we, Andrew?'

'Go,' said Portia dully. 'We'll talk later.'

He stroked his finger against her pale, tired face and turned to go. Portia could hear Julia clear as crystal as they drifted off.

'I so wish she'd found the time to smarten up a bit, you know. That new dress you bought her in Khan must have cost a fortune.'

'Another large gin and tonic there, George, easy on the tonic.' Lucasta was perched on a bar stool in the Long Gallery, deep in conversation with poor George, or Gorgeous George as she'd affectionately nicknamed him, who as well as trying to serve the remaining guests, had to listen to her ladyship's tale of woe.

'Nothing against Portia and Andrew now,' she was twittering on, 'they've done a wonderful job on the old place, full credit there. But, Jesus Christ, neither one of them has the first clue how to organize a good old-fashioned piss-up. I don't know a sinner here tonight. The place is full of actors I've never heard of and gobshite politicians. There's a string quartet in the hall, for fuck's sake. Where do they think they are? Church?'

The Last of the Great Romantics

One of Lucasta's main grievances was that both Andrew and Portia had expressly forbidden her from launching into one of her customary sing-songs at the grand piano. She was particularly pissed off as she'd gone to a lot of trouble to compose a song in honour of the occasion entitled 'Whoops there, Vicar, you're sitting on one of my artichokes'. Vegetables were a big motif in her musical repertoire this year.

'And they've banished all my kitties to my bedroom and now the poor little things are totally disorientated and they keep weeing everywhere. Apparently they're not good enough for Portia and her poxy hotel. I wouldn't mind, but Mr Fluffles was the Shah of Iran in a past life.'

'Lady Davenport?' She turned round to see Robert Armstrong standing beside her, extending his hand.

'Jesus, you gave me a fright,' she answered. 'I'm only ever called that in court.'

'I just wanted to say how sorry I was to hear about your husband's death.'

'Why's that?' asked Lucasta, taking a slug of her drink. 'Did he owe you money or something?'

Ever the diplomat, Robert just nodded and smiled, well aware that grief did funny things to people. 'I'm a widower myself, you know, and I just wanted to say that the pain does get easier. You must miss him dreadfully.'

'Easy come, easy go,' she replied, bored now with play-ing the grieving widow. She was squinting at him intently, racking her brains to figure out why his face was so familiar. 'I know you. Are you that idiot who does the National Lottery draw on a Saturday night? If you are, then your chakras are a complete disgrace. I've lost count of the number of spells I've done for my numbers to come up and they never bloody do.'

Although the President had probably never been spoken to like that before in his entire life, he didn't seem to mind. In fact, this eccentric-looking creature in her oilskin jacket and wellies was the first person really to make him laugh all evening.

'Oh, I know, did we sleep together in the sixties?' asked Lucasta, signalling to Gorgeous George to top up her gin.

'I'm afraid I'm going to leave you guessing,' Robert replied, kissing her hand politely as he took his leave. 'But I'm very glad to see that you're not entirely prostrated with grief.'

'Weirdo,' Lucasta muttered drunkenly. But at least she waited until he'd left the room.

Much later, he and Eleanor were back in the presidential limousine zooming down the motorway to Dublin, heading for Phoenix Park House, their official residence.

'So what did you think?' Robert asked his daughter.

'Perfect,' she replied with her eyes shining. 'Oh Daddy, it's absolutely perfect.'

'That's settled then. We have a plan B.'

Chapter Four

The night had been an overwhelming success, but that was the last thing on Daisy's mind. She'd slipped away from the party at about midnight and gone straight up to the estate office on the fourth floor to start making the necessary arrangements for Blackjack to come home. There was an eight-hour time difference between Ireland and Las Vegas, so at around four in the afternoon US time, she started making phone calls. Even though it was a weekend, everything was handled with typical American efficiency; by the time she contacted the Bellagio Hotel, where her father had been living for the past year, his body had already been released from the post-mortem inquiry. All that remained for her to do was sign a note of permission and fax it through so that his cremation could go ahead. It did flash through her mind that this would probably all cost a fortune, but she was too upset to care. She'd talk to Andrew about that later. All that mattered now was getting her dad home.

'We'll all miss him here,' the manager had sympathized with her. 'Your pop sure was a real one-off.'

Even on such a long-distance line, the manager could still hear the sound of a hooley in full swing in the background. 'Sounds like you folks got a real Irish wake happenin' there, Miss Davenport. I know that's just what your pop would have liked. A right good send off to the heavens above, without any weepin' or wailin' or gnashin' of teeth.'

Daisy put the phone down, knowing full well that apart from hers, there'd be precious few tears shed over her father's passing. There were a lot of big decisions to be made and she made all of them alone, knowing that if it were left to her mother, Blackjack would be buried in bin liners in the city dump.

'I wouldn't even dream of sullying the Grand Canal by dumping that bollocks in it,' had been Lucasta's final pronouncement on the subject, the previous day. 'The sewer rats deserve better bedfellows.'

There was no point in even trying to talk to Portia about the arrangements. For a start, she hadn't set eyes on her all evening and anyway, she and Blackjack had never really seen eye to eye. One of Daisy's earliest memories was of the sixteen-year-old Portia standing in the Library in her school uniform, bawling her eyes out because her father had gambled away her boarding school fees and she had been sent packing just before her exams. It had to be said that when Daisy's turn came to be sent to school and there was no money for her fees, it never really bothered her much. She had never been remotely academic like Portia and the loss of an unwanted education barely knocked a feather out of her. Spoilt rotten and thoroughly indulged by her father, she was perfectly happy to stay at home helping out with her beloved horses whenever the mood took her.

Since her early teens, she'd had a string of unsuitable boyfriends, spotty local adolescents mostly, who, like Daisy, had great difficulty in holding down any kind of job. But instead of being given the third degree, or shown the door as they would in any normal home, Blackjack had always welcomed them with open arms, taught them how to play five-card stud and introduced them to the advantages of having a single malt whisky still in the cellar. Her memory flashed back to one particular ex-boyfriend who would have made any normal parent's blood curdle.

He was a twenty-year-old recovering heroin addict whom Daisy had drunkenly picked up in a bar in Kildare and who'd subsequently given her a crossbar home on a stolen bike.

'So, you're on the dole then?' Blackjack had breezily

asked when Daisy first introduced them. 'Wonderful. Got any cash on you? Even better. You cut the deck and I'll deal.'

Not exactly a conventional upbringing, she knew; in fact Portia often used to say that if a social worker had ever visited the Hall, both she and Daisy would have been sent into a children's home immediately. (The ten-year-old Daisy was temporarily swayed by this notion; mainly because there was a pool and a trampoline in the kids' home.) But Blackjack was the only father she had and now he was gone and she never even got to say goodbye properly. Even the last conversation she ever had with him hadn't exactly been a golden memory. 'My test results came back clear!' he'd raved from across the Atlantic. 'And they're negative!'

There would be a small, simple memorial service in Ballyroan church, she decided, and then the family Mausoleum would be his final and proper burial place. A magnificent eighteenth-century folly perched on top of a gently sloping hill, it commanded breathtaking views of the land for miles around. Nine generations of the Davenport family were buried there and now there would be ten, she reflected, starting to sob again. It was a wonderful, peaceful spot though and it gave her some comfort to think that her father would finally be at rest there.

The Irish consulate in Nevada had also promised to

contact her as soon as his remains were en route to the mortuary at Vegas McCarran international airport, from where they'd make their final journey home. His body would probably arrive at Dublin airport in about two days' time, Daisy calculated, where she'd be waiting to meet him. With or without the rest of her bloody family.

For the second morning in a row, Portia woke up without her husband in bed beside her. She gazed sleepily up at the bedroom ceiling, thinking about last night and about everything she had to do that day, willing herself to snap into action. Funny how the whole night seemed like one big blur, she thought, still in that dreamy, half-asleep, half-awake state. Robert Armstrong being all regal and Augustan, Susan de Courcey being her usual snide self, Julia bossing her around, a string quartet playing, the heat, the overcrowded rooms, celebrities she'd never heard of wafting around, her stuck in that God-awful, stinking bloody tracksuit and then Andrew . . . There was something she was trying to remember, something life-alteringly huge he'd dropped on her last night . . . and then with a jolt, she was wide awake.

New York. He'd been offered a contract there *and had accepted it*, without even talking it over with her first. Bloody hell, she thought, dreading the discussion/argument/screaming match which lay ahead. Suddenly the phone on her bedside table started to peal. It was just seven-thirty, she noticed on the alarm clock as she stretched across to answer it. It was Daisy, sounding teary and snuffly as though she'd been bawling all night.

'Look, I just wanted to let you know that Daddy's arriving into Dublin airport, probably the day after tomorrow. I'm going to drive down to meet him. All by myself. On my own. But that's fine, I understand you probably have much better things to get on with. But if you could just find the time to pick up the phone and contact the parish priest about arrangements for the memorial service, though, that would be great . . .' More hysterical tears. In fact all Portia could glean through the sobs were the words 'airport' and 'parish priest'.

'You know I'll come with you, darling,' Portia said in a classic Pavlovian response to the emotional blackmail being laid on with a trowel. Besides, Daisy was liable to wrap her car around a lamppost on the long drive to Dublin, given the state she was in. 'That's not something you want to do alone. And I'm sure Andrew will drive us.'

'And someone's going to have to pay for all this.'

'Don't you know we'll take care of that?'

'You're a star,' came the muffled reply as Daisy blew her nose down the phone. 'Andrew was here, actually. I think he's just left. He should be with you any minute.'

In a leap, Portia was out of bed and into her dressing gown, kicking aside the famous tracksuit which was now strewn across the floor. She hadn't had a chance to say two words to him since last night. He'd spent the evening giving guided tours of the Hall to various guests and freeloaders while she'd done her best to keep out of sight. She had stayed till the bitter end, though, helping Tim with the big clean-up in the kitchen before realizing it was well after four a.m. By the time she'd got home, Andrew was out for the count and snoring so loudly you'd think there was a large Zeppelin passing overhead. Small wonder, she'd thought, slipping into bed beside him. He smelt like a brewery.

Tripping down the stairs, she was just in time to hear his car pull up at the front door of the lodge. She opened the whitewashed wooden barn door to see him stepping out of his Range Rover, laden down with the morning papers.

'I declare the evening to have been a veritable triumph!' he called out theatrically, sounding like a ham actor in a Victorian melodrama. 'We're in every single paper, fantastic photos, brilliant write-ups, all of them raving about the Hall, how it's going to attract all the jet-set glitterati. What did I tell you? Julia Belshaw is worth her weight in gold!'

He absent-mindedly kissed Portia on the forehead as he made his way down the dark, narrow passageway which led to their bright and airy kitchen, expertly dodging the overhead beams so as not to thump his head.

Portia followed him, amazed as always by his boundless energy and enthusiasm. Particularly as he was functioning on only a couple of hours' sleep, not to mention the monster hangover he must be nursing.

'Isn't it fantastic?' he said, spreading the papers all over the long pine kitchen table. 'You just couldn't have bought press coverage like this, not in a million years. Eleanor Armstrong's plastered over every paper, no surprises there. Here's a great one of Robert Armstrong making that big speech and doesn't the Ballroom look well in the background? Hey, look at this!' he said, folding over one of the tabloids as his eye fell on something else: a colour photo of Tiffany Richardson posing in her hot pants. 'WHAT A CHEEK!' ran the banner headline. 'All publicity is good publicity,' he added, clocking the blank look on Portia's face. 'Oh, look, here's one of Lucasta,' he said as Portia peered over his shoulder. It was indeed a full-length photo of her proudly standing in front of the new bar in the Long Gallery, looking as though she'd just put down hammer, nails and a power drill having gone to IKEA and then built it from scratch out of a flat pack all by herself.

'We should have it framed,' Portia said, dryly. 'Be nice to have a photo of Mummy without a drink in her hand.'

He roared laughing, but didn't lift his head from the papers.

Portia moved over to the kettle and filled it with

water, looking out of the window on to her tiny kitchen garden as she did. It was a gorgeous, sunny morning and a gentle mist was beginning to lift from the distant fields. Spring had come early to Kildare, it seemed.

'By the way, everything's running like a dream up at the Hall,' Andrew went on, still not making eye contact with her. 'Tim's cooking up the most fabulous breakfast: eggs *en cocotte*; marinated kipper fillets; he's even baking poppy seed bagels from scratch. Too bad none of our overnight guests are out of bed yet.'

He was beginning to sound a little edgy now, as though playing for time. Portia continued to gaze out at the early morning mist, not responding.

'Fantastic, though, to have all thirty-six rooms full on our first night, isn't it, darling? OK, so they're all freebies, but one hundred per cent occupancy is what I call starting as we mean to go on.'

She still didn't answer. It was as though there was a huge white elephant in the middle of the room which both of them were completely ignoring.

'God, Eleanor Armstrong is really something, isn't she?' he said, noisily turning over the pages of a tabloid paper. 'She's so photogenic, it's almost impossible to take a bad picture of her. I gave her the full tour last night and she was well impressed with the place. Asked me all sorts of questions about guest capacity and how many the

Dining Room could seat and what the outdoor facilities were like, she's really well clued in.'

Portia took a deep breath. Clearly, it would be up to her to raise the subject he'd landed on her so suddenly last night. 'So. New York,' was all she said, still looking out at the garden.

He gave a long-drawn-out sigh and turned to face her. 'Come and sit down,' he said.

She obediently did as she was told, steeling herself for what was coming. There was a silence while he ran his fingers through his floppy fair hair, something he only ever did when he was nervous, Portia knew of old. Nervous or evasive. She let the silence continue, determined that he should speak first and knowing that, in a head-to-head situation like this, whoever broke the silence automatically put themselves into a much weaker position. Marriage to a lawyer had taught her one or two tricks as well.

'Portia,' he began before breaking off. For the first time that morning, she noticed how tired he looked. Exhausted. 'OK, OK,' he said, rising to his feet and beginning to pace the room, hands in his pockets, as though he were opening a case in the High Court and she were judge and jury. 'We both know how much the restoration of the Hall has set us back. Money well spent if you ask me. I know the venture is going to be a huge success and that we'll die rich and happy. But . . .' He turned to face her now, resting his hands on the back of a kitchen chair and looking at her square in the face. 'Darling, we have major cash-flow problems. It could take up to three years for us to start recouping our investment capital. In the meantime, we run up more debts paying staff and keeping the Hall afloat, never mind trying to meet our mortgage repayments. I'm being offered a small fortune to handle this case for Globex; they've headhunted me personally. It's only for twelve weeks, that's nothing. You could come with me, you'd love New York. God, I can just see you now, parading up and down Fifth Avenue laden down with shopping bags, going to all the art galleries and the Broadway shows . . .'

Portia looked away. Andrew could be so persuasive when he wanted something. And he really wanted this job . . .

'Portia, the plain and simple fact is that I can't afford not to take this contract. We need the money.'

'How can we leave here for three whole months with no one to manage the place? You know I can't go with you. One of us has to stay.'

'Daisy can take over when we're gone. Bit of responsibility will do her no harm.'

'Daisy? Do you want us to be out of business by Easter?'

'Honey, we've been married for, what, all of eighteen months? Three months is roughly a sixth of that. I'm sorry if I sound selfish, but I'm not prepared to be away from you for that length of time. It's just too long for us to be apart.'

She looked at him, softening. No, she didn't want to be separated from him for all that length of time either, that went without saying. He had moved around the table and was now standing behind her, massaging her shoulders. She rolled her head back, allowing his strong fingers to unravel the knots of tension there.

Andrew, she knew, was the kind of man who adored nothing more than a challenge. It had been a huge challenge to him to restore the Hall and open the hotel, one he'd relished and thrived on. But now that he'd accomplished that . . . in a flash of insight, she realized exactly what he was thinking. He'd successfully completed one feat and now was anxious to move on to the next; simple as that. After this case in New York, it would be something else and then something else and on and on and on . . . Like all high-achieving people, he bored easily and was now impatient to scale the next mountain peak.

How can I prevent him? she asked herself, suddenly flashing forward to life if he stayed at Davenport Hall. How can I hold a conversation with him about laundering the linen table napkins and blocked U-bends in the toilets when he's longing to be sitting at a high-powered business lunch in the Plaza Hotel? 'Back in the game', as he'd drunkenly let slip to her last night. If I make him stay, she thought, he'd only end up resenting me for it and anyhow, it's wrong to try to hold another person back. After all, he'd financed her in the pursuit of her dream and now it was her turn to return the favour. There was nothing else for it. That's how marriage worked.

She turned to face him, forcing a bright smile. 'So tell me again about the apartment on Park Avenue?'

Two days later, Andrew and Portia, accompanied by a snivelling Daisy, were driving towards Dublin airport and the grim task that lay ahead. Dressed in a long, black hooded coat, with her wild blonde curls tied back in a ponytail, Daisy looked like a beautiful study in grief. She had the foresight to bring a man-sized box of Kleenex with her and started to sob almost as soon as she clambered into the back of the Range Rover.

'Try and remember the good times you shared with him, Daisy,' Andrew had said kindly, looking in the rear-view mirror and seeing the state she was in.

'Thanks so much for that, but how many parents have you lost?' Then, remembering herself, she muttered, 'Sorry, Andrew. It's just hard seeing him so unmourned at home.'

It was a tough call to try and remember something good about Blackjack Davenport, but Portia was racking her brains in an effort to console her sister. It was no use though. Every time she thought about him, it resurrected painful memories she preferred to keep buried. The time he gambled a college fund bequeathed to her by her grandmother and she had to be unceremoniously yanked out of a degree course she loved; all the Davenport treasures he'd flogged for almost nothing just to pay off his debts; there was even an occasion when he ended up in court for non-payment of his account at his club in Dublin – the list went on. Daisy, in fairness, tended to see her father through rose-coloured glasses by virtue of being fourteen years younger than Portia. She was just too young to remember Blackjack at his very worst.

'Come on, girls,' Andrew said gamely, 'focus on your happy memories.'

There was a long, long silence. They'd gone through three sets of traffic lights before Portia spoke.

'Well, I remember at my Confirmation he did something nice.'

'What?'

'He turned up. Sober. And he didn't gamble all of my Confirmation money at the races later that day. There was lots left over.'

There was a hint of a watery smile from Daisy. Andrew took up the baton next. 'And didn't you once tell me a hilarious story about how he smuggled one of his girlfriends into the Hall and she ended up staying for about three weeks? About your mother thinking she was one of her spirit guides that she'd manifested into human form by accident? The clincher being that the girlfriend never spoke, so Lucasta was fully convinced that she was from the other side.' He made himself laugh then suddenly stopped, seeing a well-known hurt look on Daisy's ghostly pale face.

Another three sets of traffic lights and a roundabout passed them by before the silence was broken again.

'He had wonderful hair . . .' Portia trailed off lamely.

The arrangements at the airport mortuary were impeccable. They were met by the undertaker who told them that Blackjack's final flight had been slightly delayed at Heathrow, but was expected on the tarmac in the next few minutes, where a hearse was waiting for him.

'Would you like to wait for Daddy on the tarmac?' he asked.

'Right, come on then,' Daisy said snappishly, his gluey professional sympathy clearly getting on her nerves. The undertaker merely nodded gravely and led the way outside.

It was pitch dark by now with an icy wind beginning to whip up a gale. Andrew slipped his arm around Portia and she clung to him, delighted that he'd come and only wishing that her baby sis had someone to support her. Daisy just looked so frail and alone as she strode ahead of them, wiping her snotty nose with the back of her hand

and not caring who saw. They walked a few hundred yards over to where a small commuter 737 aircraft, safely landed from Heathrow, was slowly taxiing to a halt. Following the undertaker like shivering sheep, all three of them moved over to the waiting hearse, which was parked right beside the aircraft's cargo hold.

'Daddy will be coming out in just a few moments,' said the undertaker in his gloomy monotone, sounding as grave as a newsreader on the six o'clock bulletin. Daisy flashed her blue eyes angrily at him and then began to rummage inside her big leather handbag. A few seconds later, she produced what looked like a few raggedy tea towels stitched together with some sort of coloured picture on it.

'Oh darling, no, not that,' said Portia, alarmed.

'What on earth is it?' asked Andrew.

'It's the Davenport family standard,' replied Daisy, clinging to it as reverently as though it were the Turin Shroud. 'All of our ancestors who died abroad had it draped over their coffins on the way to the Mausoleum. It's our way of honouring the dead.'

Portia thought that there was a bit of a difference between dying gloriously on the field of battle, as many of their antecedents had, and dropping dead in a casino in Las Vegas, but she said nothing for fear of Daisy clocking her one. When fully unfurled, the standard bore the family crest, an image of two cats chasing each other with a Latin motto inscribed underneath. However, after years of wear and tear, not to mention being torn apart and then very badly stitched up again, it now looked like nothing more than a pair of mangy strays bonking.

By now, dozens of tired-looking commuters were treading down the steps of the plane, braving the harsh wind on their way inside to the warm, bright terminal building. Suddenly, the hydraulics on the cargo door cranked into action and Daisy, Portia and Andrew all braced themselves for what was coming. The undertaker moved forward, head tilted and hands loosely clasped, as though ready to say Mass.

A very small tin box, barely large enough to hold a mobile phone, came clattering down the conveyor belt. Nothing else. Portia and Daisy glanced at each other in shock as the undertaker moved forward to examine it. There was a tiny brass plate on it which read, simply, 'John Davenport, 1945-2004'.

Too stunned to speak, they were barely aware of an Amazonian giant of a woman, dressed in a clinging black mini-skirt and tight spangly black jacket, who had just disembarked and moved over to join them. No one could see her face as she was wearing a large feathery, plumed black hat, with a thick veil which entirely obscured her features. 'You all mus' be Miss Daisy and Miss Portia,' she said, in a breathy southern drawl. 'Your papa has told me just so much about you folks, I do declare I feel a kinship with you already.'

Portia looked to Daisy whose jaw was about to drop.

'Were you a friend of his? Have you come all this way for the funeral?' Portia asked, dreading the answer.

'I sure have,' replied the stranger. 'I come to bring ol' Jackie home and to meet my new family. I know this must be a big surprise for you all but . . . I'm your new stepmother!'

Chapter Five

'Well, I suppose the old bollocks must have divorced me. He certainly sent me enough bloody forms to sign.'

'Mummy, did it occur to you for one minute that maybe you could have passed on this particular nugget of information to Daisy and me? It's not at though it's none of our business.'

Portia was at her wits' end with Lucasta, who sat calmly at the grand piano in the deserted Ballroom, squalling away and occasionally taking slugs from her overflowing gin and tonic. She'd spent the day happily working on a new composition, entitled 'They're No Undersized Mangoes, They're My Prize Brussels Sprouts', and now greeted the news that Blackjack had remarried with the same mild irritation as when she ran out of fags.

'Oh, for Christ's sake, Portia, do you honestly expect me to remember every teensy boring little thing that happens? You'll be harping on at me for forgetting to tell you that it's bin day next.'

'Hardly the same thing, Mummy.'

'Amazing, isn't it,' Lucasta went on, 'how your father can still act like such a tosser even from beyond the grave? Well, all I can say is I hope he comes back as a hair louse on a filthy five-year-old child's head in his next reincarnation. Serve the bastard right. Where is his new bit on the side anyway?'

'In the family room with the others. Come on, Mummy, you're going to have to meet her and get it over with. She's staying for the memorial service, you know.'

'Bugger,' replied Lucasta, taking another large gulp of gin. 'What's this one called, anyway?'

'She's called Shelley-Marie. Oh, and one more thing: I think you'd better prepare yourself for a shock. Andrew's already christened her Miss Plastic Fantastic.'

'Oh, you have art!' Shelley-Marie exclaimed as she walked over to a giant tapestry in the family room. 'I *love* art!'

Mrs Flanagan merely grunted in reply, eyeing this upstart new arrival suspiciously, as though she was going to rob them blind at any moment. Daisy, true to form, had saddled up a horse and ridden as geographically far as it was possible to get from Davenport Hall. Unusually for her, she barely said two words on the whole dismal journey home and didn't even bother going into the house when they eventually arrived back. She just headed for the stables, white-faced and red-eyed, still clinging to the family standard as though it were a security blanket. Shelley-Marie, meanwhile, continued to waltz around the room, exclaiming in wonder at everything that caught her eye. 'Oh my good Lord, WINDOWS! I have never set eyes on windows that big in all my born days!'

By now, she had taken off her veiled hat and coat and thrown them over the back of an armchair, making herself completely at home. She couldn't have been more than about thirty years old, although she looked older, mainly because of the heavy pan-stick make-up she was wearing. She was big in every sense of the word, six feet tall and large-boned with big brassy blonde hair backcombed to within an inch of its life, Dolly Parton style. She was a good hefty clothes size to boot and the miniskirt she wore with three-inch-high hooker boots was at least two sizes too small for her. She had long false fingernails with a diamanté stud in each of them, worn with a wedding band and an engagement ring the size of the rock of Gibraltar on the third finger of her left hand. She was happily galumphing around the Drawing Room, declaring that there as sure as hell were no homes like this in her home town back in South Carolina and that if only her poor family could see her now, they'd darn well bust with pride.

'Cos you're finally in a house with a roof on it?' muttered Mrs Flanagan under her breath from the far corner of the room, where she sat slumped in an armchair watching the sideshow.

'I sure wish you were here to see me now, Jackie my darlin',' Shelley-Marie went on, addressing the tin box containing his ashes on top of the fireplace and shouting, as though all those who'd reached the afterlife were hard of hearing. Her voice was like a southern version of Marilyn Monroe's, breathless and little-girlish, totally at odds with her colossal frame. 'Can you hear me, Jackie my love? Here I am, welcomed into the lovin' bosom of your first family like I truly belonged. It's just so fittin' that I can give them the deep comfort of knowin' how happy you were in your final few days with me—'

At this morbid thought, she broke off, fluttering her hands in front of her face as though to indicate deep emotion. 'Oh, I sure do apologize,' she said, her voice trilling like a soprano's, 'it's the grief hittin' home. I declare I'll never find another lover like ol' Jackie as long as I live. Why, right up till the morning of the day he passed on there was no stoppin' him. He had the sex drive of a high school teenager.' She began to sniffle, dabbing the corners of her eyes with a long, floaty

81

chiffon scarf she was wearing, being extra careful not to rub off her industrial strength eye make-up.

'Jaysus,' muttered Mrs Flanagan, 'it's *The Jerry Springer Show* come to life.'

Meanwhile, Portia and Lucasta bumped into Andrew on their way down the long corridor which led to the family room.

'Bad news, I'm afraid,' he said, slipping an arm around each of them. 'I've finally got through to the registrar at the Little White Wedding Chapel and her story checks out. Shelley-Marie married your father exactly ten days ago. Even the serial number on her marriage cert. is authentic.'

Shelley-Marie wasn't quite so grief-stricken on the long drive back to Davenport Hall that she forgot to whip a copy of her marriage certificate out of her faux-crocodile handbag. That and a wedding photo clearly showing her towering over Blackjack, beaming at the camera and waving her bouquet while her bridegroom looked as though he was having great difficulty standing erect. There was no best man in the picture, but she had five bridesmaids, all of whom must have been related to her; they were all Amazonian giants, well over six feet tall, all with the same big hair, big teeth and big boobs. Her enormous fluffy white train must have been about fifteen feet long; it cascaded over all of the bridesmaids' feet like there'd just been a foam fight, virtually obscuring her new husband.

'The registrar particularly remembered the wedding,' Andrew went on, 'because he said the bride had a ludicrously long train with her dress which didn't even fit through the door. He didn't recall much about your father, just that he was a bit the worse for drink.'

'Shower of bastards!' said Lucasta, suddenly furious. 'And now the trollop thinks that she can just waltz in here, waving her marriage certificate and that we'll welcome her with open arms? Does she honestly think that's what deathbeds are for? Remarriage? Where is she? I'll wrap the wedding train around her deep-fat-fried neck.'

'Mummy,' said Portia warningly but it was too late. Lucasta swept into the family room as though clad in battle dress ready to see off the upstart invader and not dressed in her customary floor-length nightie with an oilskin jacket thrown over it.

'Fag!' she commanded as soon as she burst through the heavy oak door. Mrs Flanagan immediately sprang into action, waddling over to the fireplace and grabbing a box of Marlboro Lights which were sitting there.

'Light!' Again, Mrs Flanagan did as she was told, sniffing that there was a battle royal ahead. Shelley-Marie turned to flash her toothy smile at her, a bit unsure of what to make of this weird-looking woman glowering at her. Then the fog lifted as she put two and two together and, without hesitating, rushed towards Lucasta, throwing her arms around her neck.

'Oh, Lady Davenport, it's just so wonderful to meet you! Your ex-husband, I mean my husband, oh hell, you know I'm talkin' about ol' Jackie, well, he told me so much about you! He always used to say that his first wife was a deeply spiritual person who had a real connection with the other side and not just a washed-up ol' booze hound like some unkind folks said.'

There was a long silence as Portia and Mrs Flanagan looked at Lucasta to see how she'd take this. Andrew moved over towards them, ready to leap in and break up a fight at any second.

'Did the old git really say that about me? That I was deeply spiritual?' she asked, pleased.

'He sure did, my lady,' replied Shelley-Marie without a trace of guile. 'Why, as a matter of fact, I was gonna ask you to do my star chart for me. I'm an Aquarian.'

She'd hit a home run.

'Well, I'm Libra but I do have Aquarius rising,' replied Lucasta, totally disarmed. 'That means we get on.'

'Oh my Lord above, I am mighty pleased to hear that,' gushed Shelley-Marie, hugging her tightly in a big bear grip. 'Jackie talked 'bout you all the time, said he was sure that you and me would have a whole lot in common. You wanna know somethin'? I'm a little bit clairvoyant myself and I'm wonderin' if you and me maybe met up in a past life somewhere? I just feel such a strong connection with you. Have you ever been regressed?'

Yet another bull's eye.

Lucasta was known to be a great believer in past lives and regularly visited a new age spiritualist in Kildare in the hopes that it would unearth something spectacular which she could brag about for years to come. Not with great success, however: up to this point she had only discovered, after several very expensive hypnosis sessions, that she'd worked as an assistant dung-gatherer during the Black Death. Ever the eternal optimist, though, she continued to fork out large chunks of cash, convinced that one of these days it would turn out she'd really been Queen Elizabeth I.

'Oh, you really won't believe this,' said Lucasta, completely taken in, 'but I get my regression done as regularly as other women get highlights. How very interesting. And what have you uncovered so far, my dear?'

'Why don't we Irish up some coffee and I'll tell you all about it,' said Shelley-Marie, linking arms with Lucasta companionably. 'You know, already I have the strongest feelin' that you're a kindred spirit with my ol' grandma back in Kentucky. Why, you could even be her celestial twin.'

'Really? How astonishing.' Lucasta was mesmerized.

'For sure. She used to wander around the projects

85

wearing nothin' but her nightgown too. It's a sure sign that you're in touch with the angelic realm.'

'Have you ever seen anything like it?' Portia whispered to Andrew and Mrs Flanagan. 'She's playing her like a violin.'

'She's certainly done her research all right,' said Andrew grimly.

'Yeah, she has the poor unfortunate eating out of her hand,' said Mrs Flanagan. 'It can't be right, though, to take advantage of the afflicted like that. Yer mother's bad enough without being encouraged.'

It was hours later when Daisy finally hacked back to the Hall, frozen to the bone. The Hall was in darkness as she stumped her way up the great oak staircase, still clutching her riding crop, with her boots caked in mud. She kicked her way up as far as the second flight of stairs, knowing full well that her muddy boots were destroying Portia's brand-new Persian carpet and, for once, not caring. She was well beyond tears now, too emotionally drained for anything but sleep. As she thumped her way across the landing which led to the family bedrooms, she heard a voice coming from Lucasta's room. There was a light shining under the door which emboldened Daisy to knock.

'Oh, there you are, sweetie; I was just doing my nightly release meditations. Where on earth have you been all evening?' said Lucasta, standing at her dressing table enthusiastically mixing a drink and studying the measures as meticulously as a scientist in a laboratory.

'Out.' Daisy sounded sullen, like a wounded child with no shoulder to cry on.

'Well, you silly goose, you completely missed Shelley-Marie's cocktail-making lesson. Apparently she's worked in bars all her life to support herself through . . . beauty school, I think she called it; anyway, she's certainly picked up a trick or two. That's how she met your father, you know.'

'So mixing drinks wasn't the only thing the bitch picked up.' Daisy's temper, never far from the surface, was really starting to flare up now.

'She's just taught me this wonderful new way of making a g. and t.,' Lucasta rambled on, concentrating on the bottles in front of her and ignoring the fountain of bile spewing from Daisy. 'You add crushed ice, then a pinch of vermouth over the gin and then shake the bejaysus out of it before serving. Revelation. A most talented young lady. Wish I'd had the foresight to send you off to work in a bar when you were a teenager, you might have got yourself a husband by now.'

'Where is she?' asked Daisy furiously, the riding crop in her left hand starting to twitch dangerously. Not just at her mother's customary lack of tact, she was well used to that, but at the fact that she appeared to have been won over with so little effort on Shelley-Marie's part.

'Well, the Mauve Suite was free so I've put her in there. Portia almost had a fit because she wants to keep it ready for proper paying guests, but I told her to get lost. I mean, now that the opening night freeloaders have all buggered off, they're not exactly battering the door down to come and stay here, are they? Anyway, Shelley-Marie is family now, whether you bloody well like it or not. Perfectly lovely girl. And let's face it, anyone who'd go and marry your bollocks of a father without a gun being put to her head deserves sainthood.'

Poor Father Finnegan, parish priest at Ballyroan for over thirty years, had never seen a memorial service like it. Quite apart from the low turnout (aside from the family, only a dozen or so people had turned up to pay their last respects, most of whom had got the date confused and thought they were coming to parish bingo) there was the delicate question of who the chief mourner was going to be.

It was unprecedented, certainly in Ballyroan, for the widow of the deceased to be accompanied by his considerably younger second wife, especially as it seemed that the ink was barely dry on the marriage licence. Most irregular, he thought, although he knew the Davenports to be, well, an eccentric family to put it mildly. They certainly weren't regular churchgoers, that was for certain. And if Father Finnegan had one pet hate, it was parishioners who didn't show their faces inside the tiny church of Saint Claire from one end of a decade to another, until they wanted a religious service on demand, be it a wedding, a christening, or in this case, a memorial service. True, he had married Portia Davenport himself the year before last, but she was such a gentle, lovely person, always so friendly and warm-hearted, that it was hard for him to refuse her. Her mother Lucasta was quite another story though.

He could still recall the time, years ago now, when she set up a rival church in the grounds of Davenport Hall. The Temple of Isis she had called it, although it was really just a fancy word for paganism as far as he could see. There was a lot of nudity involved and cavorting in Loch Moluag on the estate and, pretty soon, a whole load of undesirable types had descended on Ballyroan, new-age hippies who were systematically destroying the peaceful calm of the town. They all seemed to have tattoos and drove dirty great camper vans that smelt of marijuana. Then there were the women who openly breastfed in public as they signed on for social welfare in the tiny village post office, which did little to impress the more conservative element of the parish. Word had quickly got back to his bishop in Kildare who demanded that poor Father Finnegan put a stop to this lunatic debauchery once and for all. However, it took a brave man to talk sense to Lucasta Davenport, he reflected, a braver man than him. She'd unceremoniously thrown him out of the Hall in language no lady should ever use.

'You'll be looking for tithes next, you narrow-minded fascist bastard!' she'd screeched at him as his Fiat Panda backfired its way down the driveway. 'As far as I'm concerned, my tithes are something that are attached to my buttocks.'

And now here she was standing outside the tiny church with her family waiting for the service to begin. 'Now look here,' she'd said to him imperiously, as if she were doing him a great favour in gracing the church with her presence, instead of it being the other way around. 'It's all very straightforward really. This is my husband's wife, simple as that,' she said, waving at Shelley-Marie who was hovering by her side like Mrs Danvers. 'I know, I know, it would have been a lot easier if Blackjack had just been gay, like the rest of the aristocracy, but there you are. Now let's just get this over with and pray that none of the retarded cousins show up.'

As if this wasn't bad enough, there appeared to be an altercation of some sort, Father Finnegan couldn't help noticing, between that pretty young Daisy Davenport and the new widow.

'No member of my family has ever gone to their final resting place without this being laid over them,' Daisy was snarling at Shelley-Marie, waving the tattered standard threateningly under her nose. 'If you don't like it, you can shove it up your lardy arse.'

'Why, all I said was that it looks like a picture of two cats doin' the business, that's all. I'm pickin' up so much hostility from you, Miss Daisy, when all I want is for us to be friends. Your papa often visits me in my dreams and I know that was his dyin' wish. Don't take it out on me just because you don't have a boyfriend.'

'Perhaps we might get started now?' Father Finnegan, trained in conflict resolution, judged this to be an opportune moment to intervene. The priest was at his wits' end, however, to think of something respectful he could say about the deceased in his eulogy. It was doubly hard, given that he had barely known him and also that his private life seemed so, well, colourful to say the least.

'John Davenport was, emm—' He broke off as his eye wandered down along the front pew. There were his two wives, sitting companionably side by side, Portia and her husband holding hands and then young Daisy looking distraught and sitting all by herself at the very end of the pew. Mrs Flanagan, whom he knew only slightly, was sitting in the back row by the door, and kept popping in and out for a cigarette. 'John Davenport was a family man,' he said without very much conviction. 'He valued his family above all else and, emm . . .' He silently racked his brains to think of more. 'He was a compassionate man, he certainly cared about, emm, about . . . those he loved.'

Portia glanced across at Andrew, deeply embarrassed at a priest having to lie so blatantly from the pulpit. Agnes and Lucy Kennedy, two elderly spinster sisters from the nearby town of Newbridge, were sitting behind them looking equally at sea.

'Excuse me,' Agnes whispered to Portia, leaning forward in her seat. 'Are we at the right funeral?'

Portia nodded, not blaming her a bit for being confused.

'Sure, God love poor Father Finnegan,' said Lucy, who was a bit deaf, in a loud stage whisper clearly audible around the church. 'What a dreadful job to have to eulogize Blackjack Davenport. Do you remember the time, Agnes dear, he can't have been more than ten years of age, when he called around to our house and ate my gerbil?'

There was a stony silence as the tiny congregation turned to look at her.

'Oh, for God's sake, can somebody just say one good thing about him, please!' hissed Daisy, at the end of her tether.

'Well, there is one thing you can't take away from him,' replied Agnes after a long pause. 'He had the most wonderful head of hair.'

'Yes, you're quite right,' said Lucy, nodding at her, 'just like Clark Gable's. Not a bit oily at all.'

Pretty soon the whole awful ordeal was over and Blackjack's remains were being ceremoniously carried down the aisle by a red-eyed Daisy. That was, until Shelley-Marie overtook her and snatched the tiny tin box out of her hands, marching triumphantly ahead of her like a rugby player who'd just scored a try. Lucasta, meanwhile, had made her way around to the church organ behind the altar, but instead of playing a suitable hymn, she was bashing out one of her favourite songs: 'Make a Bonfire of Your Troubles'.

'I honestly don't know whether to laugh or cry,' Portia whispered to Andrew as they made their way down the aisle and out into the biting February cold.

'Just think,' he replied, putting his arm around her, 'in a week's time, we'll be strolling down Park Avenue together and, I promise you, we'll look back and laugh.'

A sharp stab of worry struck her, but she wisely let it pass, for the moment anyway. There's a time and a place for that conversation, she thought as they moved out through the portico and down the stone steps outside the church.

Agnes and Lucy were still there and warmly shook hands with both of them. 'You're freezing!' Portia said kindly. 'You must both come back to the Hall for a cup of tea.'

'And you can see the renovations for yourself,' said Andrew, holding open his car door for them both.

'Oh, how sweet of you,' they chimed in unison, gingerly stepping up into the back seat of his jeep. 'I read all about your lovely party there the other night,' said Lucy, sounding just a tad peeved. 'It looked wonderful.'

'Yes, imagine Robert Armstrong being there, I'd have loved to meet him,' replied Agnes.

Portia winced at the barb but felt it was better to say nothing than to launch into a whole explanation about party planners and A-list celebrities and the kind of drivel Julia Belshaw would come out with. An awkward pause hung in the air as they turned sharp left past the gate lodge and on up the long driveway to the Hall. There was only one other car ahead of the hearse, which was Mrs Flanagan driving Lucasta, Shelley-Marie and Daisy, with great clouds of cigarette smoke spewing out of the windows. The convoy had almost reached the forecourt at the main entrance to the Hall when Lucy eventually spoke.

'Do you know what I was just wondering, Portia dear?' Portia turned around to face her. 'Well, I know your father signed the Hall over to you the year before last, when you were married,' she said very deliberately, as though bringing up a distasteful subject.

'And we're all so pleased about that, best thing your father ever did,' said Agnes diplomatically. 'It rightfully belongs to you and now Andrew too, of course. That's quite as it should be.'

'Least Blackjack could have done,' said Lucy in her loud deaf old lady's voice. 'The girls can't inherit, you know, the title only goes through the male line. You were very lucky he signed the Hall over to you when he did, Portia dear. Can you imagine some usurper coming along now and trying to turf you all out?'

'So what was it you wanted to know?' asked Portia, baffled and dying to know where all this was leading.

'Why, who the new Lord Davenport is, of course, dear.'

Chapter Six

' "Cecily! At last!" '

' "Gwendolen! At last!" '

' "My nephew, you seem to be displaying signs of triviality." '

' "On the contrary, Aunt Augusta, I've now realized for the first time in my life the vital Importance of Being Earnest." '

A thunderous roar of applause broke out as the cast stepped forward to take a well-earned bow. The audience got to their feet and the clapping grew to a deafening crescendo as the prison Governor rose from the front row and up on to the stage, patiently waving for a bit of hush. It took ages for everyone to calm down; even the armed prison officers dotted throughout the auditorium were going bananas.

'Thank you, thank you all very much for such a wonderful response,' he gushed when eventually the applause died down. 'All I can say is that based on tonight's performance, I think we can safely say the All-Ireland Padraig Pearse award for drama in the prisons is ours, for the fourth year running!'

More ear-splitting, raucous cheers from the audience, forcing the Governor to wait for several minutes before he could continue.

'Thank you very much. Now, I'd only love to be able to take credit for this remarkable feat, but I'm afraid all the accolades rightfully belong to one person and one person only. It is with great sadness that, only the other day, we heard that the best director this theatre has ever seen is unfortunately not going to be with us for very much longer.'

There were a lot of disappointed oohs and ahhs from the audience. Clearly, not everyone had heard this news.

'The time has come for this incredibly talented individual to, as actors would say, exit stage left.' The governor paused for laughter, delighted at his own gag, but none came. 'But all I can tell you is the outside world's gain is the inside's loss. Will you please put your hands together for the show's director, Jasper Davenport, our very own Mad Jasper!'

Mad Jasper stayed resolutely in the wings, apparently

97

preferring the shadows to the bright glare of the spotlight.

'Ah, come on out and take a bow,' the Governor coaxed, beaming at him as the cheering continued. 'I think he's a bit shy,' he said to the audience, teasingly. 'Maybe he's only waiting on me to address him by his fancy new title.'

More puzzled oohing and ahhing from the audience.

'Oh yes, indeed,' the Governor rambled on. 'We had a solicitor's letter only the other day with the big news. The most talented director this prison has ever seen is now entitled to call himself by a very grand new name, you know. So come on out and take a bow, Mad Jasper, your lordship!'

'Portia, for God's sake, Daisy is twenty-two years of age. It's high time someone handed her a bit of responsibility. It'll be the makings of her. Will you trust me on this?'

It was bloody hard to argue with Andrew when he was all fired up thus, Portia knew of old, not to mention the fact that he had a stubborn streak as long as Lake Geneva. Once he'd made his mind up about something, that was it. No going back. They were driving back from Kildare town where, among other things, they'd just been to collect their airline tickets from the local travel agency.

'Your flight is at two-thirty tomorrow afternoon,' the

heavily made-up agent had cooed at Andrew, unable to take her eyes off him as she passed over the business-class tickets with perfectly manicured fingernails. 'Check in is two hours prior to departure.'

'Thanks, I'm familiar with the routine.' Andrew grinned back at her, taking the tickets and slipping them into the breast pocket of his leather jacket. Right, Portia had said to herself, that gives me exactly twenty-four hours to sort this out.

It wasn't that she didn't want to get on that flight with him the next day. A huge part of her had been swept along in his usual tidal wave of enthusiasm for what lay ahead. New job, new faces, three blissful months together in one of the most exciting cities on earth. What more could she possibly want? It was sorely tempting to fantasize about the adventure that was in store and the sheer adrenalin rush of being part of that adventure with him. But like it or not, there was no shifting the awful sinking feeling she had deep in the pit of her stomach that she shouldn't go. Half of her knew how devastated she'd feel, watching him bound into the airport terminal without her, unsure of when she'd see him again, but the other, more practical side of her was resolute. The way things were at Davenport Hall at present, she considered herself lucky to get as far as Ballyroan, never mind the bright lights of Broadway.

The memorial service had been three full days ago and

Shelley-Marie showed absolutely no inclination to go anywhere. Nor could Portia put her continued presence down to plain old-fashioned gold-digging. The reading of Blackjack's will had come and gone and, unsurprisingly, he had left nothing of any value behind. Any money he'd won, he'd gambled and lost again, equally quickly. Lucasta got nothing; his lucky deck of cards and his lucky cigarette lighter he bequeathed to Mrs Flanagan; and Portia had to make do with a bill from the Bellagio Hotel for some three months' bed and board, which he'd let accumulate. To add insult to injury, Daisy wasn't even mentioned in the will. She hadn't been born when he'd written it and he'd never gone to all the bother of making a new one.

'I sure am mighty glad old Jackie didn't leave me nothing,' Shelley-Marie had pronounced, unconvincingly, Portia thought, as they all made their way back from the solicitor's office. 'Now no one can ever say that I married him for material gain.'

'Quite right too, darling,' Lucasta replied. 'There's far more to being a widow than just the jewellery.'

In the same short space of time, Daisy's behaviour had gone from distraught daughter to harridan from hell and not without just cause. Things weren't helped along by the fact that Shelley-Marie seemed to be one of those people who had an innate knack for ingratiating herself with those around her. She was already bosom buddies with Lucasta, who even went to the bother of giving her a guided tour of the Hall, a rare honour seeing as how she herself rarely got beyond the bar these days.

'And you know, darling,' she'd said to Shelley-Marie, pouring her a stiff gin, 'my idea is that every year we host a sort of bachelor festival on the grounds here in one of those big stripy circus tents. A little bit like the Lisdoonvarna bachelor festival, except that it'll be for bachelor girls too, or singletons, or desperados or whatever it is they call themselves these days. You know what single people are like; they'll fork out any amount of money if they think it'll buy true love. Their loneliness is our villa in Greece. We'd clean up.'

'Why, Lucasta, you truly are a financial visionary! I have never in all my born days met anyone with your business savvy. You know, you are gonna be a mighty wealthy woman some day.'

Lucasta beamed, totally unused to compliments. 'And you know I have great plans for in here,' she went on, sweeping her hand across the bar in the Long Gallery. 'You know how all those Hollywood stars spend fortunes going into detox in those ferociously expensive glorified health spas? God-awful places where you can't even have a drinkie or a ciggie, twenty-first-century concentration camps really.'

'I sure do,' replied Shelley-Marie, coughing slightly on the gin.

'Well, this room should be called the *retoxification* centre, where they can all come to top up on nicotine and booze and, well, name your poison really. Of course I suggested all this to Portia and she told me to sober up and bugger off.'

Shelley-Marie's expression instantly turned from gushing to aghast. 'Why, I simply cannot believe that your wonderful suggestion was brushed aside! You know, Portia' – which she pronounced 'Purrsha' – 'sure seems like a mighty good person, but . . . well . . .' she hesitated, deliberating, and then flashed her biggest, brightest, toothiest smile. 'I should learn to hush my mouth, shouldn't I? She is your daughter after all.'

'Oh, don't be so ridiculous. You're like a daughter to me now, darling, we're connected on quite another plane entirely. All that crap you read about how a mother should be bonded with perfectly ghastly people just because they've been down your birth canal is utter bollocks, if you ask me. Anyway, it's bad luck not to share gossip.'

'Well,' replied Shelley-Marie, dropping her voice conspiratorially, 'I know I've only known her a short time but I'm pickin' up such a lot of tension from her. I wonder if the stress of running a fancy big hotel is all gettin' to be too much for her. That handsome husband of hers must have spent a fortune on the place. She must be mighty worried that they won't make all that money back. How long has she been married to him for?'

'Oh I don't know, sweetie,' Lucasta giggled. 'About two stone?'

Portia had walked in on this cosy little tête-à-tête just in time to hear the tail end of the conversation. Shelley-Marie heard her footsteps on the polished wooden floor and had the wit instantly to shut up, beaming angelically at her, as if she and Lucasta had been discussing nothing more innocuous than the weather.

'I didn't know you drank neat gin,' Portia said, coolly taking in the scene.

'Why, as I was just remarkin' to your mama, it's never too late to learn a new skill.'

'We'll be seeing you go around the Hall in your nightie and wellingtons next, bashing out show tunes on the grand piano,' Portia had replied, silently boiling and wondering just how much more of her she could take.

Shelley-Marie didn't answer her, just smiled condescendingly as if to say: I understand exactly where you're coming from and I forgive you. She held her gelatined smile until Portia was out of sight and then shot a significant 'told you so' look at Lucasta.

It was as though she'd quickly assessed the pecking order at Davenport Hall and, having won Lucasta over, she next went to work on Mrs Flanagan. Andrew was the one who discovered them this time, sitting companionably together in the family living room watching daytime TV.

Mrs Flanagan had the rare gift of being able to follow about eight soap operas all at once, be they American, Australian, English or home-grown, as well as being fully abreast of what was happening on each and every one of the daytime talk shows. It was useless to ask her anything about current affairs – US Presidential elections could have been won and lost and she wouldn't know – but ask her who'd just had a makeover on *Live at Five* or who was about to have an affair with whom on *Coronation Street* and not only would you get a full report, but an in-depth analysis of future storylines to come as well. She could barely tell you the names of all the new household staff that she was supposedly supervising at the Hall, but when it came to characters on her favourite soaps, her memory was encyclopaedic. She was like a human computer: if you programmed in just one soap character's name, she'd immediately give you their fictitious date of birth, place of education, number of sexual partners past or present, number of marriages, brain tumours, occasions when they were left at the altar – the list went on and on.

'Now, you know so much more about TV than I do,' Shelley-Marie was saying, 'but it's my opinion that Oprah Winfrey is a prophet for our time. In another hundred years or so, I believe she'll be deified.'

She'd hit another home run.

'I'm hoarse saying that and no one ever listens to me,' replied Mrs Flanagan, delighted. 'If it wasn't for Oprah, I'd never have lost the half-stone.'

'Well, you'd better just be mighty careful not to smoke yourself too skinny now, you hear?' replied Shelley-Marie, affectionately patting the TV guide beside her. 'Now, would it bother you to tell me again all about the character of Ken Barlow in *Coronation Street*? I never tire of hearing you talk about him.'

Somehow, she'd even managed to get around the humourless Tim in the kitchen. A great snob and an even greater stickler for the niceties of protocol, he doggedly insisted on referring to Shelley-Marie as 'Lady Davenport' and Lucasta as 'the elder Lady Davenport'. He'd made the cardinal mistake of saying this to Lucasta's face the morning after the funeral when they were all having breakfast together in the Red Dining Room. The jar of homemade raspberry jam she flung across the room at him in response only missed his impeccably starched, crisp white chef's jacket by a hair's breadth.

'Elder my arse!' she snarled as Tim sensibly beat a retreat into the relative calm of the adjoining kitchen.

Recognizing her cue, Shelley-Marie followed him, carefully closing the door behind her. 'You must find it in your kind heart to forgive her,' she said, as though she'd known Lucasta all her life. 'She's still a little shocked, it's my opinion.' Then, perching herself on a stool, she flashed him her toothiest grin (which was reserved for men only) and hoisted up the thigh pelmet which passed for her Lycra mini-skirt. 'Tim, I wanna compliment you on that wonderful breakfast. Truly, that is the nicest meal I have been privileged to enjoy since I came to the Emerald Isle,' she half whispered in her breathy little girl's voice, being careful to point her breasts at him. Although it was a freezing morning in mid-February, she wore a see-through black gauze top through which her double D assets were clearly visible, with only the flimsiest scarf around her neck for warmth.

'Would you mind covering up, please? It's unhygienic not to wear the correct sanitary uniform in the kitchen,' he sniffed, flinging a chef's jacket and gauze hairnet at her.

Instantly copping that the sexy approach wasn't going to get her anywhere, she abruptly changed tack.

'Say, Tim? Would you have the time to show me exactly how you made the *deeeelicious* poached eggs with hollandaise and caviar? Where I come from, everything is just deep-fat fried till you can't barely taste nothin' but the grease. It sure would be a right honour for me to see a master chef like you in action,' she drawled, gamely trying to stuff her thick backcombed hair into the tiny hairnet.

Tim rarely smiled but he did now, delighted to have such a willing guinea pig, especially as one of his long-term ambitions for the Hall was to have a cookery school where he'd give hands-on demonstrations to guests who'd pay a fortune for the privilege.

Meanwhile, Andrew's jeep was just zooming past the outskirts of Ballyroan and still the debate raged.

'Do you know that when I was Daisy's age I was well on my way to being a junior partner in Macmillan Burke?' Andrew was saying, glancing sideways at Portia, who knew it was best for the sake of peace to let him have his say without interrupting. 'Her trouble is that she's just coasted along through life, indulged by your father, dropping out of school when she felt like it, messing around in the stables and calling it work because no one has ever pushed her to try and make something of her life. Don't you see? You and I are presenting her with a golden opportunity to impress everyone, not least herself. Up until now, she's been flakier than a bar of Cadbury's.'

Portia looked over at him to see if he had finished his pep talk, but there was more to come. She knew he didn't mean it, but there were times when he sounded just like one of those American self-help motivational experts, the 'you can change your life in seven days' type.

She looked out the car window just in time to see Lottie O'Loughlin, who ran Ballyroan's local Spar, chatting with Danny Maguire, their postman on the street corner. Portia instinctively smiled and waved at them, but both of them utterly blanked her, turning back to their conversation. They'd seen her, she was sure of that. More noses out of joint for not being invited to the opening. It was hard to blame them, given how long she'd known them and also the massive press exposure the Hall was getting. They were neighbours and should have been asked, simple as that. Honestly, she thought, I could kick myself for not standing up to bloody Julia Belshaw . . . There and then, she made a silent resolution not to be such a pushover in future. A little assertiveness would go a long, long way, particularly at Davenport Hall.

'And, let's face it, it's hardly nuclear physics, is it?' Andrew was still in full flow. 'Tim's running the kitchen like a dream and Molly and the rest of the staff have the place looking spotless. Bookings for the Hall are beginning to come in thick and fast. For God's sake, all Daisy has to do is answer phones politely, meet and greet guests and try and keep your mother as far out of sight as possible.'

'Honey, I know exactly what you're saying and I agree with you. Daisy hasn't exactly been a model career girl so far and under normal circumstances, I'd have no difficulty encouraging her to take a bit of responsibility for a few months. But no matter what way you look at this, these are not normal circumstances.'

'Portia, you are getting on that flight with me to-morrow and I won't take no for an answer.' Andrew was grinning, but his tone was deadly serious. 'We've worked our asses off getting the Hall up and running and we both need the change of scene. I want you in New York with me, simple as that.'

She could tell he was getting tetchy with her because he took the sharp left turn which led to the main gates of the Hall at breakneck speed, jolting her roughly against her seatbelt. 'Do you think I don't want to go? Do you think for one minute that I would choose to be apart from you?' She deliberately kept her voice cool and calm. 'But my point is that we have both worked too hard and invested far too much money for this not to work. The first few months that the Hall is open for business are critical. If I go away with you, the way things are at the moment, when we come back either Daisy will have stabbed Shelley-Marie or the other way around or one or other of them will have set fire to the Hall. A blood-bath or a massacre is the only outcome to this situation, and somehow I don't think that's the kind of publicity for the hotel that either of us wants.'

They drove on in silence for a bit, both of them at deadlock. They'd got as far as the tennis courts before, eventually, Andrew spoke. 'OK. OK. Say I talk to Miss Southern Fried brass neck as soon as we go in. If I can persuade her to leave quickly and quietly, as soon as possible, then will you come with me? Do we have a deal?'

He'd pulled the car up outside the main entrance by now and switched off the engine, turning to face her. He looked at her with that boyish, adorable, turn-me-down-if-you-dare glint in his eye which made her smile. Impulsively, she leaned forward across the passenger seat to kiss him. 'Then we've a deal,' she murmured, stroking his cheek with the back of her hand. Playfully, he caught her hand and was moving in to kiss her when there was a loud thud on the roof of their car. Another one followed immediately and then there was a deafening crash right beside where they had parked.

'Jesus Christ!' said Andrew as they both leapt out of the jeep and looked up to see what the commotion was. From a third-floor window above, which looked down directly on to the forecourt, Daisy was unceremoniously hurling bulging black bin liners like missiles and not caring where they landed.

'Bitch!' she screamed, flinging yet another one out of the window, which only missed the windscreen of Andrew's car by inches. 'Do you see wheels on the side of this Hall? Do you?' She was screeching like a demented banshee by now, Portia could only guess for Shelley-Marie's benefit. 'Well, let me tell you something! There ARE no wheels on the side of this house, there-fore it is not a bloody trailer so you can take all your tarty rubber mini-skirts and the rest of your slapper-wear collection and you can BUGGER OFF!'

In a flash, Shelley-Marie came running out of the Hall door, totally ignoring Portia and throwing herself helplessly into Andrew's arms. 'I'm detectin' so much hostility from your sister-in-law; I'm beggin' you to help me. Her papa died in my lovin' arms callin' my name—'

'That's a tiny bit of an exaggeration, actually,' Portia interrupted; annoyed with Daisy for physically throwing Shelley-Marie's stuff out of the window like this, but well able to see where she was coming from. 'My understanding is he died alone at a card table.'

'Oh, who are you, his biographer?' wailed Shelley-Marie, for once letting her guard down. 'I brought love and comfort to him in the twilight of his life and this is how his daughters thank me!' She could really turn on the tears at will; they were flowing freely down her cheeks now, making her thickly applied mascara run and giving her panda-bear eyes. Then came the trump card she'd been waiting to play for days. She hugged Andrew even tighter so that her make-up was now dribbling on to his jacket. 'After all, I am family now and there's no place else I çan go.'

'Oh, good luck,' Portia called over her shoulder to him as she tripped up the steps and into the Hall, leaving Andrew to deal with it. She couldn't, she just couldn't.

Any more of Shelley-Marie and she thought she'd physically be sick.

Hours later, Andrew still hadn't returned to the gate lodge but every time Portia started to worry, she'd brush it aside just as quickly. This is where he excelled himself, she'd reason. If anyone could talk Shelley-Marie into going quickly and quietly, it was him. With a bit of luck, Andrew's legendary persuasiveness would have worked like a charm and Miss Plastic Fantastic would be leaving tomorrow too, or so Portia fervently hoped. It did strike her as a bit odd that it all seemed to be taking so long, but then he was probably tying up other loose ends at the Hall before leaving in the morning, she reasoned.

She was upstairs in the bedroom, frantically stuffing clothes into a suitcase when she heard his car scrunch up outside. Immediately throwing the case off the bed, she hotfooted it down the stairs to meet him. God love him, she thought, he's probably thinking that New York will be an oasis of peace and tranquillity compared with all the recent goings-on at the Hall . . .

'Well?' she said, hugging him as he stooped to come through the barn door. He smelt a bit boozy, she noticed, but let it go. 'So when is the she-devil leaving?'

Andrew released her grip and ran his fingers through

his hair. Never a good sign. 'She's not. She's staying. Now, don't overreact, OK?'

'What?' Whenever anyone told Portia not to overreact, it immediately made her want to fling the nearest cat against a wall.

'The thing is . . . well, you see . . . I've hired her.'

Chapter Seven

Bookings for the Davenport Country House Hotel were really starting to come in thick and fast but nothing, absolutely nothing could have prepared any of the family for what was to come. It was first light the following morning and, as usual, Molly was the first out of bed and hard at work. Breakfast didn't begin until seven but that didn't stop her from rising a good hour before that so she could arrange all the morning papers neatly on the green baize side table in the Dining Room and also give the kitchen a final once-over before she deemed it hygienic enough for a master chef like Tim to work in. 'If you can't perform an operation on it, then it's not really clean,' was her constant mantra.

She was one of those fastidious people who took great pride in their job, the sort of person who permanently wore Marigolds and won 'employee of the month' awards. Naturally, this was a great bone of contention with Mrs Flanagan, who was rarely out of bed before ten and only ever began work after she'd channel-surfed her way through each and every one of the breakfast TV shows in the family living room.

'If that bleedin' Molly one thinks she's going to show me up, she can feck off,' she'd griped. 'I swear to Jaysus she'll be out polishing the gravel next. She opens doors with her elbows, for Jaysus' sake.'

Given that Mrs Flanagan's standards of hygiene once involved a famous occasion when she wiped wet cutlery against her bum to dry, no one was ever going to challenge her about her attitude to poor hard-working Molly.

'Do you know she's getting through six industrial-sized cases of Domestos a week?' she'd asked Tim incredulously on one of the rare occasions when they were speaking. 'When I had the run of the place, the one normal-sized bottle used to last months.'

'And you think that's something to brag about?' sniffed Tim in response. He was wise enough not to take the argument any further with her, though. All he asked was that Mrs Flanagan stay as far away from his pristine kitchen as possible and just let the professionals get on with it, an arrangement which suited everyone.

The first wintry rays of light were just breaking over

the Hall and, true to form, Molly was up and about, painstakingly polishing the brass door knob on the main door until it gleamed. Suddenly she looked up, hearing the unexpected sound of a car thundering down the driveway at speed. It was too early for a delivery van, she thought, and although they were expecting guests that day, they weren't due to arrive until well after breakfast. With a screeching handbrake turn which sent gravel hailstoning every which way, the car scrunched to a halt. Both doors opened and Molly immediately recognized Eleanor Armstrong, the President's daughter, stepping out of the passenger seat, accompanied by an older woman who looked vaguely familiar but whom she couldn't quite place.

Eleanor was dressed casually in jeans and a cream cashmere sweater with her long dark hair loose around her shoulders, looking as effortlessly stunning as she always did. Her companion, on the other hand, was wearing a bright lime-green trouser suit and clearly had absolutely nothing on under the jacket, except maybe two expertly positioned pieces of toupee tape to hold her in place. She looked as though she'd come straight from a nightclub as she strode imperiously towards Molly, whipping her sunglasses up into her chic blonde bob.

'I told you there'd be somebody up at this hour, Eleanor,' she said. 'It's the country, for God's sake, they're probably all out milking cows. Good morning!' she trilled at Molly as she tottered up the stone steps in her high heels, shivering against the early morning mist. 'We're here to see the bookings manager or, failing that, one of the Davenports will do. Well, except the mother, obviously.' Then, barging past Molly with an embarrassed-looking Eleanor trailing behind her, she added, 'Just tell them Julia Belshaw is here.'

The penny dropped as Molly realized this was the same ghastly woman who had organized the opening party and had had the cheek to hand her a cleaning schedule, as if she needed one. However, she said nothing, just nodded and showed them into the Library, wondering what on earth they wanted and whom she could possibly get to speak to them. Portia and Andrew were the obvious choice, but she knew they were both travelling to New York that day and that this would be the last thing they'd need. In their absence, her instructions were clear: Daisy was acting manager until they got back. Without hesitating any further, Molly scuttled up the four flights of stairs to the family bedrooms and knocked discreetly on Daisy's door.

'Come in,' said a muffled, half-asleep voice. Daisy and early mornings did not mix.

'I'm very sorry to disturb you,' said Molly, addressing the mound of tossed bedsheets under the huge counterpane, 'but Eleanor Armstrong is waiting to see you in the Library.' Then, as though describing something disgusting, she added, 'With Julia Belshaw.'

Daisy sat up, suddenly awake. 'Oh shit. What do they want?'

Although Molly strongly disapproved of bad language, she let this pass. After all, this was something of an emergency. 'I've absolutely no idea what brings them here,' she replied, 'but you should just see the mud on the soles of their feet. I don't care if she is the President's daughter, you're going to have to ask them to take their shoes off. Otherwise I'll have to disinfect the entire Library floor the minute they're gone.'

Five minutes later, Daisy had shoehorned herself into the hotel's new uniform, a neat black woollen jacket and skirt with a crisp white shirt underneath. She hated wearing it, naturally, but as both Portia and Andrew had resolutely insisted that it was compulsory for all staff, she had no choice. As an act of rebellion, she left her huge tousled mane of curls to tumble loose but did at least remember to clip on the nametag she'd been issued with: 'Daisy Davenport. Acting Manager'.

She legged it down all four flights of stairs two at a time before pausing for a brief moment to catch her breath beside the huge gilt mirror on the lower landing. An unaccustomed surge of pride filled her as she took a lightning-quick glance at her reflection. In a million years she wouldn't be caught dead in a two-piece suit.

Like her mother she hated formal clothes and was infinitely more comfortable in her jodhpurs, but now that she saw herself in all her glory, she had to admit she didn't look half bad. Ivana Trump eat your heart out, she thought to herself with a giggle. She knew exactly how much Portia and Andrew were trusting her with to keep the place going in their absence and, although she was nervous, she was determined to do them proud. I can cope, she whispered to herself before going into the Library. I've never had a job in my life, but I can cope. I'm a wonderful manager and I can cope . . .

Eleanor Armstrong, a natural diplomat like her father, immediately rose to greet Daisy as she burst confidently through the door. 'We've already met, actually,' she said in her soft quiet voice, shaking Daisy warmly by the hand. 'At your wonderful opening-night party, in fact. I remember thinking how brave you were to be there at all, considering you'd just heard the awful news about Lord Davenport.'

'Thanks, that's so nice of you,' replied Daisy, genuinely touched and instantly liking her.

'So you're some sort of manager now?' said Julia incredulously, not even bothering to greet Daisy. 'Where's Andrew? I was really hoping we could have a word with him.' Then as an afterthought, she added, 'Or with Portia, of course.'

'Off to New York, today as it happens,' replied Daisy,

doing her best to sound authoritative. 'I'll be in charge till they get back.'

Julia rolled her eyes to heaven as if to say that didn't quite suit her, then imperiously beckoned for Daisy to come and sit down on the sofa beside her, as though she owned the place and Daisy worked for her. She eyed Daisy up and down, apparently weighing up whether or not she could be trusted and then, realizing she had no choice but to deal with this inexperienced-looking slip of a girl, took the plunge. 'Can you keep a secret?' she snapped, briskly whipping a leather Filofax and a news-paper clipping from the depths of her Kelly bag.

'Emm, yes, of course,' replied Daisy, lying through her teeth. She knew perfectly well that you'd have to go a long way to come across a less discreet person than her. In fact, Portia used to tease her that she was nothing more than a gossipy aul' one with curlers in her hair trapped inside a beautiful young girl's body. If you wanted a rumour spread far and wide, all you had to do was tell Daisy, sit back and relax. Even labelling some-thing highly confidential didn't work, that meant she'd only tell one person at a time.

Eleanor blushed and smiled as she took off a pair of leather gloves to reveal the most stunning engagement ring Daisy had ever seen.

'Wow! What a knuckleduster!' she couldn't help exclaiming before reminding herself that acting managers like her should try and behave with a bit more decorum.

'I know, my father says you can't even see where the *Titanic* scraped it,' laughed Eleanor. 'I've lost count of the number of times I've scratched my nose on it, it's so big. The ring, that is.'

'Can I do the thing where you twist it round your finger three times and make a wish?' asked Daisy. Eleanor nodded happily and slipped the ring off her finger and on to Daisy's. It was a perfect fit and Daisy couldn't stop herself squealing like a schoolgirl in excitement. 'Look at me, I'm Liz Taylor! I have twenty-five husbands and thirteen chins! Say, look what Richard Burton just bought to celebrate me getting out of the Betty Ford Center!' she said, putting on a bad American accent and jokingly waving the rock under Eleanor's nose.

'Now you turn it three times towards your heart,' said Eleanor, delighted with her reaction, 'but you can't wish for either a man or money.'

'Oh bugger,' replied Daisy, 'there was me hoping I could ask for a fella.'

'*You* are *single*?' Eleanor said in total disbelief. 'You're joking, right? Don't tell me someone as stunning as you doesn't have guys queuing up for you?'

'This is Ballyroan you're in now, not exactly the night-club capital of Europe. If a single, eligible man rode into town we'd have him stuffed and mounted. So, tell me everything, who's the lucky guy?' Although this was the first time she'd spoken to Eleanor, Daisy found herself instantly bonding with her, she was so lovely and easy to chat to, one of those people it was impossible not to like.

'Well, it's been a bit of a whirlwind, actually,' began Eleanor before Julia gently but firmly cut across her.

'Eleanor darling, there's plenty of time for all that later. We're under such time pressure that perhaps we should get down to business?' Julia's tone when speaking to Eleanor was sugary-sweet and just a shade sycophantic, a woman who knew only too well which side her bread was buttered on.

'Oh sorry, yes, of course,' said Eleanor politely. 'Right then, to work. No doubt you're wondering what brings us here at this ungodly hour of the morning. Well, there's your answer,' she said, thrusting the newspaper clipping at Daisy who eagerly snatched it up. It was a headline article from a tabloid paper, dated that day, which read: 'EXCLUSIVE! TOP TOTTIE TO WED! ASHFORD CASTLE TO HOST SOCIETY WEDDING OF THE YEAR AS ELEANOR ARMSTRONG SAYS "I DO" TO HUNKY OLDCASTLE UNITED STRIKER MARK LLOYD.'

'Oh my God, you're marrying Mark Lloyd!' squealed Daisy in an ultrasonic voice, so high-pitched that Julia visibly winced and covered her ears. 'Oh my God, oh sweet Jesus, I think I have to have a lie-down! You are the luckiest girl alive!'

Eleanor beamed and blushed very prettily as would

any bride-to-be at a reaction like this. 'Oh, so do you support Oldcastle United then?' she asked politely as soon as Daisy let her get a word in.

'Emm, not exactly . . . No, I mean, I know *of* them, that they're a team and that they play in matches and wear tight shorts and things but I know exactly who Mark Lloyd is,' replied Daisy enthusiastically.

Indeed, there were probably only about two people in the Northern hemisphere who hadn't heard of Mark Lloyd. At just twenty-five years of age, he'd been Oldcastle United's star striker since the tender age of nineteen, and one of the main driving forces which consistently kept them at the top of the premiership league. He'd even been tipped for captaincy of the English team in the World Cup and successfully brought them to the semi-finals before they were knocked out in a nail-biting last-minute penalty shootout by the marginally classier Brazilian side. As far as public opinion went though, it hardly mattered. Mark Lloyd was a hero who continued to walk on water and who could do no wrong, one of those rare people on whom the gods smile and for whom they save their most lavish gifts. He was regularly hailed as an athletic genius on the pitch and his private life was no less colourful off it. Blessed with the body of an Adonis and the dark, brooding good looks of a movie star, he had already made millions from the endorsement deals for which advertisers were queuing up to sign him.

His few critics regularly griped about his over-exposure and indeed it was virtually impossible to go anywhere without seeing his black eyes and deeply suntanned face beaming out at you from billboards, magazine covers, shampoo bottles, even milk cartons. You name it: Mark Lloyd endorsed it; from designer sunglasses to men's underwear to an entire clothing line which one manufacturer had named especially after him. Outside Oldcastle's stadium in North London, one wily business-man even made a packet from selling tin cans labelled 'Mark Lloyd breath'.

In short, he was the man who had it all: looks, money (his personal wealth was estimated at seventy million pounds and he regularly appeared in 'The Hundred Richest' lists) and talent to boot. Ask any young kid kicking a soccer ball around his estate what he wanted to be when he grew up and chances are the snotty-nosed answer would be: 'Play for Oldcastle and score for England and make a fortune and sleep with loads of models like Mark Lloyd.' He was constantly topping 'Sexiest Man Alive' polls and numbered two Academy-Award-winning actresses among his recent list of ex-girlfriends. Even gossip magazines like the *National Intruder* had lost count of the number of high-profile celebrity page-three models, pop starlets and 'It' girls his name had been romantically linked with. And now he was marrying Eleanor Armstrong.

'That's right, I remember seeing a picture of you with him in *Dish the Dirt* magazine,' said Daisy, bright-eyed with excitement. 'And they said you were an item, but that was only, like, a few weeks ago . . .'

'We met a month ago and he proposed last week.' Eleanor was blushing scarlet by now, as though she was scarcely able to believe the news herself. 'I know, it's been a whirlwind and if any friend of mine was getting married to someone she'd barely known for four weeks, I'd be the first to try and talk sense into them. But Mark's the one. I just know. I knew from the moment I met him. I always used to think all that stuff in women's magazines about love at first sight was complete rubbish, but, oh no, it's not.'

'OH MY GAWD! That is the single most romantic thing I have ever heard!' squealed Daisy at a decibel level that made Julia wince again. 'So how did you meet?'

'Through my best friend, Simon Allonby. He's the team physician for Oldcastle and he invited me to a sporting achievement awards ceremony in January and, well . . . there was Mark. The funny thing is, poor old Simon doesn't even know about the engagement yet. He's on safari in South Africa and I can't get in contact with him. He'll be over the moon though, I know he will.'

'OH SWEET GOD, I JUST WISH IT COULD HAPPEN TO MEEEE!' Daisy's voice had risen another octave so the chances were that only dogs could hear her now.

'Must you? That hurts like a hangover. I had a very late night last night,' Julia snapped at her like a narky headmistress dealing with an irritating teenager. 'Anyway, I don't have time for pleasantries, so if we could just get to the point please?'

The contrast in the way Julia spoke to Daisy as opposed to the unctuous way she oiled around Eleanor was so marked it was almost rude. Daisy let it go, however, reminding herself that acting managers didn't snap the heads off visitors. Particularly really scary ones like Julia.

'Now, as I was leaving a certain A-list function which I'd organized in a well-known Dublin hostelry last night . . .' she continued.

'She was in a lap-dancing club,' Eleanor silently mouthed over at Daisy who had to pretend to cough to disguise her giggles.

'I received a call from a contact in the press,' Julia went on, oblivious, 'to alert me to the fact that not only had the news broken about Eleanor's engagement but that the media had also got hold of the fact that the wedding was to be held at Ashford Castle. So you see where that leaves us.'

'Emm . . .' was all Daisy could say, not seeing at all.

'You see, the wedding has to be a secret,' explained Eleanor, 'because both Mark and I—'

'Have already signed an exclusivity deal with *Gotcha* magazine,' said Julia, finishing her sentence for her. 'But now that the tabloid rat pack are on to us, Ashford Castle is out. So we need somewhere fabulous, naturally, and within easy commuting distance of Dublin because of the number of celebrity guests who'll be flying in, somewhere where the magazine can have tight control over security—'

'And I absolutely fell in love with Davenport Hall the minute I came here,' Eleanor chipped in. 'I can't think of anywhere more magical to be married. Mark's going to love it here too, I know it.'

'Oh bloody Nora, you mean you want to marry Mark Lloyd here? Sweet mother of all that is good and pure, I can't believe this!' Daisy was well and truly hysterical by now and kept pacing up and down the room like a woman possessed, unable to stand still for two seconds together.

'And you wait and see if I don't get you fixed up with one of Mark's friends!' Eleanor beamed at her, causing Daisy to go even more apoplectic.

'YES! YOU'RE RIGHT! The Hall will be crawling with big sexy hunky footballers!' she shrieked. 'Just wait till I tell everyone, no one is going to believe it!'

'That's exactly what you can't do,' said Julia scribbling furiously into her Filofax, 'tell anyone. Assuming the Hall is available and that you're quite capable of taking this on, then *Gotcha* magazine are insisting on absolute secrecy, or the deal's off, plain and simple.' She stopped scribbling for a moment to glare across at Daisy, coolly assessing this scrap of a thing who didn't seem responsible enough to take charge of a dormant hamster never mind the society wedding of the year. 'Look, Daisy, this is going to be the single biggest thing that's happened in the countryside since your last shit-shovelling contest or whatever it is people who don't live in the city get up to when they're not worrying sheep. I'm talking a guest list of at least two hundred, I'm talking about taking over the entire Hall for the wedding, I'm talking about a marquee in the garden stacked with enough champagne to send shares in Veuve Clicquot skyrocketing and as if that weren't enough' – she threw her head back and shook her bobbed hair imperiously – 'I'm talking about Saturday March the twentieth, barely four weeks away. Are you absolutely sure you're up to this?'

Daisy eyeballed her, drawing herself up to her full height. 'On behalf of the Davenport Hotel group,' she pronounced, with Ivana Trump as a role model not far from her thoughts, 'we're honoured that you've chosen us for your wedding. You've made the right choice. And, of course, it goes without saying that we can fully cope.'

Exactly ten minutes after they'd driven off, Daisy was on the office phone sobbing hysterically. 'Oh Portia, you have to help me, I have the most unbelievably big news and I can't cope with it, I really can't, it's too much for me. You HAVE to help me! I know you're supposed to be heading off to New York today but I really need for you to swing by here and explain to me how I'm supposed to deal with this. Oh God, oh God, I know I've only been in charge for half an hour, but I really think I'm having a nervous breakdown or even a heart attack; I'm having pains in my chest and it hurts me to breathe and I'm all dizzy and this is just all too overwhelming—'

'Now, I need you to calm down, darling,' Portia interrupted soothingly, all her years of experience in dealing with Daisy when she panicked like this coming to the fore. 'Just tell me what's happened and, whatever it is, we'll deal with it.'

'OK, OK, OK,' said Daisy, forcing herself to take long, slow, deep breaths. 'I think you should be sitting down for this though.'

Between gulping for air and hyperventilating, eventually Portia managed gently to extract the news from her. The society wedding of the year was to be held at Davenport Hall. Signed, sealed, delivered, in the bag, one hundred per cent confirmed. Portia slumped down on the bottom stair beside the phone. And this was before she was even told the news about Shelley-Marie?

'Daisy, will you do something for me?'

'I'll try. I might pass out, but I'll try.'

'OK, great. Just get in the car and come over to the gate lodge. I've something to tell you too and I don't want to say it over the phone.'

'I'm on my way.' And she'd hung up.

When Andrew arrived back at the gate lodge the previous night, it transpired that during the course of his 'little chat' with Shelley-Marie, she'd impressed on him how guilty she was feeling about staying on at the Hall and how much she'd love to contribute.

'You know there sure is so much I could do for you folks,' she'd whispered in her breathy little girl's voice to him. 'Why, by trainin', I'm a technician.'

'Oh really?' he'd answered politely. 'Do you mean you're some kind of engineer?'

'Why no!' she giggled, playfully punching his arm. 'A nail technician.'

In the gospel according to Shelley-Marie, the only facility lacking at Davenport Hall was a good old-fashioned beauty salon, US style.

'There's no treatment I'm not qualified to do,' she'd argued. 'Yoga classes, holistic facials, skin consultations, blow-dries, tattoos, Hawaiian massage – why, I began my career as a masseuse. I can wax, tint, pluck and scrub like a drag queen. My speciality is a deep-cleansing organic mud wrap. Andrew, these folks are paying you'all good money, don't you think they deserve to be wrapped in cling film and submerged in mud?'

And so after several strong whiskies and very much against his better judgement, Andrew somehow found himself not only agreeing to the salon being set up, but also to forking out for the old nursery suite on the fourth floor to be converted for the purpose. 'No problem, absolutely no problem in the world, marvellous, delighted with the whole beauty thingy,' he'd drunkenly slurred at Shelley-Marie on his fourth attempt to put his car key into the ignition before snaking down the drive-way, well and truly over the limit. 'Just have a word with the missus, she'll sort everything out.'

'The missus', predictably enough, hit the ceiling when he told her the news. Andrew had been apologetic bordering on grovelling, while Portia drummed into him the enormity of what he'd just agreed to.

'You do realize that Daisy will go ballistic when she hears this? How will we ever get rid of Shelley-Marie now?'

'I know, I know, oh Jesus, I am so sorry,' he had said as his ever-patient wife plonked two Solpadeine into a glassful of water by the bedside table for him. 'It's just . . . I don't know what it is, but it's like she has this way of getting around people. I think I'd have agreed to any-thing just to get away from her. Shame she went into the beauty business, she'd have cleaned up as a corporate lawyer.'

That bit Portia could understand. After all, she had witnessed first hand how Shelley-Marie had wormed her way around just about everyone else up at the Hall . . .

'Anyway, it won't be as bad as you think,' Andrew went on, seeing her tense, worried look. 'Think about it. She'll be so up to her eyes getting the salon organized, it'll keep her well out of Daisy's way. And we'll be back in twelve weeks and we can sort it all out then. Miss Plastic Fantastic had absolutely no intention of going anywhere for the time being, you know. At least this way she's making herself useful.'

'I know, I know,' Portia had sighed, clambering into bed beside him. 'It's just, well, I'm the one who's going to have to break it to Daisy, aren't I?'

The sound of Andrew in the shower, happily cater-wauling *New York, New York* at the top of his voice, brought Portia back to the present. He was no Luciano Pavarotti, but what he lacked in singing ability, he more than compensated for in sheer volume and could now be heard loud and clear throughout the tiny gate lodge. Without even stopping to think, she leapt up the stairs and tapped at the bathroom door. 'Can I come in?'

He was too busy wailing to hear her gentle knocking, so she went in anyway. He was just stepping out of the shower and was wrapping a towel around his waist when he saw her. 'Hey, sexy lady,' he said, playfully pulling her towards him. 'You know I'd like nothing more than a quickie, but I'm expecting my wife any second.'

'You're drenched,' she said, ruffling his wet hair as she wrenched out of his strong grip and perched on the edge of the bath.

'Oh baby, baby, can you believe this? In less than twelve hours, you and me will be sipping cocktails in the Plaza and the only thing you'll have to worry about is whether to begin your shopping in Macy's or Saks the next day.'

He sounded so buzzy and excited, so full of enthusiasm for what lay ahead, that she dreaded having to burst his bubble. Get it over with quickly, her instinct told her. 'OK, I have news. Big news.'

'Give me the last sentence first.' He was looking at himself in the tiny bathroom mirror now, liberally splashing on Burberry aftershave.

'Remember us wondering why Eleanor Armstrong was so anxious to have a full guided tour of the Hall, the night of the opening?'

'I surely do. Far more important question. Do you think we should eat at Sardi's or at the Rockefeller Center tonight? Or maybe we should stay local? I know this great seafood place just around the block from the apartment, you'd love it . . .'

'You're not listening.'

'I am. Eleanor Armstrong and the grand tour. And there was me thinking she was just trying to get me alone.'

'She's getting married to Mark Lloyd and she wants to have her wedding at the Hall. Exclusivity deals with a magazine who are paying for the whole shebang, the works.'

'Wow!' Andrew turned to face her, gobsmacked. 'She's marrying Mark Lloyd? *The* Mark Lloyd?'

'In about four weeks' time, yeah. But, darling, don't you see what this means?'

'I certainly do. It means, my sexy one, we are RICH! We're home and dry, baby!' He had pulled her up to her feet and was now waltzing her round in circles. 'What did I tell you, oh ye of little faith? The Davenport Hotel is going to be the biggest success story of the decade! YIPPEEEEEE! So how does it feel to be married to a multi-millionaire, you lucky girl?'

'Be serious. You know what this means.'

'No I don't.' He was looking at her, genuinely puzzled, and then the penny dropped. 'Portia, if you think for a minute that I'm going to let you stay behind to work on this wedding, you're very wrong.' His eyes were twinkling at her, but he sounded deadly serious.

'Andrew, listen. One of us, and by one of us I mean me, will have to stay. How can we leave Daisy in charge of this? I haven't even broken it to her yet about Shelley-Marie, and you can guess the reaction that'll get. I've just put down the phone to her and she was practically hyperventilating. Julia Belshaw has just landed this on her—'

'Julia's organizing the wedding?'

'Yeah, but—'

'No buts. Problem solved. Julia could run the country with one hand tied behind her back. Best wedding planner in the business. You know, you're going to have to learn to delegate here, what will your staying on achieve? The two of us apart, you slaving away behind a reception desk here, me missing you in New York . . . No, no way. We're going away together as planned and that's all there is to it. I want you there with me, simple as that.'

God, he could be so stubborn when he really wanted something, Portia thought. And he really, really wanted them both to go to New York . . .

'Sweetheart,' he said, perching on the edge of the bath beside her and really giving her his full attention, 'quite apart from anything else, you need the break. We both do. You worked so hard for the opening, over my dead body am I letting you stay on here to worry about bridesmaids and ushers and bloody flower arrangements and all that jazz.'

He was playing with her hair now, and Portia let him. The thought of being a continent away from Julia and her bossiness was sorely tempting . . . although she did feel a sharp stab of guilt at dumping this on Daisy's

135

inexperienced shoulders. Talk about feeling torn between the two people she loved most . . .

She blushed prettily as he coiled a long strand of her hair round his finger. After all, he had given up so much for her, and now it was payback time.

'I'm sorry to force you into an A or B situation, babe,' said Andrew in his most persuasive I-could-sell-sand-to-the-Arabs tones, 'but don't I come before the Hall?'

'Of course you do. I'm just worried about landing all this on poor Daisy, that's all.'

'That's what email is for. That's what phones are for. Worst-case scenario: something awful goes wrong. You can fly back in a matter of hours, so where's the problem? This is where Julia excels herself and at the end of the day, what do either of us know about planning big fancy weddings?'

Chapter Eight

Saying that Lucasta was a teeny bit eccentric was a bit like saying that the Leaning Tower of Pisa was ever so slightly off-centre. Before the Davenport Country House Hotel had ever opened for business, it was a great source of worry to all concerned exactly how she'd behave in the company of guests who were paying a fortune for the privilege of staying there. In the hectic days leading up to the opening, both Portia and Andrew had drilled it into her long and hard as to what was and, more importantly, what wasn't acceptable behaviour whenever there were visitors around. Poor Portia had even suggested at one point that they go shopping to buy Lucasta a new wardrobe, in the hope that it might lure her out of her customary nightie and wellies worn under a smelly oil-skin jacket.

'You don't need to dress like that any more, Mummy,' she'd gently pleaded. 'The central heating inside the Hall is state of the art now, not like in the old days when we all had to wear six layers of clothes each so as not to get frostbite. It's boiling now, all the time, so what about getting rid of the wax jacket and letting me buy you something, well, you know, a bit more suitable?'

'But this is my look, darling, why should I change what works? Are you suggesting there's something wrong with me as I am?' Lucasta replied, fishing in her pockets for the remains of a battered pack of cigarettes. 'Yes! Two left!' she said, jubilantly stuffing a fag into her mouth and lighting it. 'You see? My outfit is functional as well as flattering. I can fit five packs of ciggies in the pockets as well as little treats for my kitties. You know, darling, if you're going to insist on smartening us all up you really should invest in a full-length mirror for yourself, you know. I don't give a tuppenny shite what Andrew says, the happiness fat most definitely does not suit you.'

And so, looking like an extra from *One Flew Over the Cuckoo's Nest*, she tripped down the stone steps at the front of the Hall just in time to see Eleanor about to clamber into the passenger seat of Julia's nippy sports car. 'Good morning, Lady Davenport!' she called up the steps to her. 'My father said if I saw you I was to be sure to pass on his very best!'

'Who the hell are you now, I wonder?' muttered

Lucasta, blowing cigarette smoke into the early morning mist and squinting suspiciously at her. Fortunately, Eleanor couldn't hear as Julia was revving up the engine, impatient to move on to the next appointment she'd carefully scheduled for the bride-to-be.

'I think he's quite taken with you actually!' Eleanor added before hopping nimbly into the tiny two-seater and zooming down the driveway.

'Well, your father's only human, whoever he is,' Lucasta shouted back, oblivious to the fact that two more guests were coming down the steps behind her, out for a stroll to work off their enormous breakfast. They were a youngish couple, city types by the look of their brand-new 'his and her' matching tweed jackets and spotless walking shoes.

'I mean, like, I can handle the quiet of the countryside OK,' the girl was saying in a whiny, nasal, south Dublin accent, 'but it's the smell that drives me, like, totally nuts, you know?'

'Exactly, babe,' replied her boyfriend in an equally irritating accent. 'It smells like, I dunno, like raw sewage or unemptied bins or something, like, really putrid, you know?'

'It's only horse manure from the stables, you idiots,' said Lucasta as they walked by her. 'This is the country, for Christ's sake, what do you expect? That the horse shit smells meadow fresh? What do you want me to do? Go down there and spray them with air freshener? Arseholes.'

She was in a foul humour that morning and not without good reason. Lucasta was the proud owner of at least two dozen cats, including an army of strays she fed and who frequently slept in bed beside her. However, since the Hall had reopened, her absolute favourite cat, Martini, had vanished. She'd searched for him high and low and had even sneaked into guests' bedrooms, half the time not caring whether they were there or not, but no sign. She placed the blame for poor Martini's disappearance firmly and squarely at Portia's door; if she and Andrew hadn't insisted on all her cats being confined to the family rooms once the hotel was open, then this wouldn't have happened.

'They've been used to having the run of the Hall and now the poor angels are completely disorientated since you've so cruelly banished them from their natural habitat. What in God's name is wrong with them anyway, I'd like to know?' she'd screeched at Andrew on one of the rare occasions when he'd firmly put his foot down with her. 'These animals have a damn sight more pedigree in them than the bloody middle-class snobs you want to come and stay here. I've a good mind to report you to the ISPCA, you unfeeling bollocks.'

Martini, however, had proved himself to be something of a daredevil in the past. When the builders were in, he'd vanished for a full day before one of the workmen discovered him stuck at the bottom of a cement mixer. But by now a whole week had passed without any sign of him, which led Lucasta to conclude the very worst. With her chin up and her head held high, she decided that if Martini had indeed passed over to the other side, then she should try to make contact with him to make sure he was being fed and minded properly in the spirit world. It was the least a loving pet owner could do and far more than she would have done for her ex-husband (who often used to goad Lucasta by saying that the only good cat was a dead one squashed on the side of the road).

And so, armed with a tatty book she'd fished out of the Library entitled *The Amateurs' Guide to Conducting a Séance*, she made a beeline for the old cowshed at the bottom of the kitchen garden. It was just about the only spot on the estate which hadn't been renovated and she felt that Martini's spirit would feel at home with the leaky corrugated roof, the bales of hay strewn around and the overriding stench of dung, away from the pristine cleanliness of the house proper. This was a process which demanded absolute privacy and quiet and it was nigh on impossible to get either at the Hall these days. It was barely nine in the morning and already she could hear the whine of Molly's hoovering wafting through an open window, not at all conducive to getting in touch with the spirit world, she sighed, flicking her long grey mane over her shoulders and going inside the shed.

It was almost pitch black as Lucasta shut the door behind her and groped her way inside, plonking down on her hands and knees and spewing out the contents of her pockets. A moment later, she had successfully lit four tiny tea lights and had expertly sprinkled some sage and marjoram in a circle connecting them. 'Now, before we get started, spirit guides, I need you to pay very close attention,' she ordered, as though the other side were no further off than a long-distance phone call. 'It says in this book that I need to sprinkle the droppings from a virgin unicorn on the ground for the spell to work. Well, I'm awfully sorry but I couldn't get any so Oxo granules will just have to do instead.' Squinting in the candlelight at the tiny print in her book, she began to chant, 'Feline Goddess of the North, I salute you. Feline Goddess of the South—' She broke off suddenly and strained to listen. There it was, a very faint, weak meowing noise and close by too, by the sound of it.

'Oh Christ,' sighed Lucasta in exasperation. 'I'm inclined to forget how talented I am. One line of a spell is all I need utter successfully to break through to the other side.' Then, raising her voice, she called out, 'Martini, my little cherub, it's Mummy. Can't you hear me, sweetheart? Are you at peace, darling? Are there any messages you want to give me from beyond the grave?

Racing tips, lottery numbers, that sort of thing? Meow once for yes and twice for no.'

There was a rustle of hay which caught her attention and, as she turned sharply around, there was Martini, limping towards his mistress.

'Oh my little darling, you've come back to Mummy,' she twittered, delighted, scooping him up in her arms and kissing him full on the lips. 'What on earth happened to your paw, my angel?' she cooed, noticing the tiny splint that had been carefully bandaged to Martini's hind paw.

'I'm terribly sorry, but I'm afraid it could be broken,' came a man's voice, speaking very politely from the gloom. 'I've done my best with the paw, but I really think he should see a vet.'

Lucasta knelt in silence, still as a statue for a moment, before the realization finally dawned on her. 'Do you know, Martini,' she whispered, cradling him close, 'I've always suspected that there was a vortex on the estate where spirits from the other side could port through. Well, there must be because how else do you explain the way all my ciggies keep disappearing? But never, never, never even in my wildest dreams did I imagine I'd stumble on it at the back of the old cowshed.' Then, raising her voice and trying her best to conceal her excitement at this rare find, she shouted up to the roof, 'Now, I'm quite sure you're a very benign spirit and I'm so pleased that Martini's brought a little friend with him from the other side. Are you some sort of spirit guide? Or perhaps you're a poor lost soul who's found his way through the vortex by accident? A sort of spiritual tourist or day-tripper, that sort of thing, you know?'

'Ehh, something a bit like that, yes,' came the puzzled reply from behind a mound of haystacks.

'Oh now, where are my manners,' said Lucasta as though she were hosting a society dinner party. 'Is there anything I can do for you to make you more comfortable?' she cooed at the leaking roof. 'Perhaps you'd like me to do an energy clearing or burn some incense or maybe do a little chanting to make you feel at home while you're passing through our world?'

'I'd hate to put you to all the bother of chanting,' came the voice unenthusiastically, 'but now that you mention it, I'm absolutely starving. A few sandwiches would be brilliant, thanks. The smell of food from the Hall is driving me insane.'

Lucasta could hardly contain her excitement. 'Unbe-fucking-lievable,' she said, awestruck. 'An ectoplasmic manifestation with an appetite!' Raising her voice again, she added, 'I'll be right back. Stay here and be at peace whilst I'm gone. Be a dear and keep an eye on Martini for me, will you?'

'I'd be delighted,' came the reply. 'Oh, and by the way, I'm strict vegetarian; I don't eat anything that ever had a face. I hope that's not a problem, is it?'

The grandfather clock in the gate lodge had just chimed ten as a scene of a very different sort unfolded. Portia had just finished breaking the big news to a hysterical Daisy, already on the verge of a breakdown over Eleanor Armstrong's impending wedding to Mark Lloyd. They were sitting in Portia's sunny little kitchen, surrounded by bulging suitcases while Andrew stomped around on the wooden floors upstairs, swearing aloud when he couldn't find clothes he specifically wanted to bring.

It had been the worst, bitterest, most God-awful row the sisters had had in years. Daisy had always been headstrong and obstinate about getting her own way when it came to arguments, and nine times out of ten Portia would cave in to her, usually wanting nothing more than a quiet life. But the row over Shelley-Marie was different. Daisy was a great one to scream and shout and hurl things around in arguments and now was all the more effective for being furious in an ice-cold way. Far, far scarier.

'You're telling me that Andrew went and *hired* Shelley-pisshead-Marie? And that not only am I left in charge of the Hall for what will be the biggest wedding of the year, but on top of that, I still have to deal with that two-faced, manipulative, conniving bitch? Tell me you're joking. Please, Jesus, tell me this is April Fool's Day.'

145

'Darling, I'm no happier about this than you, but just think, it could be quite useful to have a beauty salon on hand for this wedding—'

'An A. and E. department to stitch heads would be a damn sight more useful. You're insane even to think about letting her near guests, unless you want it to look like a Dollywood wedding in all the photos.'

The sound of another holdall being dumped on the hall outside broke the awful silence.

'Daisy, will you just hear me out?' Portia pleaded, aware that time was ticking by and that she and Andrew would have to leave any minute. 'You know how important it is for us that this wedding goes as seamlessly as possible. We couldn't buy the publicity it's going to generate; it'll put Davenport Hall on the map for the rest of our lives. And,' she added, 'it's not as if we're completely leaving you high and dry. Julia Belshaw will be running the show with you and just look at the marvellous job she did organizing the opening of the Hall.'

'Bugger Julia anyway. Don't you realize the longer Shelley-scumbag-Marie stays, the harder it'll be to get rid of her? At this stage, she'll probably claim squatter's rights. Not for one second would I put it past her.'

Portia sighed. Just this once, she was going to pull out all the emotional stops. No matter how shifty she felt about it, this time she had no choice. 'Darling, I know how hard it is for you having her loitering around the place, but let me make a deal with you. If I faithfully promise you that the morning after the wedding you can personally show her the door, then will you just put up with her until then? I need you onside, Daisy, I can't go away unless I know you're OK with this. Andrew and I have practically bankrupted ourselves just to get this far with the Hall and if this wedding goes well, then we're home and dry. Please, darling?' Then came the ace she'd kept up her sleeve. 'Will you do it for me?'

She looked across the table at her sister, trying to gauge her reaction. With Daisy, you never could tell how she'd react when faced with a situation as unpalatable as this one. There was a good chance that she'd tell the lot of them to get lost and continue hurling Shelley-Marie's belongings out of windows and generally making life a living hell for those around her.

'Well?' Portia asked gently. 'Do we have white smoke?'

Daisy had been staring into space, lost in her own little world, and Portia deliberately didn't break the silence. A revolting crystal carriage clock, a gift from Andrew's mother, chimed eleven, but she still said nothing, even though she knew their taxi would arrive any minute.

'You know I hate the bitch's guts,' Daisy eventually said, looking Portia in the face.

'I had noticed that, yes.'

'And you know I think she's using you for free bed

and board now that she's discovered Daddy had sweet bugger all of any value in Ireland.'

'I know, darling. I agree with you.'

'And you know I don't buy into her bloody daytime TV tale of woe.'

'Neither do I, not for a moment.'

'But against all that . . .' Daisy rolled her big baby blue eyes the way she used to when she was a small child and was caught doing something naughty. 'I know how much you've ploughed into the Hall and what big news this wedding is. And of course I know how important it is to you that it goes off OK, to you and Andrew, I mean,' she added hastily. 'And I know you should be all excited about going to New York with him now, not sitting here at the last minute, worrying about whether or not the place will become famous for being the first hotel in Kildare to have a homicide on the premises within a few weeks of opening.'

Portia smiled, sensing the conversation was going her way.

'So, all right then, we have a deal. I'll promise to swallow my pride and behave myself until Eleanor Armstrong is safely married, on the condition that I get to fling bitchface out of here personally the next morning.'

'You're an angel.' Portia beamed. 'I knew you'd come through for me.'

They both looked up to see Andrew bounding through the kitchen door with his overcoat on, finally ready to go. 'So, do we have a Pax Romanus?' he asked, looking at Daisy a bit nervously.

'Everything's OK,' said Portia, rising to go.

'Ahh, Daisy, you're just the best,' said Andrew, sounding more than a little relieved. 'You're going to make a brilliant acting manager. And you know Shelley-Marie has some wonderful ideas for the Hall. I think she'll prove to be a real asset.'

Daisy had to bite her tongue from replying that the only asset that conniving wagon seemed interested in was free bed and board for as long as no one saw through her. In the Mauve Suite too, only the best and most expensive in the Hall . . . She let it pass, not wanting to sour this goodbye.

There was a maniacal thumping at the front door.

'That'll be Tom,' said Portia, zipping up one of her bulging bags. 'Be hell to pay if we're not in that car in exactly thirty seconds.'

Tom was Ballyroan's local taxi driver who was famous for always being ridiculously early to collect customers. He would then thump on their front doors and windows while people broke their necks to get ready and not keep him waiting; then he'd spend the entire journey berating them for delaying him, as though they weren't paying through the nose for the privilege; then he'd inflict 'the lecture' on them, about how unpunctuality was a form of disrespect bordering on bullying. There was probably no one in the entire village who hadn't been subjected to 'the lecture' at some point, with the result that most people simply booked him for about a half-hour after they actually needed to be driven anywhere.

'I'll phone you every day,' said Portia as they stepped out into the chilly, misty morning. Andrew and Tom were frantically lugging bags into the boot of the car and the sisters hugged each other tightly. Although wild horses wouldn't have kept Portia from flying to New York that morning, she was such a natural worrier that of course she felt huge pangs of guilt at leaving her sister with so much responsibility, particularly after the events of the last twenty-four hours. Daisy knew this too and with that unspoken bond that exists between sisters, that gift of knowing what the other is thinking without anything actually being said, she knew full well her job was to send Portia off with as many reassurances as she could give her. Whether she believed them herself or not was entirely another matter.

'And I'll email you every night,' she replied, trying her best to sound confident and managerial.

'That's it then,' said Andrew eventually, when the last suitcase had been hauled into the car. 'Jump in, or we'll be late.'

'You take good care of her,' Daisy said, pecking him

warmly on the cheek. 'And don't worry about a thing here. Everything is going to be just fine.'

Portia rolled down the window and waved after her, silently blessing her for being such a trooper. She waved like minor royalty until the taxi had turned out through the gates and on to the main road. Everything *is* going to be fine, she thought, banishing aside any lingering last-minute worries she felt about leaving Daisy in charge. Of course she was doing the right thing in going away with Andrew. After all, she reasoned, the Hall and all its attendant problems would still be waiting there for her when they came home. And at the end of the day, it was only for a few weeks, really . . .

'You OK?' said Andrew, slipping his hand around hers.

She beamed back at him, knowing she'd made the right decision. 'I'm fine.' After all, she figured, didn't her marriage come first?

Two hours later, she and Andrew were ambling through the wide, busy duty-free area of Dublin airport, hand in hand and looking for all the world like a pair of newly-weds.

'Do we have time for a coffee?' Portia asked, always a bit antsy about being late.

'Plenty of time,' Andrew replied, steering her towards a Butler's café on the concourse. 'My tummy's rumbling so loudly, you could mistake it for Concorde's final flight.'

The café was packed with passengers, bags, buggies

and baggage, but they queued up, ordered steaming hot lattes and two sinful, sticky chocolate-covered Florentines and eventually managed to find seats at a bockity table beside a youngish couple, who grimaced up at them, reluctantly hauling their plastic bags from seats which were clearly free.

'Thanks,' Portia said politely, starving and dying to tuck in. She had just begun to munch on her Florentine when she felt Andrew urgently squeeze her knee under the table. 'What?' she mouthed.

He winked at her and nodded his head in the direction of the girlfriend's newspaper, spread out on the table in front of them. There was a huge, full-colour photo of Mark Lloyd, clearly taken on a soccer pitch as he was wearing his full Oldcastle kit, arms raised exultantly in triumph, as if he'd just scored a winning goal in a World Cup final. 'MARK TO WED!' screamed the banner headline, 'AND ELEANOR ARMSTRONG IS THE LUCKY GIRL!!'

'I never could stand that stuck-up feckin' bitch Eleanor Armstrong,' said the girlfriend, scanning the paper in disgust. 'Mark Lloyd is off his bleedin' head to have anything to do with her. Sure, what kind of life will he have with her? Stuck in bleedin' Phoenix Park bleedin' House, listening to boring speeches by . . . whatshisname . . . the father . . .'

'Robert Armstrong,' grunted the boyfriend, engrossed

in another paper, which this time had a picture of a tearful Eleanor looking about ten years younger. Probably taken at her mother's funeral, Portia reckoned. 'ELEANOR'S TEARS OF JOY' ran the headline, 'AS MARK PRESENTS HER WITH A £100,000 DIAMOND ENGAGEMENT RING'.

'Yeah, well, I voted for the woman in the election,' the girlfriend went on, unaware that both Portia and Andrew were hanging on her every word. 'And Mark deserves better than that snotty cow. He shoulda stayed with that lingerie model, she's miles better for him any bleedin' day. Better-looking than Eleanor up-her-own-arse Armstrong as well. I mean, what in the name of Jaysus does he see in her anyway?'

Now it was the boyfriend's turn to get annoyed. Slowly folding his newspaper with studied venom, he was all the more threatening for not making direct eye contact with her, and just staying focused on ironing out imaginary creases in the *Daily Sport*. He was wearing a chunky gold sovereign ring on just about every finger, and each one reflected the light, bouncing it right back into Portia's eyes. 'Imelda, I am too hung over to be listening to your shite. Eleanor Armstrong is a very classy bird and that overpaid prick, who hasn't played one decent game this season, isn't even in her league. Now shut up and let me finish me breakfast in peace.' Sovereign-ring man sat back with his arms folded, as much as to say: If you're looking for a row, I'm your man.

'I did not leave our four kids at home with me mother so I could be spoken to like this.'

'Then go back to yer mother and let me go to Lanzarote in peace. I might ring Eleanor Armstrong and offer her yer ticket. Be a nice change for her to be with a real man, not some bleedin' over-styled hairdresser's model.'

'Don't you say that about Mark Lloyd.' Imelda was roaring by now, unaware that just about everyone in the café was enjoying the sideshow. 'Ya jealous git. Just cos you couldn't score a goal against the under-elevens in a five-a-side out on the green.'

Sovereign-ring man was busy thinking up a suitably cutting retort when he felt Portia's eyes on him and turned the full force of his bulldog stare on her. 'What are you looking at?'

'Oh, nothing,' stammered Portia nervously, 'nothing at all.'

'In fact, darling,' Andrew said, helping her up, 'we'd better get going or we'll miss our flight.'

She rose and in her haste to get away as fast as she could she stumbled over one of their duty-free bags, which were strewn carelessly across the floor. There was a loud clatter as one bottle clunked off several others but, luckily for Portia, nothing smashed.

'Sorry,' she said lamely, gathering up her own bag.

They both glared viciously at her. 'Well, enjoy your holiday,' said Andrew, aware that everyone in the café was watching.

'This isn't a holiday,' growled Imelda. 'It's our honeymoon.'

They waited until they were well away from the café and safely past the duty-free area before the pair of them collapsed into helpless fits of giggles.

'I thought he'd haul you outside and beat you up,' said Portia, hysterical with laughter, when an announcement came over the tannoy.

'Aer Lingus is pleased to announce the departure of flight EI106 to Kennedy International Airport, New York. We'd like to invite our Premier Class passengers to begin boarding through gate B25.'

'That's us, babe,' said Andrew. 'One of the perks of working for Macmillan Burke is that only business-class travel is good enough.'

'I have to warn you, I could get *very* used to this lifestyle,' Portia laughed, happily linking arms with him as they made their way down the gangway and stepped on to the aircraft.

No sooner had they taken their seats in huge, over-sized leather armchairs by the window, than they were both immediately offered a chilled glass of champagne. 'Yup, I think the high life definitely suits me.' Portia smiled, clinking glasses with him and thinking herself the luckiest woman alive. Not even when the air hostess offered her a choice of morning papers and she noticed that every single one of them carried the story about Eleanor and Mark's engagement did she flinch. Ordinarily, she'd have been riddled with guilt about leaving poor Daisy to shoulder the burden, but not now. For a few glorious weeks, she was leaving all her worries behind her and by God she'd earned it.

As the aircraft slowly began to thunder its way down the runway, the roar of the engines building to a shuddering crescendo, she gazed out of the window, watching the runway disappear beneath her, houses becoming tiny dolls' houses and green fields slowly fading into pure white cloud. She felt exhilarated, ecstatic to be getting away and thrilled to have Andrew sitting beside her, knowing she'd have him all to herself for the next few glorious weeks. Just like a second honeymoon.

Taking a luxurious sip of champagne and feeling like a movie star, she stretched her long legs out on to the footrest in front.

Life, she thought, just doesn't get much better.

Chapter Nine

The following day, with bags under her eyes so heavy you could carry luggage around in them, Daisy found herself in a power meeting sitting across the hunting table in the Library from Julia Belshaw at her formidable best. A great one for early morning starts, Julia had scheduled the meeting for seven a.m. and arrived at the Hall a full ten minutes early, then spent the remaining time pacing up and down the marble hallway and glancing impatiently at her watch every two minutes. When eventually she heard the sound of Daisy thud-thudding down the great oak staircase, she stood impatiently waiting for her at the bottom, as though she'd been standing there for hours, despite the fact that it was seven on the dot.

'Right, come on then, lots to do and very little time to do it in,' she barked down at her, sergeant-major style, ignoring the fact that there just might be guests who were still asleep. 'If you snooze you lose, you know,' she added, clicking her fingers at Daisy for her to hurry up before she turned on her heel and headed for the warmth of the Library.

'And good morning to you too, Julia,' Daisy muttered as she sleepily trailed in her wake. 'It's *lovely* to see you and you're looking so well. I'm sure Jimmy Choo designed those six-inch heels you've on specifically to be worn in the countryside.'

Never a morning person at the best of times, Daisy was particularly ratty and cranky that day, and anyway, Julia looked like she always did: ready to go either to a business meeting or a nightclub; she was suitably dressed for either occasion. Today she was in a tight red satin suit with shoes exactly the same shade, which, with her bright blonde hair, made her look like country Barbie against the huge hulking stone walls of the Hall.

'Sit down,' Daisy said, closing the Library door behind them to keep in the warmth. 'I'll ask Molly to send us in some coffee, or perhaps you'd like some breakfast?'

'Thank you, no,' replied Julia, clip-clopping ahead in her killer heels down the long wooden parquet floor. 'I don't have time in my schedule to get to the gym today and the golden rule is no workout, no food. Besides, breakfast is a luxury we don't have time for.'

Daisy rolled her eyes to heaven behind Julia's back and

resisted the urge to stick her tongue out at her. Why did she always make her feel like a recalcitrant schoolgirl who hadn't done her homework? She was starving and one of the biggest treats for her these days were the amazing breakfasts which Tim whipped up in the kitchen: mouth-watering, delicious confections . . . She was almost drooling at the thought . . .

'So what's the story with Andrew and Portia?' demanded Julia, dumping her briefcase at the top of the reading table as though she were chairman of a board of trustees.

Daisy knew the question was unavoidable but still dreaded having to answer her. Better to get it over with, she thought, slipping into a chair opposite Julia and trying her best to sound casual. 'They've both gone to New York. Andrew had to go on business and Portia went with him. They left yesterday and will probably be gone till May.'

Julia was in the middle of pulling a great wad of files from her briefcase, but stopped immediately. 'And they left you in charge?' she asked, eyeing her sharply.

Daisy racked her brains to think of a cool, confident way to make light of the situation, then gave it up as a bad job. She took a deep breath and reminded herself that she was a manager now, so telling Julia to get bent, as she'd ordinarily have done, was out of the question. 'Well,' she began, hating the fact that she had to explain herself, 'Portia and Andrew both have full confidence in me and will be in touch with the Hall every day and then with you organizing the wedding . . .'

'OK, OK,' said Julia, not even waiting for her to finish. 'It's clearly none of my business so I'll just say this. It's only seven a.m. and already my day is off to a bad start. The fact that you're going to be around is not exactly music to my ears. I'm sure you're a lovely person and I'm not saying a word against you, but the thought of handling this wedding with you is almost enough to have me reaching for the beta-blockers.' She was leaning on the table with both hands spread out, eyeballing Daisy so as to really hammer the point home. 'This is the single biggest event I've ever had to coordinate and I'm afraid that dealing with hormonal girlie-girlie squeals every time Mark Lloyd's name is mentioned frankly gives me a headache.'

Daisy was about to jump in and defend herself but Julia just barrelled right over her. 'But, like it or not, you're the acting manager here and there's nothing I can do about it. So let me just paint you a little road map of your future, honey. For the next few weeks, I need you to be what I call a "good little corporal". I don't expect you to make any kind of decision, but when I give you an order, I expect it to be carried out to the letter. You do what I tell you, when I tell you and you never, ever question me. And we'll get along just fine.'

She strode over to the sideboard and helped herself to a large bottle of mineral water, unscrewing the top and taking big gulps straight from the bottle. 'But on the plus side, I will say this. As a single woman and someone who respects the sisterhood, I think your sister is a very smart lady to go to the States and stick by a man like Andrew. Believe you me, there are women out there who would gnaw through the back of Portia Davenport's head to get at a guy like that. If she'd been idiot enough to let a man like that out of her sight, then I'm sorry but he'd be fair game. There are single women who would happily propel your big sister's ass into the divorce courts in the blink of an eye and she'd never even know how she got there. Clever, clever lady to say sod the sodding hotel. What pile of bricks is worth more than a marriage? But that's neither here nor there because as far as you're concerned, until the big day, I own your soul. Right. Down to work.'

She fished a leather-bound notebook from the depths of her briefcase and unclipped a gold pen from the side of it, being ultra-careful not to chip one of her scarlet talons. 'Well begun, half done, I always say. Now, *Gotcha* magazine's foremost concern is security. For obvious reasons, it's critical that no photos appear as spoilers in any newspapers or magazines before the wedding issue hits the stands, or do the words Plaza Hotel and Catherine Zeta Jones mean nothing? There are going to be over two hundred guests and each and every one of them will have to be frisked on entry to make sure they're not carrying cameras, tape recorders or those infernal picture phones. A thorough sweep will have to be done of the entire estate . . .'

She continued to drone on about guard dogs and security huts and marquees and salsa bands while Daisy frantically scribbled notes, desperately trying to keep up with her. Give me ten Trinny and Susannahs instead of this one, she thought. Why is she wasting her time working as a wedding planner when her talents would be put to much better use in Guantanamo Bay? Julia wasn't exactly her favourite person, but there and then, Daisy made a silent vow to show her what steel Davenport women were made of. She was acting manager now and by Jesus she'd show Julia bossy bloody Belshaw . . .

'Can I interrupt for a moment?' she asked in a valiant attempt to match Julia's businesslike tones.

'Yes?'

'Were you serious when you said you wanted all the toilet paper to tone in with the wedding colours?'

Breakfast had successfully been served and, as per usual, Molly was run off her feet toing and froing in and out of the kitchen relaying guests' compliments to the chef. 'That honeymoon couple at table seventeen said that the vanilla perdue with quince jelly was absolutely historic,' she gushed at Tim while flicking a minuscule piece of dust off one of the lights above the warming plates. 'He said if he ever found himself on death row, that would definitely be the last meal he'd request.'

Tim was one of those people who thought that no matter what superlative praise was heaped on him, it was never anything less than his due, so Molly was quite used to him paying absolutely no attention to all the effusive compliments she dutifully laid at his feet. After all, he was forever chopping, flambéing, whipping, mixing, blending or stirring something whenever she was trying to talk to him, and when he wasn't, he was barking orders at his poor overworked sous-chef. So when he didn't even acknowledge her, she thought no more of it and went back to scouring the Newbridge cutlery, even though it was already so over-polished the silver sheen had completely worn off.

On one occasion, she had even whipped a fork out of an unfortunate diner's mouth and polished it there and then at the table, unable to bear seeing her handiwork sullied with food. She had even queried why they were allowing guests to use the good silver in the first place. 'I have to scald them for hours afterwards to make sure they're up to operating theatre standards,' she'd griped at Daisy a few days previously. 'Plastic disposable cutlery is far more suitable. And hygienic. I mean to say, would you want to eat off something that a complete stranger had used? It would be as bad as urinating in a public toilet.'

At this point, Daisy really started to worry about her.

That particular morning, though, flattery was the furthermost thing from Tim's thoughts. The moment the last breakfast had been served, he left Molly happily disinfecting every available kitchen surface and off he went in pursuit of, of all people, Mrs Flanagan. It was just after ten in the morning, which could only mean one thing: she'd be holed up in the family living room, fag in gob, flicking between ITV and Channel Four and shouting at *Trisha*.

'Imagine yer husband coming home with pink G-strings in a size twenty and not copping on that he's a transvestite?' she was bellowing at some poor, distraught woman on the TV. 'Did the Evans bags lying all over the house not give you a clue? If ya ask me, ya deserved what ya got, ya roaring eejit.'

'Glad to see I'm not interrupting anything,' Tim said in his nasal voice. 'God forbid that I'd actually find you supervising the housekeeping or anything drastic.'

'Piss off, baldy,' she replied automatically, not even bothering to raise her eyes from the TV. She was barely listening to him. 'Now, do ya see them pair sitting on the sofa beside Trisha?' she asked, lighting up yet another cigarette. 'I'm telling ya, they should never have had a baby together. Apart from the fact that they're cousins, they're both minging ugly. Wait, look, watch this. She's going to have to peel that chair off her just so she can stand up.'

Tim sighed and came straight to the point. 'Mrs Flanagan, in your capacity as, ahem, housekeeping supervisor,' he whined, repulsed by even having to articulate her work title, 'I have no choice but to make an official complaint through you. I'm loath to distract you from your work, but things have reached a point where—'

Mrs Flanagan turned to face him, blowing cigarette smoke right at him and not caring. 'Have you a problem with the way I work, sonny?' she growled. 'Is it my fault that I'm able to get through my day's work in half the time it takes you to boil one of yer bleeding Michelin-starred eggs? The nearest you'll get to another Michelin is if you get run over by a truck.'

Tim chose to ignore this jibe and came straight to the point. 'The fact is that my kitchen is my artist's studio and each plate I present a meal on is like an artist's palette to me and each meal I present is like—'

'The statue of David. Go on.'

'Since yesterday, food has started to go missing from the kitchen, Mrs Flanagan,' he said, patting his bald head as though checking the comb-over was still in place. 'Vital, essential ingredients as necessary to me as nicotine and television appear to be to you. Today alone, a fresh delivery of organic fruit has completely vanished from the pantry. What am I supposed to do for my baked cherry sponge pudding with port compote? Not to mention my apple and rosemary tart with Lancashire cheese, which I may as well shake my hat at now. How am I expected to concoct desserts for tonight without the basic staple of fresh fruit?'

'Ahh, just get them pissed and serve them a few tubs of ice-cream,' cackled Mrs Flanagan, not taking him remotely seriously. 'Worked for me for forty years.'

'I don't think that you appreciate the gravity of the situation,' he snivelled, although not raising his voice. 'Someone is pilfering from my stockroom, Mrs Flanagan. I've conducted a thorough check of all windows and doors throughout the kitchens and pantry area and there appears to be no sign of a break-in. It would appear to be highly unlikely that any of the guests or staff would steal into the refrigeration room at night in order to make off with a full crème Chantilly, fifteen meringues and almost four pounds of Parmesan cheese as happened last night. I have no idea who is doing this or why, but that's your responsibility as, ahem, housekeeping supervisor to find out.'

He had a way of spitting out her work title that was starting to wear a bit thin with Mrs Flanagan. 'So what do ya want me to do about it? Buy ya more fruit? Go out the back yard and pick some yerself, ya lazy fart, I have telly to watch,' she growled.

'The only organic fruit that I would consider worthy of working with comes from Smithfield market in Dublin, so no, picking a few mouldy cooking apples from the kitchen garden isn't an option. What I require you to do—' He broke off for a moment, having caught sight of Mrs Flanagan's impression of him reflected in the TV. 'Your job is twofold. Firstly, to find out precisely what's happening and who is thieving from the kitchen and secondly, for the sake of all concerned, to prevent it from ever occurring again.'

'Who in the name of Jaysus do ya think I am, Sherlock Holmes?' she snarled, lighting up another cigarette to try to keep her blood pressure down. 'Am I being followed by a Mr Watson?'

'No, but then you are of a Miss Marple vintage,' sneered Tim, delighted that he could throw back a witty rejoinder. 'But I'll give you your first clue. Whoever is pilfering from me hasn't once gone near the pheasant or game or any of the cold meats that are hanging up in the walk-in freezer. I think you just might be looking for a vegetarian.'

Chapter Ten

In the end, it was Julia of all people who gave Shelley-Marie the stamp of approval and ensured her survival at Davenport Hall, at least temporarily.

'Fabulous idea,' she decreed to Daisy. 'The only thing missing at the Hall is a good beauty salon. I was absolutely dreading the thought of having to bus the wedding guests to some sawdust-on-the-floor hick beauty parlour on the morning of the wedding. My God, have you seen some of the women going around Kildare? I know that the eighties revival is back, but these people are pure first-hand 1980s, big gelled hair and New Romantic heavy eye make-up. No, this'll have a fantastic trickle-down effect.'

'Which is?' Daisy asked, tentatively.

'It solves a big problem for me, which makes me

happy, which in turn makes me less abusive to you. Fabulous suggestion, don't even think about changing your mind. I presume Andrew thought of it?'

Daisy was also to discover that Shelley-Marie's talent for ingratiating herself had won her other powerful allies in the battle to allow her to take up permanent residence at the Hall. Her principal supporters in the red corner for letting her stay on after the wedding were Lucasta and Mrs Flanagan, both of whom vocally protested to Daisy about what an asset she was to the hotel, what a pleasure it was to have her around and, not least, the fact that she had nowhere else to go.

'Your bollocks of a father left her virtually penniless, you know,' Lucasta had said. 'All that poor girl has to her name are the leather mini-skirts and all that interesting rubber underwear she arrived with, and you want to turn her out of the Hall as soon as this bloody wedding is over? I wouldn't allow one of my kitties to be treated with such disdain.'

Mrs Flanagan's tack was slightly different, though no less persuasive. 'If ya let that poor unfortunate young one go, I'm handing in me resignation here and now. After the hard life she's had? Do you know that she was in foster homes for the first ten years of her life cos her aul' fella was in prison and her ma was in and out of mental homes her whole childhood? And then she was put in an orphanage or children's home or whatever the hell they

call them now and the carers there never stopped harass-
ing her, she was telling me, cos they were all mad jealous
of her. But she made something of her life, she hauled
herself out of the shite and got all her beauty therapy
qualifications and everything was finally going great for
her . . .'

Her voice was starting to wobble a bit now so that she
sounded like a voiceover on one of those 'watch our
heroine pluck triumph from out of the mouth of
adversity' biopics. The type of movie that Miramax
would sweep the board with at Oscar time.

'Then she met yer da, talked him into marrying her,
God knows how, and just when her life had turned a
corner' – she sniffed, dabbing her eyes with the corner of
her housecoat – 'just as a little bit of luck was finally
going her way and her dreams were finally becoming
reality, what happens? The selfish bastard goes and drops
dead. Honest to Jaysus, it's like something ya'd see on
Oprah.'

Daisy knew better than to contradict her, but in fact it
was something she had seen on *Oprah* while she was
going through some accounts in the family room only
the day before, and she felt pretty certain that Shelley-
Marie had too. Something else had also struck her: that
each and every time Shelley-Marie related her back
history to whoever would listen, it changed. Only
slightly, but enough to raise the hackles of suspicion on

the back of Daisy's neck. One day she'd breathlessly whisper the foster home story; another, she'd have grown up in the projects with nothing but a Miss Fantasia's in her local town . . . stuff that wouldn't sound out of place in a Celine Dion tearjerker. Words her father used to say kept coming back to haunt her. 'To be a good liar,' he used to pontificate, 'you need the memory of an elephant.'

In all fairness to Daisy, though, she was really trying her best to make a decent fist of her new job as acting manager. Without even knowing it, she'd genuinely impressed Julia not only with her enthusiasm for all the hard work that was involved but also with the way she'd thrown herself headfirst into helping with preparations for the big wedding. They had only had one significant argument and that was over Julia's irrevocable decision to hire a marquee for the reception.

'But the Dining Room seats eighty!' Daisy had protested during one of their early morning power breakfasts. 'Not to mention the fact that the Hall has eight lovely great big reception rooms. I don't understand why on earth you'd want to squish all the wedding guests into some freezing, smelly old tent.'

Julia smiled condescendingly at her, as if she were addressing a very slow-witted five-year-old. 'What you need to realize, Daisy, is that these "wedding guests" as you choose to call them are not ordinary people like you and me. They are celebrities. I think you'd do very well to bear that distinction in mind. They're as different from you and me as low-fat butter is from the real thing and the marquee I'll be hiring, believe you me, is no stinking wigwam. Take a look at this,' she said, thrusting over a thick colour brochure with her long scarlet talons. 'Is that what you'd describe as a poky little tent? It comfortably seats two hundred, which makes it almost three times the size of the Dining Room here, it has a dance floor the size of your Ballroom, it even comes with its own fake grass, for Christ's sake.'

'Fake grass?' asked Daisy innocently. 'Why would you want fake grass in the middle of the country?'

'Because fake grass is more grass-like than actual grass,' she replied in such a rude tone of voice that she may as well have added, 'you thick hick.' She went on, by way of explanation, 'It has the decided advantage that your heels don't sink into it and that you don't spend your time dodging sheep droppings. Just think of it as a big green carpet cunningly disguised as grass, without the revolting country garden smell. Honestly, when I was organizing the opening party for the Hall, I must have destroyed about six pairs of Jimmy Choos. I should have waived my fee and just presented you with my shoe bill instead.'

Daisy eagerly seized the glossy brochure to have a look. The marquee did indeed look astonishing in the photos, utterly opulent and absolutely vast. It even had crystal chandeliers embedded in a star cloth hanging like a huge canopy from above which gave the glittering effect that you were partying under a clear night sky.

'OK then,' she had said, well and truly won over, after she'd finished oohing and ahhing. 'So tell me where you think the best place would be to put it and I'll start talking to the gardeners.'

'You really are working out very well, you know,' Julia said to her later as they walked across the forecourt to where her sports car was parked. 'Three weeks to go and I'm only on four milligrams of Valium a day. Well done you. Keep it up.'

Daisy could only presume that this was meant as a compliment.

FROM: <u>daisydavenport@davenporthall.ie</u>
TO: <u>portiadavenport@aol.com</u>
SUBJECT: Just to let you know that the Hall hasn't burnt down and I haven't stabbed our wicked stepmother yet and Julia and I are actually getting on OK, sort of, ish . . .

Hi Portia!!!!
  I sat down to write you this email but then realized I've said everything I want to say in the subject box at top.

Basically, all's well so far. This
wedding is going to be unbelievable and
you never know, I might even meet a
fella at it. All the Oldcastle team
are invited and most of them have
confirmed. Yummy, yummy!!!!

How's the Big Apple??? Done any
serious shopping??? Which is a heavy
hint for . . . have you bought me a
really fab Donna Karan yet???
Love to Andrew,
Daisyxxxxxxxxxxxxxxxxxxxxxxxxxxx

FROM: *portiadavenport@aol.com*
TO: *daisydavenport@davenporthall.ie*
SUBJECT: *Well, thank God for that!*

So glad everything's OK at home, you're
a sweetie to put my mind at rest. We
arrived safely and (you'd have been in
seventh heaven!) were met by the
longest stretch limo you ever saw,
tinted windows, a mini-bar inside . . .
the whole works . . . I love being a
corporate wife! As soon as the driver
heard this was my first time to New
York, he insisted on giving us the

full guided tour . . . Oh Daisy! I
can't tell you how amazing it was
seeing the Manhattan skyline for the
first time! It's everything you imagine
and more. Breath-taking, awe-inspiring,
I've run out of superlatives to
describe how astonishing it looks.
(Tell me if this is driving you mad?)
We drove by loads of the big land-
marks, the Chrysler, the Flat Iron and,
would you believe, I can actually see
the Empire State from our bedroom
window! The apartment is lovely, if a
bit on the bachelor pad side for me,
but A adores it and can't believe he's
back living here with wifey in tow.

   Got to dash . . . big dinner coming
up with some of A's colleagues (in
Cipriani's at the Rainbow Room, if you
don't mind) and I need to buy something New Yorky to wear . . . don't
want to let the side down!
Much love to my baby sis.
Portiaxxx

FROM: <u>daisydavenport@davenporthall.ie</u>
TO: <u>portiadavenport@aol.com</u>
SUBJECT: *Well, don't let me keep you!!!*

Have to admit I got a bit confused at
your last email. Thought I'd somehow
got wires crossed with Carrie Bradshaw
. . . Bitch!! So jealous!! Enjoy!! Would
LOVE to hear more about your flashy,
glam lifestyle but the outside drains
are blocked again and I'd swear the
septic tank has a leak in it . . . the
difference in our lives . . . !
Dxxx

Chapter Eleven

By Christ, Daisy thought to herself, it's not often you see the cool, calm, über-efficient Julia Belshaw in a flap.

It was mid-morning the following day and the Hall was in its usual state of organized chaos. Daisy was rushing off to a meeting with a hotel supplier in Dublin and both Molly and Tim were in the kitchens, clearing up after breakfast and preparing for lunch respectively. Lucasta had completely vanished; she was never anywhere to be seen these days, not even for her usual tipple during happy hour in the bar. She would appear back at the Hall very late at night, smelling even worse than she normally did and explaining her absence with a dismissive wave of her hand.

'Get bent,' was all she said to Gorgeous George when he had the temerity to ask her if she was all right as she swished into the Long Gallery well after eleven p.m. one night. 'I'll have you know I'm on the brink of announc-ing a very exciting discovery to the world so until then, you'll just have to leave me be,' she said, stuffing the pockets of her wax jacket with as many airline-sized bottles of gin and miniature tins of tonic as she could, before stomping off to bed. Given that her last 'exciting discovery' had been a cure for ingrown hairs involving the use of rose quartz crystals, no one paid too much heed to her.

Mrs Flanagan too had disappeared, but into the family sitting room; a toasted sandwich in one hand, a box of twenty cigarettes in the other and the TV guide tucked under her arm, leaving strict instructions that under no circumstances was she to be disturbed. 'I'm working on a top-secret project,' was all she gave away, 'and I need to do a bit of research first. So in the meantime, youse can all feck off.'

'Honestly,' Daisy had grumbled to Amber, the very young and very pretty day receptionist, before she left for her meeting, 'some people in this house wouldn't last a wet day in the workplace.' (It was hard not to laugh aloud at this coming from Daisy of all people, of whom, up to a week ago, it could have reasonably been said that she had never done an honest day's work in her whole life.)

They were both standing at the elegant Louis XVI reception desk in the main entrance hall when two guests, an elderly French couple, came tottering down the staircase, Louis Vuitton bags in hand, all set to check out. Daisy immediately snapped into action, beaming angelically at them and asking if they had enjoyed their stay as she expertly tapped the computer and printed off their bill. 'I'll handle this,' she said with great confidence to Amber, delighted to have a chance to show off her new-found professionalism.

'Ehh . . . my Engleesh is not so good as it used to be,' said the woman, smiling and nodding, 'but we have many times been staying at the Ritz, Paris and, may I say, the dining here is incommensurable.'

Daisy and Amber glanced at each other; neither one's French was good enough to give a sophisticated, bilingual reply, but they thanked them effusively for the lovely compliment and, judging by their guests' big, happy smiles and by the warmth of the handshakes they exchanged, it could safely be said that their stay was a success and that they might even be back.

Both Daisy and Amber walked them to the top of the steps outside and gamely waved them off like old friends.

'Nothing like a satisfied customer,' Amber remarked, shivering a bit against the biting cold.

'You know what we could really do with around here?' Daisy asked, only half listening to her. 'Now don't laugh, but I feel I wouldn't be doing my job as acting manager unless I gave these things proper consideration.'

'What's that?'

'A hotel porter. We badly need one, I almost broke my back helping those guests from Dublin carry luggage to their car the other day. Honest to God, they were only here for two nights and they had five suitcases between them. They must have changed clothes about eight times a bloody day.'

'They did. One of them was aghast that we didn't have a strict dress code for dinner. Apparently she'd brought three possible evening gowns to choose from and by gowns I really mean gowns, with ridiculous trains and everything. I think they confused this place with the Kodak Theatre on Oscar night.'

'I'm being serious,' replied Daisy. 'We could really do with the extra help and you know what else? We could hire a big, beefy, sexy-looking guy and then give him a bell-hop uniform to wear with a little pill-box hat – you know, like in 1930s movies?'

Amber giggled. 'Now that would make my early morning shifts all the more bearable. Can we get one that looks like Colin Farrell? Please?'

'Let me talk to Portia about it,' Daisy laughed, really savouring her new responsibilities. 'Right, I've got to dash,' she said, suddenly remembering the time. 'Probably not a good idea to keep someone we owe money to waiting.'

She was just about to trip down the stone steps to her

car as Julia's distinctive red two-seater came whooshing up the driveway, doing one of her trademark gravel-scattering handbrake turns. The woman herself then dumped the car at right angles to the bottom of the steps and came running up, barely taking the time to bang the car door behind her. 'Code red emergency!' she was shrieking at the top of her voice, taking the steps two at a time, no mean feat in five-inch stilettos.

'Oh Christ, what fresh hell is this?' Daisy muttered when right on Julia's heels came a brand-new, showroom-condition Porsche.

'OK, OK, I need you both to remain calm,' said Julia breathlessly, sounding anything other than calm herself. 'It's them. Eleanor and Mark Lloyd in person. He had a day free in his schedule and wants to see the Hall for himself. OK, OK, OK . . .' she continued, thinking aloud. 'Here's what I need you both to do. Evacuate the Hall, tell all the nobodies staying here there's a fire or something, I don't care, just get rid of them. Mark can't have plebs bothering him when his time is at such a premium.'

Keep cool, Daisy kept saying to herself, keep nice and cool and remember you're a manager. She took a deep breath and was about to point out calmly that under no circumstances could she subject guests to that kind of appalling treatment when Eleanor herself called out from the passenger window of the Porsche.

'Good morning, everyone! Please, please excuse us for

landing on top of you like this and promise me you won't make a fuss? We'd hate to think that we were putting anyone out.' A lady to her fingertips, Daisy thought as they all went down the steps to meet and greet.

Eleanor looked as naturally beautiful as she always did, dressed down in jeans and a simple white shirt under a black leather jacket. She shook hands with Julia warmly and gave Daisy a big bear hug, like an old pal she hadn't seen in years.

'Mark was supposed to be training all day,' she blushed, 'but it was unexpectedly cancelled so he called me from Oldcastle this morning and flew all the way to Dublin by helicopter just so he could see the Hall. I hope that's all right?' she asked, addressing Daisy. 'If it's not a good time for you, we could easily come back again.'

Touched by her politeness and humility, Daisy was about to reply that there was no problem at all, they were only delighted to see them, when the man himself appeared from the driver's side of the car.

Eleanor beamed at him, linking his arm. 'Come and meet everyone and you can apologize for landing on top of the poor Davenports without warning like this.'

Daisy could feel Amber's hand gripping her arm tightly as the man himself stepped elegantly out from the driver's side. Eleanor graciously made the introductions, singling out Daisy as the Hall's acting manager.

'Great to meet you,' said Mark in an unmistakable

south London accent, dark eyes glinting at her. 'What a great pile of bricks you got here.' He took his gaze off her for a moment to survey the front façade of the Hall then turned his full attention back to her. 'I just love it,' he said, really impressed. 'Yeah, I'm lovin' it. I'm a big fan of neo-classical architecture. Doric columns, yeah, great, cool, man, I really dig. Fantastic choice, Ellie, my mum's really gonna love this.'

As they all made their way inside, Daisy found herself struck by the twin illusion of familiarity and estrangement with Mark. Celebrities must experience this all the time, she thought, total strangers feeling as though they know you intimately, because you're a household name and your face is so well known. They all stood companionably in the Hall chatting, or babbling like the village idiot in Amber's case, the way people do when they meet really famous people in the flesh. Daisy excused herself for a moment and slipped off to the reception desk to see if she could hastily reschedule her appointment with Portia's particularly snotty hotel supplier. As she stood with the phone in her hand, interminably on hold, she had a good chance to observe the famous Mark Lloyd close up.

He wasn't particularly tall, but was lean, lithe and athletic with that golden glow about him which super-fit people always seem to have. He was dark-skinned and tanned with deep, dark brown eyes which didn't so much dance when they looked at you as do a wild Latin American salsa. Although it was a chilly March morning, wild and windy, he was only wearing a light, Lycra T-shirt which clung to his powerful muscles as though designed for no other purpose, with a pair of army-fatigue-style combat trousers slung low at the hips which clearly showed his knicker elastic. (Calvin Klein: what else?) Instead of this seeming like a major fashion *faux pas,* however, he carried the look off as though he'd just happened to step off a catwalk during London fashion week. In a nutshell, he looked every inch the off-duty superstar, Daisy thought, although she was half expecting him to turn around and start plugging men's aftershave at any second. He was parading around the entrance hall as though he was surveying it and would soon put in an offer when the hotel supplies manager butted in on her thoughts, telling her crisply and in no uncertain terms that she'd reschedule the appointment to facilitate her just this once, but under no circumstances could this be allowed to happen again.

'Thank you so much,' said Daisy, feeling that she at least owed her an explanation. 'My sister would kill me if she knew I'd cancelled on you, but, you see, can you keep a secret? Mark Lloyd has just arrived and wants to see the Hall—'

'MARK LLOYD?' came the astonished reply. 'Oh my God, tell him I love him SOOOO much! Will you tell him that my boyfriend and I got the DVD of *Mark Lloyd's Greatest Goals* for Christmas and that we've watched it about a thousand times between us? And will you be sure to tell him that his equalizer at Stuttgart in the European Championships was the MOST AMAZING piece of ball control I have ever seen?'

'Ehh, yeah, I'll be sure to pass that on,' Daisy said, marvelling that just the magic of his name could transform even the snottiest old battleaxe into a gushing, star-struck teenager. Even Julia had abandoned her usual bossy, narky persona and was smiling sweetly at the happy couple as though she had nothing better to do all day than stand around making small talk. Clocking that Daisy was finally off the phone, she snapped into action.

'Mark, Eleanor, I know how little time you both have, so I suggest that we start at the top of the Hall and work our way down. That way, you can see all the best bedrooms for yourselves and allocate them accordingly. I remember one particular wedding I planned where the groom insisted on the bride's family having the bedrooms in an old coach house about five miles away from anyone else.'

'Actually, Julia,' Eleanor gently interrupted, on catching a look of raw panic flitter across Daisy's face, 'I'm not so sure that's really necessary. The last thing we'd want to do is bother the other guests. Maybe if we could just take a peek at the reception rooms and then we could show

Mark the spot we've chosen for the marquee in the garden? We can easily leave the bedrooms for a more convenient time.'

Really impressed by her thoughtfulness, Daisy led the way, beginning with the Yellow Drawing Room to the left of the reception on the ground floor. Mark was the only one who had never seen it before, and his reaction was all that his bride-to-be could have hoped for and more.

'Oh wow, now you're talkin'! This reminds me a bit of Buckingham Palace, 'cept it's miles nicer. Classier. And it don't have the disadvantage of corgi hair all over the furniture.'

Eleanor grinned and blushed and glowed behind the silk curtain of her long, straight hair.

'I was there, you know, last year,' Mark went on as Daisy shepherded them on through to the Red Dining Room, 'when the Queen gave me my OBE. In fact, this place reminds me of there a lot, actually. 'Cept I think your taste in art is a lot better. They've just got pictures of horses and foxhunts and that, which wouldn't be my scene at all. Wow! Come here, Ellie, look! They got a Graham Knuttel! That is so fantastic!'

Eleanor, however, was over by the French windows deep in conversation with Julia and didn't hear him. He made a beeline for the painting (one Andrew had bought at auction) and surveyed it expertly. 'Cool! What wouldn't I give to have this hanging in my place! Don't you love the sharp, angular thing he's got going on? And that great, really bold use of colour? How old is this one, then?'

'Emm . . .' Daisy hadn't a clue, to her it was just a big blobby yoke on a wall, but didn't want to sound completely thick.

'Early eighties, I'd guess,' said Mark, squinting up at it. Then, turning his jet-black, dancing eyes back to her, he said, 'If you're ever selling it, will you give me first refusal? I'll make it worth your while.'

Daisy found herself gazing at him and had to say to herself forcefully: Don't go all girly, don't go all girly . . .

'It's just that I'd really love to see that hung up against my wall.'

Oh Jesus, she thought, I'd love to see how you're hung up against any bloody wall . . .

'Mark? Can you come over here please?' Julia commanded, although she did tone it down a tad, given that she was addressing Mark Lloyd. 'It's just that we really need to discuss Georgian sugar sculptures and whether you want them encased in white or red roses for the table centrepieces.'

'On the way,' the man himself replied, ambling over as if there was nothing else he'd rather be doing.

'Empire line, Jane Austen style,' Eleanor was whispering to Julia about her wedding dress, 'very plain and simple, with just my mother's pearl necklace. I'm only having one bridesmaid, my best friend Karen, and her dress is going to be a similar style. Timeless and classical, you know; after all, I don't want to wince when I look at my wedding photos in twenty years' time. Oh, and I need to speak to your head chef about the food, if that's OK,' she said, turning to Daisy as she and Mark rejoined them. 'I have this idea that the meal should hark back to Georgian times, in keeping with the surroundings.'

'Whatever you want, my love,' said Mark, slipping his arm around her shoulder. 'Sounds like it's gonna be a real classy do. There'll be nothing tacky or cheap about our wedding, will there? Not like poor old Shane Donohue's, eh?' He correctly interpreted the blank looks from Julia and Daisy. 'You know Shane? Oldcastle striker? Equalized against Arsenal in the last minute of the FA Cup Final last season?'

More blank looks.

'Repeated groin strain injury? Got sent off ten minutes into the last Man U match of the season?'

Even Julia was beginning to sweat a little now. Who in the name of God was this guy?

'Married to Falcon Archbold?'

'Oh yes, him!' Daisy and Julia chimed in unison, the mystery solved. Falcon Archbold was a glamour model and minor C-list celebrity who had just been crowned queen of the jungle in a reality TV show called *We Are*

Famous, Try and Shame Us. She had won her way into the nation's heart by spending two weeks in the Australian rainforest eating slugs and cockroaches and, on one occasion, a live eel. She'd even spent over an hour buried in a coffin full of live rats, which, expert opinion went, is what finally sealed the competition for her. She had married Shane Donohue shortly afterwards, in what had to have been one of the tackiest weddings ever seen this side of Hollywood.

'Oh God, that was a ghastly affair.' Julia winced. 'Didn't he have this whole "Maharajah for a day" theme going on? With a live elephant?'

'I remember reading about that in *Dish the Dirt* magazine!' said Daisy. 'And she dressed up as Pocahontas in a bra and sari and all her bridesmaids were like concubines. Awful!'

'You should have been there,' said Mark. 'That wasn't the worst of it, not by a long shot. The Jewel in the Crown restaurant on the Tottenham Court Road did all the food for it, on platters of solid gold. I'm not kidding. We all had to sit on cushions on the floor, looking like right plonkers, while Shane and Falcon sat on these giant gold thrones drinking out of golden goblets. "King and Queen for the day" type vibe, you know.' He stopped, catching the slightest hint of an embarrassed blush from Eleanor. 'Nothing like that for you and me though, Ellie. Class, all the way. Whatever you want, I'll go along with.

If you want to get married on top of the Himalayas with Michael Palin himself doing the ceremony, I'll be there.'

Much later that night, Daisy was in her room getting ready for bed when the phone on her bedside table rang. She glanced at her watch. Midnight. Has to be Portia ringing from the States, she figured as she bounded across the room to answer it. Eejit still mustn't be used to the time difference, she thought, although she was absolutely dying to chat to her. She was itching to tell all about her day, about Mark Lloyd and how fab he was; how unlike the usual stereotype of the thick, rich, tasteless footballer. Eleanor Armstrong was the luckiest girl on the planet . . . that was official.

'Portia, that you?'

'What? Have I got the right room number?'

A man's voice. A south London accent.

'Who is this?'

'Daisy, that you?'

'Yes, who's this?' Jesus, my nerves, she thought.

'It's me, Mark. I really hope it's not a problem, me ringing you so late.'

She nearly dropped the receiver. 'Yes! I mean no! I mean . . . it's great to hear from you, Mark.' Stop hyperventilating, she told herself. And whatever you do, stop gushing; you're starting to sound like Geoffrey Rush in *Shine*.

'Only I'm back at Oldcastle now for training, you see, and I won't get a chance to go back to Ireland till the week of the wedding.'

'Oh right. Well, happy training!' *Jesus!* said her inner voice. *Happy training?*

'This is a bit delicate, you see, and I didn't want to mention it in front of Eleanor today. She gets embarrassed dead easy, you know.'

'Is everything OK, Mark?'

He sighed. 'Well, it's just that I really want Ellie's day to be perfect for her, you know? Money is no object, none at all.'

'Aren't the magazine paying for it?' Daisy was getting confused as to where this could be leading.

'Technically, yeah. But what Ellie doesn't know is that I'm gonna donate all their money to my favourite charity and foot the bill myself. I'm saving it for a surprise for her though. I think she'll be dead chuffed with me.'

'Oh Mark, of course she will! That's an overwhelming gesture!'

'You think?'

Daisy said nothing, just reflected, for about the fortieth time that day, on how JAMMY Eleanor was to have landed a guy like this.

'What's the charity?'

'One my friend Alessandro set up. S.A.C.'

'Sorry?'

'Sexually addicted celebrities. Don't laugh, it's a big problem for a lot of people I know.'

Daisy was far from laughing. If Mark Lloyd had told her he was donating his entire fortune to help the lesser-spotted eel, she'd still have swooned like a teenager with a major crush.

'So here's what you can do for me, Daisy. I need you to call me every day and keep me posted on everything that's being decided, is that OK?'

'Of course! I know how much Eleanor has on her plate. Anything I can do to help.'

'Great, that's great. So, is it OK if I give you my personal mobile number?'

Chapter Twelve

'Say, lady, you've gotta be having a *Pretty Woman* day,' the doorman at the Park Avenue apartment said as Portia wafted by him, laden down with carrier bags.

'You said it, Sam,' she laughed. 'Big night tonight!'

She'd just spent one of those rare, blissfully happy days where you honestly feel you must have done something spectacularly good in a past life, like been a nun in a comptemplative order or else done voluntary work in a leper colony, to merit such good fortune now. Andrew had had to go into his office first thing that morning and had left her with strict instructions to spend, spend, spend and then meet him later that night for dinner. Which she had gleefully carried out to the letter.

She had spent most of the day excitedly exploring Fifth Avenue: Saks, Bergdorf Goodman, Lord and Taylor, and had even treated herself to a colour and cut at the famous Elizabeth Arden Red Door salon. She really wanted to look good for Andrew that night and was thrilled with the outfit she'd bought: a beautifully cut black shift dress and an exquisite tweed coat. Sinfully expensive but it made her look and feel a million dollars.

'Ma'am,' the sales assistant in Saks had cooed at her, 'you look just like Carolyn Bessette Kennedy. And she was my style icon!'

Who could resist a sales pitch like that? Sold, ten seconds later.

Andrew had arranged to meet her at Cipriani's in the Rockefeller Center at seven, and so on the dot, she stepped out of a yellow cab and made her way inside the cool, marble building, following the signs which read: 'Cipriani's, top floor'.

Meanwhile, as the express elevator rocketed skywards and Portia's eardrums were popping once every twenty-five floors, Andrew sat at the best table in the whole restaurant, eagerly glancing over towards the door every few minutes. With him were his old friend and colleague, Ken Courtney, and another lawyer assigned to the case, a New Yorker, Lynn Fairweather. When Andrew eventually spotted his wife arrive, he immediately excused himself from the table and went over to where she was standing by the restaurant door, asking the maître d' which table she should go to.

Ken and Lynn said nothing, just watched the romantic reunion being played out in front of them as husband and wife hugged each other tightly like they hadn't seen each other in weeks, rather than hours, neither one caring that they were on view for the whole restaurant to see.

Ken sat back, tossing the menu carelessly aside. 'So what do you think?' he asked.

Lynn didn't lift her gaze from Portia, not even for a second. 'Meet my new best friend.'

'Good to see you again, Portia, you look well.' Ken rose to kiss her on each cheek and unconsciously eyed her up and down as he did. It was an irritating habit of his, Portia knew well, something he had always done, and not just with her, with all women. Ordinarily it annoyed her, but not tonight. With Andrew beside her, clasping her hand and knowing she looked great in her new finery, who cared what the Ken Courtneys of this world thought? Ken, she knew of old, was a great one for judging women solely in terms of looks, but tonight Portia was far too happy to give a shite about being in the company of her least favourite of Andrew's friends.

'Good to see you too, Ken,' she lied.

'I'm sure you wanted Andy all to yourself tonight, but I'm afraid you're stuck with us, for dinner anyway. Don't worry, Lynn and I have no intention of overstaying our welcome.'

195

A perfectly innocuous statement, but somehow, coming from Ken, it managed to sound sleazy and patronizing. And it really bugged her the way he always called Andrew 'Andy'. She didn't know why, it just really annoyed her. It was as though this was his way of subtly reminding her that he and 'Andy' went back a lot further than she did. (They'd been at boarding school and then both went on to study law at UCD together.) His accent grated with her too, almost like he'd studied every film James Dean ever made and then copied him, vowel for vowel.

'You really are looking well,' he added, this time dropping his neck to check out her cleavage. Yet another delightful habit of his.

'Thanks, Ken, you too,' Portia lied, noticing that he was even more pot-bellied than the last time she'd seen him. 'It's so fantastic to be in New York. I can't tell you how much I'm loving it,' she added, beaming at her husband and, this time, not lying.

'It's great to be back and all the better that you're with me,' Andrew said as he squeezed her waist and kissed her cheek, not caring that half the restaurant was staring at this very uncool spontaneous show of affection. Very un-Cipriani's. 'Sit down, honey, and I'll order you a drink,' he said, gallantly pulling out a chair for her, 'and let me introduce Lynn.'

'Welcome to New York, I've heard so much about you.'

'And you,' Portia lied again, shaking hands with her across the dinner table. Andrew had never mentioned anyone by the name of Lynn; she'd have remembered. Probably one of Ken's many bits on the side, she thought, smiling pityingly at her while Andrew caught a passing waiter's attention. She certainly looked like someone Ken would have a fling with; she seemed to fulfil all of his requirements to the letter.

Lynn was a) young, barely thirty Portia guessed; b) beautiful, with wide even features, blue eyes, cheekbones that could have doubled up as a cheese grater and a neat, trim figure to boot; but above all she was c) blonde. Ken had a big thing about blonde women. He had even tried it on with Daisy once, during one of his whistle-stop trips to Ireland, when he'd stayed with Portia and Andrew at the gate lodge, conveniently leaving his lovely wife back at their beach house in the Hamptons.

Daisy had gamely taken him up to the Hall for a tour, so that he could see all the renovation work which was still in full swing and the pair of them then spent the night getting rat-arsed drunk. One thing led to another and, according to Daisy, he started kissing her, claiming he was way too pissed to find his way back to the gate lodge and wouldn't it just make more sense if he bunked down with her for the night? Needless to say, she had unceremoniously thrown him out of the Hall telling him in no uncertain terms to fuck right off, that she didn't do married.

'The only exercise you're going to get tonight is the two-mile walk home, fatso. Besides, you're far too old for me and, just for the record, my type does not include married pot-bellied pigs with irritating affected accents. You're from Limerick, for Christ's sake, not Long Island.'

It was probably the one and only time in his life he'd been rejected.

Of all the many things that bugged Portia about Ken, chief amongst them was the cheating. He was married to a gorgeous woman and had two beautiful little daughters. Ordinarily she wouldn't have minded – after all, Ken's extra-marital affairs were thankfully no concern of hers – but Jennifer Courtney was such a lovely person, beautiful inside and out, the sort of woman any guy would be proud to be with, that it broke Portia's heart to see her so flagrantly made a fool of.

She and Andrew often talked about it, with Portia taking Jennifer's side and saying things like, 'He's so lucky to have her in the first place, why does he do it? Is he stupid or does he actually want to get caught?'

Andrew would treat the whole thing as a joke, always sticking up for his old pal and invariably winding up the whole discussion with, 'Ken's Ken. He's always been a playboy and he'll never change.'

'Just don't let him give you any ideas,' Portia would

playfully joke back at him, 'or I'll do a Lorena Bobbitt. And I'll get away with it too. A judge would take one look at my mother and let me off on the grounds that insanity runs in the family.'

So as the drinks arrived and the chat went on, Portia began to feel almost sympathetic towards this gorgeous creature, destined to be nothing more than another notch on Ken's bedpost. Probably a model, she thought, looking over at her, or an off-off-off-Broadway actress, or even a dancer; that was the type he normally went for, she knew of old. Some poor wannabe who'd be impressed by all Ken's name-dropping and money and swagger.

Andrew, typically, had ordered champagne to toast his wife's first visit to New York and the sommelier kept topping them all up, so before Portia knew where she was, she began to feel a bit woozy and light-headed. Wonder if the old gitface has even mentioned the fact that he has a wife, she wondered silently as Ken launched into an anecdote she'd heard a thousand times before about the time he went on a drunken razz with a gang from Cape Cod and had somehow ended up in the Kennedy compound, in the pool with Ethel and Ted. Hilarious . . . the first time.

Lynn dutifully tittered and Portia thought she'd throw up. Just then, Andrew's cell phone rang. 'Do you mind my taking this?' he whispered to her. 'It's probably Globex. I'll be back in a moment.'

She smiled at him as he left the table and went outside in search of a little quiet. A silence fell and she decided to seize her moment. 'So, Ken, how's Jennifer? I really hope I get to see her while I'm here.'

'Oh, she's very well,' Lynn answered for him, in a crisp, cultured East coast accent. 'I had lunch with her only yesterday. She's invited all of us up to the beach house some weekend soon. That's if you're free, of course. Andrew certainly seemed keen when I mentioned it to him at work today.'

Portia just looked at her, a bit shell-shocked. 'Oh, is Jennifer a friend of yours too?'

Lynn contemplated the question as she added sparkling mineral water into her champagne. (That gesture alone should have me running for the hills, Portia thought. The one piece of motherly advice Lucasta had ever passed on to her elder daughter was never, ever trust anyone who waters down their drink.) 'Well, I suppose I'm pretty friendly with all of the Macmillan Burke wives, yes. You and I are going to become great buddies too,' Lynn laughed. 'Whether you like it or not.'

'Oh, you work at the firm too?' Legal secretary, Portia thought? She seemed a bit young to be one of the high-rolling attorneys Macmillan Burke usually hired . . . not to mention too pretty.

'I'm a senior tax consultant, freelance mostly, but

Macmillan's paid me a fortune to come on board for the Globex case.'

'Can you believe Lynn's only early thirties and yet she's earning more than me?' said Ken, looking at her googly-eyed. 'Me or Andy.'

'I'm really glad you've arrived though,' Lynn went on, not even bothering to acknowledge the compliment. 'Straight up, I have such a huge favour to ask you—'

'Sorry about that, darling,' Andrew interrupted, rejoining them and slipping his arm lightly around Portia's shoulders as he sat down. 'That was Dick Feinberg from Globex, I had to take the call. That meeting has been moved forward to seven a.m. tomorrow, Ken, he needs to go over the Feinman deposition before the plenary session at nine. That OK?'

'No problem, Andy.'

Shit, thought Portia, who had been looking forward to a good long leisurely morning in bed with her husband, but she quickly reasoned herself out of the disappointment. After all, they had weeks and weeks ahead of them to look forward to . . . What more could she ask for, she thought, squeezing his hand and gazing at him in that glazed loving way that couples do, which never fails to make single people want to throw up.

'Ken, switch seats with me, I wanna talk with Portia,' Lynn ordered in the manner of someone who's used to getting her own way.

Ken obediently hauled himself up and moved over so that he was now facing Andrew, while Lynn could command Portia's full attention.

'So, may I ask you something?'

'Fire away.'

'Can you tell me about every single male friend you and Andrew have?' she asked. 'Age, address, education, occupation, earnings and dating history. That's all I need to work on, for the moment.'

'Bloody hell,' said Portia, winded and totally unused to the directness of your average Manhattanite.

'Oh, I'm sorry.' Lynn laughed, revealing a row of flawless pearly white teeth. 'I always forget you've gotta preamble things with Europeans. Basically, Portia, I'm getting married this year.'

'Oh, well, congratulations. Who's the lucky man?'

'I don't know yet. If I knew that, I wouldn't need your help.'

'I'm afraid I'm not with you.' Portia was raging that Andrew was so deep in conversation with Ken; she'd have loved him to overhear this, so they could have a great giggle over it afterwards.

'OK. My life coach says I'm totally ready to be in a loving, committed marriage and, astrologically speaking, I am one hundred per cent certain that it'll happen this year.'

'Based on what exactly?'

'Something a fortune teller told me back in nineteen ninety-seven. But everything else he told me came out right, so why wouldn't this?'

Portia found herself double-checking her glass to try and ascertain exactly how tipsy she was. Was she really having this surreal conversation?

'He was right about my mother's facelift, and he was right about my moving apartment and changing hair colour and he was deadly specific that two thousand and four was the year I would marry. He said it would happen the same year *Friends* came to an end.'

Portia was about to say that, since 1997, it might conceivably be a fairly safe bet to assume that one might move, or dye your hair a different colour, but she kept quiet, remembering how seriously some women took these things. Lucasta would give you a black eye for even daring to suggest that her tarot cards readings weren't so much accurate forecasts of the future as a series of lucky guesses. Lucky and not very difficult to predict. ('You may take a shower, very soon. You may also enjoy a social occasion, but that could happen any time within the next five years. I'm afraid I can't be more specific than that. That'll be eighty euros, thanks.')

'So here's where you come in,' Lynn went on, now drinking unadulterated mineral water. 'In January, I took a night class called 'How to find a husband when you're over the age of thirty'. It's all about applying the principles of marketing taught at Harvard Business School to finding a life partner.'

'But you're so fabulous looking, I can't believe they're not queuing up for you,' Portia blurted out.

'Welcome to Manhattan, honey, the town where single women outnumber men by a ratio of six to one. Know what that means?'

Portia shook her head, absent-mindedly fiddling with her wedding ring.

'It means that, statistically, I'm more likely to die in a car crash than I am ever to get one of those,' she said, pointing at Portia's wedding band.

'Have you tried internet dating?'

'Weirdos, saddos, sickos and whackos. Yes, I have tried it and it's a waste of time and time is what I don't have. I am thirty-five years old. If I don't look it, it's thanks to the fabulous oxygen facial they do at Bergdorf Goodman's – you've gotta try it, one session a week and they start IDing you in bars. But, anyway, like it or not, I'm looking down the barrel at forty. I want two kids, one dark and one fair, so, working backwards, that means I need to be pregnant with my first by next year, which means I need to get married this year which means I need to find the right guy and go through the whole dating thing *now*. Also, as soon as I meet him, I need to book the Plaza straight away for my wedding reception and the wait is almost ten months.'

Portia shot another glance over at Andrew, raging that he was missing all this, but he was still deep in conversation with Ken.

'Anyhow, one of the things they taught on the course was to change your reference group to reflect your desired status.'

'Sorry?' Portia was well tipsy by now and was having a tough time keeping up.

Lynn smiled patronizingly, as if explaining Stephen Hawking's *A Brief History of Time* to a slow-witted pass maths student.

'Single people want you to stay single. That way they don't feel so bad about being alone themselves. Married people, on the other hand, want you to be married too, particularly when they're childless. It's so that they can have adult company to talk to when they get bored with each other. All of which makes you my new best friend, Portia. You are my personal pipeline of opportunity. So, will you tell me all about the single guys you and Andrew know? I'm not looking for perfection either, you know. On the course, we're all taught to lower our standards to realistic levels. Just as long as he can use a knife and fork, that's OK with me. At the end of the day, they're all bastards. What you have to do is try and find me a nice bastard.'

Hours later, as Portia lay snuggled up in Andrew's arms in the enormous emperor-sized bed back at their Park

Avenue pad, she relayed the gist of the conversation to him.

'I know, isn't she a howl?' he said, rubbing her bare back and gently massaging her shoulders as he stared at the ceiling. 'I knew you two would hit it off. Lynn's great, best tax consultant in town. She's going to win this case for us, I know it.'

'I couldn't believe how she had everything all worked out, right down to the gynaecologist she was going to book for her delivery. It's not just that she'd like to meet someone, she's looking for a husband in the same way that Scott was looking for the Antarctic. God help the poor eejit, whoever he is. Talk about having your whole life mapped out for you . . .'

'Some guys like that. A woman who'll take control and make their decisions for them. Men are so crap at all that.' He sounded drowsy now, ready to drop off.

'Yeah, well, just so long as she doesn't target married men, my darling,' Portia replied. 'At least, not this married man,' she added, kissing his earlobe seductively and brushing away a stray piece of hair.

But it was too late. He was out for the count.

Chapter Thirteen

FROM: _daisydavenport@davenporthall.ie_
TO: _portiadavenport@aol.com_
SUBJECT: Mark Lloyd is a bona fide sex god and I fancy him like you wouldn't believe and Eleanor Armstrong is just so lucky and he's knickers mad about her and WHY CAN'T I MEET A GUY LIKE THAT???

Hi Sis,
Yet again, I've said it all in the subject box. Jesus, you should see him. I swear, his eyes are the colour of coal, jet black. Honest.
Yours, in a hot flush,
Daisyxxxx

Claudia Carroll

FROM: *portiadavenport@aol.com*
TO: *daisydavenport@davenporthall.ie*
SUJBECT: *Hands off!*

Dearest Daisy,
Just remember he's on the verge of
marrying someone else and you'll be
fine. As Mummy would say, it's bad
karma to go poaching another woman's
man. Be cool, calm and professional,
remember you're an acting manager and
all will be well. I don't mean to pry
or appear overly inquisitive but was
kind of hoping you'd have some news
about the running of the Hall for me??
Apologies if this appears in any way
nosy . . .
Much love,
Portiaxxx

FROM: *daisydavenport@davenporthall.ie*
TO: *portiadavenport@aol.com*
SUBJECT: *Oh yeah, the Hall, sorry.*

Hi again Sis,
Am in a mad rush as am late for one of
Julia's bloody power meetings, so here

is the news in point form.

1. Miss Plastic Fantastic has finally settled on a name for her beauty salon: 'The Retreat'. Ironic, don't you think? Given that the only retreat she'll be beating is when I kick her lardy arse out of here the morning after this wedding? Bring it on . . . This has one big advantage though. It's keeping her well out of my way, for the time being at least.

2. Mrs Flanagan had been roped in to helping her. I wanted to get our own builders in to renovate the old nursery but Shelley-Marie just smiled and simpered and took matters entirely into her own hands. Herself and Mrs Flanagan headed off to Atlantic Homecare in Dublin and the next thing, a truckload of furniture arrived, mostly chairs and tables and God knows what else. To be honest with you, apart from having about ten thousand million other things to be getting on with, I'm half

```
afraid to go up there to see
what's going on for myself. I
think I'll just hold off until she
hands me another invoice and then
I'll rant and rave and demand to
know where our money's going.
```
3. There is no third point. Did I
   mention Mark Lloyd gave me his
   PERSONAL mobile number???!!!

```
Love to Andrew. Hope all the sex and
shopping isn't completely wearing you
down, you jammy bloody bitch.
Dxxxxx
```

It turned out Daisy didn't have to wait long to discover what Shelley-Marie had been up to. The following morning, just as she was tucking into one of Tim's divine full Irish breakfasts ('a health-conscious fry-up' she'd call it, or else 'a heart attack on a plate'), Shelley-Marie galumphed up to where she was happily ensconced in the Dining Room.

'Well, good mornin' to you,' she stage-whispered in her breathy, baby-doll voice.

Christ, Daisy found herself thinking, that little-girl-lost act is going to wear so thin by the time you hit forty.

'I do declare you are the easiest person in the whole

house to find. Come mealtimes, you're always gonna be in the Dining Room, aren't you?'

Daisy, who was starving and had been really looking forward to the mouth-watering confection of rashers, fried eggs and sausages she'd just helped herself to from the buffet, felt her appetite instantly evaporate.

'So what can I do for you?' she asked curtly, pushing her uneaten plate away and feeling a flush of irritation at Shelley-Marie for ruining her breakfast, the one meal of the day she could enjoy in peace without Julia barking up her bum.

'Why, nothin', except to settle up a couple of accounts I seem to have run up. Furniture mostly, but the hairdressin' sinks are arrivin' any day now and I think you better prepare yourself for a shock. They're mighty expensive, and that's before you even get goin' on all the products I'm gonna be needin'. Now, I've gone and ordered some, but I'm gonna need a heck of a lot more.'

Daisy impatiently began to leaf through the threeinch-deep pile of invoices in front of her and almost fell off her chair in shock. 'Ninety-five euro for a jar of moisturizer? You've got to be kidding me. Who in their right minds is going to fork out that much for a pot of bloody face cream?'

'Why, that's just cost price. I intend to retail with a fifty per cent mark-up, which makes it one hundred and forty-two euros and fifty cents to the consumer, I think you'll find.'

Not for the first time, Daisy got a brief glimpse of a shrewd, hard-headed business brain under the meringue-head image Shelley-Marie normally presented to the world. Busy and all as I am, she silently vowed, I'll make it a priority to watch you like a hawk until the happy day you're sent packing.

'I'm very sorry, but I absolutely cannot permit our guests to be overcharged in that shameless manner,' she said, putting on a very posh accent as though this would intimidate Shelley-Marie further. 'You'll have to explore other product ranges which are more, shall we say, realistically priced.' Now I'm starting to sound like the Duchess of Devonshire, she thought, resisting the temptation to grab a Danish pastry from the freshly baked pile on the buffet table and opting instead to try and make a dignified exit without stuffing her face.

'Crème de l'océan was formulated by scientists workin' at NASA, you know,' said Shelley-Marie, hot on her heels. 'Each and every gram of it is extracted from royal jelly and its results are truly miraculous; you oughta try it. Why, I believe it could take the desperation lines off your face and, who knows, maybe even get you a boyfriend.'

Daisy did a lightning quick scan of the Dining Room to double-check that no one could hear. Apart from

Molly furiously scrubbing the sideboard with what looked like a wire brush and a youngish, honeymooning couple from Galway who were sitting in the bay window giggling at some shared joke, the room was empty. 'Shelley-Marie, let me explain in words of one syllable just so you're absolutely clear. I don't care if your over-priced bloody face cream is personally hand squeezed by the Pope from the liver of a Grand National winner, under no circumstances will our guests be ripped off. Got it? Good.'

She felt fantastic as she tripped down the long corridor leaving an open-mouthed Shelley-Marie in her wake. Well whaddya know, she thought, enjoying the unfamiliar spring in her step. Maybe I'm finally learning managerial skills after all.

'D-Day minus seventeen days,' trilled Julia, 'and so far, none of you are pissing me off, which must be some kind of record. I'm still only on three milligrams of Valium a day, so well done, all of you.'

'Is that a lot?' Daisy piped up innocently.

'It is, when washed down with a bottle of ninety-five Talbot and a half a pack of beta-blockers, believe me. Anyway, our next power breakfast will be at exactly seven a.m. tomorrow and until then, keep up the good work, everyone!'

The meeting broken up, everyone sitting around the

213

long table in the Library duly scattered to the four winds, half afraid of incurring the wrath of Julia for failing to hop to it. They were a motley crew that morning, Daisy thought as they all set about working on their allocated tasks. Apart from herself, Mrs Flanagan was there in her capacity as housekeeping supervisor, although her sole contribution was to ask about Alessandro Dumas, Oldcastle's legendary midfielder, and to make sure that the bedroom he was allocated was on the first floor, as close as possible to her own, coincidentally.

'Each of his legs is insured for about a hundred grand, ya know,' she had said by way of explanation. 'Yis can't expect him to be able for too many flights of stairs.'

Tim was there too, of course, having really outclassed himself with the menu he had devised for the twelve-course wedding banquet. It would truly be a historic meal, Daisy knew, delighted at the reflected glory that the Hall could look forward to basking in.

There were a few people from *Gotcha* magazine there too, including the editor-in-chief and 'It' boy-about-town Joshua Byron-Smyth, the first time he'd bothered turning up. Ostensibly, he was there to decide which photographs should be taken where and to begin interviewing the bride-to-be with just over two weeks to go. However, he arrived at the meeting late, swaggering into the Library with his sunglasses on and offering no other explanation than a thumping hangover from a launch party he'd been at the previous night.

'You're looking as fresh as a daisy, Joshua darling,' Julia chirped, keenly aware of which side her bread was buttered on and not daring to tear strips off the person who was actually paying for the wedding.

Smooth liar, Daisy thought, consciously having to suck in her cheeks to stop herself from giggling at the sight of him. He looked more like a pineapple that was a good two weeks past its sell-by date, with bleached blond hair gelled into a 1950s vertical quiff and ridiculously dark fake tan plastered (patchily) all over his face and hands. Daft as a brush.

'Tell me, Josh darling, what was the launch for?' Julia trilled over to where he was standing at a hunting table, plonking two Solpadeine into a tumbler of sparkling water.

'Aromatherapy toilet roll,' he replied in a surprisingly deep, gravelly voice. 'Sorry if I sound like the Exorcist, must have smoked about forty cigarettes last night.' Then he just plonked himself down on one of the Library's comfy armchairs and spent the rest of the meeting dozing peacefully in front of the fire. Surprisingly, Julia let him be; all she did was shrug her shoulders at everyone else as though to say: well, he is paying the piper.

'Believe it or not, he is the best in the business,' Julia hissed over to Eleanor as soon as the snoring started. 'I'm sure he'll begin interviewing you the minute he starts to feel . . . well, a little more like himself, shall we say. I know he's planning a big feature on the beautiful bride, blissfully happy in the lead-up to her big day.'

Eleanor didn't answer, just nodded and sipped on a hot lemon tea she was cradling between her hands. If ever anyone looked stressed in the lead-up to her big day, it was her, or so Daisy thought, glancing across the table at her. Nerves, most likely, she decided, and who could blame the poor girl with all this fuss and commotion going on all around her?

'And how is Mark getting on?' Julia asked her. 'Training going well?'

'Yes, I think so,' she replied softly. 'Although I haven't spoken to him properly in a few days. He's up to his eyes with this big match coming up.'

They were interrupted by Amber, who stuck her head around the Library door. 'I'm really sorry to interrupt,' she said, terrified to venture any further into the room with Julia in full flow. 'I know you told me not to put any calls through to the Library, but it's just . . .'

'Just what?' Julia snapped irritably.

'It's just that Mark Lloyd is on the phone at reception.'

'Oh, thank you,' replied Eleanor, visibly brightening as she rose to take the call.

'Emm, well, actually, he asked to speak to Daisy.'

'He probably just wants a progress report,' said Daisy, aware that Eleanor's big soulful eyes were following her all the way out of the room. Two minutes later, her trembling hands picked up the phone at reception, her nerves not helped by Amber flapping in her ear. 'Hi, Mark! It's Daisy here. Sorry to have kept you waiting.'

'All right, no worries. How are you?'

'Well, the wedding plans are coming on really well, we're in great shape for the rehearsal . . .'

'Great, great, fab. Look, I know this might seem a bit odd, but how do you fancy coming over to Oldcastle this weekend to give me a progress report? There's a great hotel here that me and all the lads stay in, you'd really like it. *And* you could fill me in on what's happening.'

'What?' Daisy almost dropped the phone. Was she hearing things?

'It's just – I know how stressed Ellie is about the whole thing and it would really be great for me to be kept in the loop, so to speak. I feel so out of touch over here.'

Daisy took a very deep breath. 'That's very sweet of you, Mark, but I'm afraid I can't possibly take off for a weekend like that. We're all working flat out this side of the wedding, it wouldn't be fair for me to leave everyone high and dry.' I deserve the Victoria Cross for saying no to him, she thought.

Mark was charm itself. 'No worries, I totally understand. Guess I'll just have to keep calling you then, won't I?'

Gotcha magazine's security team had arrived that day

too. A big van with 'A1 Security' on it pulled up in front of the Hall and two beefy, burly men, all dressed in black, immediately began scanning the Hall and grounds. They looked and acted just like a SWAT team as they paraded down the driveway communicating with each other via walkie-talkie even though they were only a few feet apart. They had an odd way of talking too; from what Daisy could hear, it sounded as though they were just shouting song titles at each other.

'Ten four, ten four, looks like we got us a convoy,' one bellowed on seeing the postman cycling up the driveway followed by Tom in his taxi.

'Roger that,' replied the other, waving at them to bring them to a halt. 'Yeah, looks like the boys are back in town.'

Within minutes of their arrival, Lucasta had christened them Tweedledum and Tweedledee.

'Is security really necessary?' Daisy had asked Julia, in total exasperation. 'You're in Ballyroan you know, not Baghdad.'

'Abso-fucking-lutely,' replied Julia, 'and this is only the start of it. All of the hotel staff will have to be issued with ID tags to authorize them to gain access to the Hall and then they'll each have to be interviewed individually.'

'Interviewed?' Daisy had a mental picture of the security team tying people to chairs and then shining lights in their faces, like the KGB did in Bond movies.

'Oh, calm down, it's perfectly standard procedure before an event like this. It's just in case someone is got at by a rival magazine and bribed to take candid photos, which they'd publish ahead of *Gotcha*'s wedding spread. Spoilers, we call them. Or else stupid asshole bastards, entirely depending on my mood.'

'I think I can safely assure you that no member of staff would accept any kind of bribe, no matter how tempting. We value loyalty here, you know.' Here I go, sounding like the Duchess of Devonshire again, Daisy thought. But bugger Julia anyway, she really had overstepped the mark this time. When she thought of poor Molly and Tim, slaving day and night so that the wedding would be a success and then Mrs Flanagan . . . This was a slightly more sobering thought.

'I wouldn't put it past that bloody family retainer of yours. Quite apart from the fact that she doesn't appear to actually do anything apart from watch TV and smoke, can you honestly look me in the eye and tell me that if she were offered fifty thousand euros for a few photos and juicy titbits about Mark and Eleanor . . .'

'Out of the question,' replied Daisy firmly. Convincing herself proved to be a bit more difficult, though.

As soon as that morning's meeting had 'wrapped' (in Julia's words), Mick the head gardener bolted. He made his escape through the Yellow Drawing Room which led directly out on to the terrace and then into the marquee via a long, snaking overhead canopy, just in case the one thing Julia couldn't control, the weather in March, let them down on the day. She had issued poor, hard-working Mick with one of her legendary schedules, so that not one idle, stray leaf would befoul the driveway on the big day, and so the surrounding lawns would be at their elegant, manicured best, with time to spare.

'Any particular style or cut?' he'd asked her sarcastically at the end of the meeting.

'As close to a Brazilian as fucking possible,' replied Julia in a get-to-work-and-get-out-of-my-sight tone of voice.

'A what?' he muttered, removing himself from the line of fire.

'Just short and neat,' Daisy whispered back to him, 'a bit like a number one haircut.'

Andrew often used to say that Julia Belshaw could run the country with one hand tied behind her back and, it had to be said, he wasn't far wrong. With just days to go, everything had been organized with all of her usual super-efficient professionalism. The Hall, both inside and out, quite simply had never looked better. Even the tiresome distraction of actual paying guests had thoughtfully been removed by *Gotcha* magazine.

Insisting that their team have the full run of the Hall in the lead-up to the big day, they had requested that any visitors who had booked rooms at the Hall that fortnight be cancelled. This meant a bunch of white lies from both Daisy and Amber, as they contacted guests and pleaded overbooking, with the sweetener of a freebie weekend later in the spring, by way of an apology. It seemed that the entire estate was a huge, buzzing hive of activity, everyone hot-footing around the place desperately trying to stick to the impossible schedules Julia had issued them with. 'I'm not asking anyone to do anything I'm not doing myself,' had been her justification. 'If I can put in fifteen-hour days, we all can.'

Even Mrs Flanagan had been prised out of the family room, the TV guide ruthlessly snatched from her, and sent to make sure the bedrooms were at their pristine best. Luckily for her though, she was paired off with Molly, who happily scrubbed every spare surface in each and every room while Mrs Flanagan stood outside the front door smoking fag after fag.

'Could you kindly refrain from smoking out there?' Molly sniped at her, sticking her head out of an upstairs window. 'The smell carries, you know. It's stinking out this room and it's aggravating my asthma.'

'Do ya think I enjoy smoking, do ya? I'm doing this to get rid of the midges.'

'What midges?'

'My point exactly, I'm after smoking them all away for ya. Try and keep up, will ya, luv?'

It was well after eleven one night when Daisy wearily

walked the indefatigable Julia across the driveway to her car.

'You've got exactly eight hours turnaround time before our next breakfast meeting,' Julia was saying, 'so do at least try to get some rest. We're in tip-top shape, you know; I'm very pleased. Naturally, there are major things like flower arrangements to sweat about, but not until D-Day minus three days.'

'You'd think you were launching the space shuttle,' Daisy yawned, marvelling at Julia's energy and wondering a) what she was on and b) if she could get her hands on some of it.

'Straight to bed now, you look exhausted and I need you firing on all cylinders for the rehearsal ceremony tomorrow.' Even after a fifteen-hour day, Julia could still sound bossy.

Ja, mein Führer, Daisy thought, suddenly getting an urge to goosestep all the way to her car, although all she said aloud was, 'Thanks, Julia. I'll just send Portia a quick email and then I'll be out like a light.'

'Give her and Andrew all my love,' said Julia, considerably more perked up. 'And tell them that I have everything under control here. I hate to tempt fate, but for once, I really feel confident that nothing, absolutely nothing can go wrong.'

As though on cue, a loud, wailing, screeching noise that sounded a bit like a demented banshee pierced the still night air. 'GET YOUR FILTHY PAWS OFF HIM, YOU IGNORANT BOORS, HE'S MINE AND I DEMAND THAT YOU LEAVE HIM ALONE!'

'All units alert, we have an SOS on our hands, I repeat an SOS. Request immediate back-up.'

'I'm standing beside you, you fucking eejit, will you for Jaysus' sake stop quoting Abba song titles?'

From around the side of the garden path came both security men, followed by a maniacal Lucasta screeching at them for all she was worth. 'All you're doing is frightening him, you BRUTES! Now he'll never trust me again!'

Daisy and Julia peered into the darkness and, between them, could just about make out a huge, hulking man's silhouette looming dimly out of the dark night.

'And you needn't think you're off any hooks either,' one of the guards yelled at Lucasta. 'You've a right load of explaining to do.'

'Ah, give the aul' one a break,' replied the other. 'She's probably some harmless local bag lady from the village. Look at the state of her, she must have been sleeping rough for years.'

'This is my mother, Lady Davenport,' said Daisy, judging it wise to step into the fray. 'It's quite all right, she lives here and poses no security threat.'

'Thank you, darling, I was beginning to feel like a

terrorist there for a moment,' said Lucasta, fumbling in her pocket for a cigarette.

'Can you identify this man?' asked Tweedledum, indicating the Yeti beside them.

Daisy squinted into the darkness and one of the men obligingly shone his torch into the stranger's face. He was a giant of a man, impossible to put an age on, heavily bearded and filthy dirty. He said nothing, just blinked at the harsh light which must have been blinding him.

'I'm really sorry,' said Daisy, beginning to get nervous. 'I've never seen him before in my life.'

'Right, in that case,' replied Tweedledee, 'I'm calling in the local guards to deal with you, for trespassing on private property.' He went to grab their hostage roughly by the arm and then immediately backed off because of the revolting stench from him. 'Urghhhh, the bleedin' whiff off you!'

'I'm terribly sorry, lads, but theoretically, I'm not actually trespassing,' replied the Yeti politely.

'You can explain that to the guards,' said Tweedledum.

'Yeah, and maybe you'll decide to give them your name,' said Tweedledee, sounding like one kid that was about to tell on another over some bit of playground messing.

'Right so, lads,' said the Yeti in the tone of one who knows the game is up. 'Now, I have to tell you that, although I'm opposed to titles and ownership of land and all of that malarkey, as it happens, I do have a fundamental right to be here and—'

'Jesus, will you just give us your feckin' name and let us get in out of the freezing cold!'

'Well . . . in that case, I suppose I'm Lord Davenport.'

Chapter Fourteen

'It's a sitcom. I'm stuck in the middle of a bloody sitcom.'
Julia was sitting at the bar in the Long Gallery staring
into space and shivering from head to toe, as though
she'd just been in a car crash.

'I think she could use a very large brandy,' Daisy said
to Gorgeous George behind the bar, who instantly
hopped to it.

'Give me anything, rubbing alcohol, anything,' Julia
said numbly. 'As long as it's fermented, I don't give a
fuck.'

'This is only a minor setback,' Daisy said firmly, trying
to convince herself more than anyone, 'and we'll sort it
out somehow, so just try and relax, OK?'

It was utter chaos in the Long Gallery, but fortunately
for Daisy, years of living at Davenport Hall had inured

her to dealing with complete bedlam. Tweedledum and Tweedledee had carried out their threat and called the guards, who were now questioning the intruder. Or at least trying to, given that Lucasta was still shrieking at the top of her voice and invoking the curse of the Davenports on all present. (No one batted an eyelid though, as Lucasta's curses were so ineffectual that they were generally thought to bring good luck to the object of her wrath, usually someone she owed money to.)

'I discovered him, he's my friend and he was incredibly sweet to Martini and we've been having some lovely chats so therefore he belongs to me so therefore YOU CAN ALL BUGGER OFF,' she screeched, as though this were a stray dog she'd found on the side of the road.

'Just a few questions, Lady Davenport, and then we'll all be out of your hair,' replied Ban Garda Noreen Reynolds calmly, well used to dealing with Lucasta and the various spectacular scrapes she'd got herself into over the years. In fact, the goings-on at Davenport Hall were almost the stuff of legend at Ballyroan's tiny Garda station and over the years had morphed into a kind of blooding ritual for new and inexperienced recruits, the theory being that if you could handle Lucasta, Bin Laden would be a comparative stroll in the park.

Noreen herself, as a young rookie some twenty years ago, could still remember getting a call from Lucasta to say that her husband, Blackjack, had just dropped dead having accidentally shot himself while cleaning his rifle and could the police please come and clear up the awful mess. Poor Noreen was there within minutes, puzzled by the sniggers of her colleagues when she told them she was headed for Davenport Hall. She did think it a bit odd though when Lucasta asked her to stop off at Devaney's pub on her way to pick up cigarettes and a fresh case of gin but put it down to the understandable shock of a newly grieving widow. Her years of training at Templemore weren't entirely wasted though; she began to smell a huge rat as soon as she arrived at the Hall and discovered the mother and father of all parties in full swing. She later found out that it was Blackjack who had let her in, looking in the pink of health and not lying in a pool of blood with a single gunshot to his head as she'd been led to believe. When Noreen eventually tracked down the Lady of the house, she found her pissed drunk under a billiard table, being felt up by a considerably younger man. The only explanation she could get out of her was: 'Oh, I didn't think you'd mind popping over with fresh supplies, officer. I'm far too locked to drive myself so just think, you've actually prevented a crime, you clever old thing.'

A charge of wasting police time was utterly ignored; Lucasta didn't even bother turning up in court and her solicitor got her off on an insanity plea. Not that she learnt any lessons; over the years she had even called out the fire brigade to help her take down a painting she couldn't reach ('I've simply got to pawn it before my husband does, darling. If he gets to this before me, the silly bugger won't even buy me as much as a box of ciggies'). On one famous occasion, she had sent for an ambulance sounding panic-stricken and saying that Daisy had been thrown from her horse and broken her neck. The ambulance duly trundled out all the way from Kildare only to discover that she actually wanted them to administer CPR on her favourite cat, who was a bit poorly. As far as she was concerned, the emergency services were nothing but unpaid staff, at her twenty-four-hour beck and call.

Professional as she was though, poor Noreen was utterly unprepared for this. For a start, the suspect completely panicked when he was taken inside the Hall and insisted on being questioned in a small, private room. Daisy leapt in and donated her office for the purpose, dying to sit in. She asked Noreen if she could be there for what she presumed would be an interrogation of sorts and was told no.

'We shouldn't be too long,' Noreen calmly told her, 'and I may have to make a few phone calls to verify his story. You just wait in the Long Gallery and I'll give you a shout the minute we're done.'

Secondly, the stench from him was so disgustingly overpowering that Noreen and her partner, a junior garda, had to take turns to run out of the tiny office and on to the upper corridor for gulps of air. Not exactly how they'd been trained to deal with a suspect being questioned for trespassing with intent, but then, this was Davenport Hall, always a bit of a black hole as far as the normal rules were concerned.

Mrs Flanagan had been woken up by the commotion and came waddling sleepily into the bar, where they were all waiting. 'So is it true what Tweedledum and Tweedledee are saying? That there's some escaped lunatic claiming to be a relation whose been living in the cow-shed for weeks?'

'How did you know about that?' said Tweedledum, sidling up beside her. 'That's classified.'

'Because you've been bellowing it all over the Hall on your walkie-talkies, ya feckin' eejit, that's what woke me.'

'I told you to cup your hand over the mouthpiece when you're talking,' Tweedledee griped at his partner.

'Jaysus, the smell of him would knock ya sideways, so it would,' she said, plonking down in an armchair beside a distraught Lucasta. 'I nearly passed out when I went by yer office just now, Daisy luv.'

By now, Julia had cooled down a bit and was deep-breathing in between taking big slugs from the neat brandy in front of her. 'Just what the world needs,' she muttered under her breath, 'another fucking Davenport.'

'Oh, get lost the whole buggery lot of you,' snapped

Lucasta, waving over at Gorgeous George to come and refill her gin and tonic. 'If it wasn't for me looking after him so well, you'd have found a rotting, maggoty old corpse in the shed instead of a real live human being. Shower of ungrateful bastards. Only for me, this would be a game of Cluedo, with dead bodies being found in cowsheds.'

'Excuse me, with or without you, I'd have got to the bottom of this sooner or later,' said Mrs Flanagan. 'I was just on the verge of finding out who was nicking all the stuff that's been going missing from the Hall . . .'

'You were?' said Daisy.

'Course I was, luv. Why do ya think I've been holed up watching all the old Sherlock Holmes fillums and *Murder, She Wrote*, not to mention the odd *Miss Marple*? For the good of me health? What, do youse all think I enjoy watching seven hours of telly a day or something?'

'Anyway,' said Lucasta, rudely ignoring her. 'If he is who he says he is then he's family, so you should all be thanking me, really.'

'But is he family, Mummy? That's exactly what I'm trying to figure out. He could be absolutely anyone. Why would any relation of ours sneak around the old cowshed for weeks and then turn around and claim to be the new Lord Davenport? Why not just come and tell us who he was in the first place like a normal person?'

'I don't know, sweetie, but I do know that there are an

awful lot of lunatics on your father's side, perhaps he's one of those Davenports. A dreadful shower of gits, but then, show me any man connected to this family who isn't. Now, I haven't set eyes on any of them since my wedding day, but I do distinctly remember thinking that they were all complete mental cases, every last one of them. When I was courting your father, he used to tell me about a cousin of his who was thrown out of the IRA for being too mad. Of course, at the time, I thought that was just one of his chat-up lines, although now I'm wondering . . . Mad Dog Davenport they used to call him. So maybe now he's escaped from an asylum or something and the cowshed reminded him of his cell. You mustn't worry though, he's perfectly harmless, I'm sure. I'll do a spell tonight to keep us all from dying violently.'

By now, Daisy was on the verge of an anxiety attack. If her mother could describe someone as mad, then they could only be eye-rollingly, torch-the-Hall-down-in-five-minutes barkingly certifiable.

'Sweet baby Jesus and the orphans,' said Mrs Flanagan, echoing her panic, 'we'll all be stabbed in our beds. It'll be a bleedin' massacre.'

'Ah, give over,' said Tweedledee, 'or else I won't be able to sleep tonight with all this scary talk.'

'I think you're right,' said Daisy. 'Whoever he turns out to be, they'll have to keep him in the station in Ballyroan, it's not safe otherwise. I mean to say, he could turn out to be anyone.'

Just then, the door opened and Noreen came in. All heads turned anxiously towards her as she clip-clopped across the long wooden floor to where they were all gathered beside the bar. 'I'm sorry to have kept you waiting so long,' she said briskly, addressing Daisy. 'But we had to make a few phone calls to see if his story checked out.'

'And?' Daisy was on the edge of her seat.

'Well, either he's the most well-researched actor I've ever seen or he's your cousin, Jasper Davenport. Also known as Mad Jasper.'

'Oh, now I remember,' said Lucasta as though this was a cocktail party and there was a last-minute arrival whose name she'd temporarily forgotten. 'Mad Dog and that awful wife of his were killed in a car crash, so this can't be him. But he had a baby son, a good few years older than you, Daisy. The social workers called here after the accident to see if we'd take in the baby.'

'His parents were killed?' Daisy didn't know which part of the story to be more alarmed at.

'Yes, darling. Oh, donkeys years ago,' replied Lucasta, who was a great natural storyteller and was really enjoying her captive audience, which comprised Daisy, Noreen, Julia, Mrs Flanagan, Tweedledum and Tweedledee. 'I remember the social workers thought we should look after the boy. Next of kin and all that stuff, you know. But I think they must have called on a bad day. You were only a baby too, Portia was away at boarding school and I was hosting one of my Goddess of Isis naked initiation rituals for a few new and very dishy male members, if I remember. Anyway, the buggery old social workers rejected us as foster parents, if you can believe that. They said that I was an alcoholic and that your father was insane. Or perhaps it was the other way around, I really don't remember. Gorgeous Georgie-porgy? Be an angel and top up my gin, will you?'

Daisy found herself brushing away a tear, stunned by her mother's callousness and consumed with curiosity as to what had become of the orphan baby in the meantime.

'Oh, stop blubbering,' said Lucasta. 'Who the hell do you all think I am, Mia Farrow?'

'That's exactly what ya said to the social workers at the time,' said Mrs Flanagan. 'I remember.'

'He probably ended up in some foster home or other,' said Lucasta, knocking back the dregs of her gin.

'And been a lot better off,' said Mrs Flanagan.

'Noreen, can I see him now?' Daisy asked, a bit red-eyed as she rose to her feet. She was well aware that, bar Tweedledum and Tweedledee, everyone there was well used to Lucasta's heartlessness, but she herself felt she'd heard quite enough. It hurt like a cold stab to think about this tiny baby, a relation she'd never even known she had, who was a Davenport and who should have grown up at the Hall with his blood family instead of . . . what? What had become of him in the intervening years?

'Certainly,' replied Noreen, 'of course you can see him. But I'd like a quick word with you in private first.'

Daisy followed her as she clip-clopped back down the length of the Gallery, closing the heavy oak door firmly behind them.

'Now, please don't be alarmed,' said Noreen, 'I've spoken both to his parole officer and the Governor of Portlaoise prison and he's not going to harm anyone. In fact, they both talked about him in unbelievably glowing terms; you'd think he was an old friend. The Governor said that the prison drama society just hasn't been the same since he got out.'

'He's been in prison?' Daisy was horrified.

'He was released last month. He's just served a ten-year sentence.'

Daisy didn't quite know what to expect as they obediently trotted after Noreen all the way up four flights of stairs, along the family corridor and down as far as the office door. Her partner, a junior garda who still looked young enough to be ID'd in bars, was waiting patiently on the narrow passageway outside.

'Would you believe he's still on the phone?' he said to

Noreen, jumping to attention the minute he heard footsteps coming down the corridor.

'To who?' asked Daisy.

'The Governor of Portlaoise. They're nattering away like two aul' ones sitting at a basin getting their hair done.' He was spotty and his voice sounded like it had barely broken. Noreen rolled her eyes to heaven. 'I only stepped outside to give him a bit of privacy,' he added apologetically. 'And because of the smell.'

Noreen just glared at him and opened the door without knocking. Daisy was glued to her shoulder, filled with trepidation about meeting this long-lost cousin she never even knew existed until ten minutes ago. He was sitting comfortably on a leather swivel chair with his back to them, deep in conversation with the Governor.

'Will you just listen to me, Michael? I'm telling you, Bertie Dwyer is totally wrong for the part of Henry Higgins. And, God love him, but he hasn't a note. Many's the time I had to listen to him squalling in the showers and you just take it from me, he sounds like a constipated crow. He hasn't been the same vocally since Tooler O'Shea walloped him in that fight over the rice pudding in the canteen back in ninety-five, do you remember? And never mind what Bonecrusher says, he just doesn't have the range for Eliza Doolittle. He looks shite in a corset and he's not able for Edwardian. Do you remember him doing the Widow Twankey in last year's panto?

Brutal, sheer brutal. Jesus, the only time the audience laughed was when the show was over. I'm telling you now, Machete O'Malley is your man. He can just shave his legs and fit into the Eliza Doolittle costume and shut up with his aul' nonsense. Lighting now is another thing altogether, especially for the Ascot races scene—'

He broke off as some sixth sense told him that he wasn't alone. Swivelling slowly around in the chair, he turned to look at the two faces staring at him. Without a trace of embarrassment he rose to his feet, making an I'm-really-trying-my-best-to-wrap-up-this-conversation face at them, and indicated for them to grab a seat. But for the fact that he looked like the result of a one-night stand between a cavewoman and the Abominable Snowman, you would almost think he was the chairman of a busy corporation instructing the Chinese cleaners to take a seat while he took a conference call from Tony Blair. Daisy didn't bother sitting, she just stood rooted to the spot, open-mouthed.

He was an enormous man, big in every sense of the word and physically built like a Tipperary shithouse. It was near impossible to put an age on him, he could have been anything between twenty and fifty, mainly because of his heavy, scraggy beard and long, matted hair. The raggedy hobo look was completed by the clothes he was wearing: frayed denim jeans with big holes in embarrassing places and a huge chunky, cable-knit Aran sweater

237

which on a normal man would have looked oversized but on him only just stretched to fit. The sleeves barely came as far as his elbows. The sight of the jumper triggered a memory in Daisy: she'd definitely seen it somewhere before . . . then the penny dropped. She *had* seen it before – on Tim. Christ Almighty, she thought, what else has Lucasta been filching for him?

He was still chattering on the phone, in no rush to wind up the call, giving Daisy plenty of time to have a good long stare at him. It was hopeless to try and discern any kind of family resemblance, there was far too much facial hair going on for that, but the more he made eye contact with them, the more she thought she could see a resemblance to herself around his eyes. Clear, wide, bright blue, the kind of eyes that focused directly on you, unflinching, just as hers did, particularly when she wanted something.

'Listen to me, Michael, I'm going to have to get off the phone now. Long story, I'll tell you all when I see you. Oh God, of course I'll be there for the opening night, just try and stop me. And if you need help with stage managing the show, just give me a shout. I'll be staying at Davenport Hall for the next while. All the best now, Michael, and give Margaret a big hug from me, won't you? And the kids too? Tell them I'm really looking forward to Easter Sunday dinner with all of you. All right, so. Good man.' As he hung up the phone, there was an awkward moment when they just stared at each other in embarrassment, no one wanting to be the first to speak. Eventually, Daisy piped up.

'So you're going to be staying at the Hall then, are you? Nice of you to let me know.'

He turned to face her and looked at her with blue eyes so like her own that it unnerved her a bit. 'You're Daisy,' he said softly. 'I've often seen you out riding early in the mornings. The stables are a credit to you; I've never seen such fine, healthy-looking horses.'

Daisy glanced across at Noreen, temporarily wrong-footed, but he was a step ahead of her.

'I have so many apologies to make to you, I don't know where to start,' he said, smiling warmly, 'but I'm really sorry if I freaked you all out downstairs. It's all those big rooms, you see, they give me desperate panic attacks. I'm a million times more comfortable in a small space like this one, so thanks for letting us use your office for my chat with the gardaí. You're a star.'

Daisy shook the hand he offered her and he seemed impressed that she didn't recoil from him. There was something so friendly and sincere about him, she found herself listening to him and letting him talk on.

'I'm sure Noreen there has filled you in on my, eh, background. And I know it must all seem a bit mad, what with me living in your cowshed ever since I was paroled, but you see, the thing is, I had nowhere else to go. I copped on that it was a desperate time for you, what with the big wedding and all, so I thought I'd just lie low, for the time being at least. Your mother was kindness itself, I swear I've put on more weight since she started feeding me than I did in ten years inside. Not to mention all the clothes she smuggled out for me. I must owe you a fortune.'

'You don't owe us anything, Mad— sorry, I mean, Jasper,' said Daisy, stopping herself just in time. He smiled back down at her.

'Don't you worry; didn't I have ten years in prison of being known as nothing other than Mad Jasper? I'm well used to it.'

'OK, then, M— Jasper.' Try as she might, Daisy couldn't bring herself to call him by this awful moniker. 'It's just that . . . well, I'm very sorry about this, but . . . you see the thing is . . .' Come on, her inner voice lectured her sternly, you're in charge here. We've already been emotionally blackmailed into taking in one home-less waif and look where that got us. Enough's enough. An involuntary shudder went down her spine even at the thought of Shelley-bloody-Marie.

'Now, just hear me out. I've a proposal for you that I think might interest you,' said Mad Jasper, taking control of the situation. Daisy was too dumb-struck to do any-thing but raise her eyebrows inquisitively.

'Here's you with this big wedding in little over a week

and with damn all security to talk of. Laurel and Hardy
are only shite, you take it from me. Sure, for God's sake,
I was living under their noses for days and neither of
them even copped on, not even with the smell of food
that must have been coming from under the door of the
shed. I was out having a slash in the paddock yesterday
and the baldy one asked me for a light for his cigarette. I
could be a great help to you here. I'd mind the grounds
for you and keep you all safe. Sure if someone like me
can break in and stay here for weeks on end, think how
easy it would be for a professional thief. I'm hardly a
criminal mastermind, but I have learned a thing or two
from my time inside and I could help you. Show you all
the weak points in the Hall and how you can make them
more secure. And you can trust me. I'm a nice guy. Just
ask my parole officer.'

'I already took that precaution,' said Noreen.

'What did he say?' asked Jasper politely, like someone
looking for a reference.

'Sent you all his love and says he'll see you at his
daughter's twenty-first.'

Jasper nodded. 'You see, you have such a grand hotel
going here, why would you ruin it by making it a target
for thugs? And believe you me, there's a lot of gougers
out there would only love to make off with the family
silver, so to speak.' He instantly clocked the look of panic
which flittered across Daisy's face. 'I meant your family, of

course, not mine. I mean I am a Davenport and all that but I'd never in a million years want to stake my claim here.'

'You couldn't,' Daisy blurted out. 'The Hall belongs to my sister Portia.'

'I mean all that guff about titles and that shite. I'm not joking you, but I honestly swear that if anyone called me Lord Davenport, I'd punch their lights out. And I'm a pacifist. So you needn't be worrying about me having a go at any of your guests,' he added, nodding respectfully at her.

For a split second, she felt as if she were conducting the weirdest job interview in history. 'If you're a pacifist, then how come they put you away for ten years?' asked Daisy. 'What in God's name did you do?'

She was so innocent and direct, he completely failed to take any offence at his criminal past being dragged up. It was odd, Daisy felt, that she was the one who was embarrassed. He never batted an eyelid, just answered her with that disarming mix he had of honesty and humility.

'You're dead right to ask me that, Daisy. If I'm going to be giving you a hand about the place, you need to know my back history, so to speak. I'm an animal rights activist and, well, it's a long story and I don't want to bore you, but let's just say I was staging a peaceful protest outside a furrier's shop above in Dublin and it got a bit out of hand.'

'What happened?' Daisy was intrigued, especially as he seemed like the type who wouldn't harm a fly.

'Ah, I was unlucky. All I wanted to do was chain myself to the railings, nice and peacefully, and sit there for the day with my placard: "Wear your own pelt". But then a whole load of professional May-Day rioters joined in the protest and turned it into a full-scale demonstration. Total disaster. The police had to be brought in, there was even tear gas used to disperse the mob, windows were smashed, the crowd were baton-charged – God Almighty, it was the lead story on the six o'clock news that night. I was singled out as the ringleader and the judge said he had to make an example of me. Gave me five years in the Joy.'

'So how come you ended up doing ten?'

'Well, you see, I started a protest inside about how there was no vegetarian option in the canteen, a peaceful demonstration, but there was an awful rough element in the Joy, you wouldn't believe it. And before I knew what was going on, a right crowd of messers had dragged us up on to the roof to demonstrate; Christ, there were helicopters circling around us and everything. So I sort of got labelled as a troublemaker and they extended my sentence. Wrong place, wrong time, you know? Then I got transferred to Portlaoise and the Governor there got me all interested in the drama end of things, so it never really bothered me when I never made parole. I was always in the middle of directing something and I never minded.'

Daisy just stared at him, open-mouthed. Finally, she began to see why his nickname was Mad Jasper.

Chapter Fifteen

Bright, late-morning sunshine was streaming through the window by the time Portia finally woke from a sleep deeper than the seabed around the *Titanic*. For a split second, she had that awful where-am-I feeling you get when you're still not fully used to the time difference and wake up in an unfamiliar bed, but then memories of last night came flooding back to her in one big, blissful deluge. She was here. In New York. In Andrew's fabulous apartment with him beside her. Except that he wasn't exactly beside her.

No matter, she thought, woozily remembering him muttering something about an early morning meeting. They had weeks and weeks ahead, just the two of them, in New York together.

Lazily, she dragged herself out of bed, pulled on one of

the T-shirts that Andrew had dumped across the back of a chair, and sauntered over to the high sash window. It was a perfect Manhattan morning, bright and cloudless, and for a second she struggled with the heavy clasp on the window before throwing it open and impulsively sticking her head out. 'Oh Jesus!' she gasped, still not used to quite how high up the apartment actually was.

Way, way down below her were swarms of people, like tiny weenie free samples, all full of hustle and bustle as they went about the business that's demanded of a professional Manhattanite. Park Avenue was jammed with mid-morning traffic, yellow cabs noisily honked horns and everywhere she looked, people seemed to be in a mad, tearing hurry.

She almost hugged herself, high on life, feeling that this was probably the closest she'd ever come to being in an episode of *Sex and the City*, and also loving that guilty pleasure you only get when you're on holiday while everyone around you is working their ass off.

She sighed with pure pleasure, pulled the window shut behind her and sashayed around the apartment, which she was slowly coming to love as much as Andrew seemed to. He'd lived there for years before he'd met Portia and had simply plonked his bags down and gone back to his old office, as if he'd never been away. Old-fashioned in design, it had high, coved ceilings, a walk-through closet, a wonderful cream-tiled en-suite bathroom with a Victorian pedestal bath, and a tiny galley kitchen, with only a microwave in it, she noted, smilingly. Andrew was a wonderful husband, a supremely talented whiz-kid lawyer and an Olympian lover to boot, but when it came to cooking skills, he was useless bordering on dangerous. Unless you counted tea and toast or ripping open the top of a cereal box, Gordon Ramsay could sleep easy. The one and only time he tried to make her dinner, she ended up with vicious food poisoning for a full week.

'And I wouldn't mind,' he'd moaned at her, 'but I defrosted that chicken at least three times before I microwaved it, just to be on the safe side.'

Macmillan Burke had obviously spent a fortune on the place; the breathtaking views of the Park from the living-room windows alone must have added a fair whack on to the rental cost. A luxurious perk such as greenery was utterly wasted on a country-bred girl like Portia though. She spent her life looking at fields, mountains and fabulous views; what was making her heart race were the city sights, sounds and smells; the nervous energy, the buzz; and the feeling that you might turn a corner and bump into Woody Allen at any moment. She couldn't contain herself, she just had to get out there once again, hit the shops, grab some food, buy some clothes, walk the streets and just be a part of all that life.

She showered and dressed and went to check her emails to see if there was a progress report from Daisy. Nothing. No matter, she thought, figuring that no news was good news. She threw on a warm jacket and bounced over to the hall table to fish out a spare set of keys Andrew had cut for her. She rooted around under a pile of junk mail to see if he'd left her a note, but he hadn't. Which was odd. He was a great Post-it writer, even if it was only to tell her silly stuff like *Don't forget to tape* The West Wing *tonight*, or *I don't care what you say, those outside drains really need to be looked at*. Or even, *I love you*.

She thought for a second, hesitated, then picked up the phone and rang his direct line. Bugger it, she figured. Yes, he's up to his armpits in work, but he'll want to know I'm out and about and when we're going to meet up later. As the number rang, she drifted off into a mini-day-dream where they were having a cosy, gorgeous, romantic dinner in some chi-chi Italian restaurant that he knew of old, where only real New Yorkers dined, just the two of them this time, holding hands across the table with Sarah Jessica Parker and Matthew Broderick talking to Tony Soprano at the table next to them, Will and Grace cracking jokes beside them, as Yoko Ono serenaded her from a white grand piano, just like in the 'Imagine' video . . .

'Mr de Courcey's office, how may I help you?' A woman's voice, crisp and businesslike.

'Oh, hi,' she said, roused from her meandering little fantasy. 'Can I speak to Andrew please? This is his wife calling.'

'Oh, you must be the famous Portia we've all heard so much about.' The voice sounded warmer, friendlier. 'I'm Glenda, one of the legal secretaries here. Welcome to the city.'

'That's very nice of you, thanks. I was just wondering if I could speak—'

'Oh, I just love your cute little accent! Say something Irish.'

'Emm, the top of the morning to you?'

Hysterical laughter followed. 'I love it! I love the lilt, it's a scream! You know I'm one-quarter Irish on my grandmother's side?'

'Emm . . . really?'

'Sure, honey. She came over after the war, hoping for a better life, but got caught up in the Depression. Then she met my grandfather who made all his money from bootlegging but he got drafted into the Second World War and was killed in action in Normandy. I'm welling up just thinking about it. How they've never been on the biography channel, I'll never know.'

Jesus, Portia thought, will I ever get to talk to Andrew? 'I just wondered if Andrew was around . . .'

'So what are your first impressions of the Big Apple?'

'Oh, it's just everything I ever thought it would be. I can't tell you how much I love exploring. I just wanted to have a quick word with my—'

'Oh well, honey, I just have six words to say to you. All the B's. Bergdorf's, Bloomingdale's and Barneys for your brazilians, Birkins and Bellinis.'

'I'm sorry?'

'Shopping tips, sweetheart. If I had a rich husband like Andrew, they'd have to open up a branch of Barneys right in my front room. You take my advice, honey, and go max out his credit card. If he's anything like my guy, he'll pay it just to keep the peace. Say: Ah sure, to be sure, to be sure. Every time I try to get Andrew to do it for me, he leaves the room.'

'Speaking of Andrew, I was really hoping to talk to—'

'Wait up, honey, Lynn's right here beside me, wants a quick word.'

Portia rolled her eyes to heaven as the phone was passed over, clearly hearing Glenda whisper, 'You know what these Irish are like, they'd keep you chatting on the phone all day. You can't ever get a word in.'

'Hi there, Portia, I hope you're not feeling under the weather after last night?'

'No, I feel wonderful, thanks. Dying to get out and see the city. Maybe you can help me, Lynn, do you know where Andrew is?'

'Tied up in meetings all day, I've barely seen him myself.'

Not to worry, Portia thought, he'd be back at the apartment that evening; she'd see him then for a lovely, romantic evening, just the two of them this time.

'So how about you let me take you to lunch?'

'Oh, well, that's very sweet of you, Lynn, thank you.'

Given the choice, Portia would have preferred to be out and about exploring the sights and sounds of Manhattan by herself, but it was really good of Lynn to offer her lunch. Friendly. And, after all, she had the whole day ahead of her. She could always do touristy stuff afterwards.

'Great. How about the King's Carriage House at one p.m., that'll give you thirty minutes to get there, which is plenty. I'll book a table now. It's on East Eighty-second Street between Second and Third.'

'Sorry?'

'I forgot you're not used to the grid system yet. Just jump in a cab at Park Avenue and give the address. It's only five blocks from you.'

At exactly one p.m., Portia stepped out of a yellow cab and into the crisp sunshine. 'Have a nice day, ma'am,' the taxi driver called after her, sounding as though he really meant it.

'Thanks,' she smiled, 'you too.'

A uniformed concierge gracefully held the door open

for her and she stepped inside, squinting a bit till her eyes got used to bright overhead lights. The restaurant was big and bustling, high-ceilinged and elegant, with waiters and bus boys running around. It was obviously very trendy too, as a long queue had already formed at the reception desk.

'Portia, darling, lovely to see you.' It was Lynn, shoving Versace sunglasses into the breast pocket of her crisp linen jacket as she entered the restaurant doors, a bit breathless from having rushed to get there. 'Hi Paul. God, if you get any more gorgeous I'll make your wife divorce you.' Lynn strode confidently up to the top of the queue and kissed the maître d' warmly, leaving Portia to trail in her wake.

'May I say how stunning you're looking today,' the maître d' toadied to Lynn as he escorted them to a window table and helped her off with her jacket. She did indeed look a million dollars in a smart black linen trouser suit, with a low-cut sleeveless top which revealed her perfectly tanned, toned, athletic shoulders.

'I'm really sorry about this but I only have about forty minutes for lunch, so if it's OK with you, can we get straight down to it?'

'Ehh, yes, of course,' Portia answered, wondering: Get down to what exactly?

Lynn fished about in her Hermès bag for a very stuffed-looking Filofax and whipped it open in a blinding flash of French-polished nails. 'Firstly, let me emphasize that geography is not any kind of barrier between me and my goal. If you can tell me of any single, eligible guys that you might know of in Ireland, I am so there.'

OK, Portia thought, we're in for a continuation of last night's discussion. So this lunch wasn't about Lynn being friendly towards her at all. It was just another chance for her to pick Portia's brains. She took a sip of her mineral water and braced herself while Lynn rabbited on.

'If you think that Ireland is where I need to go, then that's where I'll go. I'm fully prepared to invest time and energy in this project. You gotta speculate to accumulate. And if Andrew is anything to go by, then Irish guys are hot, hot, hot.'

'Lynn, I need to stop you right there. I am from a tiny village in a backwater of County Kildare. It's hardly Las Vegas.'

'Think.' Lynn was impatiently rapping a gold pen against her Filofax.

'OK, let's see. Well, there's Tom O'Donnell, he's definitely single.'

'Age?'

'Oh, you know how it is with balding men in their fifties, it's nearly impossible to put a definite age on them, particularly when they start losing their teeth.' What the hell, Portia figured, might as well have a bit of fun with this.

'Occupation and an estimate of his earnings?'

'Let's see now.' Portia sat back and deliberately took her time. 'He's our local taxi driver and claims he owns a fleet of taxis, but it's actually just a Nissan Micra that failed the NCT and his mother's second-hand Volvo. In fact, I think that's your main problem with Tom.'

'What?'

'He still lives at home with his mother. Very close to her too; he drives her to mass every Sunday.'

'Any special talents or interests I should know about?'

'Well, I've never seen it myself, but they say he can sink a pint of Guinness in under five seconds. And my mother swears she once heard him burp the national anthem.'

Lynn's face fell as she angrily put a neat line through his name. 'Who else have you got?'

'Let me think . . .' Portia took another long sip of mineral water and really started to enjoy herself. 'Oh I know. God, why didn't I think of it before, it's so obvious, it's staring me in the face.'

'Who, what?'

'Single, straight and absolutely loaded. He's probably the most eligible bachelor in the county. He's got loads of women running after him.'

'Other women are not a variable which concerns me. Describe him.'

'Well, he's what you might call gothic-looking. You know, tall and skinny. Mid forties, I'd think.'

'I *love* that look, you mean like that actor Richard E. Grant?'

'More Herman Munster, really. Quite reserved, always very well dressed. Oh, and he works with his hands. Loads of women want to date him, from as far away as, oh, Carlow. Let me put it this way, I don't think he'd have any problem finding his way around a naked woman's body.'

'Did he ever come on to you? When you were single, I mean.'

'I wouldn't really be his type. Well, not yet anyway.'

'So what does he do?'

'Oh, didn't I say? He's the local undertaker. Hugely successful too – he did my father's funeral and we were all delighted at how smoothly the whole thing went. Even my mother was forced to admit it was a far better send-off than the old bastard deserved.'

Lynn sighed deeply and decided to change tack. 'Why don't I leave you to think a little further about *suitable* guys from the Emerald Isle and in the meantime, here's a list of the Macmillan Burke men I need information on. Basic stuff, really: status, income, which Ivy League school they attended, college grades, general dating history and whether they're leg or breast men.'

Portia looked at her, wondering if she was messing

around. It was only when Lynn tore out a neat list of names from her Filofax and handed it over that she realized she was being deadly serious.

'Don't look so dumbfounded, Portia, I need your help here. You can't expect me to find all this out for myself, can you? As a married woman, you can get away with asking anything you want and guys will tell you straight out. If I ask, they just smell the agenda and clam right up.'

Or maybe they just see the shark fin sticking out the back of your neck and that gives them their first clue, Portia thought as lunch was served. A buffalo mozzarella salad with Parma ham and caramelized onion marmalade . . . unbelievably delicious but as far as Portia was concerned it may as well have been boiled tripe on toast. Funny, she thought, how company can sometimes make you completely lose your appetite.

Precisely forty minutes later, Lynn pecked her once on each cheek and strode back to the office, leaving Portia with the same feeling the Free French resistance fighters must have had after ten minutes of being interrogated by the Gestapo. She felt bulldozed over, bossed around and, worst of all, used. Wait till I tell Andrew, was all she could think as she waved down a yellow cab and said the only words in the English language calculated to make her feel better.

'Hi there.' She beamed at the driver. 'Can you please take me to the poshest, swishest and trendiest store on the island of Manhattan? The kind of place where nothing costs less than five hundred dollars and no matter what I buy, my husband will fall in love with me all over again?'

Hours later, she arrived back at the apartment, laden down with shopping bags, all thoughts of loopy Lynn well and truly banished. After the taxi driver had said, '¿Qué?' a couple of times and Portia gesticulated wildly and pointed at her clothes like she was having a small seizure, eventually he'd deposited her in front of every true Manhattanite's raison d'être: the Madison Avenue entrance to Barneys.

Portia was instantly in girl heaven and raced around the contemporary casuals floor like a high speed Mack Sennet chase scene on speed, never in her life having seen anything quite like this. Ballyroan's sole contribution to world couture was 'Nuala's Valu-Fashions' on Main Street, where eighties originals were still sold. Not as any kind of tongue-in-cheek retro revival, they were the real thing, right down to the fuchsia-pink puffball skirt in the window, white stilettos and boiler suits, all with shoulder-padded jackets to match. It was like comparing a mangy stray dog with a Cruft's champion: everything you picked up here was a work of art, right down to the exquisite-coloured cashmere jumpers beautifully laid out on glass-topped tables. Even the freebies in the ladies' room were all Jo Malone.

'You realize US sizes are a little bigger to what you got in Europe?' a stunningly pretty assistant asked Portia, passing another mass of clothes into the changing room for her to try on.

'I know, isn't it just the best thing ever?' Portia was in seventh heaven, twirling around in a beautifully cut black bootleg trouser suit. 'This is the first time I've fitted into a size ten since I got married!'

She well and truly shopped till she dropped, the novelty of it adding to the adrenalin surge. For the first time in her life she could really appreciate Joan Rivers' comment that a woman only ever really has an orgasm when she's shopping. Portia was looking and feeling a million dollars, wearing the black trouser suit with a cream cashmere halter neck top and the most translucent Giorgio Armani make-up she'd treated herself to in the make-up hall. In one blissful afternoon she'd completely obliterated all thoughts of loony Lynn Fairweather and now just couldn't wait for the romantic dinner for two with Andrew which she'd been looking forward to all day . . .

She almost fell in the hall door and dumped her newly acquired finery on the carpet, just as the answering machine picked up a call. She was about to lift up the phone, presuming it was Andrew, when the one voice which could turn her bowels to the consistency of a mushy pea rang out, echoing around the high ceilinged hallway. 'Andrew, my darling, this is your number one lady calling! Wonderful news, I'm coming to see my baby boy and I'll be arriving tomorrow, so do send a car to JFK for your old Mummy, there's a good boy.'

FROM: <u>*daisydavenport@davenporthall.ie*</u>
TO: <u>*portiadavenport@aol.com*</u>
SUBJECT: You really won't believe this.
In fact, you should probably make sure
you're in a sitting position before
reading any further . . .

Hi Big Sis!!!
   Hope all's well in the Big Apple and
that you have to buy new suitcases to
carry home all the stuff I JUST KNOW
you're buying for me . . . The funniest
thing. Now whatever you do, don't
panic, OK? You remember after Daddy's
funeral how everyone was wondering who
the title passed on to? And the
lawyers were madly trying to trace some
distant cousin who none of us had
heard of? And you know how I've been
saying to you for ages that we could
really do with a bit of extra muscle

round here for lugging baggage around and doing all the shitty jobs? Well, surprise, surprise, two birds killed with one stone . . . He's called Jasper Davenport and he's just the sweetest guy. There's a sort of family resemblance between him and me, a bit like Viola and Sebastian in *Twelfth Night* type thing. Mummy says we're like two completely dissimilar things in a pod.

Anyway, in my official capacity as acting manager, I've hired him and he's staying. Absolutely nothing for you to worry about at all, he's totally trustworthy,

Love and a big hug to Andrew, Daisyxxx

PS. Is it OK if I lend him some of Andrew's clothes? It's just that we don't have time to go shopping for a uniform for him this side of the wedding . . . hope you don't mind!!!

FROM: *portiadavenport@aol.com*
TO: *daisydavenport@davenporthall.ie*
SUBJECT: *How extraordinary!*

OK, I should have guessed there was
something up when you hadn't done your
usual trick of writing half the content
of your email in the subject box at
the top. *Unbelievable* news! What's he
like? And, more to the point, what's
he been doing all these years? Don't
suppose by any miracle he's been
training in hotel management?? No, that
would be too good to be true, wouldn't
it? Let me know everything's OK with
him, will you? It's just that when you
write sentences like 'don't panic' and
'nothing to worry about' it has
precisely the opposite effect on me.
Love,
Portia

FROM: <u>*daisydavenport@davenporthall.ie*</u>
TO: <u>*portiadavenport@aol.com*</u>
SUBJECT: *Of course he's completely trustworthy, what do you think, that I went and hired some convicted criminal straight from Port laoise prison, out on parole?*

Am insulted that you think I'd give a job to someone who wasn't 100% kosher. Good coming from you seeing as it was your husband who went and landed us with Shelley-Marie. No, smart arse, Jasper hasn't exactly trained in hotel management but he has held a lot of responsible positions. He's an absolute godsend. Not only will he be brilliant at security for the wedding but he's dead handy with a hammer and nails too. He's been involved with the theatre for years, so he can also help with the entertainment side of things here. (Don't worry, I'm not planning on setting up a cabaret, at least, not yet . . .) I think he likes it here. And he's not even taking up one of the family rooms, he insists on sleeping in

262

the old storage room downstairs.

I'm a manager now and I made the call and that's all there is to it.

Dxxx

FROM: *portiadavenport@aol.com*
TO: *daisydavenport@davenporthall.ie*
SUBJECT: *Oh dear . . .*

You know I trust your judgement implicitly. Sorry if I gave the wrong impression. If you say he's OK, you know that's good enough for me. Further apologies if my last email was a bit on the curt side. Just got a bit of bad news. Susan de Courcey arrives tomorrow for an indefinite stay. My nerves are in flitters.

Pxxx

FROM: *daisydavenport@davenporthall.ie*
TO: *portiadavenport@aol.com*
SUBJECT: *Oh no!! You poor thing! What are you going to do? Cheer up, though, it mightn't be as awful as you think. It's a full moon in a few days and I'm sure she'll be out on her broomstick*

ripping the heads off orphans and torching bloodbanks, or whatever it is the old witch gets up to in her spare time.

Hi Sis,
   Said it all in the subject box.
   Have to go, or Julia will plaster my innards all over the tennis courts.
   Dxxx
PS. May I remind you, at least you're in New York with your loving, adoring husband . . .

Chapter Sixteen

The following morning, punctual to the minute for the midday meeting she'd scheduled, Julia's zippy sports car whooshed up the driveway, she did one of her ninety-degree handbrake turns and then tut-tutted when she saw the mess she'd made of the gravel. Eleanor, who was safely strapped into the passenger seat, almost concussed herself as her head jerked violently against the side window. If she was expecting an apology though, she had another think coming. Julia was in particularly rotten form that day, not helped by the fact that it had been well after two a.m. before she'd got home after the shenanigans of the previous night. She had then collected Eleanor from Phoenix Park House on the dot of eight a.m. and whisked her off for a final dress fitting with her designer in Dublin and so, in addition to everything else, was functioning on only a few hours' sleep.

'Can you believe it?' she was ranting at poor Eleanor as though somehow this was her fault. 'D-Day is looming and some Neanderthal Davenport relation turns out to have been living in an outhouse for the last few weeks. Fresh out of prison, if you don't mind, although if someone told me he was fresh out of a mental home, I'd have believed it.'

She glanced sideways just in time to catch a worried look on Eleanor's pale face. 'Oh, it's nothing for you to be concerned about, sweetie, I'm sure Daisy will have sent him packing to the nearest home for the bewildered by now. It's the kindest way to deal with the in-bred aristocracy, really, just lock the whole shower of them up. How Lucasta Davenport has managed to escape a padded cell all these years is completely beyond me.'

'But if he is their cousin, then doesn't he have a perfect right to be here?' asked Eleanor, concerned. 'He is family, after all.'

Julia breathed deeply with her eyes closed, as though she were doing a yoga move. 'Eleanor, you are so like your father, both of you are almost too soft-hearted for your own good. Let me reiterate, this is only a tiny blip and absolutely nothing for you to lose any sleep over. In fact, it's a good sign. Before every big wedding, it always feels like you're on a one-way street to certain disaster with nothing but one catastrophe after another to pave the way. Nothing worse than this can possibly happen now. I'm sure the Neanderthal man has been sent on his way and we'll never have to set eyes on him again.'

Julia's day was about to take a nosedive for the worse, however. Just as she and Eleanor hopped out of the car, Jasper came striding around the side of the Hall from the paddock. 'HALT! DO NOT PROCEED!' he was bellowing. 'No unauthorized personnel beyond this point. State your name and business and kindly produce identification.'

'Holy crap, it's Brad Pitt,' said Julia, suddenly switching into flirtation mode. 'I don't believe we've met.' She proffered an elegantly manicured hand only to have it remain floating in mid-air, ignored.

'You've a short memory,' he replied. 'I only met you last night.'

Julia looked at him, gobsmacked, and you couldn't really blame her. The transformation was truly astonishing. Instead of the giant moth-eaten caveman from the previous night who, if you were unfortunate enough to be downwind of him, could knock you sideways with the smell of stale BO, here was a bona fide Greek god. His light, fair hair had been washed and cut short and the manky beard was gone, revealing an almost babyish face, with lightly tanned skin and those piercing ice-blue eyes so like Daisy's. The transformation was completed by an extremely expensive-looking black suit, very well cut, which accentuated his height and huge, chunky frame. And this time, the only thing he smelt of was Calvin Klein's Obsession For Men.

'Ah, you're all right, I don't blame you for not recognizing me,' he said, correctly interpreting the stunned dead-fish look on Julia's face. 'The barber in Ballyroan nearly passed out when Daisy took me there this morning. I hardly recognized myself in the mirror after he'd finished with me. And then this gear is all Daisy's brother-in-law's stuff, you know? I'm not really much of a jacket and trousers man, myself. Sure I've been wearing nothing but boiler suits for the last ten years.'

'Well, clever old Daisy,' purred Julia, unable to take her eyes off the bulging pecs which were fighting a losing battle to stay restrained inside his jacket. 'You know, as wedding planner, I'm going to be staying here from tonight until after the wedding. You must let me know what room they've given you. Maybe you can tell me a little more about those boiler suits.'

If she'd just come out with it straight and said, 'Take me now, big boy,' her tone couldn't have been any clearer. As it happened, though, Jasper was having none of it. 'Positively no entry without authorization. I need identification for yourself and your friend there.'

'I'm Julia Belshaw and this is the bride,' she replied

briskly, but still managing to sound flirty. 'There wouldn't be a wedding without her.'

'It's lovely to meet you,' said Eleanor, smiling coyly and extending her thin white hand to him. 'And it's so great to know how professionally you're handling all the wedding security. My father will be thrilled.'

It had been a long, long time since Jasper had come into any kind of social contact with such an attractive member of the opposite sex and shyness now hit him like a ten-ton stage weight. He was saved, though, from any further embarrassment as Daisy came bolting down the stone steps. 'Jasper, it's quite all right, Eleanor and Julia are wedding party,' she said, out of breath.

'Right, so,' he replied, sounding almost relieved to revert back to demented bouncer mode. 'I'm only letting them in because you're vouching for them, Daisy, but I'm telling you, the retina scan is the only way to go. And they both still have to sign in. I need a permanent record of all personnel within the building at all times. If you wouldn't mind.'

Daisy nodded and led them both inside, leaving Jasper gazing after Eleanor as she tripped lightly up the steps, as if he'd seen a vision.

'Have him scrubbed and sent to my tent,' whispered Julia when they were safely inside the door. 'Come to Mama.'

'I'm afraid he's a little institutionalized,' Daisy

explained as they all signed a visitors' book on the hall table which Jasper had left out. 'He's, emm, been away for a long, long time,' she added for Eleanor's benefit.

'I don't give a shit if he's just out of Alcatraz,' said Julia. 'Clever old you to reveal his inner sex god. It's the most fabulous transformation I've seen since Carol Vorderman, so kudos to you. Right. To work. Ice sculptures.'

As they trooped out through the Yellow Drawing Room and into the marquee, Daisy couldn't have been more stunned. She'd been expecting a battle royal with Julia over poor Jasper and was astonished not to have met with at least a degree of resistance. But no, Julia was happily chirping on about how drunk she was planning to get as soon as the newly-weds were safely helicoptered off on honeymoon and how Jasper was exactly the TLC she had in mind.

'Probably been a good decade since he had sex,' she was chirping, 'so I can fill him in on all the advances there have been, if you catch my drift.'

'I'm just glad to have someone to help with the bags,' replied Daisy, astonished. 'He even offered to take care of any guests who didn't pay up, but I had to turn him down. I was afraid he meant "take care of" in a *Goodfellas* kind of way, whereas I want him to take care of people in a more Julie Andrews way.'

'Oh Christ, just as things were looking up,' sighed Julia on seeing one of the ice sculptures which had melted and now looked like a bent willy. 'You see, Eleanor darling, this is why we dress rehearse all of the ice centrepieces. They can so easily begin to look semi pornographic . . .' she happily chirruped on.

Her day had just brightened up considerably.

'So now we have a convicted felon working at the Hall. That just about beats Christmas.' In the build-up to the big day, Tim was stressed enough about the Georgian banquet he was preparing without having to deal with this.

'Appalling. I couldn't agree with you more,' said Molly, putting down the pile of napkins she was neatly folding into cone shapes. Had Tim said that black was white or that Mosney was this season's chicest holiday destination, she would have backed him up one hundred per cent.

'Well, the pair of youse would want to get feckin' used to it then, wouldn't ya?' said Mrs Flanagan, stumping her way through the kitchen on her way outside for a fag. 'Cos take it from me, he's here to stay.' Then, clocking the looks of disgust flittering between the other two, she added mischievously, 'He's just done a ten-year sentence for violent disorder, he's a complete mental case and he's been living in the cowshed for the last three weeks. Sounds a bit overqualified to work here, if ya ask me.'

Daisy, on the other hand, was beside herself with excitement, loving having him around. 'Finally, after all these years, I get to have a big brother,' she beamed at Jasper as they sat companionably in the Dining Room over lunch one day. Or rather, as Daisy sipped on a frothy cappuccino and Jasper wolfed back a cheese sandwich as though he'd just been sentenced to the electric chair and this was his last meal.

'You're putting me off my food, looking at me like that,' he said, not lifting his head from the plate he was hunched over.

'Sorry, it's just that the last time I saw anyone eating like that, I was in boarding school.' It was as if he thought the food would be snatched away from him at any second.

'Where I've been, you either eat quick or not at all.'

Daisy had been filling him in on everything that was going on at the Hall, including the onset of Shelley-Marie. She was amazed at him though; even though he'd been hiding out for the past few weeks, he was surprisingly well clued up on the various comings and goings.

'I've seen her all right, and I've seen all the workmen traipsing inside the Hall with basins and big heavy-looking boxes of supplies. Yeah, I figured she was doing some women's beauty thing, all right. She's kinda familiar-looking, did she used to be an actress or something?'

'Who knows, she changes her story every time she tells it. Nothing about her would surprise me.'

'It's driving me mental where I've seen her before . . .'

'Well, round here she's known as Miss Plastic Fantastic. You'd better watch out for her, seriously. She is without doubt the most conniving, devious, two-faced see-you-next-Tuesday you've ever come across, and you've been in a maximum security prison.'

'That's lovely language for a lady like you to be using. Bet you wouldn't catch Eleanor Armstrong swearing like that. Right, I'll go up to the beauty place and introduce myself when all this wedding malarkey is over, so she doesn't get a fright when I start fingerprinting all indoor personnel, like. So she must only have been married to your father for a few days when he passed on then?'

'Mmm.' Daisy nodded. 'But my own personal theory is that he sobered up and took an instant heart attack when he realized what he'd married. Makes sense. But you can't slag her off or even breathe a word against her in front of Mummy or Mrs Flanagan. They think the sun shines out of her lardy arse.'

'And what about you, Daisy? Why is there no man on the scene for a lovely-looking girl like you?'

She sighed. 'How long have you got?'

'I'm serious. What's wrong with all the fellas around here not to be queuing up for someone like you?'

'Portia says I'm geographically challenged in that there isn't an eligible bloke around here for miles. But personally I think I'm just really, really unlucky. Let's face it, Jasper, all the good guys have taken their grade A loins off the meat market,' she replied, with Mark Lloyd's black eyes not a million miles from her thoughts. 'But then Mummy just tells me to shut up and stop whingeing. She says if Portia can get a husband, then the dogs on the street can.'

'You must have had boyfriends though. Who's the last fella you went out with?'

She put her coffee cup down with a clatter, shuddering involuntarily at the very thought of her last foray into the shark pool of dating.

If there was one thing Daisy had going in her favour, it was her willingness to put herself out there and really take risks, so when Andrew de Courcey had swanned into all their lives, she wouldn't let up badgering him into matching her up with one of his single friends. 'And it's not like I'm in a position to be fussy or anything,' she'd said, 'I've been single for a full year, so, just as long as they can walk erect, they're in with a chance.'

Ever the gentleman, Andrew had obliged at first, but even his patience wore pretty thin after one set-up too many, when she lambasted him for only ever arranging blind dates with wrinkly old men, as she put it.

'They're all in their thirties, same age as me,' he had defended himself. 'Now excuse me while I figure out where I parked my Zimmer frame so I can hobble to the post office and collect my old-age pension.'

'You're nearly forty!' she had screeched at him.

'I'm thirty-seven.'

'Yeah, that's what I said. Nearly forty.'

'Thirty-seven is still mid-thirties.'

Andrew was highly sensitive about his age and, unfortunately, Daisy did herself no favours with him as a matchmaker if she thought this was the way to go. He eventually called an abrupt halt to the whole find-Daisy-a-fella stakes one night a few months back, when he'd gone to a particular amount of trouble to set up a dinner date for her. This time the target was an old school friend of his, a charity aid worker, just back from Belarus and keen to meet Andrew's stunning sister-in-law. The date was to take place in the Lemon Tree restaurant in Kildare and Daisy dutifully trooped off, looking like a goddess in a borrowed little black dress, borrowed jewellery and a purse stuffed with borrowed money. About an hour later, Andrew's chum rang to say that they'd barely finished their starters when Daisy excused herself to go to the loo and never came back, leaving him looking like a right gobshite surrounded by adoring couples eyeing him up sympathetically.

'For starters, he had red hair,' she had drunkenly explained to a furious Andrew when she did eventually crawl home, pissed and almost falling out of her taxi. 'Red-headed guys *hic* just don't do it for me. Remind me of Chris Evans. And his name kept making me giggle.

David Vale? Sounds like a *hic* housing estate in Swords. Then he bored the arse off me. He kept going on about his charity work, you know, sending kids with cancer to Disneyland and setting them up on *hic* dates with Britney Spears, that kind of thing. And I felt like such an utter cow for not fancying him that the simplest thing was just to head for the hills. Anyway, a few of my mates were in R.I.P.'s nightclub just beside the restaurant, so you mustn't worry about me, Andrew. I still ended up having a really nice *hic* night.'

Not a tale she was particularly proud of.

'Well?' Jasper was gentle, but probing.

'Do you know, whoever Mr Right is, I wish to fuck he'd hurry up.'

'Language.'

'Sorry. It's just that I'm twenty-two. I'm practically pensionable at this stage.'

'Of course you'll meet someone. Off the top of my head I can think of at least four pals of mine who are due for release very soon. Course, you might prefer to find a boyfriend from among the law-abiding, and I can understand that.'

She laughed.

'You'll be with someone in no time, Daisy.'

'I bloody hope you're right. I keep telling myself – what is that phrase? – for every old sock there's a shoe.'

'Listen to you,' he replied, 'the last of the great romantics.'

'I'm too bloody romantic for my own good, that's the trouble.'

'Right so,' he said, suddenly springing to his feet. 'Lunch break over. Back on the job.'

Daisy watched in astonishment as he picked up the Villeroy & Boch plate, cup and saucer and marched to the sideboard with them where he tidily brushed off crumbs and stacked the china in a neat pile. 'Jasper, you really don't have to do that. We have staff to clear up for us.'

He turned to her and smiled. 'You work eight years in a kitchen and, I'm telling you, you'll always appreciate people cleaning up after themselves. Respect for others never does any harm, Daisy. Remember that, in case you ever end up inside.'

'Unless I stick a machete into Shelley-Marie one of these fine days, that's hardly likely,' she laughed, linking his arm as they made their way down the corridor and back outside into the drizzly day.

It was so lovely to have him around the house, she thought, glancing sideways at him as they tripped down the stone steps. Not for the first time, she found herself marvelling at what an amazing person he seemed to be. Between foster homes and prison, he's had easily the hardest life of anyone I've ever met, she thought, and I have yet to hear a single moan pass his lips. 'Hope the weather improves for the wedding,' she said, breaking the easy silence which had fallen between them. 'Or else Julia'll have one of her turns.'

'A very highly strung woman right enough.' He nodded in agreement, bending down to pick up a stray sweet wrapper that was littering the driveway.

'I think she might have an eye in your direction, you know,' said Daisy mischievously. 'So would she be your type then?'

'I'll tell you, my type is about as far away from a woman like that as you can get— Uh, who's this now?' he broke off, much to Daisy's annoyance. She'd really have loved to continue this fascinating conversation, but a car which had just passed the gate lodge had come zooming up the driveway.

'Flower delivery?' asked Daisy. 'Or an early arrival maybe?'

'The first guests aren't scheduled to arrive until six p.m. sharp tomorrow, according to my timetable,' replied Jasper, puzzled. 'I swear to God, the minute all this wedding malarkey is over, I'm going to insist that we install electronic security gates right down the bottom of the drive. It's a disgrace the way any eejit can come up the driveway in an ice-cream van if the mood takes them. Security needs to start right back at the gate lodge if I'm to keep track of all the comings and goings effectively. No messing around.'

It was a bit of a puzzle though as to who this early arrival could be. Absolutely no one who worked at the Hall was exempt from one of Julia's famous schedules, which came colour-coded this time and which clearly stated that six p.m. the following evening was the earliest they could expect guests.

In addition to this, Julia had also dispatched Tweedledum and Tweedledee all the way down to the front gates to monitor security, delighted with Jasper's extra muscle and equally delighted that *Gotcha* magazine didn't have to pay him. Jasper had resolutely refused to accept a single penny from anyone; all he asked for was bed and board in return for an honest day's work. He'd finally been coaxed in from the cowshed but insisted on sleeping down in the basement, in an old disused pantry which had only a tiny window, with bars on it.

'Those big rooms upstairs freak me out,' he'd explained to Daisy, who was encouraging him to opt for more comfortable quarters. 'This'll do me grand. Sure all it needs is a simple camp bed and a couple of posters up on the walls and it'll feel just like home.'

He'd been the first up that morning too and was already outside, pacing around the perimeter of the Hall by six a.m. 'I'm just identifying the weak points of entry,' he'd explained to Julia when she arrived an hour later. 'It's not exactly Fort Knox here at the minute, is it now? Take a look at that,' he said, indicating the French windows at ground-floor level which led into the Library. 'I know fellas who could break in there in around five seconds. Bars on all doors and windows, that's what's needed here.'

Given that the wedding was just days away, Julia was so stressed and hassled that, unusually for her, she didn't even pause to flirt. She just shoved a schedule at him and barked that she'd see him later.

As ever, she had coordinated everything right down to the last, teeniest detail. There was even a coloured map indicating where everyone should park, in reverse order, so that the first guests to arrive were left with the longest distance to walk to the Hall. Nor was this a coincidence. Julia wouldn't have been the ruthless PR supremo that she was without first categorizing her guests and arranging their arrival times accordingly. And so the D list were scheduled to turn up first and were to park behind the tennis courts, about half a mile from the hotel reception, whereupon they would be shown to their rooms in either the slightly less salubrious, cold, north-facing part of the Hall (if they were lucky) or else in the converted stable block; entirely depending on their status in Julia's eyes. Those privileged enough to have made it on to her A list, however, had carte blanche to arrive whenever they felt like it and could park in front of the Hall door, if the mood took them, whereupon they would be shown into one of the swishier, more luxurious suites where a welcoming basket of goodies courtesy of *Gotcha* magazine was awaiting them. It probably would have caused great offence to most of the guests to learn how they were prioritized. For example, a number of the Oldcastle wives and girlfriends, whose careers had begun in the pull-out colour section of the *Sunday Sport*, were in for a nasty shock when they found themselves allocated lesser rooms in the converted stables.

By now, the car had pulled to a halt and the driver leapt out. He was a young man, in his late twenties, of medium height and build. He had light brown hair with eyes almost exactly the same colour, trendy designer stubble on his lightly tanned face and, in the normal run of things, might have been considered attractive rather than drop-dead gorgeous. Might have been. As he stepped out of the car and made his way towards them, Daisy noticed that he was as white as a ghost, with a stressed, tired-looking expression in his bloodshot eyes.

The poor guy had barely got to the bottom of the steps when Jasper lit on him. 'State your name and purpose of visit,' he snarled, towering over the new arrival. 'And produce photo identification instantly.' If he had added: 'Or I'll set fire to your house and your hired car,' he couldn't have been scarier.

'You know, I've just been through this whole drill with your colleagues at the main gates,' replied the stranger wearily, totally unintimidated by Jasper's sledgehammer, take-no-prisoners approach. He spoke with a soft, lyrical Scottish accent and the more Daisy got to look at him, the sorrier she felt for him. Even under all the stubble, his face looked ashen and drawn, almost as though he'd just been in a car crash.

'It's Allonby,' he went on, as though for the thousandth time. 'Simon Allonby and, yes, I know I am a wee bit early, but you see—'

'Allonby with an A,' replied Jasper, expertly leafing through the thick wads of paper Julia had presented him with, scanning the guest list for his name. 'Yeah, there ya are now, under the As,' he muttered, adding, 'It says here you're Dr Simon Allonby,' as though this was deliberately concealed information which automatically made him a likely member of the Corleone family.

'Team doctor for Oldcastle, that's right, but if you'd just let me explain. I've decided to come a couple of days early and stay here for the match as well as the wedding on Saturday—'

'Now you just shut up and pay attention,' Jasper barked with his glowering face only inches from Simon's and practically raining spit down on top of the poor guy. 'For all I know, you could be Saddam Hussein with the beard shaved off. Full identification this instant and then you can go back to the front gates and stay well away till your allocated arrival time. And,' he snarled, his eyes still locked on Simon's but nodding towards his car, 'you can remove that heap of crap from the front drive, that's strictly for limousines and A list only. When your allotted arrival time comes, you can park on the far side of the tennis courts. And let that be a lesson to you for annoying me.'

'So it's the traditional Irish welcome then?' Simon sounded too exhausted to be remotely offended by Jasper. He just fumbled about in his jeans pocket for a wallet, fished out his driving licence and handed it over with an air of patient resignation. Jasper snatched it from him, ripped it out of its plastic container and held it up to the light.

'I know fellas who'd knock off a fake driver's licence as quick as look at you,' he muttered, scrutinizing it like a master forger.

Daisy turned to shrug her shoulders at Simon and an embarrassed silence fell. 'The magazine doesn't want us taking any chances,' she laughed in a vain attempt to make light of the situation.

'Not even with close friends of the bride?' He sounded far too tired to be annoyed.

'Oh, you wouldn't believe the measures they expect us to take. We even have to search everyone's luggage, just in case some smartarse tries to smuggle in a camera . . .' Daisy broke off as the penny slowly began to drop. 'I'm sorry, did you say your name was Allonby?' A distant bell was ringing in her head . . . Where had she heard that name before? Then it suddenly came to her: this was the best friend Eleanor had told her about, the one who had introduced her to Mark Lloyd in the first place.

'Yes, Allonby. A.L.L.O.N.B.Y. Now if you're both quite finished giving me the third degree, I'd very much like to see Eleanor. That's presuming I'm allowed see my best friend without being fingerprinted first.'

After what felt like an eternity, Jasper eventually handed back the drivers licence and grudgingly admitted it to be genuine.

'Thank God for that,' replied Simon dryly. 'Well, much as I've enjoyed this wee chat, I'm afraid I really must be getting along.'

'*Car keys*,' snarled Jasper. 'Your car's a security threat parked there. Give me the keys and I'll move it for you.'

Simon tossed them over and wearily made his way up the steps.

'SAY THANK YOU OR I'LL FLING THE KEYS INTO LOCH MOLUAG,' Jasper howled after him.

'Thank you soooo much,' muttered Simon, not even turning back.

'That's grand so,' said Jasper calmly, tramping off to shift the car. 'Bit of manners, bit of respect, that's all I'm asking for.'

Mortified, Daisy raced up the steps to catch up with Simon just inside the hall door. 'You'll have to excuse Jasper,' she said breathlessly. 'He's, emm, been away for a long time and emm . . .' She racked her brains to think of a tactful way to explain.

'I don't mean to be rude, but I think your brother might need to brush up on his social skills just a wee tad.'

'We're cousins.' Daisy blushed, although given how alike she and Jasper were, this was a relatively easy mistake to make.

Simon was standing at the reception desk by now, impatiently tapping his fingers on the visitors' book, waiting to be helped. Daisy jumped to, remembered what was expected of her as acting manager and hopped around to the other side of the desk, nervously leafing through the room allocations which Julia had practically sweated blood over. 'Allonby . . . Allonby . . .' she mumbled, scanning the list for his name. 'Yes, I've found you. You're a day early checking in, but it's OK, your room is ready for you. You're not actually staying in the Hall itself, you've been given a room in the old outhouse . . . I'm sorry, I mean in the newly refurbished part of the hotel which is only a short walk away.' She checked herself just in time, wondering why in God's name this guy was making her so jumpy. Yeah, sure, he was kind of cute, but not in the Mark Lloyd category, not by a long shot. 'So you're the team doctor for Oldcastle then? Wow, I'd say you could tell a few stories.'

'A few.'

'So how is Mark? He was here you know, to have a

look at the Hall, and he was just so charming and lovely
. . . and . . . well, Eleanor's *soooo* jammy, isn't she?'

'Speaking of Eleanor, do you think I could see her? If
you could tell me where she is, I'll find my own way.' He
wasn't even looking at Daisy, just staring intently at the
staircase, impatient to be gone.

'I'll call her room for you and see if she's there,' she
replied coolly, picking up the reception phone and
checking for the room number. Was this guy rude or
what?

'I'd hate to see you break a sweat or anything, but it is
urgent.'

Daisy stopped dialling to glare at him. 'Excuse me?'

'Now, I know when you look up the word "urgent" in
an Irish dictionary, it says: "Ah sure, what's your rush,
there's time for another six pints of Guinness yet", but
this really, really is a crisis, so if you just give me her room
number, I won't detain you from terrorizing more guests
on your driveway.'

'She's in the Edward the Seventh Suite, being interviewed,' replied Daisy, curtly replacing the receiver and
deliberately keeping her cool. 'It's on the second floor on
the left,' she added, not even bothering to show him the
way.

'Being interviewed?'

'Yes. For the wedding. About how lucky she is to be
marrying Mark Lloyd. Normal bridal stuff, you know.'

'Lucky is not a word I'd use.'

'Ignorant git,' she muttered under her breath as soon as he was safely out of sight. 'If he doesn't watch it, I'll introduce him to Shelley-Marie.'

It was late, well after eleven o'clock that night, before Lucasta and Mrs Flanagan arrived back at the Hall after a long-standing commitment which had occupied the pair of them for the past few days. They were attending a protest rally in Dublin to demonstrate against the smoking ban which the Irish Government proposed to introduce at the end of the month. They'd both sat on the organizing committee and their march was to take them from Parnell Square right to the main gates of Government Buildings. 'We'll bring our campaign right to their doorstep, see how the fascists like it,' Lucasta had snarled. She and Mrs Flanagan had spent many happy hours in the family room designing and making dozens of banners with slogans like: 'Honk if you hate the ban!', 'If you've a problem with smoke, stay home', 'Nicotine Nazis, Out!' and, the pièce de résistance: 'Puff Off!'

So just after breakfast had finished, the pair of them trundled off, clattering their signs loudly behind them and boasting that this could very well be the first bloodless coup in the history of the state. However, things had not entirely gone according to plan and by the time they wearily trudged back to the Hall, they were both in the depths of depression at the complete and utter failure of their mission. Apart from the fact that only a tiny handful of stragglers had joined in their protest march (some of whom were semi-professional protesters and arrived fully dressed in May-Day riot gear), the publicity generated was little short of dismal.

'One fecking paragraph on page twelve of the *Blanchardstown Bugle*?' Mrs Flanagan moaned. 'Tucked away under the weather report, so ya can hardly see it? And the bastards even cut me out of the photo; they just put in you looking like a mental patient with a banner that says "we all have to die of something". Is that what I walked me bleeding feet raw for? I could have done Lough Derg today, I'm that knackered.'

'Oh, shut your bloody whining, where's the Dunkirk spirit?' Lucasta snapped. 'It's just a minor setback, that's all. We need to regroup, rethink our strategy . . .'

'A *minor* setback? That copper at Government Buildings said that in the history of lunatic demonstrations, this one was up there with the "how do you know St Patrick wasn't gay" Lesbian Alliance march, and you're calling this a minor setback?'

'Your negativity is knocking my aura off kilter, now shut up and let's pour ourselves a nice, soothing couple of g. and t.s at the bar. Might as well drink ourselves senseless and be thankful that at least we have one small pleasure the bloody Government can't throw us in jail for.'

They were about to trounce upstairs to the Long
Gallery when the phone at reception rang. Mrs Flanagan
was over like a bullet, sore feet notwithstanding. 'I listen
to the red–hot sound of Sun FM, Kildare's coolest radio
station by miles.'

Ever since Portia had left, this was her standard way of
answering the phone, whenever she could get to it before
either Daisy or whatever duty manager happened to be
on. It was an ongoing battle between them; Mrs Flanagan
was hoping that she might win a cash prize or, better still,
a holiday abroad ever since the station started running
this stupid promotion and kept grabbing the phone
whenever she could. It led to endless bickering between
them as Daisy quite rightly maintained that if either
Portia or Andrew were to find out, they'd have a fit. This
time, however, they weren't around to hear.

A crisp, clipped woman's voice on the other end of the
phone said, 'This is Phoenix Park House calling. Could
you put me through to Lucasta, Lady Davenport, please?
I have a call holding for her. Thank you.'

'Yer not looking for the cash call amount for this hour
then, are ya, luv?'

'I'm afraid not.'

'Ahh, no bother then, luv, just hang on to yer knickers
for a minute. She's right here beside me,' Mrs Flanagan
replied, waving like a lunatic for Lucasta to come and
join her.

'Who is it?' said Lucasta, taking the phone from her.

'Dunno. Phoenix Park House was all yer one said.'

Lucasta gasped and covered the mouthpiece of the phone with her hand. 'Do you think they heard about our protest today and now they're phoning to complain? Or arrest us, even?' Her tone was hopeful, as though the column inches this would generate could only boost their campaign.

'Lucasta Davenport speaking,' she said grandly, 'Acting President of the Nicotine Nazis' Puff Off campaign. May I help you?'

'Please hold for a call, thank you.'

'Hello?' A man's voice, deep and resonant.

'Yes, who is this?'

'It's Robert Armstrong here. Please excuse me for ringing so late, but—'

'I know that name from somewhere.'

Robert laughed. 'We met only a few weeks ago, actually, at your opening night launch party, perhaps you remember? Anyway, the reason I'm calling is . . .'

'Oh bugger,' Lucasta whispered, this time not bothering to cover the mouthpiece. 'It's that head case from the opening night piss-up. The one who kept saying he was the President of Ireland or some load of shite like that. Hello?'

'Yes, I'm still here,' Robert replied patiently. 'The thing is, you see, my future son-in-law, Mark, is playing in a friendly soccer match against Ireland on Thursday, and I was wondering if I could organize some tickets for you, and your family, of course. Unfortunately, I won't have the pleasure of your company as I have to go to Beijing on a trade mission but Eleanor tells me this is the least we can do after all your kind help in organizing what I'm sure will be a wonderful wedding.'

'Oh dear, oh dear. Are you some sort of retard?' Lucasta cooed sympathetically. 'Does your psychiatrist know that you're making these phone calls? Yes, a football match sounds absolutely delightful and I'll tell you what. Why don't you send Apollo Thirteen around to collect us?'

Chapter Seventeen

A few days earlier, a continent away . . .

The day had started out all right, as Andrew hurriedly pecked Portia on the cheek on his way out of the door, overtired and late for work, as usual. 'It's all going to be fine darling,' he said. 'I've organized a car to collect her from the airport, she'll be in town by about fourish, so all I'm asking you to do is call her hotel and see if she's OK. That's all. Promise.'

Portia nodded. Like she had a choice.

'So, maybe we could have dinner with her later on?' He ran his fingers through his hair in that nervy way he had.

'Of course,' she said automatically. Like we're going to leave Baroness Thatcher on her own, her first night in New York?

'The three of us, I meant.'

'I know.'

'And maybe you'd spend a bit of time with her when she gets into town? I know she'd really love that.'

Portia couldn't bring herself to answer that one, knowing full well that Susan de Courcey would prefer a night in Fallujah to an afternoon in her daughter-in-law's company.

'Thanks, honey. Dunno what I'd do without you. I'll make it up to you, I promise.'

He bent down to kiss her, and she would have loved nothing more than to slide her arms around his neck and hug him tight, but just then, right on cue, Consuela, the cleaning lady, arrived.

'*Holà, buenos días,*' she grunted, shoving past them. Consuela was used to having the run of the apartment and it bugged her to have irritating distractions such as the people who actually lived there cheekily getting under her feet.

'Later, hmm?' was all Andrew said as he absent-mindedly pecked her on the cheek and was gone.

Portia closed the door behind him, made for the bathroom and snapped into action. OK, OK, OK, she reasoned with herself, so this isn't exactly how she thought her romantic trip to New York would pan out, but what could she do? Nothing. Susan was, after all, Andrew's mother; she was probably only going to be in town for a short stay and that was all there was to it. And anyway, she figured, it wasn't as though she was staying with them; Andrew said she always stayed at the same hotel, so at least that was something. She stepped into the shower, shuddering at the thought of what lay ahead over the next few days. Bad enough that she'd barely had any time alone with him since she arrived, bad enough that Lynn bloody Fairweather seemed incapable of wiping her bum without first consulting Portia, but now this . . .

She sighed and let the power shower gush all over her, the carefully positioned jets hitting her muscles in places where she didn't even know she had places. Just a few more days, she thought, just a few days and then she'd finally have her husband to herself . . .

Andrew had given her a cell phone, which was both a blessing and a curse. A blessing to be able to keep in contact with him all day; a curse because Lynn the human stick insect had managed to inveigle the number out of him.

She had just wrapped a towel around her and was heading for the bedroom when it rang. 'Jesus Christ.' She jumped, still not used to the bloody thing. 'Hello?' she answered, dripping on the carpet. 'That you, honey, did you forget something?'

'No, it's me, Lynn. I'm very busy, this is just a quickie.' She was whispering, as though she were phoning from the toilets and didn't want anyone to overhear. 'So a new guy has just started here, his name is Ross Chamberlain, about thirty-five I'm guessing but I need you to find out all about him for me. I haven't clocked a wedding ring, but you know how some guys never advertize their status, so that doesn't mean a thing. OK, so a crowd of work colleagues are going to the Tribeca Grill tonight, in the village, which is the perfect opportunity for you to suss him out for me. I'll meet you at your building at seven sharp—'

'I'm very sorry to cut you short, Lynn, but I'm afraid I can't.' Portia spoke slowly, savouring the deliciously new sensation of telling Lynn where to get off.

'I don't understand.'

'My mother-in-law is in town and we're taking her out.'

'Andrew's mother? Well, that's even better! Nothing like an old lady to matchmake . . . this is so matriarchal, it's perfect! Oh, look, my learning-impaired assistant is here, I gotta go. You leave all the dinner arrangements to me and I'll call you back. Love you, mean it!' And she was gone.

Portia had planned on spending a leisurely morning all around Fifth Avenue, maybe climbing the Empire State and then browsing in the famous Barnes & Noble bookstore, her idea of heaven on earth. But she was in too much of a temper after Lynn's phone call to do anything but sit in a Starbuck's café sipping on a latte and trying her best to cool down.

What did she need to do to get a little quality time alone with her husband? She knew how much he adored the buzz and the sense of being on the go twenty-four hours a day, and she loved it because she loved seeing him happy, but she was starting to feel walked on, hemmed in and thwarted at every turn. This she could probably have dealt with; what was really getting her down was the fact that she'd barely even seen him since they arrived. Of course, he was working all the hours God sent, she knew, but it was upsetting her to think that they were turning into two flatmates who shared the same living space and hardly ever saw each other, rather than a husband and wife who should have been ripping the clothes off each other like they were on a second honeymoon . . .

It was a sobering thought. She'd even gone to the bother of buying a fabulously sexy nightie in Barneys the previous day, a beautifully designed creation, all lacy and low-cut, which accentuated her womanly curves beautifully whilst still holding her tummy in nice and tight. Any designer who could achieve that should be working at NASA, she thought, annoyed at what a total waste of money it had turned out to be. She'd gone to so much trouble to make it a special evening too, dotting expensive aromatherapy candles around the apartment and having a good long soak in a hot tub before slathering every inch of herself with the Jo Malone body lotion he loved the smell of.

And then waited. And waited. His direct line clicked through to his voicemail when she eventually rang before she fell into bed herself, exhausted and still not fully used to the time difference. It wasn't a good sleep, though; she woke every hour on the hour until the digital alarm clock on the bedside table read one a.m. and still the bed was empty and cold beside her. Early morning sunlight was streaming through the bedroom curtains when she woke again, realizing that he had come home and was snoring like a tram yard beside her. She instinctively snuggled into him, but woke him up, by accident.

'I'm sorry, sweetheart,' she whispered. 'I was so worried about you. When did you get home?'

'Whattime's it?'

'Six-thirty. Did I wake you?'

'Yes, you woke me.' He was out of bed now, on his way to the bathroom.

'Sorry. I didn't mean to.'

'Jesus, Portia. Ken and I are in court this morning and we had to prepare all night last night. I just could really do with an uninterrupted night's sleep, you know.'

She let it pass, knowing how cranky he got without sleep and that, even at the best of times, he was never what you'd call a morning person. Back home, she had a rule never even to try to engage him in conversation until he'd had at least two cups of coffee, by which time he had reverted to his usual charming, wide-awake self. But God Almighty, she thought, rolling back over to her side of the bed, if ever there was a couple who needed a bit of quality time together, it was them.

'Susan, it's lovely to see you, welcome to New York.' Portia wasn't a natural actress, but she really tried her best to fake sincerity as she kissed her mother-in-law on each cheek. 'You must be exhausted,' she added politely although Susan was one of those women who always looked exactly the same, irrespective of health, time of day or what she was wearing. Probably something to do with the Maggie Thatcher helmet hair-do, always impeccably chiselled into place and lacquered enough to put a sizeable dent in the ozone layer.

'Do you think she sleeps on her back with the hair in one of those long wooden slats, like they did in the eighteenth century, like Marie Antoinette?' Daisy mischievously used to ask – behind her back, of course.

'Nonsense, I'm not in the least bit tired. I'm absolutely dying to hit the shops, in fact,' Susan snapped, briskly handing her mink coat to Portia to arrange on the empty chair beside her. 'One quick pick-me-up and I'll be off.'

They had met in Teddy's Lounge, the cocktail bar in Susan's usual hotel, the Roosevelt. It was an old-fashioned, timelessly elegant building tucked away in a discreet corner of Madison Avenue and East Forty-fifth

Street. Sweeping staircases, oak-panelled walls and high ceilings groaning with lead crystal chandeliers: Portia thought it was exactly the kind of place where Susan *should* stay. Even the staff seemed to remember her from her last visit and were suitably fawning towards her.

'What may I get you, Mrs de Courcey?'

'A chilled glass of Sancerre, thank you very much,' she replied, never for a moment thinking that there was another Mrs de Courcey present. Not that this bothered Portia, she hadn't changed her name when she got married, precisely to avoid there ever being any confusion between the two of them.

'Now, here's the plan of action,' she said, not quite as bossily as Lynn, but not far off it. 'I'm having my hair done at Elizabeth Arden's on Fifth as soon as we leave. I can't possibly go to dinner with Andrew with it looking like a bush, which it always does after a long-haul flight.'

Portia said nothing but an image flashed into her head of some poor unfortunate hairdresser with a blow torch, hammer and chisel attacking Susan's scalp, the only conceivable way she could imagine it shifting by even a millimetre.

'And then after dinner, I want to see a show.'

'Won't you be tired? With the time difference and all, I mean? I find it gets to about nine in the evening here and I'm completely wiped.'

'Andrew always takes me to a Broadway show on my

first night. I feel I'd be letting him down if I didn't go.'

Susan had a horrible habit of excluding Portia from any of her plans, even though she knew Portia'd have to be there, whether she liked it or not. Like the awful Christmas Day the previous year when Portia and Andrew arrived at the de Courceys' house for dinner to discover that there wasn't even a place set for Portia. It was almost as though Susan regarded her as her son's much disliked live-in girlfriend, one who was unlikely ever to rise to the rank of the new Mrs de Courcey. Ninety per cent of the time, Portia could laugh at it and let her legendary rudeness pass, mainly for Andrew's sake. The remaining ten per cent of the time, though, was tougher. A lot tougher.

'So, I thought you'd go to that ticket place on Times Square and get that out of the way while I'm at the salon,' she barked on. 'Just on no account get seats in the stalls. I suffer dreadfully from claustrophobia.'

Twenty minutes later, having been given careful directions by the hotel concierge, Portia found herself standing at the bottom of the longest snaking queue she'd ever seen. It was already freezing cold and before she'd even inched her way up to the 'YOU ARE ONE HOUR AWAY!' from tickets sign, it started to pelt rain – one of those near torrential downpours so peculiar to New York that seem to come out of nowhere. Bugger, bugger, bugger, she thought, whipping out the cell phone to seek advice. 'Hi. You have reached the voicemail of Andrew de Courcey. Sorry I can't take your call right now, leave a message and I'll get back to you.'

Two hours later, not only had he not got back to her, but Portia was drenched to the skin, frozen to the bone and so pissed off she thought she'd kill someone. The only thought keeping her sane was that a nice long hot soak in the bath with a chilled glass of Sauvignon Blanc was only minutes away.

The first sign that something was amiss was when she let herself back into the apartment only to discover the hallway strewn with suitcases and luggage. Then poor Consuela came out of the kitchen, a bit panicked-looking, to put it mildly.

'*Ay, señora*, I so sorry, *lo siento mucho, pero no podía echarla de la casa*. I can do nothing to stop the lady.'

Portia was about to tell her to calm down, that nothing could be that dreadful, when she realized that, yes, unfortunately, there was something that could be.

The kitchen door swung open to reveal Susan, in a pair of Marigolds, scrubbing away at the insides of the microwave. 'Oh, there you are, Portia. I've been trying to explain to that useless maid of yours that a good squirt of lemon juice in boiling water is the only thing really to disinfect the inside of any microwave. I almost fainted when I saw the state of it. And the fridge! Barely enough milk for a decent cup of tea. No food to speak of, just full of booze, if you don't mind. How Andrew can be expected to work the hours he's putting in and then come home to a smelly kitchen and a rubbery old microwaved dinner, I don't know.'

Portia kept her cool and was about to tell her that they ate out most nights, as did most New Yorkers, but she never got the chance.

'Did you get the tickets?'

'Eventually, yes. I had to queue for them for the last few hours, in bucketing rain—'

'Good. What show? We'd better get a move on if we're to have dinner first.'

'*Phantom of the Opera*. It was the only thing I could get three seats together for.'

'Oh dear God, you are joking.'

'What?'

'Do you honestly think I've come all the way to New York to sit through an *Andrew Lloyd Webber* musical? Are you mad?'

'Susan, this is all that was available. I've just got soaked to the skin getting them for you at a cost of almost three hundred dollars—'

'Of your hard-earned money, dear? Is that what you were about to say?' She always enjoyed making a point out of the fact that it was Andrew's earnings which Portia lived off and usually managed to get in a dig or two about Davenport Hall, that it would still be the crumbling shithole nature intended had she not had the very good luck to marry into money.

Portia had to bite her lip hard. Very bloody hard. She took a deep breath and changed the subject. 'As you quite rightly say, Susan, we'd better go if we want to make dinner reservations.' It was the same tone of voice mental health professionals use to coax psychiatric patients in from skyscraper ledges. 'And I see you've got some bags with you. Shouldn't we grab a taxi and go via the Roosevelt Hotel, so you can drop them off?'

The silence alone should have alerted Portia.

'The Roosevelt? Oh no. I've checked out, dear. My usual suite wasn't available and they put me in this ghastly room beside a lift. Well, you know how rattling noises set off my migraines, so I moved out immediately. Far more sensible for me to take the spare room here anyway. Otherwise it was just going to waste.'

Chapter Eighteen

'And where the hell is Eleanor, might I ask?'

With just days to go, Julia could be forgiven for being even tetchier that usual. She, Daisy, Joshua and Lucy his wedding photographer were all patiently waiting for the bride-to-be in the Library, for the day's briefing session.

'Probably in her room,' said Daisy, instantly hopping to it. 'I'll give her a shout.'

'If you would, thanks.' Julia nodded appreciatively. 'I'm afraid my patience is wearing very thin today. She's losing so much weight; she's starting to look like a heroin addict. I've had to reschedule an extra dress fitting just to make allowances; the designer nearly had one of his tantrums. Here we all are, waiting patiently on her, busting a gut to make sure her big day is perfect and do you think I've had as much as a smile all morning?'

'On my way,' Daisy replied, amazed that Julia could be so sweet and smarmy to Eleanor's face and as caustic as a tin of baking soda once her back was turned.

Five minutes later, she was racing down the corridor to the Edward VII Suite, which was Eleanor's for the duration, when she bumped into Simon, gingerly closing her door behind him.

'Hello there,' he said as soon as he'd seen her.

'I'm looking for Eleanor. She's late for a meeting.'

'I'm afraid you'll be a wee while waiting on her to join you. Meetings are probably the last thing on her mind right now. Give her a bit of time, will you?'

'What's up? Is she OK?'

He said nothing, just looked, if possible, even more worn out than when he had arrived.

Daisy was about to ask if this was just a case of pre-wedding jitters when the beep beep of her pager went. It was Amber at reception. 'MARK LLOYD ON LINE THREE FOR YOU, LUCKY BITCH,' flashed the message.

'Oh, sorry, will you excuse me?' she said, making her way back downstairs. 'That's Mark, wanting a progress report.'

'Mark Lloyd is phoning you?' Simon began to look a bit more awake.

'Yeah.' She began to get defensive. 'Why wouldn't

he? He wants to be kept posted on all the preparations.
Like any normal groom would.'

'You think?'

'And all together now . . .

> On top of spaghetti [to the tune of 'Old Smokey']
> All covered in cheese,
> I lost my poor meatball
> When somebody sneezed.
> It rolled up the garden
> And under a bush
> And now my poor meatball
> Is covered in mush . . .'

Lucasta was absolutely delighted with herself. She had
single-handedly organized a fundraising concert in aid of
her 'Ban the Ban' pro-smoking campaign and she herself
was headlining. It wasn't exactly what you might call a
stellar line-up; apart from herself, she had so far only
managed to inveigle a few locals like Jimmy Joe Doherty
who agreed to bash out a couple of tunes on his tin
whistle and Lottie O'Loughlin's ten-year-old son who
said he'd bring along his magic kit and try and do a few
tricks. But as far as Lucasta was concerned, she might as
well have been organizing the Glastonbury festival.

She was busy rehearsing, or rather, screeching out a

few of her own compositions at the grand piano in the family room, with blatant disregard for any unfortunate guests who might still be in bed, when Mrs Flanagan interrupted. 'Jaysus, Elton John will shit himself when he hears you.'

'Bugger off, I'm rehearsing.'

'I was wondering what the racket was. You'd want to watch it or some of the guests will start asking for a reduction in their bills.'

'Has the post come yet?'

'Yeah. No joy though.'

Lucasta had personally written to a number of famous people, not so much politely enquiring whether they'd be available to perform at her fundraiser, as demanding it of them, claiming it was no less than their duty as Irish citizens. The tone of the letter was bossy, bordering on threatening, and the final paragraph invoked the curse of the Davenports on anyone who failed to give their services gratis. Needless to say, Bono, the rest of U2, Van Morrison, Westlife and the Corrs had all, so far, unanimously failed to reply.

'What a ghastly shower of un–civic–minded bastards. I want you to personally set fire to any of their albums lying around the house and I'll think up a spell to keep all of them out of the hit parade for decades to come.'

'Right so,' sighed Mrs Flanagan, lighting a fag at the piano. 'Terrible shame the Corrs can't make it. I would have enjoyed trying to fatten the three sisters up a bit. Skin and bone is all they are. They should be modelling for the Concern ads.'

'Listen to this, I've been working on it all morning.' Lucasta coughed and flexed her fingers as though she were performing at the Royal Albert Hall.

'Like a rat in a drainpipe
Or a vampire in a bloodbank,
You must have been something God-awful in a past life
Cos, baby, look at you now.'

'Oh, move over Liber-fecking-race. What happened to all yer songs about vegetables anyway?'

'Because if you were in any way musical or had a note in your philistine head, you would appreciate that I'm bored stupid with that as a running theme of mine this year. A bit like Picasso went through a blue period, and then went completely off it. Same thing.'

'Ah right, yeah, you went through a Brussels sprout period, I get it.'

'Will that be all? I really do need to practise, you know.'

'Yer telling me. I only came to tell ya that yer wanted on the phone.'

Lucasta banged down the piano lid impatiently. 'Right, I'm coming. Christ Almighty, I bet John

Lennon never had to put up with interruptions like this.'

'Probably not. Mind you, I never heard him singing a song called "Give Peas a Chance" either.'

'Smartarse. Any luck with the cash call yet?' she asked as they walked towards the phone at reception.

'Don't talk to me. You know yer one Bridget Mulcahy from Sallins?'

'The one who gave up being a nun to become an air hostess?'

'That's her. Anyway, she won it in the last hour. A seven-night break for two in a beach hut in the Maldives.'

'Wasted on her. That bitch could probably have got the flights for free.'

This put Lucasta into a really narky humour and she almost snapped the face off the person who had been patiently waiting for her at the other end of the line.

'Yes, who is this then?'

'Lady Davenport? This is Lieutenant Colonel Frank Jefferson calling you from Phoenix Park House. I'm President Armstrong's aide-de-camp.'

'Oh bloody hell,' Lucasta groaned, clearly audible down the other end of the phone.

'Who is it?' asked Mrs Flanagan. 'He sounded posh, whoever he was.'

'I think it's that mental case who was phoning here claiming to be the President of Ireland,' said Lucasta, covering the mouthpiece. 'If only I didn't owe money to that nice psychiatrist in Kildare, I'd get him to sort this poor delusional idiot out. It's awfully sad, really, what havoc mental illness can wreak. Hello?'

'Yes, I'm still here, your ladyship. His Excellency President Armstrong has asked me to call you with the arrangements for the Ireland versus England match tomorrow. Naturally, we will send a car for you so if you could—'

Lucasta sighed. 'Yes, yes, yes. Tell you what. The minute I see the space shuttle sitting in my front driveway I'll come running out and you can whisk me off to whatever planet you think you live on. All right?'

FROM: *daisydavenport@davenporthall.ie*
TO: *portiadavenport@aol.com*
SUBJECT: *I know all brides are supposed to get ants in their pants before the big day but, Jesus Christ, Eleanor really takes the biscuit.*

Hiya Sis,
   Hope all's good with you and that Susan's not driving you completely spare. Eleanor is acting like a right prima donna in the run-up to the final

furlong. She missed all the briefing
sessions today and now Julia's having a
shit fit because she doesn't have a
final decision on the entrance music.
And she's taking it out on me. What is
wrong with everyone???? Eleanor
Armstrong should be on cloud nine,
marrying a big hunk of sex like Mark
Lloyd. He rings me every night wanting
to know what's going on, right down to
the teeniest detail . . . wouldn't any
girl be thrilled to be marrying a
bloke that attentive and devoted and
ROMANTIC? (Quite apart from the fact
that he's a big ride and a multi-
zillionaire???)

Some awful friend of hers arrived
too, Simon somebody, the guy who
introduced the jammy cow to Mark in
the first place. In fact, now that I
think of it, she's been acting like a
moody adolescent ever since he arrived
. . . Maybe he fancies her and is
trying to talk her out of the whole
thing???? They certainly spend an awful
lot of time in her room together . . .
Hmmmm, the plot thickens.

311

Much love, from the hub of intrigue
that the Hall has become . . .
Daisyxxx
PS. Forgot. Robert Armstrong has asked
us all to some boring old football
match tomorrow. I'm only going to get
a glimpse of Mark in tight shorts and,
before you email back . . . I KNOW!!!
HE'S GETTING MARRIED IN 3 DAYS' TIME!!
But I'm allowed to look, aren't
I . . .?????
PPS. How are you??

FROM: portiadavenport@aol.com
TO: daisydavenport@davenporthall.ie
SUBJECT: Sound advice

Poor girl. You go to that soccer match
tomorrow and try and find someone
single. You're wasting your time ogling
a man that's as good as married.

Things not great here. Susan has moved
in. My stress levels are through the
ceiling. I'm not kidding. Counting the
days till she decides to go home, but
there's no sign of that happening yet.
Love, Portia

FROM: *daisydavenport@davenporthall.ie*
TO: *portiadavenport@aol.com*
SUBJECT: *OK. You win the 'which of us had the shittiest day' contest.*

Hear you loud and clear. Will behave at the match tomorrow. Will only have one drink. Promise.
Dxxx

The wintry sun was just setting that evening when Jasper found himself striding outside, heading in the direction of Loch Moluag, on the edge of the estate.

Five minutes later, he had caught up with Eleanor, who was walking round the perimeter of the lake, bundled up in a huge heavy tweed coat which made her look tiny and, if possible, even more frail. She jumped involuntarily when she heard his footsteps marching towards her.

'I'm sorry,' said Jasper gently, 'I didn't mean to startle you.'

'It's OK,' she said, gazing wanly out on to the lake. 'I didn't think anyone had seen me slip out here.'

'Kind of my job,' he said, keeping at a respectful distance from her, 'to be aware of all the comings and goings around here.'

She looked at him, as though wondering if he could

be trusted. 'I just needed a bit of time out. I need to think.'

'You're grand,' he said, stepping back, as if not wanting to intrude any further on her privacy. 'I just wanted to make sure you were OK. Not going to throw yourself into the lake or anything dramatic.'

She had just turned to smile at him, glad that he hadn't quizzed her any further, when he noticed that she'd been crying.

'Ahh, don't be upsetting yourself. Nothing can be that bad.'

'Maybe not,' she replied. 'Thanks.'

'You're welcome. Just know that if there's anything I can do, Miss Armstrong?'

'You could start by calling me Eleanor.'

Chapter Nineteen

'Low lie the fields of Lansdowne Road [to the tune of
   'The Fields of Athenry']
Where once we watched the King Keano play
With Duffer on the wing.
We had dreams and songs to sing
About the glory round
The fields of Lansdowne Road.'

A cheer erupted the like of which Daisy had never heard before in her life. She and Jasper had just arrived in the Players' Box at Dublin's magnificent Lansdowne Road stadium, having bickered the whole way from Ballyroan.

The first row was over Eleanor, who had sent a message downstairs, via Simon, to say that she wasn't coming. A car had been sent from Phoenix Park House to bring Lucasta, Daisy, Jasper and Simon to the match, but there was no budging Eleanor.

'She's exhausted, very stressed,' was all Simon said, coming down the stairs to where they were all gathered, patiently waiting on her.

'Won't she want to see Mark play?' Daisy blurted out. 'I'm sure he'll be really disappointed if she just doesn't turn up.'

'Do you think?' Even through his lilting Scots accent, Simon's tone cut.

'Fine, then,' Daisy snapped, steering Lucasta out of the door and into the waiting limo. 'If that's what she wants.'

'Frankly, I don't think any of this is what she wants.'

Daisy's temper, never far from the surface, began to simmer. 'Look, I don't know what your problem is, but I've been aware of a vibe from you ever since you got here. For God's sake, what have I done?'

'Why don't we just get into the car?' he answered, not taking the bait. 'Or at this rate, we'll miss the kick-off.'

'Simon, why don't you take Lucasta in the limo and Daisy and I will follow in our own car?' said Jasper, intervening. 'I want to stop off on the way there. Get kitted out, like. We won't be long behind you.'

'Suits me,' said Daisy, delighted a) that she wouldn't have to endure Simon's company on the long drive to Dublin and, even better, b) that he'd be left alone with

Lucasta, who was in a foul humour and hadn't stopped moaning since she got out of bed that morning. 'I mean, a soccer match?' she was whingeing. 'What interest do I have in bloody football? If I want blood and guts and torture and senseless violence, I don't need to go all the way to Lansdowne Road. I can get that at home, for free.'

When they finally arrived, barely in time for kick-off, Simon, who'd been watching out for them, came over to where they were standing.

'I'm so sorry we're late,' said Jasper. 'If it's any consolation, it's all my fault.'

'Yeah,' said Daisy. 'Gobshite made us stop off at a sports shop just so we could both end up looking like this.'

If they'd been on their way to audition for the part of Mr and Mrs Mad Demented Fan, neither of them could have looked any better. Jasper had gone to all the bother of painting his face with the green, white and orange of the Irish tricolour and was fully kitted out in the team strip, completing the look with a giant-sized plastic inflatable hammer, with 'God Help the Queen' scrawled across it. Just in case there was the slightest shadow of doubt as to which side he was supporting, he'd also draped a full-sized Irish flag like a cloak around his shoulders.

'Might as well have a bit of crack,' he'd said to Daisy in Olahan's sport shop in Naas. 'When you're out, you're out. When I was doing solitary, I used to dream about seeing Ireland play at Lansdowne Road. I never thought I'd see the day.'

'You were in solitary?'

'Ah, long story. You know me for being in the wrong place at the wrong time. You see, a terrible row broke out in the recreation room over whose turn it was to have the remote control and, well, I tried to sort it out but I ended up being labelled the ringleader. So the Governor, who was my pal, said he'd have to make an example of me. Sure, the poor man couldn't be showing me preferential treatment all the time, could he? I'll tell you though, solitary really sorts out the men from the boys. Longest twenty minutes of my life.'

Meanwhile Daisy, a tad more subtly, had limited herself to a tight tricolour T-shirt with 'The Referee's a Wanker' written across it, and tied her hair into two big bunches held in place by tricolour ribbons.

'Very nice.' Simon couldn't help smiling appreciatively at her. 'Very Pippi Longstocking.'

She ignored him.

'Where's Lucasta?' Jasper asked him without taking his eyes off the pitch, even though the match hadn't even started.

'I couldn't get her any further than the bar in the Players' Lounge,' he answered.

'Sorry again for keeping you waiting,' Jasper went on, as if trying to make up for Daisy's rudeness in blanking him. 'Only for the fact that your one here handles a car like a getaway driver, we'd still be on the M50.'

'Game's just about to start, you're in the nick of time,' said Simon, ushering them down to their front-row seats. 'I hope you enjoy it now. Shame to have got all dressed up for nothing.' He just caught a flash of blue fury from Daisy's eyes. 'Oh come on, let's put our differences behind us.'

'I have no differences with you, Simon. I'm just not used to guests at the Hall treating me like something they stood on.'

'Do you think we could just enjoy the game? What do you say, shall we let the bugles sing truce for the next two hours? Then I'm very happy to revert back to slagging each other off like Kerry and Brian McFadden.'

She found herself smirking. There was something about the Scots lilt that made everything sound funny. A bit like Billy Connolly telling one of his 'we were so poor as kids' yarns, the accent alone could have you howling at the phone directory.

'We're in the front row?' said Jasper, starting to hyperventilate, 'Oh lads, pinch me, I think I've died and gone to heaven.'

As they took their prime seats, it did strike Daisy that she and Jasper stood out a bit. In a heaving sea of fans, kitted out in either the Irish tricolour or the red and white of England, the players' box was like a tiny oasis of corporate types: men in expensive suits and fabulously dressed, glamorous women, all dripping in flashy jewellery and looking like they should be off to an awards do and not sitting pretty on the sidelines of a soccer match.

Looking excitedly around her, the only people Daisy recognized were two very high-profile Oldcastle wives, Falcon Donohue and Shakira Walker, who were sitting side by side and looking bored out of their heads.

Falcon Donohue, she knew from her appearance on the celebrity reality show, *We Are Famous, Try and Shame Us*, not to mention the fact that she and her waist-length hair extensions appeared on magazine covers at least every other week. Shakira Walker, on the other hand, Daisy recognized from the girl band that she fronted, Nuclear Pussy, who had just had a number one hit with a gloriously alliterative song entitled 'You Done the Dirt and Now You're Dumping Me?' There was a big, busty blond woman beside them, applying lip gloss in a small compact mirror. She looked a bit familiar, but somehow Daisy couldn't quite place her . . .

'Bit weird, isn't it?' Simon said, misreading her thoughts. 'Never fails to churn my stomach, to be honest with you. All those minor celebs and fat gits in fat suits are mostly directors and sponsors with bugger all interest in football; they're just here on corporate junkets. Meanwhile, the real fans are queuing up outside shelling out hard-earned cash for overpriced tickets from the bloody touts.'

A pang of guilt struck Daisy. Being brutally honest with herself, she had to admit that she wasn't exactly a diehard footie fan herself. In fact, not only was this the first actual game she'd been to, the only ones she'd ever watched on TV had been the few World Cup appearances Ireland had qualified for. And even then she would moan at Portia and Lucasta that the matches invariably clashed with *EastEnders*. Looking around the packed stadium though, she felt a huge swell of pride, a patriotism that had never bothered her before, at the sea of green all around her, all *Olé, olé, olé*ing fit to burst your eardrums. Just being there, being part of it was an adrenalin rush like she'd never experienced. It was easy to see how fans became addicted so easily.

'So what do you think of your first game so far then?' asked Simon, seeing the way her eyes sparked with pride and excitement. 'I can spot a football virgin a mile away.'

She looked him straight in the eye. 'Unbelievable,' was all she could say, 'just unbelievable. It's the nearest thing I'll ever come to being in the Roman Colosseum. The only thing that could make this more exciting is if Russell Crowe himself walked out with his sword and sandals.'

The teams had just begun to line out to a deafening

roar from all around the stadium and the English chant went up.

> 'Oh, the famous Irish team went to see the Pope in
>   Rome [to the tune of 'The Battle Hymn of the
>   Republic'],
> The famous Irish team went to see the Pope in Rome,
> The famous Irish team went to see the Pope in Rome,
> And this is what he said:
> FUCK OFF!
> Glory, glory, glory, England,
> Glory, glory, glory, England,
> Glory, glory, glory, England,
> And the Brits go marching on.'

The Irish fans were about to come back with a similarly derogatory chant when the national anthems began, starting with 'God Save the Queen'. Everyone stood up respectfully, which gave Daisy a good chance to eye up the teams. The first person her eye fell on was Alessandro Dumas, who also played for Oldcastle but was kitted out in the England strip today. The only reason Daisy recognized him was because he spearheaded a shampoo commercial with a really crappy slogan which was on TV only about eighty times a week. '*Stallion pour hommes,*' he would croon to camera with a waterfall cascading behind him. '*Only stallion can tame your bush.*'

He looked lean and mean, shaven-headed and surly, ready for anything.

'Isn't that sweet?' she whispered to Simon, unaware that it was the height of bad manners to talk during the anthems. 'Look! He hasn't got a clue of the words.'

Simon didn't answer, just kept belting out the bit about 'sending her victorious', while Jasper glared over at her.

She didn't bother resting her gaze on him for too long though, she was far too busy squinting down the line to pick out Mark. Yes! There he was, tanned, toned and even more rugged and sexy-looking than she remembered, wearing the number nine shirt with his untamed curly brown locks of hair blowing all over the place: Heathcliff in an England shirt and a pair of shorts.

As soon as it was over, yet another raucous cheer swelled the stadium and then it was Ireland's turn. Tears of pride ran down Jasper's cheeks as he burst his lungs singing 'Amhrán na bhFiann', which he kept wiping away with his shovel-sized hands, forgetting that his face was painted, so that he ended up covered in big green and orange swipes. He might have looked like a Halloween horror mask gone wrong, but the expression in his eyes was beatific.

The anthems over, the referee moved out to the middle of the pitch and they were off. '*Who's the wanker in the black?*' both sides chanted in unison, as the whistle blew and the game got under way. Straight away, England were up and at it, with Mark ruthlessly taking possession and kicking a long ball over to Ryan Walker who made it past Ireland's defences and had got almost as far as the penalty spot when Alan Heap, Ireland's youngest striker and something of a teen sensation, headed it back up the pitch and away from any danger of England scoring. In no time, the English chant went up:

> *'He's fat, he's round, his arse is on the ground,*
> *He's Aaaaaaaaaaaa-lan Heap.'*

'That's vicious!' Daisy exclaimed, hardly able to believe her ears. 'Suppose Alan Heap heard?'

Simon roared laughing at her. 'That's nothing. Wait till you get a load of some of the chants they hurl at their own players.'

Shane Donohue had possession now for Ireland, leading to a raucous chorus of:

> *'You're nothing but a tosser,*
> *You're nothing but a thug,*
> *You can't see the ball*
> *And your wife eats slugs.'*

'And that was probably before she even went into the jungle,' said Simon. Daisy turned around to see if this reference to her performance in *We Are Famous, Try and Shame Us* had upset Falcon, but she was just staring blankly ahead of her, unmoved and bored-looking.

'Wait till the fans start having a go at Shakira Walker. Let's just say I've never heard so many words rhyme with 'Nuclear Pussy'.

As the first half wore on, England's strategy seemed to be to form a five-man midfield when defending, taking their high-energy game to the flanks and literally giving the Irish no room to manoeuvre. Even with Daisy's inexperienced eye, she could tell that Alan Heap was easily Ireland's most dangerous player, yet every time he tried to make a break or create an opportunity, he seemed boxed in, giving the impression that England could suddenly strike.

Which they did.

It was all over in a blur, but in a fraction of the time it took Daisy to drop her jaw in astonishment, Shane Donohue had kicked upfield, passed to Mark who in turn kicked it to Alessandro who scored. Half the stadium stood rooted to their seats in muted horror while the other half raised the roof. '*Are you Malta in disguise?*' the English fans chanted, nearly losing their reason as the scoreboard officially confirmed England 1: Ireland 0.

'I don't believe this, how did that gobshite of a goalie let it in?' Jasper was apoplectic with rage.

'I thought this was a friendly?' Daisy asked innocently.

'Between England and Ireland?' Simon laughed. 'Is there such a thing?'

Half-time and Ireland had failed to equalize as Daisy and Jasper followed Simon into the Players' Lounge, to find Lucasta plonked at a table, happily moving on to her third g. and t.

The English fans' chant still rang in their ears as they joined her: '*Can we play you every week?*'

'It's a really good match, if ya ask me,' Shakira could be heard saying as she made her way to the bar. 'It's tragedy, it's entertainment, what more do the Irish want?'

'What, apart from a win, you mean?' chirruped Falcon, running a French manicured talon down the cocktail menu. 'Too early for a cosmo, do ya think, girls?'

'Are you mental?' replied the busty big-haired blonde who'd been sitting with them. 'It's never too early for a cosmo.'

That's where I know that girl from, Daisy thought. She's Buffy Tompkinson, the glamour model, as she styled herself . . . wasn't she a girlfriend of Alessandro Dumas?

The table Lucasta had bagged was as geographically far from them as it was possible to be and Simon, for one, didn't seem a bit sorry.

'The bitches of Eastwick, we call them back at Oldcastle,' he muttered to Daisy. 'Do you think they ever take poor, wee Cinderella out?'

She giggled.

'Seriously, though,' he went on, 'you want to watch out. Buffy, Alessandro's girlfriend, is lethal after a few drinks.'

'Did you have to mention that gobshite's name to me?' moaned Jasper, inconsolable. To say that he was devastated by the half-time score was an understatement on a par with saying that George Dubya Bush was an eensy bit of a dimwit. 'I don't know how he got past Alan Heap, for starters. And for Dumas to score, of all people! Normally, that eejit couldn't hit a cow's arse with a banjo.'

'Over here, sweeties!' Lucasta cooed. 'I'm awfully sorry I missed the first half, but I really had to G.T.F.O.O.H.'

'G.T.F.O.O.H.?' asked Simon.

'Mummy's code for get the fuck out of here,' Daisy explained.

'So I just thought I'd have one little pint while I was waiting for you,' she went on.

'Pint of what?' asked Daisy.

'Of gin, darling.'

'You look like you could use a shoulder to drink on, what'll you have, big guy?' Simon asked Jasper sympathetically.

'Guinness, thanks. Here, let me give you a few quid.'

'Welcome to the wonderful world of corporate hospitality. It's a free bar.'

'Free drink? That's the worst kind.' Jasper honestly looked as though he was going to open a vein.

'And for you?' Simon smiled down at Daisy.

She was about to ask for a mineral water, given that she was driving Andrew's jeep, but just then she caught sight of the most fabulous-looking cosmopolitans being served to the bitches of Eastwick. What the hell, she figured, one couldn't hurt, could it? 'I'll have what they're having, thanks,' she said.

'And a little gin and tonic for me, thanks, angel,' chirruped Lucasta.

He winked. 'I love a woman that appreciates a free bar.'

'Oh, I never believe in going to the bar when there's a man in the company,' said Lucasta, settling into a party mood. 'All that bloody feminism malarkey ever meant for women was that they had to buy their own drinks and that men stopped offering them seats on trains. Thank Christ all that passed me by, that's all I can say. Saves me a fortune too.'

Simon raised his eyebrows a bit, as anyone would who wasn't used to her ladyship.

'You know, I say to Daisy, if some poor unfortunate hunchback with one eye and a comb-over is gobshite enough to ask you out on a date, you order a steak dinner and let baldy pay for the works. Men appreciate you all the more when they have to earn you, as it were. Before that awful Germaine Greer one came along, women weren't equal to men, they were superior and ... By the way,' she interrupted herself, squinting at Simon as though she were seeing him for the very first time.

Then it came. The killer question.

'Are you single?'

'Let me give you a hand with those drinks,' said Daisy, squirming a bit, especially when she saw Simon turn bright red. OK, so he wasn't exactly her favourite person, but, she figured, would you wish Lucasta's sledgehammer matchmaking tactics on your worst enemy?

'So your mother was filling me in about your cousin Jasper on the drive here,' he said as they waited patiently at the bar. 'About his . . . background.'

'Yeah? It's an astonishing story, isn't it?'

'Unbelievable,' he laughed, looking very grateful to have been rescued. 'The long-lost cousin, returning to stake his claim to the ancestral home. Like something out of Dickens.'

'Or *The O.C.*'

A few minutes later, they rejoined Lucasta and Jasper, plonking a trayful of drinks in the middle of the table.

'If I ever get my hands on Dave Gemell, I swear to you I won't be responsible,' Jasper was moaning.

'Who?'

'That useless, schizophrenic sad excuse for a goalie that we have.'

'Oh.'

Now the crowd's chant was starting to make sense to Daisy.

'Two Dave Gemells,
There's only two Dave Gemells . . .'

'So what's happening to the teams now?' Daisy asked innocently.

'With a bit of luck, they're getting the living lard kicked out of them by the manager. I've seen better performances from the prison warders annual under-elevens five-a-side.'

All Daisy wanted to do was enjoy her day out but Jasper's morbid depression was really beginning to drag her down.

'Could you believe it when Kerr took O'Sullivan off twenty minutes in?' Jasper went on whining. 'And sent on that useless sack of crap, Peter Daglish? I swear, the housekeeper at Davenport Hall would have made a better midfielder, so she would.'

Simon caught the bewildered look on Daisy's face and explained.

'This is where the team manager demonstrates his sense of humour by taking off a player that's doing great and replacing him with someone untried, at an international level. Wee bit like taking Michelangelo off the Sistine Chapel job and replacing him with a humble painter and decorator. Daft.'

Daisy laughed, although she was still not sure if it was his joke she was giggling at or the accent which automatically made everything sound funny. In what felt like no time, a raucous cheer from the pitch let them know that the teams were back on, so she gulped back her cosmopolitan, fervently hoping that Ireland's performance would improve in the second half, if only to make Jasper less of a moany hole to be around.

'You all go,' Lucasta commanded waving to the fast-emptying bar, 'I'll stay here, just to keep our seats.'

'It's all really moving, innit?' she overheard Falcon say to Shakira as they filed past them on their way back out.

'Yeah, but the most moving thing was when my Alessandro scored!' said Buffy and the three of them dissolved into tipsy cackles.

They walked past Daisy, ignoring her, leaving an untouched cosmopolitan behind. Shame to waste it, she thought, checking to see that no one was watching before she knocked it back.

'If I had the wings of a sparrow [to the tune of 'My
  Bonnie Lies over the Ocean']
If I had the arse of a cow,
I'd fly over Old Trafford tomorrow
And shit on the bastards below.
Shit on, shit on, oh shit on the bastards below, below . . .'

Daisy knew about as much about football as a fruit fly knows about pure maths but even she could tell that the

Irish side had pulled their socks up considerably since half-time – or the interval as she kept calling it. Their game was far more offensive; they managed to keep play firmly around the English net; they kept their cool and then the gods smiled down on them. Mark Lloyd tripped up Ireland's key midfielder, Tony Duffy, and the ref awarded Ireland a penalty. For a split second, Ireland were back in the game and it fell to the eighteen-year-old Alan Heap to step up and take it. The English fans sang:

> *'Que será, será,*
> *Whatever will be, will be;*
> *You can't score a penalty,*
> *Que será, será,'*

But the teenager looked like an ice man as he bravely lined up to take the shot. Suddenly after all the noise and screaming and vicious chanting, the stadium went eerily quiet.

'I've heard young Alan wears his granny's miraculous medal whenever he's playing,' said Simon.

'I swear, I'll shove it down his throat if he misses this,' said Jasper.

It was as though everything was happening in slow motion as young Alan raced to kick the ball and sent it soaring . . . Twenty thousand pairs of eyes in the stadium followed its progress, half of them willing it in, half of them willing some act of God to let it go wide . . . Every spectator held their breath and then . . . the miracle . . . The ball hit off the post, the goalie dived for it but . . . it was too late . . . It passed over the line and Ireland scored.

The cheer was the loudest yet as every tricolour in the stadium went ballistic and the chant went up:

> *'You're not singing,*
> *You're not singing,*
> *You're not singing any more!'*

To which the English fans came back with:

> *'Who ate all the pies? [to the tune of*
> *'Knees Up, Mother Brown']*
> *Who ate all the pies?*
> *You fat bastard,*
> *You fat bastard,*
> *Heap ate all the pies.'*

This unsubtle dig at his puppy fat or even the cries of 'Get your tits out for the lads' did nothing to dampen Alan Heap's spirits. He danced cartwheels around the pitch and his team mates leapt on him in a human pile that left Daisy wondering if he'd broken any bones. 'You'd think we'd just won a war!' she exclaimed but Jasper was too busy sobbing like a big girl's Laura Ashley blouse even to put a coherent sentence together.

'I'll never forget this moment,' he gulped, 'not as long as I live. This is even better than Ray Houghton's equalizer in Stuttgart in eighty-eight.'

'Mightn't be the best penalty I've ever seen,' said Simon, equally impressed if a tad less emotional, 'but it's certainly one of the bravest.'

In spite of England's best efforts to get ahead, the final whistle was upon them in no time, with the scoreboard showing a very honourable 'England 1 : Ireland 1'.

*'You had joy, you had fun [*to the tune of 'Seasons in the Sun'*],*
You had Ireland on the run,
But your joy didn't last
Cos we ran too fucking fast.'

The Irish fans were as jubilant and ecstatic as if they'd just won the World Cup, an attitude summed up in Jasper's tearful comment as they made their way back to the Players' Lounge.

'Ah lads, I never thought I'd live to see the day that we'd beat England one–all.'

The corporate bar was like a cool, calm oasis of tranquillity compared with the scenes of sheer joyous madness on the stands and Daisy happily put in for another cosmopolitan. Jasper and Simon had rejoined Lucasta, probably the only person there who was oblivious to the fact that a) there had been a match in the first place and, more importantly, that b) Ireland had actually equalized.

They were all deep in conversation at the bar when a steward discreetly approached Daisy.

'Excuse me, are you Miss Daisy Davenport? I've a message for you,' he said, slipping an envelope into her hands.

She greedily ripped it open, delighted no one was around to quiz her.

So what did you think of the match then? Hope you
enjoyed it as much as I enjoyed seeing you in the box.
You and me have a lot to catch up on. How about
you come to a small private party I'm having later on?
In the Berkeley Court Hotel, at about eight.
  We'll have a laugh.
  Love,
  Mark

PS. You should read and destroy this. The last time I
sent someone a note, it ended up on eBay.

Yes! she thought, scrunching up the note and shoving it into her jeans pocket. Could this day get any better?

Chapter Twenty

Could this day get any worse?

Portia, a woman blessed with the patience of a Tibetan monk, had officially reached breaking point. It's sometimes the case in life that you can have ten thousand tiny, niggling bothersome things annoying you all at the same time, and you rise above them and just let them wash all over you. Inevitably, though, one more inconsequential trifle will come along and that one little thing is what will set you over the edge.

And thus it was with Susan de Courcey.

By now, Portia had endured day after interminable day of Susan's snide comments towards her, her legendary rudeness and her blatant disregard for the fact that, like it or not, Portia was the woman her only son had chosen to be his wife. Susan's attitude to her daughter-in-law had barely changed one jot since she first met and married Andrew: Portia may have come from a landed family but was still an *arriviste* of the highest order, who by a stroke of pure luck had happened to worm her way into her son's affections and who now lived for no other purpose than to fritter away every penny of his hard-earned cash on herself and, worse, that monstrous pile in Kildare she'd inherited from her sodden old alcoholic of a father.

'And she's an appalling wife too,' Susan would chatter away on the phone in her bedroom to her great friend Nan Keane who lived on Vanderbilt Avenue and who also had a daughter-in-law she couldn't endure. Portia used to think it was almost like a contest between them, a really sick 'whose son married worst' competition, with tea and sympathy at the Palm Court as the glittering first prize.

'Hasn't got the first clue about how to look after a man,' Susan would say at the top of her voice, not caring, in fact probably hoping that Portia would happen to overhear. 'And so poor Andrew is forced to eat out night after night, when he's working all the hours God sends on the Globex case. It's the sort of case that makes or breaks a career, you know, and then what does he come home to? A Post-it note stuck on a filthy microwave saying: "I left you some quiche." Quiche! For a grown man! I really don't know how the poor exhausted darling puts up with it.'

Portia simply couldn't win. Susan had her at every turn. The quiche episode had happened once and once only, when, surprise surprise, Andrew was working late. Portia had nipped down to Cielo's deli, just half a block from the apartment, and had bought it for him, knowing that he'd love it, that he'd have eaten earlier and that all he'd want would be some small snack when he got in. But to listen to Susan go on, you'd think she'd tried to feed him barbecued dog poo on a skewer, marinated in a puddle of rat wee.

Three days later, Portia was still listening to her go on about it. She tried to explain to Susan that yes, she did of course occasionally cook for Andrew at home, but that seeing as how he was seldom back from the office before one a.m. these days, there seemed little point in her making elaborate meals for him.

Thereby walking right into Susan's emotional trap. For the next twenty-four hours, she had to put up with a spate of: 'So you don't think it would be nice maybe to cook something for me? Seeing as how I am a visitor here?'

'Susan, we eat out every night. That's what New Yorkers do. That's what people do when they're on holiday. You love eating out.'

'Well, of course, dear, if you're happy spending Andrew's money on expensive meals, what can I say to that?'

Then there was the clothes agenda. If Portia bought a new outfit and tried her best to look smart, she would catch Susan on the phone saying something like: 'I couldn't believe it, Nan. She was in another new trouser suit today, from Saks Fifth Avenue, you know, so it must have cost an absolute packet. I really don't understand women like that who can just take, take, take . . .'

However, having overheard a couple of conversations along that line, Portia decided to dress down a bit, opting for a fleecy tracksuit with her brand-new Reebok trainers, which she'd bought at the Century Twenty-One discount store for a fraction of what they'd have cost in Ireland.

Game, set and match, Susan. Portia was in the bath that night, waiting on Andrew to come home when she heard, 'Oh Nan darling, I was actually embarrassed to be seen with her today. Like something out of a trailer park in the most revolting tracksuit you ever saw. I kept praying we wouldn't meet anyone I knew. Yes, darling, tea in the Palm Court at the Plaza tomorrow would be lovely. That's not half of what I've got to tell you and I can't really talk now, if you're with me.'

It didn't help that Andrew was working the hours he was, and it wasn't his fault either, Portia was quick to remind herself. After all, he couldn't be held responsible for his mother's personality, or lack of it. She couldn't even talk to him properly about it, seeing as how the only time they seemed to get on their own together was generally in the wee small hours of the morning, when he'd collapse into bed beside her, more often than not too exhausted to talk.

He'd rung her cell phone one day when she had a rare break from Susan, who was meeting her friend Nan and had categorically not invited Portia along with her. So they could gossip about her, Portia correctly assumed.

'So how are you surviving the onslaught of Mommie Dearest?' he asked her teasingly.

She thought for a moment, knowing she'd have to exercise extreme tact. 'It's, emm . . . Well, let me put it to you like this. Two women on their own together in an apartment, spending all day every day in each other's company, is never going to be a pretty sight.'

'Oh shit, here's Ken, I've got to go. Look, I'll see you tonight, OK? Don't worry, babe, she's not going to be around for much longer. I'm just happy that you've got company all day when I'm not around.'

She hung up and took a deep breath, wondering if he even had the first clue what she was going through.

It was the next night when the straw that broke the camel's back finally fell. Lynn had organized a girls' night out in Nico's restaurant, an Italian trattoria in the Village. Much as Lynn irritated her, Portia accepted the invitation on the grounds that any chance to get away from Susan was a gift from the gods to be seized on. No such luck, though.

'Oh, I adore Nico's, how lovely of your friend to pick one of my favourite restaurants in the city!' she said when Portia told her where she was headed. The only saving grace about what promised to be an utterly dismal evening was that Jennifer Courtney was there too, Ken's gorgeous wife.

Portia hugged her warmly when she arrived, genuinely delighted to see her.

'Oh my God, it's been so long!' said Jennifer, hugging her back. 'I haven't seen you since Lucy's christening and she's, like, walking now!'

'It's been way too long.' Portia beamed at her. 'Look at you, you look amazing. Two children and sea air suits you.'

Jennifer really did look wonderful. She was fine-boned and petite with short ringlety auburn hair cut tight to her face, which accentuated her huge brown eyes and made her look like a tiny Victorian doll. They'd first met at Portia's wedding and she had instantly liked her; Jennifer was warm and friendly with that wonderful directness that New Yorkers have.

'You're an angel to say that. I'm carrying a lotta baby blubber still. I feel like a hick country bumpkin coming up to town with all of you fancy ladies.'

'You and Ken live in West Hampton, don't you?' asked

Susan, peering over the glasses she used to study menus, which made her look, if possible, even more scary.

'When I see him, which is hardly ever these days,' laughed Jennifer. Then, turning to Portia she squeezed her hand and joked, 'So, welcome to the wonderful world of the Macmillan Burke widow. How do you like it so far?'

Portia laughed, loving the sensation of having an ally. Someone who really understood.

There were just four of them for dinner and Lynn plonked herself down beside Portia and immediately launched into her favourite topic of conversation, this time involving an Ivy League tax consultant she'd just started dating, who was going through a very messy divorce.

After an appetizer and main course of listening to: 'I don't mind that he's separated and I don't mind that his ex practically *conned* him into giving her the brownstone on the Upper East Side. I've gotten really, really skilled at bashing square pegs into round holes over the years. But what I do mind are his three pre-teenage children, who for some weird reason don't seem to like me.'

In an attempt to bond with the kids, Lynn had taken them to Toys "Я" Us on Times Square, hoping that throwing cash at them would somehow turn her into a fairy stepmother. 'Assholes. Three thousand bucks it cost me and then the youngest one insisted on McDonald's.

342

(Me? In McDonald's? Hello? Is the universe trying to tell me something?) So I took them and then the middle one got sick all over my Hermès Birkin bag. Do you know how long the wait is to get one of those? No, of course you don't . . .'

After about two hours of this, Portia could take no more and excused herself to go to the ladies' room. She switched on her cell phone, hoping there'd be a message or at least a text from Andrew, but there wasn't. So, having lingered over the freebies for as long as she could, she eventually slunk back to rejoin the others. Lynn had left the table to make a call and she found she'd arrived just in time to overhear her esteemed dragon-in-law preaching on at poor Jennifer.

'You are so lucky having children, you know. My biggest regret in life is that I'll never be a grandmother now. Well, not much chance really, with Portia the age she's at. My husband and I often talk about it; we really wish that Andrew had gone for someone a bit younger, you know. I always say to my great friend Nan that he'll regret it in a few years' time—'

She shut up when she saw Portia.

There was an awful, ugly silence broken only by a waiter plonking a trayful of teas and coffees on their table. Portia eyeballed Susan, wanting to leave her in no doubt that she'd heard everything and willing herself not to cry. At least, not in front of her.

Eventually Portia spoke. Slowly, deliberately. 'I'm glad I'm not crying, Susan, because I would really hate for you to think that what I'm going to say is in any way clouded by emotion.'

Susan took her glasses off and met her eyes, almost willing her to cause a scene. Something really juicy for her to tell Nan in the Palm Court the following day.

'I want you to know that it's not OK for you to treat me like this. Not by a long shot. How *dare* you? How dare you speak about me like that? I have bent over backwards to make your stay here as pleasant as I can and in return you've bitched about me, belittled me to my face and behind my back and generally done your level best to make my life a living hell. Well, congratulations, Susan, I have finally reached the end of my tether. Now one of us is going to have to leave that apartment tonight because over my dead body will I endure another night in your company.'

The silence was broken by a waiter arriving with the check. 'Is everything all right, madam?'

'Nothing a good funeral won't fix.' Portia was trembling but her voice held steady.

It seemed as though the tables around them had fallen silent too, having a great time enjoying this unexpected worm-that-turns sideshow.

Eventually a very shell-shocked Jennifer spoke. 'Ladies, I need the bathroom. Portia, would you mind showing me where it is? Excuse us, Susan.' She got out of her seat, linked arms with Portia and gently steered her back towards the ladies' room. 'You OK?'

Portia nodded as her eyes began to well up.

'That was some speech! Boy, remind me never to get in a fight with you. You sure are one feisty lady.'

'Oh Jennifer, I'm so sorry you had to witness that, but by God, she had it coming.' Portia was running cool water over her wrists now, in an effort to calm down.

'She's something else, all right. I don't know how you've been coping with her. When I first met her, all I could think was: Well at least now I know whatever happened to Baby Jane.'

Portia laughed, but got teary a split second later. 'I meant what I said, Jennifer. I can't go back there tonight. I can't spend one more second in that bitch's company. Oh God, what am I going to do? Andrew's just never around, ever, and I've been stuck with her from morning till night, criticizing me, harping on at me, constantly having a go at whatever I do or don't do . . .' The tears were rolling unchecked down her cheeks now.

'Oh honey, don't let her get to you. You wanna know what I think you should do?'

'Rip out her still beating heart and wave it in front of her face?'

Jennifer laughed. 'Better than that. Get into the car with me right now and come stay at the beach house with me and the kids till she's safely gone. We don't even need to go back to the table, let's just leave now. Swing by your apartment, pick up your stuff, and hit the road like *Thelma and Louise*. If we're gonna be Macmillan Burke widows, might as well do it together. Andrew's not gonna mind, is he?'

Portia smiled at her, really touched. 'I doubt he'll even notice I'm gone.'

Chapter Twenty-One

The match was over, the post-match commentary had been discussed in painstaking detail, the 'Man of the Match' had been declared (Alan Heap, who else?), the fans were falling out of pubs and clubs the length of Lansdowne Road and Daisy was DRUUUUNK. Not just tipsy, or giddy, or a bit merry, or what's euphemistically known as 'in flying form'; she was classically pissed, flopping around a bit like a cartoon rag doll.

Not long after the final whistle blew, the diehards left in the Players' Lounge decamped to the stunningly swish Berkeley Court Hotel, where the English team were sequestered in fabulous, five-star luxury. But not to anywhere as plebeian as the lounge; they were all immediately whisked off to Mark's penthouse suite, which, needless to say, boasted its own private bar.

Lucasta was in her element and immediately plonked herself on a barstool where she remained for the rest of the evening.

'Two free bars in the one day?' she squealed excitedly at Jasper. 'I think I've died and gone straight to heaven.'

Meanwhile, Mark himself had disappeared off to his bedroom to slip into something more comfortable, and was gone for bloody ages, but boy was he worth the wait when he eventually did make his grand entrance.

He'd changed out of his navy England suit and tie and now looked infinitely more relaxed in combats and a cut-off T-shirt that accentuated his taut rippling arm muscles. Daisy almost fell over when he made a beeline straight for her, ignoring the bitches of Eastwick and just about everyone else in the room. The only trouble was, he had taken so long to get himself showered and shaved that, while waiting for him, she had downed so many home-measured vodka and Red Bulls, she'd lost count. This, on top of all the cosmopolitans she knocked back during the match, was giving her a serious dose of the helicopters; it seemed as though she was standing perfectly still, while the rest of the room revolved around her.

This is hilarious, she thought, aware of Mark giving her a sexy, lingering kiss in front of everyone. She tried her best to say, 'Congratulations, Mark, you had a great game and you must be very proud.' Except that it came out something like this: 'Congattshhhhullaaatms. YOU are a fuckkkkking great foootshballerr and if shu weren't getting marrhhied in a few shays' time, I would give you one ANNNYYTIIME . . . Class act, that's what shu are. But you sheee . . . your geeshing marrhhied to Eleanor sooooo you reeeally shhhounllndt kiss me like that . . . alllthough it was a looooovely kisshhh and you're a faaab kisshhher . . .'

(Translation: Heartiest congratulations on a wonderful performance today. However, the fact that you are on the verge of matrimony unfortunately precludes any chance of a deepening friendship blossoming between us. And by the way, you kiss very well.)

She was dimly aware that other people in the suite were staring at her but was way too far gone to care. Then, like in a drunken dream, she became aware of Alessandro Dumas beside her too. 'Itshhhh's you! I think YOU are very, very VEEEEERY cutsh too. I mean cute, I receeconisssed you from shat ad you do on the telly . . . you know . . . the shampoo ad . . . .you know the one I mean . . . you're in it for fuuuck's sake . . . And shurrr going out with the tartyy-looking one . . . shhwhatssher-name . . . over shere . . . shhhitting at the bar with my shhhmother . . . Jeeezzzz . . . hope Mummy's not too shloshed . . .'

(Translation: Your appearance is familiar to me as a result of the television campaign you spearhead to advertize hair care products. In addition, it is my under-standing that you are dating the rather provocatively dressed young lady who is currently sitting at the bar in conversation with my mother, whom I fervently hope has not overindulged herself this evening.)

Then turning back to Mark, who was practically hold-ing her up by now, she gushed, 'Look at you. I meeean to ssshhhay, take a look at shu. Seeeeexy, shat's what youu-ure. I nearly caaame in my shnickers when you shhhepped on to that foootie thingggie . . . JASPER! Whadddya call the grasssyy thing they kick the ball on again? You smust know, for fuuuckk's sake, you were there.'

(Translation: You are an extraordinarily good-looking young man and I found myself attracted to you the moment you stepped out on to the . . . unfortunately, my memory fails to inform me of the correct word. Jasper? Can you assist my failing powers of recollection, please?)

Jasper, however, was out of earshot. He was sitting at the bar, hit on from both sides by Shakira and Falcon, neither of whose husbands seemed to be in the least bit bothered that their wives were almost competing for a man who appeared to have virtually no interest in either of them.

'I believe the word you're looking for is pitch,' Simon called over to Daisy. He was fairly close by, closer than she realized, watching her intently from the bottom of a staircase made entirely of glass brick. He had that look of someone who was politely trying to make an escape, but couldn't. Shane Donohue had effectively collared him, demanding to know why it had taken him a full ten months before he was officially granted a clean bill of health.

'I ain't played more than two bleeding matches for Oldcastle this whole season and I'm not blaming you nor nothing, mate, but it is all your fault.'

'Shane, you broke your foot. Be thankful I got your X-ray results in time for you to play today. And if you hadn't badgered the physio, I would have recommended waiting at least till the end of the season before you played. It can take up to six months to fully recover from a greenstick fracture.'

'You're not very well, are you, love?' Mark said to the swaying Daisy. 'I think you could do with a bit of a lie-down. Why don't I take you upstairs?'

She needed no further persuasion. She only wished she hadn't belched quite so loudly as he took her by the hand and led her to the lift.

Jasper, unlike anyone else whose surname was Davenport, had been blessed with the great gift of being able to drink those around him under the table while managing to retain a fairly clear, cool head himself.

Lucasta was bossily insisting that he top up her drink while Falcon was in full flow, drunkenly droning on about the time she was coated in honey and placed in a glass cage full of wasps on *We Are Famous, Try and Shame Us.*

'Oh, they bleeding stung like hell, like you wouldn't believe, but that weren't the worst fing that happened to me on that show at all. Wanna know what the really worst was then?'

'When you said live on telly that you thought Colombo discovered America?' sniped Shakira. 'You was nuffing but a laughing stock for weeks after that.'

'Piss off, I weren't asking you.'

'The fact that you ended up snogging that sweaty old rock singer, whatshisname?' Shakira went on.

'Oh shut up, you dirty old slag bag, pour us another one, will ya, love?'

Jasper just kept quietly topping up their drinks, having voluntarily slipped into the role of barman.

'Stop putting that Red Bull crap into my drinkie, Jasper,' said Lucasta, 'it only makes me fart. Now do go on with your story, dear. Most entertaining.'

'I wish I could remember it now,' said Falcon waving an empty glass in front of her. 'No, I don't want no champers, just gimme another cosmo, love . . . Oh . . . sorry . . . I can't remember your name.'

'Jasper Davenport.'

'In't he just so cute?' giggled Falcon. 'If my Shane weren't here, you'd be in right trouble, so you would.'

'I discovered him, you know,' said Lucasta proudly. 'All by myself. Never think to look at him now that he'd spent most of his life in prison, would you?'

'*Life in prison?*' said Falcon, enthralled.

'No, life on a tropical island,' snapped Shakira. 'What did you fink?'

Just then, Buffy, who had been trying to lure Alessandro out on the balcony (with no success), joined them.

''Ere, did you say your name was Davenport, then?'

Jasper nodded and Lucasta belched in response while Falcon attempted to get to the end of her story, which was easier said than done, considering how far gone she was. 'No. Definitely, the worst thing for me about being stuck in the bleeding rainforest was the lack of make-up. You're not even allowed mascara, you know. I tried to smuggle in some and that old bitch what reads the nine o'clock news on the telly told on me, so we all lost two days' food rations, just cos of that lippy old cow. And then my fake tan started to fade in the second week cos I never thought I'd even last that long, did I, and then the two presenters slagged me off somefing rotten so they did . . .'

'You're not anything to do with the Davenports of Davenport Castle in the country here, are you?' Buffy asked Jasper, waving an empty wine glass in front of him.

'I certainly am,' said Jasper, obediently topping up her glass. 'Except it's a Hall not a castle.'

'Shut up, Jasper, you retard!' Lucasta hissed. 'How do you know she's not from the social welfare office? Or the Inland Revenue?' Then, turning imperiously back to Buffy, she said, as tight-lipped as a Mafiosi wife, 'We might be.'

'That is such a coincidence!' replied Buffy, delighted. 'Do you ever come across an old mate of mine? We used to be actresses together in the States, years ago, you know. I often wondered what became of her.'

Jasper looked at her intently. 'I might have. What was your friend's name?'

'Well, she had a lot of names, but the last I heard of her, she'd gone and married some Irish lord by the name of Davenport. I nearly pissed myself when I heard that, I can tell you. We done lots of movies together, of an adult nature, mostly, but she was really good, she even won an award once. She played the lead in *Shaving Ryan's Privates* and she got the "best breasts" gong. Good old Shelley-Marie, I'd love to see her again, have a decent catch-up, you know.'

'Jaysus, it's after getting fierce warm in here altogether,' said Jasper, stepping out from behind the bar. 'Why don't you and me step out on to the balcony for a minute and get a bit of air?'

* * *

The lift ride to the top floor of the penthouse was smooth and seamless and the doors had barely closed over when Mark started kissing Daisy. She tried to pull back, but given the state she was in, this was easier said than done.

'Mark!! Shhoppt it!! Whatt the fuuck are you doing? You're getting marrhhied in a few shays . . .'

(Translation: Mark! Kindly refrain! You are on the brink of matrimony!)

He chose to ignore her. She was like a lead weight, but somehow he managed to take off her T-shirt and was unloosening the zip of her tight denim jeans when the lift glided to a halt. The doors opened and they were immediately in the bedroom, a room so enormous that a family of fourteen could have happily lived there, but there was only one ultra-modern circular bed on a dais, right in the middle of the room, which Mark expertly steered her towards.

'Markk! Gettoff me . . . I just need a little lie-shown. Shhat's all . . . I'll be grandshh in a bit . . .'

(Translation: Desist from pawing me. All I require is to lie in a horizontal position, wherein I will endeavour to regain my composure.)

She didn't so much slip gracefully between the Egyptian cotton sheets as collapse in a drunken stupor with a loud thud, walloping her head on the wooden side of the dais as she fell.

'Ow, owww! What in the shname of FUUUCKING hell was shat? My brain is shurting now, Shark . . . I mean . . . Mark . . . oh whatever your shname is!' she yelled.

(Translation: Oh dear. I appear to have had a mild contusion in my cranial area and am now suffering some considerable pain. I'm awfully sorry, but as a result of this mishap, I appear to have momentarily forgotten your name.)

She slumped down on to the bed, nursing her head, but lying down only seemed to make her feel worse. The helicopter sensation that had given her such a buzz downstairs was now a hundred times increased and a slow, sickening nauseous feeling was starting to come over her. None of this was helped by Mark who by now was completely naked beside her and was attempting to pull her jeans down.

The one per cent of her that had a vague idea of what was happening kept saying: No, no, no. Dear God no, don't let this be happening and please Jesus don't let me puke over him.

'Ohhhh, shtoooop it, pleeease, Marrkk . . . whatt doo you shink shu're at? Get your hand out of my knickers . . . shhhittt . . . I donn't feeeel well. Feel ill; shwill you getttme water. Need water. Shanks.'

(Translation: Could you refrain from touching me in such an intimate manner, please? I feel most dreadfully

unwell and would appreciate it if you could kindly pro-
cure some water for me. Thanks.)

'Come on, love,' was all he said, sounding remarkably
sober and in control, 'you know you're up for it.'

He paid absolutely no attention whatsoever to her
cries and continued to fumble at the stubborn zip on
her jeans. She was down to her bra by now and was
suddenly aware of him grabbing her breasts roughly
when the sober part of her said, 'No . . . pleassshhhe . . .
can you shop? I want sho be shhhcik . . .'

He was lying on top of her by now, thrashing at her
jeans and cursing when she slowly became aware that she
was simultaneously being rolled on to her side.

'Mark! I fucking shhaid shop!'

But now it appeared there was another pair of hands
feeling her boobs, another pair of hands undoing her
bra . . .

Drunk as she was, she somehow managed to
manoeuvre herself into a sitting position . . . Mark had
successfully pulled her jeans down and was kissing her
bare tummy while another man with a tattoo on his arm
was pulling her head back, biting her neck so much it
made her cry out . . .

'You must relax . . . *calme, repose-toi* . . .' she heard in a
Frenchman's voice. 'This will be . . . *très drole* . . . fun . . .'

A split second later, the overhead light snapped
on and she heard an accent she recognized. 'Get

away from her this minute or by God I'll not be responsible.'

She didn't know what happened next, just that there were mutterings, curses and then the feeling that she was on her own again. She lay back, holding on to her throbbing head when she heard the disembodied voice again, except this time the Scots accent registered. 'Bastards. Tell me if they've hurt you and I'll kill them. TELL ME.'

She tried her best to shake her head but ended up bursting into tears instead.

'Shhh, shh . . . It's OK, they're gone, Daisy. You don't have to worry one wee bit. I saw you disappear with that scumbag Lloyd and then when that low-life Alessandro Dumas trailed behind, I figured I'd better keep an eye on you. Just in case you needed rescuing.'

She tried to raise her head from the pillow but couldn't. 'Ales . . . Alesshhhhandro was sheeehere too? With . . . Mark?'

'Aye. No better than pigs, the pair of them. You, my poor drunken lassie, had a lucky escape from what they call a roasting, which loosely translates from scumbagese to a three-in-the-bed session.'

'I shjust wanted a lie-down . . . He . . . told me I could ushhee his bed to shleep it off . . . and then . . . Oh God, whatsh kind of an eeeejit am I—' She broke off, really starting to feel sick. She managed to raise herself up a little and whispered, 'Shhhanks, Simon,' but that was all she could say.

Just as he answered, 'All in the line of duty,' she bent over his feet and puked her guts up.

Chapter Twenty-Two

For the first time since she set foot on American soil, Portia was finally starting to relax and enjoy herself. Jennifer was a perfect hostess, her two little girls, Amelia and Lucy, were utterly adorable to be around and the colonial-style beach house in West Hampton was like something straight out of the pages of a glossy interior design magazine. From the moment they arrived, Portia instinctively felt that getting out of the city had been without question the right thing to do. Andrew had been bitterly disappointed when she called him from Jennifer's to tell him she was staying. Disappointed and a bit confused.

'I don't get it,' he had said. 'I thought you liked New York, I really did. I know it hasn't been easy, with me putting in all these hours, but I promise, it's not going to be for very much longer. Couldn't you just visit Jennifer another time?'

Portia had to bite her lip to restrain herself from telling him the real reason she had absconded. Rightly or wrongly, she had decided not to relay back to him the conversation she'd overheard in the restaurant on the grounds that a) it would only upset her to have to repeat what Susan had said and b) at the end of the day, she *was* Andrew's mother and he was her only child. If Susan had started a massacre at the table that awful night, nothing would alter that fact. And she was pretty certain Susan wouldn't report the row back to him either. She was probably playing the 'I'm only a fluffy, defenceless old lady all alone in the big city and my errant daughter-in-law has abandoned me and now the lions in Central Park Zoo will probably eat me alive' card for all it was worth. And let her, Portia thought, just let her.

After all, it wasn't for very much longer.

'Cheers, welcome to the Hamptons,' said Jennifer, topping up Portia's long-stemmed crystal wine glass, filling it to the brim with a delicious, crisp Sancerre. 'Boy, it is sure good to have you here.'

'Here's to our absent husbands,' said Portia, raising her glass, 'who are probably, let's see now . . . it's ten at night . . . hmm, this is really tricky . . . where on earth could they be?'

'STILL IN THE OFFICE,' they chanted together

in a tipsy sing-song, before collapsing into fits of giggles.

'Mummy, I can't sleep.' It was Amelia, who had appeared at the door of the veranda in her Barbie pyjamas clutching a tatty-looking moth-eared teddy. 'You're very noisy and I'm afraid you'll scare away the tooth fairy.'

Amelia had finally lost her first tooth earlier that day, amid great hysteria, and only Auntie Portia's gentle promise that the tooth fairy would make it all worthwhile calmed her down a bit.

'Oh, sweetie, I'm so sorry, here, come sit on my knee,' said Jennifer, holding out her arms.

'No, I wanna go back to bed. Just keep it down, will you? I don't wanna have to tell Daddy that I lost out on fairy money because of you.'

They waited till she'd gone back upstairs before dissolving into more fits of laughing.

'She is her father all over,' said Jennifer. 'For her next birthday, I asked her if she wanted a Barbie dream home and you know what she said? Thanks, Mommy, but if I'm gonna be seven years old, don't you think it's time I had my own investment portfolio?'

'She's the cutest, funniest child,' laughed Portia. 'At this rate, she'll be running her own corporation by the time she's ten.'

'She misses Ken a lot. Lucy is too small really to notice him not being around, but every day Amelia says to me,

"How many more sleeps till Daddy gets here?" It would break a heart of stone.'

Portia sank back into the soft cushions, took a sip of wine and gazed out at the sea. It was pitch dark and inky black; the flickering, rose-scented candles on the porch were twinkling like fairy lights and the only sound you could hear was the distant lapping of waves . . . It was the most blissed-out, relaxed, beautiful place you could ever imagine and for the life of her she couldn't understand why Ken would stay away from this perfect life, the statement home, this wonderful wife and two dotie little princesses like Amelia and Lucy.

Then she remembered. It probably suited Ken down to the ground only to appear at weekends or whenever he'd nothing else on. She glanced over at Jennifer, who was sipping her wine and staring out to sea, and she found herself wondering. Jennifer was a smart woman; did she have any idea about Ken's extra-marital dalliances? The models, the actresses, the single women he met in bars and whom he paraded around the town for a few weeks until he invariably tired of them and moved on to the next one. Or maybe there was some truth in the old saying that the wife is always the last to know . . .

It made her feel guilty and uncomfortable though, knowing something that poor Jennifer didn't.

Should she tell her?

Jesus, no. The thought alone made her shudder.

Would I want to know, if I were in her shoes?

Well, yes, I suppose I would want to . . .

Wouldn't a friend tell, even though it was being cruel to be kind? Didn't someone as lovely as Jennifer deserve the truth?

Right there and then she made the decision. She wouldn't say anything, for now. But if Jennifer asked the question, straight out, she wouldn't lie to her either. She couldn't, she simply couldn't.

'You thinking about Andrew?' Jennifer asked, sensing Portia's eyes on her.

'Honestly?'

'Yes, honestly.'

'It's so amazingly perfect here; I was just thinking that I could never leave if it was mine.' Only a half-lie.

'You're probably wondering how Ken manages to stay away as long as he does.'

Portia smiled and took another sip of wine.

'I think the same when I look at you. I think: what, is Andrew crazy? Married to this beautiful Irish lady and what does he do? Works day and night and leaves her all alone. But you wanna know what, honey? This is our lot, this is what we married into and, like it or not, this is the pattern for the next ten, fifteen years. They're corporate lawyers, they're at the top of their game right now so they've gotta cream off as much cash as they can before the inevitable burn-out.'

'Oh no. You see, Andrew's only here for this one contract. Once the case is finished, he's coming back to Ireland. That was the deal we made. This job is just to pay off some of the debts we ran up renovating the Hall.'

'Portia, sweetie, you gotta get real. Andrew *loves* New York, he loves the pressure, the stress, the hundred-hour weeks, it's like he's addicted. Like an adrenalin junkie. How else could he neglect you the way he does? You take it from me. This contract is just the thin end of the wedge. I know Ken is already planning to strong arm him into working on another case this summer. And there'll be another job after that and another and another and Macmillan Burke will keep adding zeros on to his salary to get him to stay. And you love him so you'll stay with him and then sooner or later you'll wake up and find yourself in my shoes. Alone, staring out to sea and not knowing when I'll see my husband again.'

Portia had sat up now and was about to contradict her, but Jennifer went on.

'And a word to the wise, honey. Lynn Fairweather? Don't trust her as far as you could spit her.'

Ordinarily, Portia slept like a log but not tonight. For once, the soothing, whooshing sound of the sea right outside her window didn't work its tranquil magic.

Hours after she and Jennifer had hauled themselves upstairs to bed, she was still wide awake and staring at the ceiling.

Suppose it was true.

Suppose Jennifer was right and Andrew really had no intention of coming home. Or worse, that he would come back to Ireland with her all right, but only grudgingly, wanting all the time to be back in New York. Could she hack it? Could she really spend the rest of her life, as Jennifer put it, as a Macmillan Burke widow? The thought of ending up alone, husbandless like Jennifer, wasn't something that appealed to her, but the thought of Andrew ending up like his best friend Ken was something much, much worse . . .

An image of Andrew and Ken out nightclubbing in some midtown hotspot flashed through her mind and wouldn't go away. Ken collecting phone numbers of the beautiful women clustered around him the way he did and Andrew with him, beside him, being his charming irresistible-to-women self . . .

She immediately banished the thought from her head. Of course she trusted her husband. That was what marriage was all about. She trusted him implicitly. It was just getting harder and harder to keep trusting someone you never saw, that was all.

Another half-hour passed and she was still tossing and turning. It didn't help that when she tried to text him, to see if he was up yet, his bloody phone was switched off.

Was this how her life was going to pan out? Away from the Hall she loved so much, never seeing the man she loved so much and trying to call his cell phone, upset and agitated and really needing to talk to him and just getting through to his voicemail? And Jennifer was certainly right about one thing.

She wouldn't trust Lynn Fairweather as far as she'd spit her either.

In the space of a few short days, Portia's stay at the Hamptons had settled into a kind of routine. Every morning at daybreak, Amelia, followed by Lucy, who could barely waddle never mind walk, would bounce into her room, hop up on her bed and demand money from her. Invariably, Portia would oblige for the sake of peace and slip five-dollar bills into her grasping hand, on the premise that the tooth fairy must have got their rooms mixed up in the night.

'Stupid dumb tooth fairy,' Amelia would say, stuffing the cash into the breast pocket of her Barbie pyjamas as discreetly as a wine waiter, to be cannily locked in her safety deposit box later, safely out of harm's way.

'You are way too generous to that child,' Jennifer would tease over breakfast and Portia would laugh and cuddle Lucy and stuff her face with the divine maple syrup pancakes the housekeeper would rustle up.

In the early mornings, before the school run, they would all pile into the huge Chevrolet and go shopping at Bert's minimart, the nearest convenience store where you could buy everything from freshly caught lobster to a kite-surfing kit, along with the wax which went with it. ('The thing for your stick.') It had a wonderful seaside-ish quality to it and made you feel like you were on a permanent bucket-and-spade holiday. Jennifer and Portia would stock up, while Amelia pestered the staff by constantly asking, 'How much is that?' about every item she could reach, then trying to haggle them down. In the afternoons, though, they took turns collecting Amelia from the Quaker school she grudgingly attended in West Hampton and then, weather permitting, would spend the rest of the day at the beach. 'School's dumb,' Amelia would whinge as she changed into her Barbie tankini. 'All the other kids in my grade want to talk about Bratz all day long. I mean, what am I supposed to do? Just take the doll's clothes off and then put them all back on again? How lame is that? I asked my teacher about investing in blue-chip shares and she made me sing a verse of "Barney".'

The days were warm now, and bright till well after eight each evening, which was easily Portia's favourite time of day. Much as she adored the girls, she found her-self exhausted by the time they'd gone to bed, which was religiously on the stroke of eight every night, no discussion. Amelia would moan about missing CNN's financial report, but Jennifer was firm. 'Time for grown-up chat,' she'd say, tucking them in before escaping out on to the veranda with Portia.

There they'd drink crisp white wine, eat barbecued shrimp freshly caught that morning, and talk about anything and everything. The more they drank, the more they giggled and invariably at some point in the night they'd try phoning their husbands and would howl with laughter if either one of them actually got through.

After the weeks and months of stressing and fretting Portia had endured, firstly about the opening of the Hall, then about whether to leave Daisy with the wedding to manage and finally about being in New York with Susan de Courcey driving her insane, this was the perfect antidote. She looked and felt far better than she had done all year too. The bags under her eyes were starting to disappear, she was lightly tanned from the sea air and all the fresh, healthy food was giving her skin back its old glow. She'd also worked through a lot of how she felt about Andrew working so hard and never seeing him. Instead of feeling second best or shunted to one side, as she had done when she first came to the States, now she just couldn't wait to be with him again. She had the days counted till Susan's departure and it was almost there.

One bright sunny morning she woke earlier than usual, feeling queasy. She lay awake for a bit, trying to ignore it and doing her usual first-thing-in-the-morning ritual, which was mentally ticking off the number of days left until Susan buggered off back to Ireland, out of Andrew's apartment and out of their lives. Not counting today, only four days to go, she figured, almost hugging herself at the thought of seeing him again. She sat up and reached across the bedside table to fumble for her watch. Five-thirty a.m. No wonder the house was so quiet. You could count on at least another hour of peace and quiet until Amelia came banging on the door, looking for cash. She was about to drift back to sleep but lying on her back seemed to make the rumbling in her tummy worse, more persistent.

Seconds later, she had her head over the toilet bowl, heaving her guts up for all she was worth.

When the house eventually woke and they were all sitting around the breakfast table tucking in, Jennifer, in full mommy mode, instantly copped that Portia had touched nothing and was just gingerly nibbling at the corner of a dry piece of toast.

'Not like you,' she remarked. 'Thought you liked our east coast blueberry pancakes.'

'Maybe not this morning,' Portia answered, white as a sheet. 'I think I may have overdone it with those scallops last night. I was as sick as a parrot this morning.

I had to go feed the chickens, as we say in Kildare.'

'You mean you had to talk to God on the great white telephone?' asked Amelia, who missed nothing.

'Into your school uniform in the next ten seconds,' Jennifer barked at her, in her cross mommy voice. 'Up the stairs, NOW!'

As soon as she'd gone, Jennifer said, 'You know, honey, I had those scallops last night too and I'm fine.'

Their eyes met over the kitchen table for a second.

'Whaddya say we go to the drugstore and buy you a pregnancy test?'

'Portia, this is not a proposal for the Nobel Prize, it's stunningly simple. Two lines, you're pregnant; one line, you're not.'

She and Jennifer were standing on the landing outside the family bathroom, having this debate in hushed tones, mainly so Amelia wouldn't overhear.

'But I just couldn't be!' said Portia, for about the fifteenth time.

'Honey, Immaculate Conceptions rarely happen outside of Old Testament movies with Charlton Heston in them. Are you on the pill? Diaphragm? Any kind of contraception?'

'Yes. I'm married to a man who works a one-hundred-hour week. Highly effective it is too.'

'In the last month, dopey.'

Portia thought back. She was too embarrassed to say aloud what she was thinking, which was that since she and Andrew had arrived in New York, their sex life had been disastrous bordering on non-existent. They so rarely saw each other and when they did, he was usually too exhausted to do anything except drop into a deep sleep beside her. Added to that, Susan landing on them had effectively put an end to any intimacy they may have had, given that she was a light sleeper and had no compunction about thumping on the dividing wall if they as much as had a conversation, *sotto voce*. 'Do you mind?' she would screech at the top of her voice. 'I'm trying to watch David Letterman.'

In the blissful days before Susan had arrived, there had been a couple of early-morning quickies – all right, very early morning, given that Andrew was usually in work by seven. But she couldn't be pregnant. Yes, her period was late, but that was nothing unusual in itself. She'd never been what you might call 'regular' in her whole life and had put being a few weeks overdue down to all the stresses she'd been shouldering. She couldn't be . . . could she? Surely she couldn't be . . .

'Honey, you're thirty-six years old, these are the fertile years. It's entirely possible. Now get in there and go pee on a stick.' Jennifer was insistent. She'd even put on the cross mother voice.

'OK, OK, I'll do it just to shut you up.' She was about

to turn on her heel when Amelia flounced by and took in the situation at a glance.

'Knocked up, huh?' she said, slamming her bedroom door behind her.

Chapter Twenty-Three

FROM: portiadavenport@aol.com
TO: daisydavenport@davenporthall.ie
SUBJECT: Wedding update please!

Didn't hear from you all day yesterday,
which is odd, but then . . . maybe
you're just up to your eyes with all
the wedding stuff. Do let me know that
everything's OK. You know me for
worrying!
  Much love,
  Portia

FROM: *portiadavenport@aol.com*
TO: *daisydavenport@davenporthall.ie*
SUBJECT: *Get in contact!*

Me again.
  OK. It's been all day and still no
word from you. Really starting to fret
now . . .
Pxxx

FROM: *juliabelshaw@davenporthall.ie*
TO: *portiadavenport@aol.com*
SUBJECT: *The wedding. Just in case anyone in this family actually remembers
that there is a wedding happening
tomorrow.*

Portia,
  I'm very sorry to bother you when
you're probably having such a wonderful
time of it in New York but I'm afraid
there's a problem. In a word, Daisy.
Bad enough that she disappeared off to
a soccer match yesterday, but I'm
reliably told that she drank her body
weight at a party afterwards and hasn't
been seen since. She's holed up in her

375

room, refusing to budge, when I need
her here, helping me. It's D-Day minus
one day, for God's sake . . . The bride
is in Dublin at her hen do, needing to
be collected and the groom will be
arriving tomorrow with a list of
demands the length of my arm . . . I do
not have TIME for Daisy's juvenile
carry-on. If she wanted to go out and
get pissed and make a show of herself,
she should have waited till after the
wedding, as I intend to do. Honestly,
of all the days for her to go AWOL on
me.

Can you have a strong word with her,
please?

Yours, in a rush,

Julia

PS. Love to Andrew.

Julia wasn't exaggerating when she said she was up to
her tonsils trying to cope without Daisy. All morning
long, she never even got a chance to draw breath. A
steady stream of wedding guests had begun to arrive,
everyone from the Oldcastle team, their manager, their
wives and assorted trophy girlfriends all the way up to the
top of Julia's A list: Robert Armstrong, the President

himself, now safely ensconced in the Library enjoying tea and scones by the fire. Only the groom was missing; he was scheduled to arrive in discreet, subtle style, by hot-air balloon, the following morning. Everyone was enchanted with the magnificent grounds, the Hall itself and the exquisite rooms they'd all been allocated. Well, almost everyone.

Just as Julia was thinking so far so good, there was a diplomatic incident which only someone with her flair for soothing bruised celebrity egos could have dealt with. She and Amber were both at reception, meeting and greeting, when ear-piercingly shrill voices could be heard wailing from the top of the great oak staircase. Even though the hall was thronged with new arrivals, all heads automatically looked up to see what the commotion was. Clacking down the stairs in impossibly high heels came Shakira Walker and Falcon Donohue, both looking exceptionally glamorous and virtually in-distinguishable, at least to Amber's eyes.

'Are you the manager or what then?' squealed Shakira in her shrill Essex girl tones. 'Cos I got a bleeding complaint to make.'

'Yeah, me and all,' whined Falcon in an unmistakable south London accent, almost falling headfirst over a Louis Vuitton matching luggage set carelessly dumped at the bottom of the stairs. Julia steeled herself as they clickety-clacked across the marble hall, oblivious to the stares they were attracting from other guests who stood calmly waiting to be served, enjoying the sideshow.

'Sweet God, it's the blonde leading the blonde,' she muttered under her breath to Amber. 'You continue checking guests in, let me pee on this fire.'

'You answer me this then,' said Shakira, pointing a fist laden down with diamonds and acrylic false nails into poor Julia's face. 'How come that dirty slapper gets a better room than what we got, wiv a view over a genuine Irish lake, when me and Ryan only get a box room overlooking the bleeding stables. I'm not joking, the smell of shit almost made me gag.'

'Smell of shit probably came off your own filthy arse, dinnit?' replied Falcon, shaking her waist-length hair extensions in fury. 'Now are you gonna explain to me why slaghead 'ere got a goodie bag in her room wiv a voucher for the Spa and all I got was a poxy bottle of Irish whiskey I wouldn't brush me teeth with? I'm a miles bigger name than what she is any day. Did I eat a tarantula on live TV for this?'

'You piss off!' shouted the other, pointing her breasts at her.

'Ladies, ladies, let's all calm down,' said Julia soothingly, sounding like Kofi Annan giving a keynote speech to the UN Security Council. That a fist fight didn't erupt was entirely down to Julia's innate tact, not to mention years of experience in dealing with celebrities and their easily bruised egos.

Shakira kept screaming that just because Falcon had been buried in a pit full of cockroaches in the Australian rainforest, that didn't entitle her to any kind of preferential treatment. Then Falcon demanded to know how come Shakira got a room with a four-poster bed when she only had a lousy headboard. Only Julia's lightning-quick action in promising both of them unlimited treatments in the Spa the following morning before the wedding saved the day. It worked a treat though; the pair of them were like pussycats for the rest of the evening.

And still no sign of Daisy.

'I had that dream again. Something catastrophic is about to befall us, there's absolutely no getting away from it this time, I'm afraid.'

Lucasta was standing in the middle of the Red Dining Room, still in her nightie, oblivious to the stares of other newly arrived wedding guests who were trying to enjoy Tim's award-winning buffet lunch. (She would have been murdered for appearing in a public area like that when Portia was around, but standards had slipped a little since her departure.)

'The one where ya find Shergar's head in the downstairs pantry?' asked Mrs Flanagan.

'No, you moron, that dream unfailingly brings good

luck. The one where I'm naked and covered in mud and that boring priest from the village is droning on about reporting me for indecent exposure.'

'That wasn't a dream, ya gobshite. That happened. Two months ago.'

'Oh shit, so it did. I'm so upset, it's bound to confuse me a bit. I meant the dream where I'm being burnt at the stake and all the munchkins from *The Wizard of Oz* are roaring laughing at me and singing "Somewhere Over the Rainbow". Something awful is going to happen. I hate that I'm always right, but that's the cross I have to carry through this life.'

'And I have to put up with ya. That's me own personal cross.'

'Oh, why do none of you ever fucking listen to me? This is like a Greek tragedy about to unfold in front of our very eyes! I feel like Cassandra, my predictions are always deadly accurate but doomed to be forever ignored!' Lucasta was screeching at the top of her voice by now, really working herself up into a state.

'Excuse me, Lady Davenport,' said Molly, coming over to the table they were sitting at like a bullet. 'But I'm afraid I must ask you to refrain from using language like that in front of guests. The gentleman at table twenty-two says you're putting him right off his flambéed frittatas.'

'Fine. Just don't any of you come crying to me when the whole place goes up in flames, or worse. The only consolation I have is that I'll be able to stand by your gravesides and say I told you so, you absolute shower of arseholes.'

Daisy physically couldn't move. All she wanted to do was stay in her room and shut out the world. Dealing with the hangover she was nursing was bad enough, but when she thought about Mark Lloyd and Alessandro and what might have happened . . .

What might have happened if it weren't for Simon, she corrected herself.

It was already lunch time, she had a thousand things to do, she knew Julia would come thumping on her door again any second now, yet somehow she couldn't even bring herself to leave the sanctuary of her room. She tried to make herself think about Portia and how she'd entrusted her with the smooth running of the wedding, but not even that amount of self-inflicted guilt-therapy worked.

No one will really miss me if I don't go downstairs, she reasoned. Between Molly and Tim and Jasper and all the staff at reception, the place was practically running itself these days. Besides, the thought of having to go downstairs and face all the Oldcastle glamour-hammers, Buffy and Shakira and the one that ate slugs in the Australian outback after last night . . . and then the one sickening thought which was really making her stomach churn came back to her. Eleanor. Yeah, sure, she'd pissed Daisy off by being a bit sullen over the last few days, but up until then she had been lovely – ladylike and gentle. And now, in less than a day, she'd be marrying that scumbag, sleazeball git . . .

Another thought struck her. Maybe that was why Eleanor's mood had altered so drastically in the last few days. Could it be that she'd heard something about Mark? And maybe now was having second thoughts about the whole thing? All of a sudden, Daisy felt ashamed for bitching about her . . . the poor girl would have to spend the rest of her life married to a lying, two-faced cheater, unless . . . Oh Christ, she thought. No matter what angle she looked at this from, the next twenty-four hours were going to be a disaster for everyone concerned.

She looked over at her alarm clock. Twelve-thirty. Five more minutes and then I'll face them, she thought, snuggling back under the heavy counterpane of her four-poster bed. She had just drifted off when the phone by her bed started to ring yet again.

Bugger it, she'd have to talk to Julia sometime. She'd plead a migraine . . . Maybe that would buy her another few minutes of peace.

'Hello?' Try as she might, she couldn't keep her voice from sounding flat and bored and uninterested.

'Still in your room at this hour? Now that can't be good.'

She smiled, instantly recognizing the Scottish accent. 'Hey, Simon, how are you?'

'More to the point, how are you? I'm asking in an official medical capacity, you understand.'

'Then, in your official medical capacity, I have to tell you that this patient has seen better days.'

There was a long pause which Daisy didn't attempt to fill. She was just too tired, emotionally, physically, every way. Besides, Simon was one of those people who seemed comfortable with silence.

'You know, those guys really are nothing but a pair of aul' bawbags, as we say in Glasgow,' he said eventually. 'I've always said it, and I'll keep saying it to my dying day. Mark Lloyd would have his arse for a perfume factory.'

Daisy found herself giggling.

'Seriously, though,' he went on, 'I'm really going to have to restrain myself from socking them both one when next we meet. You had a lucky escape, but let me tell you, you'd be astonished at the number of women who are willing participants in one of their so-called roasting sessions. Really astonished.'

'Are you being serious?'

'Daisy, my poor wee innocent, think. The likes of Mark Lloyd and Alessandro Dumas earn somewhere in the region of twenty-five thousand quid a week and only spend about four hours a day training. So they're rich and they're pricks and they have a lot of free time on their hands. And this is how they spend it. Women, women, women, all the way.'

Daisy started to get a bit teary again. She was sure Simon meant well, but the thought of being just another notch on a bedpost surprisingly didn't make her feel better.

'Have you thought about maybe talking to someone about this?' he asked gently, after a bit.

'Oh Simon, talk to who? The police? The Sunday papers? I don't think so. And even if I do, what do I say? I was almost sexually assaulted but wasn't? A roomful of people saw me stotious drunk, falling all over the place and then disappearing off with Mark Lloyd to his bedroom. If I took this further, anyone with a brain in their head would say to me: What the hell did you expect? And they'd be right. That's what's making me feel so shit. I was drunk and stupid and I should have known better. If you hadn't come into that room when you did, I'd be telling a very different story now.' She was starting to sob now and fresh fat tears were falling down her face.

'Shhh, come on, wee girl, don't go upsetting yourself any more. You've had quite enough. I'd say getting over that hangover alone was little short of a Herculean task. I recall seeing you trying to knock back Jeyes fluid you found in the bathroom at one point.'

She stopped sobbing for a moment.

'No, what I meant was talk to a counsellor. You did

nothing wrong, Daisy, those guys are just utter arseholes. Take it from me.'

'I'll be fine.'

'Sure? You don't sound it.'

'I promise. There's just one thing.'

'What's that?'

She took a deep breath. 'Eleanor. What in God's name am I going to say to her?'

There was a long pause. 'Come downstairs and have a wee drink with me, will you?'

'Simon, I can't. I can't face those people. I'm sorry, I'm just not up to it.'

'Shhh, calm down. I'm not suggesting you do a cancan through the Ballroom. Meet me downstairs. I faithfully promise, the coast is clear. We've a lot to talk about and we've only got twenty-four hours.'

Ten minutes later, still feeling shaky and headachy, Daisy led Simon into the Library, probably the only room in the Hall that was completely deserted, since most of the Oldcastle guests were, thankfully, availing themselves of the free bar in the Long Gallery. Simon wearily slumped into a leather wing-backed armchair and began to rub his tired eyes exhaustedly.

'You know, before I began working for Oldcastle I used to work in the A. and E. department in Edinburgh,' he said. 'Twenty-four-hour shifts sometimes, I kid you not. But nothing, nothing compares with what I'm feeling right this minute. I just want the next few God-awful days to be over like you wouldn't believe. Single malt whisky, if you have it, thanks. Better make it a large one.'

Daisy slipped around to the drinks table and poured him a large glass of Laphraoig, thought about it, then poured one for herself. To hell with it, she thought, if ever I needed a cure . . .

There was a buzzy, electric feeling about the Hall, hardly surprising given that the place was full to the gills, everyone excitedly looking forward to the big day tomorrow. Even though the Gallery was a full floor above them, she could hear the sound of a right pre-wedding hooley in full swing. Lucasta was bashing out one of her compositions at the grand piano, leading a sing-song clearly audible throughout the Hall. It was something she'd been working on for days, entitled 'I never even knew what a banana was till I was sixteen, if you catch my drift'. It was enough to give Daisy a panic attack. The very thought of bumping into anyone who had seen her at the party the previous night was making her nauseous all over again. And yet she'd have to face them, whether she liked it or not.

Simon seemed to be reading her thoughts. 'Don't fret yourself. You're quite safe from anyone even remotely connected with Oldcastle as long as the free bar holds out.'

Slowly, Daisy sat down on the ottoman beside him

taking a big gulp of the whisky. It felt warm and burnt its way down, and after a few minutes the colour began to come back to her cheeks. 'Simon, what are we going to do? About Eleanor, I mean. She can't marry him. She just can't. It would be a disaster.'

He smiled wryly. 'No it wouldn't. Poll tax was a disaster. The *Titanic* and the *Lusitania* were disasters. But compared with marrying Mark Lloyd, the Hundred Years War could be considered a minor mishap.'

Daisy's head started to spin a bit. Jesus, what was she going to do? Be the sole reason why the wedding of the year was called off? Wilfully ruin what should be the happiest day of the girl's life? Because Eleanor really loved Mark, she was sure of that, and up until yesterday, she would have sworn under oath that Mark loved her too . . . All his phone calls to see how the wedding plans were shaping up, his invitation for her to go and visit him at Oldcastle – yeah, sure, he was a bit flirty with her all right, but she just thought . . . what? That this was the way he communicated with all attractive women? That he was just being attentive to her to make absolutely certain that Eleanor's big day went without a hitch? Oh Christ, how could she have been so bloody thick not to see what was coming?

Simon must have realized how her head was swimming with it all, because he sat forward and spoke to her in a doctor voice. Reassuring. Gentle. 'What you need to understand,' he said softly, 'is that Eleanor happens to be my best friend. Since we met at college, all those years ago. And there's nothing I wouldn't do for her. I've no doubt in my mind that *Gotcha* magazine will gleefully make you and me out to be members of the Borgia family when this gets out and the best of luck to them if they do. But, Daisy, make no mistake about one thing. We have to tell her what happened last night. The whole story, in glorious Technicolor. It'll be hard on you, I know, but believe me, it's the right thing to do. Because I will not stand back and watch my best friend make the biggest mistake of her life.'

Daisy just stared ahead. She knew he was right. It was just the thought of actually narrating the whole bloody nightmare to, of all people, Eleanor. And yet what choice did she have?

'I introduced them, you know,' Simon went on, swirling his glass. 'All of, what, two months ago. In a million years I never thought she'd be his type, or indeed, the other way round, but lo and behold, I head off to Cape Town for a four-week break and I come home to find them engaged. If you think the press were shocked at the whirlwind romance, as they labelled it, you should have seen my reaction. As soon as I heard the news, I drove here immediately and told Eleanor straight up that she was far too good for him and that he'd never change his spots. That type never does.'

'What did she say?'

'Not much. You know Eleanor, still waters run very deep. She adores Mark and I suppose she thinks marriage will change him. But surely you noticed she hasn't exactly been leading conga lines around the place since I gave her my honest assessment of her fiancé?'

'Oh God, Simon, this is just so awful. She'll be devastated. What are we going to say to her?'

He took another deep gulp of whisky and looked out of the window. 'I don't see anything wrong with the truth, do you?'

Given that it was D-Day minus one day, Julia's stress levels can only be left to the reader's imagination. It didn't help that Robert Armstrong's personal chauffeur got waylaid into Lucasta's almighty sing-song and, when the time came for him to collect the bride herself from Dublin, could barely see straight, never mind do the forty-mile drive there and back. Jasper, luckily, came to the rescue.

'I'll be there and back in two hours,' he said to Julia as she passed him the keys to the presidential limo.

'Much appreciated,' she purred in a 'you are about to get so lucky tomorrow night when all this shit is over' tone of voice.

Exactly an hour later, he was patiently waiting in the car park of the Four Seasons Hotel in Dublin. Nothing as vulgar as a hen party in Temple Bar, with drunk women in veils and L plates and toilet seats wrapped around the bride's neck for Miss Armstrong. No, she had booked a very quiet, sedate affair: a pampering day in the hotel's fabulous health spa followed by dinner for herself and her close friends, geographically about as far from the Hall as she could get.

It was late, well after two a.m., when she eventually stepped out of the hotel and spotted the limo. She was about to slip into the back seat when she noticed that it was Jasper holding the door open for her and not her regular driver.

'Ehh, bit of a change of plan,' he said, by way of explanation. 'The poor other fella's had one too many, so I'm to take you home. Back to the Hall, that is.'

She smiled and slipped into the passenger seat beside him. 'That's so nice of you.'

'Did you have a good night?'

'Quiet. Restful. What I needed.'

They drove in silence and Jasper left her with her thoughts. They had got as far as the motorway to Kildare before he chanced a quick glance over at her. She was crying, soft silent tears. Instinctively he fished around in his pocket and produced a tissue, which he handed over.

'Thank you.'

'It's none of my business, Miss Armstrong—'

'Eleanor.'

'But I just wanted to say one thing. Any man marrying you tomorrow should think himself the luckiest man
alive. If there's something upsetting you – or if there's
some*one* upsetting you, you just give me the word and I'll
sort them out for you.'

An image flashed through his head of the state Daisy
had been in on their way home after the party. He had
asked no questions but knew instinctively that something
was up. And he had a fair idea of what or rather who the
problem was.

Eleanor said nothing, just continued staring out of the
window.

'All I'm saying is that you can count on me. If you
asked me to kick someone's head in I'd gladly do it. I
swear I'd pulverize them so they'd have to be DNA
tested to be properly identified. You only have to say the
word.'

Eleanor turned to him and in the light from a passing
truck, he could see the wet tears on her cheeks. 'I know,'
she said, gently. 'And thank you.'

'Just remember, the offer is there.'

Chapter Twenty-Four

'I gotta tell you, I think you're making a huge mistake.'

Portia stayed resolute.

'Honey, I know exactly how you feel, but you really oughta think this through. You're all excited and emotional right now, and it's understandable that you just wanna hop on a train and tell Andrew the news, but as your friend, the one who gets to say all the shitty things to you, all the stuff you don't wanna hear, I gotta remind you of something: Susan de Courcey. La Belle Dame Sans Merci herself. Waiting like a praying mantis for you in that apartment. Like Kathy Bates in *Misery*. With highlights and slightly better make-up. And two sledgehammers instead of one.'

Portia shifted from one foot to the other, the nauseous feeling she'd had earlier starting to return. Jennifer was quite right, of course. Susan would still be resident in Park Avenue, ripping the heads off dead bodies or whatever it was that she got up to in her spare time.

'And she'll think all her birthdays have come at once when she sees her sad disappointment of a daughter-in-law returning to the spider's web. Means she can get right back to her favourite hobby: bitching about you in the Palm Court with Nan Keane and the rest of her vicious sewing circle.'

'I know. I'm fully expecting her to be twice as awful as she was before I went away. With the added guilt trip that I abandoned Andrew to be here with you.'

'She's gonna have a field day with you, honey. All I'm saying is, you're newly pregnant, do you really need this in your life right now? You should be taking care of yourself, resting up and relaxing for the next while, till you're at twelve weeks and can start talking about it. I know that crone of old; she'll stress you out and wear you down and all for what? At the end of the day, Andrew's still gonna be putting in one-hundred-hour weeks, same as he always does. You're going right back into the frying pan at the one time in your life when your body doesn't need to.'

'Jennifer, I know what you're saying and I really appreciate your advice, but . . .'

'I knew there'd be a but.'

Portia looked her in the eye. Of course Jennifer only

had her best interests at heart, she knew that and loved her all the more for it. But this news was just so overwhelming, so unbelievably amazing that the thought of telling Andrew over the phone, the very idea of not being with him when he heard . . . no, she couldn't contemplate it. She was going back to the city, and that was all there was to it. For better or for worse.

Jennifer was still prattling on, undeterred. 'Sure, go tell Andrew your news but then get straight on the first train back here. I know I'm being selfish, cos I so love having you here, and the girls do too, but I really feel that it's much better for you and the baby to stay here, where it's so peaceful and relaxing. I've got a great doctor in the town, Dr York, she took good care of me during my pregnancies and I'm sure she'd be happy to see you—' Jennifer was nothing if not sensitive and broke off as soon as she clocked the look of steely determination on her friend's face. She sighed. 'OK, OK. Gimme five minutes to find my keys and I'll drive you to the station.'

Portia was in luck. There was a midday train which would get her back to town by two, in perfect time, she hoped, for her to catch Andrew at lunchtime. Jennifer, an angel to the last, had let her go with just an overnight bag.

'My insurance policy,' she explained, pulling the car into the drop-off area. 'Means I get to see you when you come back for all your stuff. Sooner rather than later, I hope.'

Both women hopped out of the car and hugged, with Portia's five-foot-ten-inch frame towering over her pint-sized pal. 'You've been such a friend. I really don't know how even to start thanking you,' she said, sincerely meaning it. 'What would I have done without you?'

Jennifer batted it off, but kept on hugging her. She was teeny weeny but freakishly strong too; eventually she released Portia from her iron-clad grip. 'Can I just give you one parting piece of advice, honey?' she said. 'As one Macmillan Burke widow to another?'

'Of course, fire away.'

'No one is happier for you than I am, you know that. And I'm sure Andrew will be thrilled too. Just don't fall into the same trap that I did, that's all I'm saying to you.'

'How do you mean?'

'Oh, phrases about leopards and spots spring to mind. Don't think that starting a family will magically transform Andrew into husband of the year, because it's not going to. A baby is the best, most wonderful news in the world for *you*. Just don't think this will change him into a doting, attentive guy who wants to be with his wife twenty-four-seven. Because it just won't.'

A full hour later, just as the train was arriving into Manhattan, Portia was still mulling over what she'd said, raging that she hadn't had time to debate with her any further. Of course, she could fully understand where Jennifer was coming from. She was married to the greatest philanderer in the Northern Hemisphere, who thought turning up at the Hamptons every other weekend made him both husband and father of the year.

Andrew was different. Right to her bone marrow, Portia knew how over the moon he'd be at impending parenthood, that he'd want to put her best interests first, that he'd cut down on his work hours, finish this case, get back to Davenport Hall, anything just to be with her and, in time, the baby . . .

Oh God, that felt weird, she thought. Somehow actually saying 'the baby' didn't make her feel in the remotest way like a mum-to-be. She was thrilled, shocked, ecstatic . . . and nauseous again.

She only barely made it to the toilet on the train and had to elbow an old lady out of the way before throwing up all over again.

In spite of Portia's impelling the train to go faster by sheer force of will, surprise, surprise, it didn't. It glided into Grand Central Station bang on the dot of two p.m. Needless to say, Andrew's phone remained switched off. The outbox on Portia's cell phone was crammed with the text messages she'd been bombarding him with the entire journey, each one more urgent and hysterical than the last, till the final one read: 'DON'T EVEN READ THE

END OF THIS MSGE! JUST CALL THE SECOND, THE VERY SECOND U GET THIS!!'

No joy. As she fought her way through the throng in the central concourse, she dialled his direct line at the office.

'Macmillan Burke, Andrew de Courcey's phone. How may I help you?'

'Glenda?' Portia had left so many messages with her over the past few weeks, she could recognize the voice instantly.

'Hey, Portia honey! I just love that lilt so much! How are you? Enjoying the life of leisure in the Hamptons?'

'Well, as a matter of fact—'

'Gee, I sure envy you and Jennifer Courtney. Why can't I have married a rich husband too?'

'Speaking of my husband, I was just wondering—'

'Instead of that lousy, no-good guy I ended up with. The closest he ever took me to a beach house in the Hamptons was a wind-blown shack in South Carolina. Which cost him like twelve dollars a night. No kidding, honey, it was just like Dorothy's house in *The Wizard of Oz*. Right after the twister.'

A burly black guy roughly knocked into Portia just as she was going through the ticket turnstile, making her feel ratty and impatient and fed up with being polite to this woman she'd never even met.

'Glenda, I hate to interrupt, but I have to know where

Andrew is. I've been trying to call his cell phone for the last few hours, but it's switched off.'

'Well, mystery solved. His cell is right here beside me, honey. Guess he must have forgotten it.'

'OK. This is a grade A emergency. I need to know where Andrew is. Now. And I'm not getting off this phone until you tell me.'

There was a pause. Glenda wasn't used to Portia putting her foot down quite this firmly. 'Well, he's in a meeting, sweetie, said he wasn't to be disturbed under any circumstances. Like that's gonna surprise you.'

'In a meeting where?'

The central concourse was noisy and packed and Portia was practically shouting, which made Glenda sound even more intimidated. Andrew's wife was usually so chatty and gentle, you could almost hear her wondering what harridan from hell was this on the other end of the phone?

'A lunch. With Dick Feinberg from Globex. Honey, all you gotta do is relax. I got the message and the second your husband walks back into his office, I'll have him call you. Where's the fire?'

If only you knew, Portia thought.

'At lunch where?' she persisted, sounding a million miles away from her usual pleasant self.

'You really don't wanna interrupt them, sweetie. You have no idea how pressured those guys are, they're due in court Monday morning . . .'

'Please answer my question, you've no idea how important this is. They're at lunch where?'

There was a pause while poor Glenda weighed up her loyalty towards her boss against the steely determination in Portia's voice. What the hell, you could almost hear her thinking. I don't get paid enough to deal with hysterical corporate wives. 'Balthazar, in the Village. It's on West Fourteenth and Eighth.'

'Thanks.' Portia curtly ended the call, ran outside the building and immediately jumped into a cab.

'That was mine!' screeched a guy in a pinstripe suit who had been about to grab the taxi at the same time.

'Emergency!' Portia called back at him, slamming the door firmly shut and barking the address at the bewildered Puerto Rican driver. It was so completely out of character for her to be this rude that she did flush a bit, but quickly put it out of her mind. This was such life-altering, overwhelmingly BIG news that nothing else seemed to matter. Absolutely nothing else . . .

'Anything else, sir? Madam?'

Dick Feinberg had just said his goodbyes, leaving Andrew and Lynn to pay the bill.

'Oh Christ, did he have to order that second bottle of fizz? My head is throbbing,' Andrew was groaning as he fished his credit card out of his wallet. 'And I have an afternoon of it ahead of me. I'm going to have to burn the midnight oil to get that deposition ready for the court hearing on Monday.'

'Listen to you. So grouchy,' Lynn purred. 'Safe to assume you're still missing wifey?'

Andrew smiled. 'Yeah. I'm going to have to prise her out of the Hamptons at this stage. God, my head hurts . . . What were we drinking? Methylated spirits? Nail varnish?'

'Someone could use a coffee,' she replied, smiling suggestively. She'd waited a long time for this and knew she'd have to pick her moment carefully.

'Great, let's pick one up on the way back to the office.'

'Or you could take a couple of hours off. There's no point in trying to work now, you'll crash out. Look, your place is only a few blocks away, whaddya say we go back there, I'll fix you a strong coffee and you can sleep it off a little.'

'Lynn, I really should get back.'

'What, are you afraid I'm gonna jump your bones? Relax. Let me take care of you.' If she'd added, 'And I won't go running off to the Hamptons once the going gets tough,' her intention couldn't have been any more marked.

The traffic was bumper-to-bumper all along Park, so, unable to contain herself, Portia paid the driver, left him an embarrassingly huge tip, hopped out and walked the rest of the way. Eventually she spotted Balthazar, across the street, neatly tucked in between two high-rise apartment blocks. She was too impatient to walk the twenty or so metres to the traffic lights, so she just ran out in front of the traffic, ignoring the cacophony of car horns and shouts of 'Get off the road, crazy lady!'

She burst through the door, panting and out of breath, flustered, agitated and anxiously looking around for Andrew's familiar, tall, fair-haired silhouette. But it was well after three o'clock by now and, apart from a few stragglers lingering over dessert wines, the restaurant was empty. In a flash, the maître d', a small, round, Italian man, had oiled his way over to her.

'May I help you?'

Portia ignored him and moved inside to the dining area proper. No. Definitely no Andrew.

'Ma'am? How may I help you?' The maître d' sounded a little more insistent, having followed this slightly panicked-looking woman into the restaurant proper, probably wondering if she was about to set fire to the place.

'Oh, I'm sorry,' said Portia, flustered and suddenly aware of the picture she cut. 'I was looking for Andrew de Courcey, actually. He would have been with a table from Macmillan Burke?'

'Excuse me?'

'A tall fair-haired man, Irish accent?'

401

'Oh, sure, now I got you. Yeah, he was here for lunch all right. Table sixteen.'

'Oh, how long since he left?' Doing a quick mental calculation, Portia figured that he and this Dick Feinberg, or whatever his name was, would be on their way back to the office and that she could nab him there.

'They left like an hour ago. He asked me to call a taxi for him and his date, cos they had both had a little too much of the sauce over lunch, you know what I mean?'

'I'm sorry, did you say his date?'

'Sure. He left with a lady friend.'

'I really miss her, you know. Place seems empty without her. Hate coming home here now. Hate it.'

Ordinarily, Andrew was a man who could hold his drink, but not today. Exhaustion and loneliness were proving to be a lethal combination, or at least, so Lynn calculated. They stood side by side in the tiny galley kitchen as he drunkenly attempted to pour some coffee for them both.

'Black for me, I don't do dairy,' she purred, moving in on him and sounding surprisingly sober.

'Jesus, sorry, I didn't . . . know you were behind me.' He had turned around to find her almost pressing herself up to him and spilt the freshly brewed coffee all over her white linen trouser suit. 'Sorry, sorry . . . oh God, I'm such a dork.'

'Hey, relax, Andrew. I think someone has had enough to drink. Why don't you have a little lie-down and I'll go soak this suit out in your bathroom. Don't want my underwear to get ruined.'

He was in no fit state to argue. Ten seconds later he was crashed on the bed, out for the count.

It's funny how the memory works, Portia thought. How something as simple and inconsequential as a song played on the radio has the power to pull you back to a specific date, time and place in your life. And with the sub-conscious mind being what it is, all the emotions you experienced, no matter how long ago, come flooding back as fresh as if you had experienced them only yesterday.

In the long months that followed, as her pregnancy advanced and she had time to think, it was Ella Fitzgerald singing 'They Can't Take That Away From Me' that would instantly bring her back to that taxi journey, on that warm, sunny, New York afternoon.

She had run out of Balthazar, hopped into a yellow cab and told the driver to take her to Macmillan Burke's head office on East Forty-third Street. But the rush-hour traffic had already begun to build, and as they turned on to Park Avenue her nausea came back with swift and sudden vengeance. The maître d' at Balthazar had to be wrong, simple as that. There was no way; absolutely no way that Andrew could have left there with a date . . . It was a simple mistake, she thought. Maybe it was some colleague or co-worker that had joined them on business, that was all. What else could be the case?

Her tummy churned over and she had that terrifying feeling that either she'd have to be sick in the back of the cab or else on a loo within thirty seconds. Thinking fast, she decided against braving the traffic jam to get to the office and made a detour. They were only about two blocks from the apartment so in a flash her decision was made.

She told the driver to pull over, just as Ella Fitzgerald was coming on the radio. I won't last, she thought. I'll get sick in the privacy of my own home, clean myself up, then grab another cab and catch Andrew back at his office . . .

'Oh no, they can't take that away from me . . .' Ella Fitzgerald's soulful voice was ringing out as she paid the driver and ran into the building.

She sprang out of the lift and let herself into the apartment, praying she'd make it to the bathroom in time. She ran down the hall and threw open the bedroom door. There were two half-drunk cups of coffee on the bedside table and the first thought that struck her was how odd that was. Consuela would surely have tidied them away. It was a few seconds later before her brain fully registered what she was seeing.

There was Andrew, stretched out on the bed, shirt un-buttoned, shoes kicked off and wearing a pair of Manchester United socks she'd given him the previous Christmas. 'Mum?' he said groggily when he heard the door.

Then Lynn came through from the en-suite bath-room, hair all ruffled, looking like a lingerie model in a very fetching grey silk bra and G-string.

Andrew sat up immediately as soon as he registered who it was. For a split second no one spoke, they just looked at each other in shock.

In an instant, he was on his feet, frantically trying to button up his shirt and getting the buttons in all the wrong holes. 'Jesus Christ,' he stammered. 'Portia . . . this . . . this really isn't what it looks like. You have to believe me.'

'You're not even supposed to be here,' said Lynn, immediately on the defensive.

Portia stood rooted to the spot, too shocked to reply and yet wanting to fill the awful silence.

'Oh, I'm *so* sorry,' was all that came out, shakily but trying her very best to sound strong. 'Did I interrupt something? Please! Continue!'

'Hey, lady, where's the fire?' said the doorman standing at the canopied entrance to the apartment. Portia ignored him and was about to hail down the first yellow cab she saw when nausea swept over her again.

Oh please no, she thought, frantically looking around her; please, please don't let me be sick all over the sidewalk . . .

There was a neat, orderly row of flowerpots on a window ledge just outside the entrance door and she barely had time to think before finding herself hurling up into one of them.

'Jeez, lady,' snapped the concierge, 'those plants are plastic! They don't need to be fertilized!'

'I'm so sorry,' she panted, trying to catch her breath and fervently hoping Andrew wouldn't follow her outside.

By a miracle, a yellow cab pulled up right beside her and an elderly lady got out. Without pausing for breath, Portia leapt in.

'Will you be leaving that there, ma'am?' the concierge shouted at her furiously. 'I'm not paid to clean that up, you know!'

She had barely slammed the car door shut when Andrew came bolting out through the revolving door, looking utterly ludicrous, she thought bizarrely, barefoot, with his shirt flapping behind him, frantically looking for any sign of her. Thank God, she thought, thank God he didn't see me throwing up into a flowerpot . . .

Even from inside the car, his cry of 'Portia!' was deafening.

'Drive!' she whispered hoarsely to the driver.

'Where to, lady?'

'Oh, will you just drive the car!'

The driver sensed the tone, did what he was told, and moved off, heading south.

Portia looked out of the window and for a second their eyes locked as her taxi sped off.

Lucasta always used to say that at times of great crisis, small mercies go a long way and, sitting in the back of the car, Portia knew what she meant. There was very little traffic and within minutes, she was Midtown, away, gone, safe from him catching up with her and forcing her to listen to explanations and excuses and all that that would entail . . . She was in deep, dull shock and not one part of her brain could make a decision.

'Lady, I sure hope you're enjoying the tour but if you could give me some kinda destination here, that would be real useful. Or you wanna just keep heading south?'

'Yes,' she said dully. 'Just keep heading south.'

The first raw wave of shock was starting to give way to a slow, sickening feeling and she instinctively knew that a dam-burst of hot tears was on the way, when her cell phone rang insistently.

The number came up in bright blue caller-ID Day-Glo. 'Andrew'.

She clicked it off.

Two minutes later, he called again. She switched it off again but this time listened in to his message.

'Oh Jesus, darling, you have to let me explain. This looks awful, I know, but I had a few drinks at lunchtime and we just stumbled back to the apartment and . . . Oh God. I know how it must have looked to you, but you have to believe me . . . nothing happened with Lynn, I swear to you . . .'

Click. The voicemail on her phone cut him off mid-sentence. Seconds later her phone rang again. And again, she immediately clicked it off so all he got was her messaging service.

'Sweetheart, you have got to take my calls. You have to let me explain. Please don't jump to conclusions . . .'

She deleted the message, unable to listen to any more. Don't jump to conclusions? What was she supposed to think? That they were in his apartment in the middle of the day with him in bed and Lynn almost naked so that . . . what? So he could give her a mole check? Then the sickening feeling came back, and with it questions that she knew would drive her insane . . . Was this a one-off or had it been going on all along? Was he in love with Lynn? Her mind flashed forward to a grotesque image of him and her, years down the line, living together, loving each other, remembering Portia as some boring interlude from the past that they'd had to get through before finding lifelong happiness with each other . . . Then she thought about the baby, and how happy she had been only an hour ago and how all she wanted now was to jump off the Brooklyn Bridge . . .

Her phone rang again. But this time when the caller's ID flashed up on screen, she answered immediately.

'Portia? It's Daisy.'

'Hi,' she said in a tiny, wobbly voice, thrilled to hear someone from home. Someone in her corner. Who'd rip Andrew's head off, with a bit of luck.

But Daisy didn't ask her how she was or what was up. 'I'm really sorry to be ringing you in New York, when you're probably having such a great time . . .' she said.

You think? Portia thought.

'And I'm sorry it's taken me so long to get back to you, but, well . . . there've been a few developments this end.'

'What? Tell me, what!' A thought flashed through Portia's head. How can things get worse?

'Now I'm sure everything will work out, but . . .'

'Is it to do with the wedding?'

'Who said there's going to be a wedding?'

Chapter Twenty-Five

Gotcha Magazine
Requests the pleasure of your company
At the wedding of
Miss Eleanor Armstrong
To
Mr Mark Lloyd
The Davenport Country House Hotel,
20 March 2004

Joshua Byron-Smyth was absolutely thrilled with his efforts. 'To the naked eye, it might look as though I'm just lying in bed recovering from a ghastly hangover, darling,' he croaked hoarsely down the phone to his editor Fifi Hamilton on the morning of the wedding. 'But in actual fact, I've composed the entire first page of the, emm . . . you know, baby, the page with the typewriting on it . . . Oh bugger, what's the word I'm looking for?'

'Copy.'

'Copy, thank you, my love. It's far too early for me to be expected to think.'

'Joshua, I hate to break it to you, but it's ten a.m.,' Fifi snapped from the comfort of her leather swing-back chair on Fleet Street, well used to dealing with his total and utter lack of professionalism. 'The photographer just called me to say she's been thumping on your bedroom door since eight this morning. And you know we need this piece within twenty-four hours if it's to make the shelves next week, so sorry to rush you and all that . . .' The unspoken part of the sentence was: 'But could you please get your lazy arse out of bed and do a bit of work for a change.' Joshua took the hint. Hauling himself up on to one elbow, he peeled off the collagen eye mask he was wearing and grimaced as the daylight hit his bloodshot, puffy eyes.

'Fifi, my love, what you must understand is that this is Ireland. It's practically considered bad form to leave a party before three a.m. Last night was a work night for me, albeit a boozy one. I've made wonderful contacts with all the Oldcastle guys and their wives and partners and I've even thought of a fabulous format for the whole day.'

'And that would be?'

Joshua stumbled out of the bed and made his way to the breakfast trolley which Molly had delivered hours earlier, and poured himself some lukewarm coffee. Thinking on his feet, particularly when hung over, was where he excelled. 'It's going to be a diary format, hour by hour. Beginning with the blushing bride having her war paint put on in the salon, the bridesmaid fussing over her, the groom arriving at the Hall, all of that. Then a countdown to the ceremony, with all the guests arriving in their glad rags, the boring religious bit I'll keep to a minimum and then the reception which – it doesn't matter what anyone thinks – is the highlight of the day. Drunk chicks with their tits hanging out doing a conga line, that's what the readers want. That and the bride blubbering at the end of the night with her make-up dribbling all over her Vera Wang. Trust me, darling, it's all under control.'

If Fifi thought she'd catch him on the hop, she'd another think coming.

'Just as well I gave you this alarm call then, wasn't it?'

'Thanks a thousand, darling. I do my best.'

'One more thing. Under no circumstances are you to miss Mark Lloyd's arrival at twelve-thirty sharp. That hot-air balloon is costing the magazine a fortune and, by God, we fully intend to get our money's worth.'

One long, pampering, invigorating shower later, Joshua sauntered up all four flights of stairs to the Salon in no rush whatsoever, with Liz, his very pissed-off photographer, in tow. 'Couple of head shots of the wedding party having mani-pedis with their hair being blow-dried straight and then we're out of here,' he directed the poor girl, who just silently rolled her eyes up to heaven. They were met at the door of the Spa by Julia, dressed up to the nines in a shimmering, figure-hugging, green lace dress, mermaid style, which perfectly accentuated her slim, curvy body. As ever, her hair and make-up were impeccable; she looked as though she'd won best-dressed lady at Ascot and had just stepped out of the parade ring, trophy in hand, without even breaking a sweat. The only accessory which looked slightly out of place was the headset discreetly clipped to the side of her head and the mouthpiece she was dictating into.

'OK, we need the FOB to the bridal suite for a photo call, it's zero hour minus four hours and twenty-seven minutes, we need him right now. Give location, please.'

'The FOB?' Jasper asked, completely audible.

'Father of the bride.'

'Relax; I have him in my sights. I've just seen him chatting to Lucasta beside the marquee.'

Joshua did a double-take, marvelling that he could hear both sides of the conversation so clearly over the headset, then, hearing the clump clump of his heavy footsteps, realized that Jasper was in fact only on the floor beneath them, thudding his way downstairs to the main entrance.

'Holy fuck, if it's not one thing, it's the mother,' snapped Julia. So fraught with nerves that you could string a guitar with her, she was in absolutely no mood for anyone who dared deviate from her watertight schedule on this day of days. She turned her full attention to Joshua, shoved a timetable into his hand and practically drop-kicked him back down the stairs again.

'The Spa is out of bounds at present, no photos, no questions. Get outside and take exterior shots while the weather still holds and report back here in precisely twenty minutes.'

Too used to her to bother arguing, Joshua merely shrugged and was ambling back downstairs shadowed by the photographer when Julia hollered at him like a sergeant major over the banister rail: 'Move it, faster, do it, now!' Then under her breath she added, 'I'll bet David and Victoria never had to deal with this crap at their wedding.'

'I know you.'

Lucasta was standing at the entrance to the marquee, fag in hand, squinting suspiciously at poor Robert Armstrong. All around them, the scene was one of tightly orchestrated chaos, with ice sculptures being ferried past, exquisite floral centrepieces being carted down the red carpet and a string quartet, all looking miserable and shivering in evening dress against the blustery March wind, beginning to set up.

'Now don't tell me, it'll come to me; I have a wonderful memory for faces,' she went on, scrutinizing him. 'Did you used to sing with the Boomtown Rats?'

Robert merely smiled and looked a bit embarrassed. He had just returned from a trade mission to China but looked very well-rested and behaved as he always did, impeccably.

'No, no, I have it, I know where I've seen you before,' Lucasta was droning on. 'Are you that gobshite who was a hostage in Beirut for years?'

'No, I'm afraid not.'

'The man who ran the four-minute mile?'

'Most definitely not.'

'Did you train the winner of last year's Grand National?'

'I wish.' He was teasing her now and really enjoying himself.

She would have gone on interrogating him indefinitely, but they were interrupted by Jasper, while Joshua and his photographer ambled behind, snapping them from a respectful distance.

'Morning, emm, Mr President,' Jasper said to Robert,

totally unfazed that he was addressing the Head of State and working on the assumption that the President should be addressed the way he was on *The West Wing*. 'Sorry to interrupt, but Julia Belshaw will have a heart attack if you don't go up to your daughter's room for a photo call.'

'Duty calls then,' replied Robert politely. Then, smiling at Lucasta, he said, 'Father of the bride and all that, you know.'

She continued to look at him, baffled.

'Oh dear me. I can't bear to see you misled any longer, Lucasta. I'm Robert Armstrong, at your service. We met at your launch party, remember? And we spoke on the phone? I organized the match tickets for you. I was so very sorry not to have been able to join you, but I've been on tour in China, you know. I hear it was a wonderful match.'

'Oh, that's where I've seen you!' she said, thumping her forehead in exasperation. 'Of course, how silly of me not to recognize you. Armstrong. You're the first man who walked on the moon.'

'Lucasta,' said Jasper, stepping in. 'He's the President of Ireland. You have seen his face before, on a thirty-two-cent stamp.'

'Well, I wish someone had said,' she replied, doing her trick of lighting one cigarette off another. 'I suppose that explains all the security men traipsing all over the place.

And there was me thinking you'd escaped from some kind of institution.'

Joshua's Diary, Davenport Country House Hotel, eleven a.m., the Beauty Salon.

How wonderful it is to see all the beautiful Oldcastle ladies being pampered here in the luxurious surroundings of the Davenport Spa! Although it's hard to imagine how any of these lovelies could possibly look any better than they already do. They kindly permitted Gotcha *magazine to photograph them as they chatted excitedly about the day ahead.*

'You're nuffin' but a stupid slaphead, Falcon Donohue!' Shakira was screeching across the washbasin over to where Falcon was having her false tan painstakingly applied by Shelley-Marie. 'You know I was supposed to get my bleeding tan done before you, get a bloody move on, will ya?'

'Ignore the old tart,' Falcon said at the top of her voice to Shelley-Marie, 'she's only jealous cos I'm gonna be mahogany and she'll look like petrified shit. Where you from anyway, you got a really funny accent.'

'Oh, I come from Texas,' Shelley-Marie simpered.

'The DIY place?'

Joshua stood where he'd been ordered to by Julia and

frantically scribbled away in his elegant leather-bound notebook, periodically muttering into a Dictaphone when something particularly inspirational struck him. The Salon was packed to the gills with guests, all women, naturally, in various states of undress, demanding blow-dries and manicures immediately, while poor Mrs Flanagan waddled around calmly telling them they'd just all have to wait their turn.

'It isn't my fault if none of these good folks made appointments,' Shelley-Marie had moaned to Julia earlier. 'I've only got one pair of hands.'

'We'll just get a couple of shots and then they'll all have to bugger off,' retorted Julia, well pissed off that here was something she hadn't made allowances for in her schedule. 'At precisely one p.m., we need the room cleared for the bride and bridesmaid. The rest of them can sever limbs themselves doing their own bikini waxes for all I care. Serves them right for not booking in advance.'

Falcon Donohue, wife of Oldcastle's star striker Shane Donohue, laughs animatedly with her old friend Shakira Walker as she has her magnificent hair washed in preparation for the big day.

'Careful with that slag's hair extensions then,' Shakira called over to Mrs Flanagan as she lathered Falcon's head in conditioner. 'Four Ukrainian bitches are bald now cos of her and they're very loose, ya know. One of them fell off and landed right in my champagne flute last night. I thought it was a king rat's tail, so I did.'

Our wonderful hostess, Lucasta, Lady Davenport, arrives in the Salon to make sure everyone's happy and to check that there are no last-minute hitches.

'So the bride's father is actually the President of Ireland, then,' Lucasta twittered, oblivious to the stares she was attracting. Surrounded by a bevy of pampered, preening princesses, she stood out like a bag lady backstage at a Paris couture show. Even the photographer, who was happily snapping anything with a pulse, took one look at her lady-ship's mucky wellingtons and stinking oilskin jacket and decided to stick with the considerably more photogenic Oldcastle women. 'I just wish someone had told me. Why, oh why am I always the last to know anything?'

Mrs Flanagan rolled her eyes to heaven. Catching Joshua's eye she calmly said, 'Ah Jaysus, it's been headline news for weeks now. It's not like it's a state secret or anything.'

'Well, you might have said. I was on the verge of having Jasper escort him off the premises. Only this morning, I was saying the sooner people like that are recaptured, the better.'

★ ★ ★

Daisy, too, was up and about bright and early. As Eleanor was so late arriving back to the Hall the previous night, she and Simon had decided they had no choice but to postpone the inevitable till the following morning. Daisy had just pulled on her crisp black uniform and was clipping on her 'acting manager' nametag when her bedroom phone rang.

'Wee girl? How you doing?' The Scottish accent.

'Hi, Simon. I'm about to become the reason why the wedding of the year gets called off and, for added entertainment, I'm about to smash Eleanor's heart into smithereens. I've been better.'

'She's in her room. Come on, let's go up there now and just get this over with, shall we?'

'Do you know, I honestly think I'd rather have a javelin up my arse and out my mouth right this minute than go through with this.'

He laughed in spite of himself. 'I'm not exactly relishing the thought meself. Come on, let's get it over with.'

She put the phone down and was on her way out of the door when it rang again. 'Simon, I told you, I'm on my way.'

'No, it's me, Jasper.'

'Are you OK?'

'Running around like a lunatic down here trying to

420

keep things under control. I just wanted to say one thing
to you.'

'What's that?'

'I know you haven't an easy day ahead of you, with
everything that's happened.'

Funny, Daisy thought. Jasper was one of those people
who instinctively knew what was going on without it
having to be spelt out for him. She silently blessed him
for it as he went on.

'But I just wanted to let you know, I might have a bit
of a surprise for you later.'

*The excitement here is at fever pitch as the groom and his
best man, French midfielder Alessandro Dumas, arrive at
Davenport Hall in a hot-air balloon. As they wave
excitedly to the crowd below, we see that Mark is clearly
relishing this, the biggest day of his life, with not a trace of
nerves to be seen.*

'Bugger me, Alessandro, I think I'm going to puke.
No one told me these hot-air balloons went up so
bleeding high. I don't like heights, they gimme a
headache.'

Alessandro, whose grasp of English was less than
perfect, peered over the edge of the basket and said, '*Mais*,
where are all of the . . . how do you say . . . bunches of
the fans? I had . . . *j'ai cru* . . . expected the fans to be here

421

to say *bienvenu . . . et là bas* – no one . . . just the house . . . umm . . . workers . . .'

Unfortunately, he was right. With just under two and a half hours to go to kick-off, naturally all of the wedding guests were far too busy pampering themselves to have any interest in being drafted outside for a freezing photo call. The staff too were so completely run off their feet that only Tim, Molly and some of the extra catering staff were frogmarched by Joshua and poor Liz over to the rose garden for the photo call.

Hordes of friends and well-wishers gather by the delightful surroundings of the rose garden, thrilled to see their hero, footballing legend Mark Lloyd, arriving in style.

'Is this charade going to go on for very much longer?' asked Tim, wearing only his chef's suit and freezing against the wild March wind. 'In case you hadn't noticed, I have two hundred people to cater for and time is of the essence.'

'And the bedrooms aren't going to clean themselves,' Molly said in agreement, with her teeth practically chattering.

'Oh, ten more seconds, just till we get a couple more shots,' replied Joshua coolly. 'And could you all cluster in together a bit more? Thank you so much, it just helps us to fill out the photos a little, you know.'

By now, the balloon was only about twenty feet from the ground as the pilot expertly guided it downwards as smoothly as he could, given the less than favourable weather conditions.

'Oh hell, get me out of this thing, I think I've got altitude sickness,' said a very green-faced Mark Lloyd. 'And I'm freezing me bleeding arse off.'

'*Jeune fille jolie* at, ehh . . . two o'clock . . . Heeello!' Alessandro only spoke pigeon English, but when it came to describing an attractive woman, his vocabulary was surprisingly adequate. As it happened, it was Daisy he had spotted, sprinting out of the French doors and racing for the rose garden as though her life depended on it.

If she had thought Mark would betray even a trace of embarrassment at seeing her again, she was mistaken.

When the basket hit the ground seconds later, he was out of it in one swift, athletic leap, his nausea completely forgotten as he made a beeline for the camera, waving jubilantly like he'd just scored a winning goal.

'Mark, Mark! Over here, Mark!' Joshua and Liz were both frantically trying to grab his attention, panicking that they wouldn't get enough shots of the groom greeting his adoring fans. His adoring fans, on the other hand, had other ideas. No sooner had the photographer finished with them, than they all scarpered for the warmth of the Hall, delighted to be out of the icy winds, leaving Joshua with no choice but to improvise wildly.

Such was the throng waiting to greet Mark, that police barriers had to be used to prevent them from crushing the groom just hours before the 'I dos'. One intrepid fan, however, managed to break through security to wish Mark the very best of luck on the occasion of his wedding.

'Well, how are you then, love?' he asked. Mark playfully patted Daisy on the bottom, clearly thinking his celebrity status endowed him with a sort of droit de seigneur. 'Good night the other night, bit of fun, yeah?'

Daisy flashed him one of her iciest blue glares. 'Eleanor would like to see you in her room immediately. And if you ever touch me like that again, my cousin will plaster your brains against a brick wall. Do you understand?'

'I think maybe you're the one who doesn't understand, love.' Mark's tone had switched on a sixpence, from flirtatious to threatening. 'I hope, for your sake, you haven't said anything to Ellie 'bout the other night, have you? Cos that would be really, really stupid of you. For a start, who's gonna believe you anyway?'

Daisy looked at him, stunned into silence.

Then Alessandro sidled up. 'You so preeetty. You are remembering me, yes?'

She ignored him.

'I was just telling Daisy here that she'd want to be very careful about who she goes telling tales to, isn't that right, Alessandro?'

Like a faithful lapdog, Alessandro nodded in agreement.

'Cos ten-a-penny dirt birds are always running to the papers making all sorts of allegations about me, aren't they, Alessandro? All the bleeding same, just a bunch of attention-seekers, all looking for their fifteen minutes of fame. Like the other night, for instance. When you practically flung yourself at me. Coming on to me like a bleeding freight train, you were. I mean, only for you turfing her out of my room in time, Alessandro, God knows what would have happened.'

For a second, Daisy really thought she'd smack him across the jaw. Ordinarily, she would have screamed, ranted, roared and yelled enough obscenities at him to colour the air blue, but right now there were bigger issues at stake. And after all, she reminded herself, revenge was a dish best eaten cold. Mark Lloyd would get what was coming to him. No two ways about it. She drew herself up to her full height and summoned up every last ounce of her dignity.

'If you could get a move on, please? Eleanor asked me to tell you it's urgent.'

Chapter Twenty-Six

With just moments to go before the ceremony, the excitement is palpable as guests gather in the Ballroom here at Davenport Hall, where the happy couple will exchange their vows at three o'clock today. Never in the Hall's two-hundred-year-old history can it have seen an event as glamorous as this, as the Oldcastle wives and girlfriends vie with each other to compete in the fashion stakes. As guests begin to assemble and take their places, the gasps of admiration for the Ballroom, transformed for this truly wonderful occasion, are audible.

'Miles better than that shithole in Sheffield we got married in any day, innit, darling?' said Shane Donohue enviously. 'Can't beat a bit of class, can you?'

'Yeah, it's all right I suppose,' moaned Falcon as they

inched their way through the other guests and took their allocated seats, no mean feat in her six-inch wedge heels. 'Don't get me wrong, love, I do love old things; I mean our mansion house dates all the way back to the seventies, don't it?'

'Careful, darling, or you'll ruin me bleeding hair with that cockatoo on your head.'

Falcon shot him a dagger look as she carefully rearranged the feathers on the Philip Treacy confection she was wearing on her head. On the terraces, Shane's nickname was 'The Mulleted Messiah' and every hard-core Oldcastle fan knew how precious his hairdo was to him. 'But, Shane darling,' she continued whingeing, 'all of these old houses are totally lacking in home comforts. There's no mini-bar in our room, the TV isn't even flat screen and I had to ask the chambermaid what that ugly fing in the corner was for. She called it an armoire or somefing and it turns out you're supposed to put your clothes in it. I thought it was for DVDs, didn't I?'

Shakira and her husband, Ryan, had just taken their seats on the opposite side of the pew and were, not surprisingly, having a very similar conversation. 'It's not that I'm nitpicking or anything, love,' she said, glancing across at Falcon to check that her outfit wasn't classier then her own low-cut, clinging sheath so short in the leg that the entire congregation could have been her gynaecologist. She was delighted to see that it wasn't.

Falcon had gone for a skin-tight white satin trouser suit and the only bit of flesh on show were her boobs, which rumour had it had recently gone from a size 34B to a 38DD overnight, courtesy of a certain Harley Street magician much frequented by the Oldcastle set. 'I mean I do like staying here,' Shakira went on, 'but I'll be ever so glad to get back to London, so I will. When the bloody maid brought us breakfast in bed this morning, there was only a copy of the bleeding *Irish Times* for me to read. How am I supposed to see my photo in some up-its-own-arse Irish paper? I asked her to bring us the *Sunday Sport* tomorrow and she gave me the dirtiest look, so she did. Snobby old cow.'

Just then, the string quartet, all dressed tastefully in black and elegantly perched on a dais by the huge bay window, began to strike up 'Air on a G String'.

'I remember they tried to get me to have that played at our wedding, darling,' said Falcon, fondly reminiscing. 'When I was coming down the aisle. But I put my foot down, so I did. "Air on a G String", I said? You must be off your bleeding bickies. I don't want no smut at my wedding.'

Wedding planner to the stars, Julia Belshaw takes a final look around the stunning Ballroom and beams with pride. How pleased this lovely lady must be, seeing all her hard work in the run-up to the wedding coming to fruition!

With just minutes to go, she must be breathing deep sighs of relief, no doubt delighted to think that nothing can possibly go wrong now. We caught her chatting excitedly with Father Patrick Finnegan, a local priest who will perform the service.

'You must be the famous Julia Belshaw I've heard so much about,' said Father Finnegan, looking resplendent in his shiny new golden soutane as he shook Julia warmly by the hand. 'Well, aren't you and Daisy Davenport two great young ones altogether?' he went on, jovially shaking her hand. 'I wouldn't have known the old Ballroom at all, the place only looks fantastic, so it does. A credit to you both.'

'I only wish Daisy could hear you, Father,' she hissed, not wanting her voice to carry over the string quartet. 'But I'm afraid she's completely disappeared. Hasn't been seen all morning. I've totally given up on her. Useless, utterly useless,' she went on, bending down to pick up some imaginary piece of fluff from the red carpet.

'Well, I've done my fair share of weddings in my time, but none in surroundings as grand as this!' Father Finnegan enthused, almost itching to get the proceedings under way.

The Ballroom did indeed look spectacular; Julia's team of florists had surpassed themselves. Huge, stunning arrangements of white lilies dominated every corner of the room, while each row had an elegant posy at the end, all in white, at the bride's specific request. Nothing as vulgar as toning colours for Eleanor Armstrong, it was pure white all the way. Even the gold–backed chairs which had been carted down from the Long Gallery were covered in plain white silk covers for the ceremony.

Although it was only three p.m., the evenings were still quite short and, given the storm that was brewing up outside, Julia's idea of having the entire ceremony candlelit was an out-and-out winner. Just about every candelabra from each corner of the Hall had been carted down to the Ballroom for the occasion so that now the entire room twinkled and glittered with sparkling candlelight. It looked like the most romantic place on earth to be married, a teenage girl's fantasy wedding come true.

'It was good of you to allow the service to go ahead at the Hall, Father,' said Julia. 'We haven't exactly been very lucky with the weather and it would have been a night-mare for me to transport everyone from Ballyroan church back to the Hall in the lashing rain. You saved me several milligrams of Valium.'

'Not a bother, it's only a pleasure to have the service here,' replied Father Finnegan. 'Once a couple have special dispensation from the Bishop, sure I could marry them on the grass verge of the M50 if that's what they wanted. I married a bachelor from Dublin there a few weeks ago on Sandymount Strand. Lovely girl he married too. Malaysian. Met her off the internet. And sure, just as long as Lucasta Davenport stays well out of harm's way, I'm sure everything will go like clockwork.' Poor Father Finnegan shuddered involuntarily, as if she was about to appear over his shoulder at any minute and set up a pagan altar, littered with human bones.

The soprano, specially flown in from London for the occasion, had just stood up to sing an aria from *La Traviata* when the first sign came that something was amiss.

Mrs Flanagan and Shelley-Marie both came galumph-ing into the Ballroom, looking like they were on their way to a world's worst-dressed awards ceremony, where they'd subsequently be battling it out for first prize. Mrs Flanagan was in a brown shift dress with the belt some-where up at her collarbone, revealing her bare, wobbly, wrinkly, dinner lady white arms, whereas Shelley-Marie looked like a transvestite entrant in an 'ugly men, uglier women' contest, dressed in a Barbie-pink rubber boob tube, with matching pink plastic orchids in her hair.

'Oh my,' she cooed to anyone who'd listen, 'I just love that song she's singin'! Don't she just sound like an angel from on high? Blackjack insisted on having it played at our weddin' too, you know.' Then, turning to flash her kilowatt smile at Mrs Flanagan, she added, 'It's from, like, this really, really famous opera, my darlin' Jackie told me. La Travolta.'

Julia spotted the pair of them, excused herself from Father Finnegan, and moved briskly towards them, smiling confidently at a bunch of very attractive Oldcastle players, who looked a bit uncomfortable in evening dress and who had yet to take their seats. She was possessed of that rare gift of being able to walk faster in Dolce & Gabbana high heels than in a pair of well-broken-in trainers.

'Well, I'm very glad to see you both had time to get yourselves ready,' she said dryly, checking her watch. 'Shelley-Marie, at this precise moment you're supposed to be in the bridal suite, applying last-minute make-up retouches to Eleanor. You'd better get straight back up there, it's D minus two minutes, you know, or didn't you read your schedule?' Then, turning exasperatedly to Mrs Flanagan, she said, 'You see? This is what happens when people don't stick to the schedule. One simple thing, that's all I asked you to do, one idiot-proof, simple thing . . .'

'I sure hate to interrupt you right in the middle of your hot flush,' simpered Shelley-Marie, 'but Eleanor called us in the Salon at about one o'clock, I think, wasn't it, Mrs Flanagan?'

'Eleanor WHAT?' This was the first time all day that Julia had raised her voice and it wasn't a pretty sound.

'Yeah, yer dead right, luv,' said Mrs Flanagan. 'It was on the dot of one o'clock that she rang. I distinctly remember, cos the Harry Hegarty hit list golden oldies show was coming on the radio—'

'What did Eleanor say!' Julia hissed, a purple vein beginning to bulge out of her left temple.

'And I'd written in with a special request for Eleanor,' Mrs Flanagan prattled on. ' "As Time Goes By", by Louis Armstrong, cos my aul' fella and I danced to that at our wedding and it brought us many happy years with nothing but good luck. Apart from him dropping dead of a heart attack at the age of thirty-seven, that is.'

'Give me the last sentence first. WHAT DID SHE SAY?' Julia was talking to Mrs Flanagan as though she were a slow-witted five-year-old.

'Ah, nothin' much. Just that she was cancelling all her appointments, that's all.'

'And it didn't occur to you that this is something you might have TOLD ME?' The bulge on Julia's temple was starting to look scary now.

'Ah relax, luv, Eleanor'll be grand. Sure all that young one needs is an aul' bit of mascara and some lip gloss and she'll look a million dollars.' Mrs Flanagan could see Julia's nervous breakdown fast approaching and had decided to enjoy herself.

'And it is her wedding and all,' Shelley-Marie chimed in. 'I mean to say, it's not like she's not gonna be the focus of attention all day.'

'And to be honest with ya, luv, sure we were so run off

433

our feet all morning washing heads and doing tans, we were only delighted with the extra bit of time to get ourselves ready. There's a lot of very cute-looking footballers wandering round the place, I wanted to be looking me best.'

'If there's anything wrong with that girl, I will hold both of you PERSONALLY responsible,' Julia hissed, turning on her heel and hoofing out the double doors so quickly she almost left a cloud of smoke in her wake.

'I wish to God that one would ever feck off,' said Mrs Flanagan to Shelley-Marie as they made their way to their seats. 'Sweet baby Jesus and the orphans, does she have to be told about every gnat that farts within ten miles of the Hall? Who's supposed to be organizing this wedding anyway, that skinny bitch or me?'

The guests have now all taken their places and are eagerly awaiting the arrival of the bride. Mark Lloyd and his best man, Alessandro Dumas, have just taken their places at the altar. As the soloist's magnificent aria swells to fill the room, we see that Mark is looking a little nervous, twiddling with the cuffs of his simple black tuxedo, impeccably cut and designed especially for the occasion by Ireland's very own Peter O'Brien. He's probably thinking that facing a World Cup final in the Stadium of Light is a piece of cake compared with waiting for his bride to arrive! Alessandro moves over to whisper something to the groom, not looking in the least perturbed that the lovely Eleanor is a little behind time. Perhaps he's reminding Mark that, after all, isn't it a bride's prerogative to be late?

Moving at the speed of light, Julia hared up the oak staircase and down the second-floor corridor to Eleanor's room. One of the chambermaids was standing outside the door, carrying a tea tray and looking ashen-faced. The poor inexperienced girl almost leapt out of her skin when she saw Julia thundering towards her.

'She's in there with her father and Daisy and that Scottish guy,' she stammered nervously by way of explanation. 'I don't know exactly what's going on, all I know is that they asked me for some nice camomile tea for Miss Armstrong and now no one will answer the door.'

'This is nobody's fault,' replied Julia, breathing deeply and forcing herself to speak in the calm, measured tones of one who's well used to dealing with nervous brides. 'I'm quite sure it's simply a case of pre-nuptial jitters and that her family will talk some sense into her. And if they don't, I will.'

She pushed the chambermaid aside and rapped firmly on the door, a don't-mess-me-around-any-more-than-you-already-have-done knock. 'Eleanor?' she asked in a surprisingly soft tone, almost coaxing her to come out. 'Sweetie, it's me, Julia. May I come in?'

Silence.

'Will I send for Jasper?' whispered the maid. Even amongst the household staff, he had a reputation for being something of a Mr Fixit.

'Shhh.' Julia glared at her, as though they were trying to coax a nervous thoroughbred out of a stable and the slightest noise might send her scurrying back to safety again. 'Eleanor darling?' she tried again. 'I wouldn't rush you for the world, you come out when you're good and ready, sweetheart, but it's just that everyone's downstairs waiting for you and Mark's already at the altar . . .'

There was a tiny, discreet click as the door opened. Julia needed no further encouragement and was in like hot snot, leaving the poor chambermaid awkwardly loitering in the doorway, not having the first clue what to do.

There was Eleanor, lying on the huge, canopied four-poster bed, still in her dressing gown, surrounded by an ocean of crumpled tissues and looking like she'd been up all night, howling to the four walls. The wedding dress remained wrapped in its plastic cover, swinging innocently from a hanger on the bedpost. Daisy was over at the window and visibly straightened up when she saw who it was. Robert was sitting on the dressing-table chair beside her but immediately rose when he saw that a lady had entered the room. Even at times of crisis, his manners were exemplary. Simon held the door open as Julia barged past him in her rush to get to Eleanor's side, as though she were suffering from a terminal illness and had only moments to live.

'I was just coming to find you,' said Daisy calmly. 'I'm sorry about the delay, but we've all been trying to decide what the best thing is to do.'

The atmosphere here in the Ballroom of Davenport Hall is electric as there's still no sign of the bride. Mark Lloyd is now slumped on the steps of the makeshift altar, looking beside himself with nervous tension. Even the string quartet seem to have thoroughly exhausted their repertoire. But just in the nick of time, here comes the Irish President, Robert Armstrong himself, striding confidently up the aisle and towards the podium where it looks like he's about to address the congregation. Put us out of our misery, Mr President and tell us what's keeping your daughter!

Robert, flanked by Simon, made his way up to the altar and cleared his throat before he spoke. He was cool, clear and, as ever, in command. Even Shakira and Falcon stopped twittering to listen to what he had to say.

'Ladies and gentlemen, firstly, let me apologize wholeheartedly for keeping you all waiting such an interminably long time. That was inexcusable of us.'

He looked down and saw Mark glaring back up at him, defying him to go on. It was a surreal moment, as both men eyeballed each other with the flash of camera lights going off in their faces.

Eventually, Robert calmly returned his focus to the crowd and continued: 'I've had to make many public speeches in my time, but none as difficult as this. The fact is, my daughter has given the matter a great deal of thought and has asked me to make a brief statement on her behalf. Ladies and gentlemen, I'm afraid there isn't going to be a wedding today.'

There was a stunned silence. You could have heard a pin drop as every eye in the place slowly turned to focus on Mark.

From the back of the room, Lucasta piped up, unaware that her voice was carrying. 'I don't fucking believe this,' she said. 'Does this mean that we won't get paid?'

Chapter Twenty-Seven

'I know this will sound funny coming from me, but I really feel I owe you a huge thank you,' said Eleanor, looking a million miles from the wretched, puffy-eyed waif of only a few hours ago.

'I destroyed your wedding day and now you're thanking me?' said Daisy incredulously. 'I just think you're amazing, the way you're taking all this. If it was me . . . well, I'd probably be in the nuthouse by now. And Mark Lloyd would definitely be dead.'

Eleanor crossed the bedroom to where Daisy was standing by the window, gave her a tight hug and launched into yet another litany of apologies for all the trouble she'd caused. 'It breaks my heart, you know, when I think of all the hard work you put in so that the wedding would be a success, I just . . . well, put it this way, it'll be a long time before I hold my head up high in public again.'

'Eleanor, let's get one thing straight. I'm the one who should be apologizing to you. I can't tell you how rotten I felt about what happened, but then I figured, if I were in your shoes, I'd want to know.'

'You did the right thing. It wasn't easy for you or Simon, I know that. But, Daisy, please believe me, you've both done me the biggest favour in the long run.'

'It takes guts to do what you're doing,' said Daisy, in complete awe at Eleanor's cool resolve, and not for the first time that day either. 'Plenty of people would have gone through with the wedding because it was the easier thing to do and then spent the rest of their lives bitterly regretting it. You get ten gold stars for courage and that's for sure.'

Eleanor smiled warmly. 'Do you fancy a coffee?' she asked, making her way over to a linen-covered breakfast trolley parked elegantly by the huge bay window.

'Lovely, thanks,' replied Daisy.

'Do you know that this morning was the first time in weeks I've actually sat down and eaten properly? My father says I've gone to skin and bone.'

'You see? Yet another reason to call the whole thing off. The dress would have made you look like Calista Flockhart,' said Daisy, nabbing the opportunity to crack a joke and lighten things a bit.

Eleanor laughed as she poured coffee from a heavy silver pot into two china cups and passed one over to Daisy. 'You know, I have another apology to make to you.'

Daisy looked at her, unsure whether she should interrupt or just let Eleanor talk. Let her talk, she decided. This is probably the first time she's really been able to get it off her chest.

'When I first met you, I was so jealous of you. I'm completely ashamed of myself now, but when I saw how Mark flirted with you and the way he'd call you up all the time . . . well, all I can say is, if I was ever rude to you or unpleasant, you know where I was coming from.'

'Eleanor, you're incapable of being rude,' Daisy replied, ashamed of herself for ever thinking that she was a moody cow.

'Mark denied the whole thing, you know,' she went on, sipping on her coffee and looking out at the marquee flapping in the wind below. 'But, as Simon drummed into me, that's what men do. Deny, deny, deny, and then only when you confront them with incontrovertible evidence will they say something like: Oh well, I never meant for you to find out. And that's exactly what Mark did.'

Eleanor was too much of a lady to go into gory details about her eleventh-hour talk with the groom, leaving Daisy to draw her own conclusions.

'And I'm sure that's the story he'll stick to when the

press are crawling all over him in the next few days and I'll come out as the heartless, cold ice queen. And you know something else? I won't care.'

Daisy took a gulp of coffee and hoped she'd go on talking.

'Do you know Mark sat almost exactly where you're sitting now, only a few hours ago? Honestly, you'd have roared laughing if you'd heard him trying to justify himself. I was drunk, darling, I didn't even know Daisy was gonna be there. She'd had one too many and I just brought her up to my room to have a lie-down, what's wrong with that? I swear on my granny's grave nothing happened. If Alessandro had other ideas then take it up with him. Nothing to do with me. That's the truth, the whole truth and nothing but the truth.'

Eleanor was a lovely girl, but couldn't do a cockney accent to save her life.

'But ten minutes later, he'd changed his story so now it was: All right then, so maybe she did throw herself at me a bit but that was it and then I threw her out but she kept trying it on, but I resisted because I love you so much and yadda, yadda, yadda. And you know what? I said nothing, just listened, and as he went on and on, changing his story pretty much every time he told it, I thought: I don't believe you. And if I don't believe you, that means I don't trust you. And how can I marry a man I don't even trust? Daddy was absolutely wonderful; once

I'd actually made the decision to call a halt to the whole thing, he really couldn't have been more supportive. Somehow I don't think Mark Lloyd was exactly the kind of son-in-law he would have wished for.'

Daisy sat mesmerized on the edge of the bed. She couldn't believe how calm Eleanor was being. It was almost as if a huge load had been lifted from her thin, fragile shoulders. 'So how do you feel now?' she asked, gently.

'Numb. Still a bit raw, to be honest. But it'll pass. Have you ever had to make a really difficult decision which you know will hurt someone you care about, and yet once the decision's actually made, it's almost a relief?'

'How did Mark take it?'

'Surprisingly well, although he professed himself to be devastated. He's a bit of a drama queen though. You only have to see the way he reacts on the pitch if a rival player as much as brushes against him. Simon claims he's the world's greatest living hypochondriac. He even threatened to head off on the honeymoon without me if I left him standing at the altar. He kept dragging my father into it. Does your old man really need all the bad publicity this is going to generate? he said. Miles easier just to go ahead with the whole thing and then sort out our differences afterwards.'

'What! You mean he still expected you to go ahead with the wedding? After all of that?'

Eleanor nodded. 'His exact words were: Look, darlin', everyone's here and everything's paid for so let's just get married and sort this out on a beach when it's all over. No one knows nothing about what happened, I mean about what didn't happen,' she went on, her cockney accent even worse than Dick Van Dyke's, ' 'cept you and me. And Simon. And some of the lads. And Alessandro. And Daisy. And most of the tabloids by now, probably.'

They were interrupted by a discreet knocking at the door. Eleanor rose gracefully from where she had perched on the bed and moved to answer it.

It was the august personage of Robert Armstrong with Simon standing behind him.

Caught on the hop, Daisy stood and automatically hid her cup and saucer behind her back, as though the mere act of drinking in front of the President was an act of disrespect bordering on the treasonable.

'Ladies,' he said politely, entering the room.

'Is it all over then?' Eleanor asked anxiously.

'All over bar the shouting.'

Daisy would happily have spent the rest of the day cocooned in the Edward VII Suite chatting with Eleanor but there was a grim task to be done. The fallout from the aborted wedding was, of course, catastrophic and there was one person, Daisy knew, who would need her help more than ever right now. Bracing herself in case she ran into any of the Oldcastle set, or worse, Mark himself, she made her way downstairs and outside into the gale that was almost a storm by now.

The marquee was already being disassembled, she noticed, feeling a huge pang of sympathy for all the *Gotcha* magazine people. After all their hard work in organizing the wedding, planning it down to the tiniest detail, not to mention forking out for it, it was hard not to feel sorry that it had all come to nothing. On the TV in Eleanor's room, every news bulletin and chat show was full of the story about what should have been the society wedding of the year. Now all that was left to show for it, Daisy reflected, was an oversized white tent flapping in the blustery March winds and a kitchen full of gourmet food which would never be eaten.

The back lawn was crawling with workmen, struggling to disassemble the marquee in fading light and in the middle of them all was Jasper, barking orders at them like a Nazi SS officer. Julia was there too, sticking out like a sore thumb in her wedding outfit as she strode back into the warmth of the Hall, carting a stunning arrangement of still-fresh flowers with her. As soon as Daisy spotted her, she immediately went over to see if she could help.

'Well, well, well, look who it is. Nice of you to put in an appearance, but everything's under control, thanks,' chirped Julia, sounding in mighty form and not at all like someone whose Herculean labours had all been for nothing. 'It seemed like such a shame to waste all these magnificent flowers,' she explained, 'so I decided I'd pilfer them for the inside of the Hall. It'll look like Kensington Palace the week Diana died by the time I'm finished with it.'

Daisy was astonished at how well she was taking it. 'I just wanted to say I'm really sorry, Julia. I mean for all the hard work you put in. You must be devastated at the way things have turned out.'

'Why would I be devastated?' Julia plonked a particularly stunning arrangement of white lilies on a windowsill in the Yellow Drawing Room and looked at Daisy as if she were a bit simple-minded.

'Well, I'd be bloody raging. For starters, look at all the money the magazine spent, not to mention the cost of putting all the Oldcastle gang up here and then there's the food—'

'You know, sometimes I'm inclined to forget how inexperienced you are in the ways of the world, Daisy. Why do you think *Gotcha* magazine wanted to buy out the wedding in the first place?'

'So they could get fabulous pictures of Eleanor and Mark and the ceremony and then the knees-up in the tent afterwards,' she answered, wondering if Julia had finally lost it.

'With the ultimate goal of?' Julia could sound unbelievably schoolmarmish when she chose to.

'Emm, selling magazines, I suppose.'

'Clever girl. And can you imagine how many they'll sell now? I would conservatively guess about six times the number they would have sold had the wedding gone ahead. This is going to be one of the biggest news stories of the year, never mind the gossip column aspect of it. And we have full spin control. For God's sake, an hour after I was finished on the phone, tipping off every editor in London and Dublin, it was the lead item on Sky News. And who's going to have the exclusive photos they'll all be bidding for?'

'Oh, I get it, *Gotcha* magazine,' said Daisy, the light finally dawning on her.

'Precisely. Wait until this issue hits the stands, it'll be their biggest seller until Prince William gets married and how long is that going to take? Joshua Byron-Smyth must be pinching himself. No, this is a win–win situation for all concerned. Can you imagine how fantastic this will be for my business? My God, royalty will *beg* me to plan their weddings after this. And as for all the spin-off publicity that Davenport Hall will get, well, you can just consider it a little farewell gift from you to me.'

It wasn't hard to see what she meant. By the time Daisy got back to the reception desk, the place was thronged with hung-over guests trying to check out and get to the airport while Joshua and Liz frantically photographed them and posed last-minute questions.

'Tell us, Shakira, is it fair to say that you were devastated at what happened here earlier today?'

'Yeah, I was, I was crying and all, weren't I, darlin'?' she said to her husband Ryan as she beamed at the camera and looked about as far from devastated as it was possible to be.

'That's great, thank you, if you could just put your arm around your husband and pose for us here, beside the mantelpiece? Lovely, that's looooovely. So what do you think is the worst aspect of the wedding being called off?'

Shakira's kilowatt smile didn't budge. 'Well, when I was gonna get married first time round, my fella, my ex I mean, called the whole thing off with just a few days to go, didn't he? So I can totally sympathize with what poor Eleanor's going through. And definitely the worst part of it is that you don't get to keep the presents nor nothing. Everything's gotta go back, don't it?'

'Yeah, she's dead right,' Falcon chipped in, their rivalry forgotten as they vied for camera time. 'But at least I get to take the present what I bought her home with me. I'm really pleased, cos I went to shitloads of trouble to pick out something dead classy. Practical too.'

'What did you buy?' asked Joshua, scribbling away.

'A tiara.'

'Everything OK?' Daisy asked Amber, relieved that the

Oldcastle girls were too busy posing to bother recognizing her from the other night.

'Absolutely under control. We'll have this lot checked out in no time. Just one thing, there's a surprise for you in the office.'

'A surprise?'

'Just someone I think you'll be pleased to see.'

Puzzled, Daisy slipped behind the reception desk and opened the office door. Could it be Simon? she wondered. A millisecond later, she brushed the thought aside. Course not. Why would he want to see me? she thought. After the complete and utter holy show I made of myself the other night? Yeah, OK, he had been really sweet all day yesterday, calling her room, coaxing her downstairs, making her laugh, but that was all probably because he felt sorry for her. And, of course, for his best friend Eleanor's sake. He's probably beating the door down to get away from Davenport Hall, and who could blame him?

Funny, but this disappointed her.

'Hello, darling.'

The one person, apart from Simon, who could put the beam back on her face.

'Portia!' Daisy flung herself at her big sister and almost sent her flying. 'I can't believe you're back! Oh, this is so fantastic; you're the best thing that's happened all bloody day. So how was the Big Apple? And where's Andrew?'

449

Portia gently released her grip and wearily sat down again. 'Not right now, OK? I'll tell you sometime, just not right now.'

Chapter Twenty-Eight

'You see? My premonitions always come out right, you know. I knew with absolute certainty that something was going to bugger up the wedding today. Whenever I wake up singing the theme tune to *Dallas*, I always know there's sure to be trouble ahead.' Lucasta was plonked at her piano in the Long Gallery, happily entertaining anyone who was hanging around or hadn't checked out yet, namely Eleanor, Robert, Simon, Daisy and a few other wedding guests who were quite happy to stay on in the luxurious surroundings of the Hall for one extra night.

'Shame ya didn't ring Ladbroke's and stick a bet on then, ya roaring eejit,' said Mrs Flanagan, who was over at the bar with Shelley-Marie, still in their wedding clobber and helping Gorgeous George to keep everyone's drink freshened. It was wild and stormy outside and the Long

451

Gallery was cosy and snug, with a huge log fire crackling away at the far end of the room.

Eleanor particularly was in great spirits, laughing and joking with Simon and Daisy. The only time she betrayed herself with the merest hint of a blush was when Jasper came bounding into the room with, of all people, Buffy Tompkinson in tow.

He made a beeline for Daisy and winked at the others surreptitiously. 'Come here to me, young one,' he said to her with a glint in his twinkly blue eyes. 'Do you remember I said I had a bit of a surprise for you? Well, here it is. Or rather, here she is.'

Daisy looked incredulously from Jasper to Buffy and for a split second thought: oh Jesus, don't tell me they're a couple? Could this day get any weirder?

Led by Jasper, Buffy then tottered the length of the Gallery in her impossible high heels to where Mrs Flanagan was standing behind the bar. With someone else who'd far rather never have set eyes on her again.

'Shelley-Marie! It's so good to see ya, darlin', look at you, you look a million dollars! You're just like Madonna, you are, a mistress of reinvention. Well, well! Aren't ya going to give your old flatmate a great big hug? Don't ya recognize me then, love? It's me, it's your old mate Buffy!'

There was a silence broken only by the tinkling of ice in Lucasta's gin and tonic.

'Oh, I am looking forward to having a good old catch-up then.' Buffy hauled herself up on to a bar stool and settled herself down. She seemed totally oblivious to the fact that Shelley-Marie was glowering at her like something nasty she'd just trod on. 'When I first met Shelley-Marie, she was already famous, ya know,' Buffy kept chattering as she helped herself to a glass of champagne, 'and I was the unknown, if ya could believe that. You'd starred in, what was it called again?'

She shot an enquiring glance over at her old flatmate, who made absolutely no attempt whatsoever to enlighten her, but just stared ahead, with her smile set firmly in place.

'Oh, now I remember!' Buffy went on, loving that Jasper and Daisy, not to mention a roomful of other people, were hanging on her every word. 'You played the lead in *In Diana Jones and the Temple of Poon*. Yeah, that was it.'

'I saw that,' Jasper interrupted. 'It was our Friday night movie for a whole month when I was inside. I knew I'd seen your face somewhere before. Never forget a face.'

Shelley-Marie flashed an automatic smile at him, but her eyes remained like slits of pure white rage.

'Oh, but then we went on to make dozens of movies together, didn't we, love?' Buffy chirruped on, happily knocking back her champagne. 'All the classics, we done. *Shitty Shitty Gang Bang, Good Will Humping, Glad He Ate*

Her, Lord of my Ring, A Tale of Two Titties. And you were always such a good actor, with all those accents you could do? Mind you, the one you're putting on now is pretty good and all, isn't it? You'd never, ever think you were from Boston. Not in a million years.'

'Thank you for reminding me, Buffy. I think you've made your point now.' Shelley-Marie's voice cut like ice. 'It was mighty nice to see you'all again, but I think we really should be getting back to the Salon. I promised my darlin' Mrs Flanagan a full leg wax and I sure do hate to disappoint the elderly.' She rose and was about to go when Jasper stopped her.

'One more thing before you go.' Then, turning back to Buffy, he said, 'I reckon now's as good a time as any.'

Buffy put her drink down and shook her head theatrically, an actress whose moment had come. 'Poor old Isabelle's been calling me night and bleeding day, so she has. She's worried sick about ya, Sheldon. Wants to know when you're coming home.'

'Sheldon?' asked Daisy, on the edge of her seat as Shelley-Marie turned as white as was possible under the thick layer of false tan she was wearing.

'Oh sorry, you see when I met Shelley-Marie first, it was before the operation, so I knew her as Sheldon, didn't I, love? But I'm still great mates with his— Oh sorry, I mean *her* wife, Isabelle. Well, why would I let a little fing like you having a sex change get in the way of a good friendship? I mean, what's a bit of gender identity disorder between friends?'

Ten minutes later, Daisy almost skipped up to the bar, feeling that the weight of the world had been lifted from her shoulders. She was just about to shout in her order to Gorgeous George when Buffy sidled up. Impulsively, Daisy hugged her. 'I really don't know how to even start thanking you for helping us out like this,' she said. 'As far as I'm concerned, you're an angel come from heaven.'

'Oh, it's all right, love,' said Buffy. 'She's not the worst, old Sheldon, I mean Shelley-Marie. I don't blame you a bit for really thinking she was a woman. That surgeon worked miracles. The only giveaway is all them scarves she wears to cover her Adam's apple. But I gotta tell you, she has got a heart of gold, you know. And she's a decent old skin, really. Apart from the bigamy I mean. Isn't it funny, though, that your old dad never twigged she was a post-op.'

Daisy winced at the thought. Given the state Blackjack was probably in, it was a small wonder he never copped on. 'He passed on shortly after they got married,' was all she said.

'Just as well. The shock woulda probably killed him anyway, wouldn't it? But I really just wanted to see if you were OK, love, after what happened at the party after the match.'

Daisy looked at her, wondering what the state of play

455

was between her and Alessandro. 'It'll take me a while to get over it,' she answered.

'Mark and Alessandro are just a pair of boyos, that's all. They both love a bit, if ya know what I mean.'

Daisy couldn't help herself. 'But isn't Alessandro your boyfriend? Doesn't it bother you that he jumped into bed with me that night?'

'No, not really, love. How do you fink I met him in the first place?'

Meanwhile, Jasper was still at the bar, talking to a very shell-shocked Shelley-Marie. 'The way I see it now,' he was patiently explaining, 'there's an easy way to do this and there's a hard way. The easy way is a bit like this. You say nothing and we say nothing to no one about anything. You just pack your bags and leave the Hall and go back to your wife, or not as the case may be, and that's an end to all this, with no questions asked. The hard way isn't quite as pleasant for you, I'm sorry to say. We're talking about dragging in the cops, not just in this country, but in the States too, and there'd be a whole lot of crap bandied about, making life awkward for all of us, but mainly yourself, I'm afraid. Bigamy on top of a same-sex marriage is a felony in the state of Nevada, just the same as it is here, and I can tell you from bitter experience that life inside would most definitely not be for you. So what do you choose?'

With her highly developed sense of survival,

Shelley-Marie naturally chose the former and the deal was done.

'Well, who'd have thought it,' said Lucasta, who'd been glued to the unfolding drama like it was a double episode of *EastEnders*. 'Shelley-Marie is really a man! Blackjack married a bloke! Oh how funny, darlings. Do you know, I think I'll pop round and visit his remains in the Mausoleum tomorrow and maybe leave out a nice bottle of whisky and a deck of cards for the old bollocks. As a thank you for giving me the best laugh I've had in years. The only thing I'm sorry about is that he bloody well went and died before he realized.'

At about the same time, a scene of a very different nature was unfolding. Exhausted, numb and still anaesthetized with shock, Portia had wearily driven back to the gate lodge.

Home.

She knew there would be a thousand things for her to do up at the Hall the next day but tonight she didn't care. All she wanted was to run a hot bath and then collapse into bed. She couldn't face seeing her mother or any of the staff or even sticking her head into the hooley that seemed to be in full swing in the Long Gallery as she was leaving the Hall . . . Everything could wait.

She'd deal with it all tomorrow, she thought as she slowly lowered herself out of the jeep. In fact, in a weird way, it was almost good that she was going to be so busy over the next few days. Amazing, she thought, how I can keep going at a time like this. The less time she had to think, the better.

The lodge was freezing cold as she opened the door, pitch dark and unwelcoming with that musty, stale smell that old houses get when they're not lived in. She sighed and hauled herself upstairs, switching on lights as she went. Anything to make the place feel a bit more like home. The winds were almost gale force by now and she was just about to switch on the heating, glad that the tiny lodge heated up quickly, when the lights of a car pulling up at the door outside made her jump.

She looked out the upstairs window and saw that it was a taxi.

Someone looking for directions to the Hall, she figured, probably coming to collect another would-be wedding guest who was anxious to get away from Lucasta and her squalling.

She was halfway down the stairs when the front door opened.

Andrew.

Chapter Twenty-Nine

If Joshua Byron-Smyth thought all his birthdays had come at once, what with the non-wedding being the biggest news story of the year, his luck was just about to go stratospheric. He and Liz had worked their asses off, painstakingly interviewing and photographing just about everyone they could about the sensational events of the past few hours. The only person who hadn't obliged, surprisingly, was Eleanor, who, when approached for an interview in the Long Gallery, only gave a demure 'no comment'. Not even brass-necked Joshua dared push his luck any further, as Jasper was glued to her side like a guardian angel-cum-bouncer and rose threateningly when they approached her as if to say: Ask her one more question and you and me will have to step outside.

So, delighted with the day's work, he and Liz were at

reception waiting to be checked out when who should come down the stairs but Mark Lloyd himself. He was wearing wraparound shades, even though it was pitch dark outside, and was just about to walk past them when Joshua, like the kamikaze pro that he was, leapt in.

'Mark? Hi, Mark! Just a very quick word if you don't mind. How are you feeling right now? Is it fair to say that you're absolutely devastated, bordering on suicidal? Do you think you and Eleanor will get back together again?'

Mark deliberately put his hand to his face so that Liz couldn't really get a decent shot. The last thing he needed was photos appearing of him looking dumped and dejected, slinking away from the Hall. JILTED GROOM headlines were something he could live without. What would that do for his image?

It was the next question though, which really sealed his destiny.

'Mark? How do you feel about what everyone is saying? That you never really deserved Eleanor Armstrong and that you'll probably end up on your own for a long, long time to come?'

Just then, as fate would have it, who came click-clacking down the oak staircase but a very dejected-looking Shelley-Marie, looking puffy- and red-eyed and dragging two very stuffed-looking suitcases behind her.

It was the 'on your own' comment that did it. How

much better would it look to be seen leaving the Hall with a statuesque, busty blonde lady in tow . . . ?

Mark was over to Shelley-Marie like a bullet. 'Here, let me give you a hand with those suitcases, love. They look far too heavy for a pretty lady like you to be carrying.'

'Why, that is mighty kind of you,' said Shelley-Marie, brightening up considerably.

'Where are you headed then?' Mark asked gallantly, fully aware that there was a battery of flashbulbs going off.

'I'm not rightly sure. Dublin, I guess.'

'My car's outside. Let me give you a lift.'

'Why, that is so sweet of you! Are you certain that I won't be inconveniencin' you at all?'

'It would be my pleasure,' said Mark, grinning at the cameras as he slipped his arm around Shelley-Marie's waist and helped her outside. 'Getting all this then?' was all he said as he passed by Joshua and Liz, absolutely delighted with himself.

'Portia, are you OK?' Andrew looked white-faced and red-eyed.

She said nothing.

'I know what you must have been thinking and I can't begin to tell you how sorry I am . . .' He gingerly reached out to touch her hand, but she snapped it back.

'Don't touch me,' she said, feeling as though she'd been electrocuted. 'How did you know to come here?'

'I was like a lunatic trying to figure out where you were, then I phoned the Hall and Daisy told me about the wedding being called off. I figured you'd gone straight to the airport and got a flight home so I followed you. I jumped on the next flight I could. Portia, you have to let me explain—'

'It's a bit late to start acting the caring husband now.'

He looked her straight in the face. 'Nothing happened. You have to believe me. We had a boozy lunch, I had way too much to drink and Lynn suggested we have some strong coffee back at the apartment. Then, like an idiot, I spilt coffee all over her. She suggested I have a lie-down and . . . well, you know the rest. That is the God-honest truth, Portia, you have to believe me.'

'Andrew, you've had over twenty-four hours to think up something. Is that honestly the best you can do?'

'Honey, I know how this sounds and I know you're angry and emotional right now—'

'DON'T call me honey.'

'Sorry, sorry. Look, I had too much to drink; I was exhausted and really missing you. And you had *left*. Yes, it was stupid of me to bring her back to the apartment, I shouldn't have got myself into that situation, but I wasn't thinking straight. I wasn't thinking at all.'

'So let me guess: Lynn threw herself at you? Pointed a

gun at your head and forced you into bed while she stripped off?' Portia's tummy was starting to heave. 'Supposing I hadn't come back from the Hamptons. Suppose I hadn't walked in when I did. What then? Would you have slept with her? Certainly looked like things were heading that way to me.'

'Let's stick to the facts. I didn't sleep with her. I didn't lay a finger on her. I know how it must have looked to you, but nothing happened between us.'

'Stop being such a corporate lawyer and let me give you a couple of facts. I find my husband in bed with a semi-naked woman prancing around our apartment in her underwear. What do you want me to do? Throw you a party?'

'Portia, I was drunk. I was lonely. I made one stupid – I admit it, one incredibly stupid – mistake in bringing her back there. But that was it. Why won't you just trust me?'

She wearily slumped into a tapestry chair in the tiny hall as Andrew kept pressing his point home, about how much he loved her, how unimportant Lynn was, how guilty he felt for neglecting her the way he had done in New York and how he'd make any sacrifice, absolutely anything, even if it meant giving up Globex and the case and Macmillan Burke just so he could be with her and sort this out and blah blah blah.

You've hit the nail on the head, she thought. It's about trust. In spite of herself, she found herself actually believing Andrew that, most likely, nothing had happened. After all, she knew only too well what a predator Lynn was and even found herself suspecting her of orchestrating the whole thing. And then, how was Andrew to know that Susan wouldn't have walked in on top of them? He was the type of guy who women always flirted with and ninety-nine per cent of the time he never even noticed. The sort who would be utterly blind to the wiles of Lynn and her kind.

But the trust thing wouldn't go away.

She thought about Jennifer. All alone in that beach house while her husband led a bachelor life in the city . . . was that how her life would pan out? Would she end up another lonely, neglected, desperate housewife? The long working hours he put in, she could endure. The separations, she could endure. If she could trust him.

After a time, she found herself concentrating on her other news . . . You don't deserve me, she thought, looking at him dispassionately. And you don't deserve to know about the baby, at least not yet. You're going to have to start all over again if you want me back. You're going to have to earn me and earn my trust, right from scratch. Show you're good enough. Prove yourself.

She found her gaze falling on a small framed photograph on the hall table. It was one of Lucasta, taken on the night of the launch party, standing proudly at the bar looking like she'd built it herself. Well, I know exactly what you'd do, Mum, she thought, smiling and suddenly feeling elevated.

'Andrew,' she said, interrupting him.

'Yes?'

'Would you do one thing for me?'

'Anything. Whatever you want. Name it.'

'Would you just go? Please?'

'What?'

'You heard me. I'm sorry, but I can't be around you right now. Maybe never. I honestly don't know. You've hurt me so badly.'

'I'll do whatever you want, you know that. Whatever it takes to sort this.'

'Andrew, it's not that simple. This isn't something that can be magically put back together again. I just—' She broke off, thinking: I just what? 'I need time.'

'I'll wait.'

Thankfully, back in the Long Gallery, the evening was progressing a little better. Over by the tall sash window, Eleanor was snuggled into the window seat, cradling a hot port while Jasper stood protectively beside her. They were deep in conversation about a production of *The Cherry Orchard* playing in Dublin, which was attracting more than its fair share of controversy as it was set on the Blasket Islands.

'I'd never be bothered going to see a Chekhov play,'

Jasper was saying. 'Load of moany women looking out windows and whingeing that they want to go to Moscow? If I was directing *The Cherry Orchard*, now, I'd cut it right down to a one-act play. I'm not joking, I've seen episodes of *Take the High Road* that were far better. First rule of theatre, Eleanor, thou shalt not bore.'

'That's such a shame,' she said.

'Why's that?'

'Just that I have two tickets for the closing-night show and I was wondering if you'd like to come.'

'Are yis watching this or what?' said Mrs Flanagan to Lucasta and Robert as the three of them sat companionably around the piano.

Robert just nodded, ever the diplomat.

'Now, you mustn't worry the teensiest bit about our Jasper,' Lucasta said to Robert, cracking her fingers in preparation for another song. 'Just because of his felonious past, I mean. He's a sweet, lovely darling of a man, even if he did do a ten-year stretch. And he was a prisoner of conscience really, you know. He was just in the wrong place at the wrong time, do you see.'

Robert laughed.

'What's so funny?'

'Just look at her,' said Robert proudly. 'Eleanor is meant to be on her way to Heathrow airport as we speak and then on to Bali. Mrs Mark Lloyd. But I don't think I've ever seen a happier-looking girl who just left a man at the altar, have you? I think this evening she seems to be in exactly the right place at the right time, don't you?'

Eleanor did indeed look glowing. Radiant. You'd almost say carefree.

'Anyway, I have something I must ask you lovely ladies,' he went on. 'I know how shocked you both are about, well, about the departure of your former friend.' Not even Robert's legendary tact could find a discreet way to say, 'who married your ex-husband then shacked up here, ingratiating herself with each of you and subsequently turned out to be a post-op transvestite.'

'Who'd have thought it,' said Mrs Flanagan sadly, staring into space. 'I'll miss her – I mean, him, terrible. We had a great laugh together and . . . AH JAYSUS!'

'What?' said Lucasta. 'Have we run out of drink?'

'No, I just remembered. Shelley-Marie did a bikini-line wax on me the other day . . . fucking hell. I could die with the mortification.'

'Your bikini line? A sight that has driven strong men to distraction,' sneered Lucasta, who was adopting a far more easy-come-easy-go attitude to Shelley-Marie's departure.

'Anyway, ladies,' Robert went on, unused to the way the pair of them could bicker with each other one minute and be the best of friends the next. 'The thing is, you see, I'm hosting an ambassadors' ball at Phoenix Park House next week and I was wondering if you'd both like to come. It's the least I can do after all the bother my family has caused you.'

'Oh goodie,' squealed Lucasta, who loved a good boozy late night out more than anything. 'Will there be Ferrero Rocher?'

'Ah, shut up,' said Mrs Flanagan. 'More to the point, will there be diplomats there?'

'Some, I'm afraid.'

'And yer going to let Lucasta loose on top of them? Jaysus, we'll be lucky if a third world war doesn't break out. She *is* a weapon of mass destruction, ya do know that, don't ya, luv? I'm only telling ya so ya know what yer letting yerself in for.'

Meanwhile Daisy was at the bar, happily chatting away to Simon and feeling better than she had done in days. 'I'll tell you one thing,' she was saying. 'Jasper calls me the last of the great romantics but he's dead wrong. After this experience, I am totally changing my whole belief system. Movie love only exists in Hollywood. Romance is just something that's peddled to us in chick flicks.'

'Go on,' said Simon, looking at her, intrigued.

'And I'll tell you something else. The last few weeks have proved to me that my judgement of men is totally up my own arse.'

'Because you thought Mark Lloyd was a wee sweetie who gave to charity and slept with birds and pet mice lulling him to sleep like in a Disney cartoon?'

'Yes.' She was giggling again. The accent . . . 'But I'll tell you another thing. I don't think I'd know a genuinely nice guy if he danced naked in front of me. I solemnly vow never again to trust my own judgement. I never want to be a pushover for any guy who just thinks he can have me like that.'

'Do go on,' he said, 'I feel like I'm having a chat with Emmeline Pankhurst.'

'You may laugh, Simon, but from here on in, things are going to be very different in my love life. No more Miss Pushover. No more Miss Sucker for any guy who just happens to give me a bit of attention. Any bloke I date from now on will be put through the most painstaking interview process. And I'll want references from all of his exes and my sensible sister will have to give him the thumbs-up before I'll as much as have a drink with him.'

'Anything else?'

'Oh, and Mummy will have to do an energy clearing on him.'

'Phew! That it then?'

'Yip, think so.'

'Shame.'

'Why?'

'Because I was going to ask you out on a movie date this weekend. The slogan outside your local cinema really made me want to go there. "The Ballyroan Grand. It's either this or else drive forty miles to the multiplex in

Liffey Valley". I have to go there purely because it is the most honest advertizing slogan I have ever seen in my life.'

Daisy looked at him, reddening. 'I'm sorry, did you just invite me out? For real?'

'Hey, but if you'd rather stay home to read Emily Dickinson poetry, I totally understand.'

'Thought you'd never bloody ask.'

'Really?' He looked genuinely surprised. Surprised and delighted.

'Well, you were my knight in shining armour the other night, weren't you? I'd be a right ungrateful cow for turning you down.'

'You see? You're prepared to go out on a date again. Now that is what I call the triumph of hope over experience. Maybe you really are the last of the great romantics.'

Epilogue

Six months later

The Davenport Country House Hotel now boasts a waiting list of at least two months even to get a reservation, ever since it was awarded a Michelin star, the only hotel outside the greater Dublin area to have merited one. As Andrew once confidently predicted, it is the hottest ticket for miles and is fully booked out for weddings until early in 2008. Tim is thrilled, the bank managers are thrilled and, to this day, Molly continues to open doors with her elbows and berate guests for leaving dirty footprints on the marble floors.

Jasper now works there as duty manager and regularly meets up with Eleanor for theatre dates, although, in his wildest dreams, it never occurs to him that he might stand a gnat's fart of a chance with her. 'Sure, why would a woman like that as much as look sideways at the likes of me?' he says to Lucasta every time she teases him, which is every time she's pissed. Eleanor still continues to call him and, in her own gentle way, is making slow but steady inroads. As she says to Daisy, whom she sees regularly, 'It's a case of how long it takes for water to wear away a stone. Just watch this space.'

Lucasta and Mrs Flanagan, meanwhile, dutifully trooped off to the ambassadors' do in Phoenix Park House and, true to form, made a complete show of themselves. At one point, a drunken Lucasta berated the Jordanian ambassador for being an oily git and there was almost a diplomatic incident when they were told that, although this was a private residence, they'd still have to go outside for a cigarette, same as everyone else.

'Fuck this,' needless to say, had been their joint re-action. Relations between Phoenix Park House and Davenport Hall were almost completely broken off after that night, when the pair of them were found to have hijacked the Italian ambassador's CD number-plated car and driven it all the way home. 'At least we can have a fag in the car, where it's nice and cosy,' had been Lucasta's reasoning. Even Robert's patience and politeness had been well and truly exhausted at this point, although he is very fond of Jasper and, sources say, is even thinking of offering him a job as his personal protection officer.

Both Lucasta and Mrs Flanagan have, to everyone's relief, a new fad to occupy them and keep them well out of harm's way. Lucasta has recently embraced the Kabbalah with a vengeance and now drags poor Mrs Flanagan to meetings of the Kildare branch in Newbridge once a month. Mind you, the pair of them rarely get beyond Shaughnessy's bar on the main street.

'But that's not the point,' as Lucasta firmly says. 'We're on a spiritual quest for enlightenment and there's nothing like a nice g. and t. to open the chakras, I always say. And we both have these lovely cottony bracelets to show for it too, you know.'

On a different note, Daisy has now been happily dating Simon for the past few months and they've just gone off to Mexico on holiday together. They both really needed the break; Daisy having worked harder that she'd ever done in her whole life, now that she's been promoted to a fully fledged hotel manager, and Simon badly needing to recover from the stresses of the Oldcastle season. The main stress being Mark Lloyd, who had his worst season yet, being plagued with injuries and blaming it all on Simon. Although the hounding he received from the press when it came out that the 'rebound girl' he was seen leaving his own aborted wedding with was, in fact, a post-op transsexual, did very little to improve his performance either. On or off the pitch.

Simon and Daisy, who does a very good impression of him, just laugh at him behind his back and plot how they can get Eleanor together with Jasper. According to Simon, she's knickers mad about him, the trouble being that Jasper remains utterly oblivious. The type of guy who would barely notice that a woman fancied him, short of her dancing naked in front of him singing 'take me now'.

There was only one slight hiccup on their outward journey. While waiting on a connecting flight at Newark airport, they were sitting at a Starbucks café, when who should come clickety-clacking her stiletto-heeled way in. She was wearing the Continental Airlines stewardess's uniform and was with a gaggle of other air hostesses but there was no mistaking her. The big hair, the inch-thick pan-stick make-up, the lip gloss: it was definitely Shelley-Marie.

'Holy mother,' said Simon, 'is that who I think it is? And do you think she's on her way to a cross-dressing convention or what?'

Daisy giggled, but just then, Shelley-Marie turned from the counter and spotted her. A moment of recognition passed, where each saw the other but neither said anything. Wordlessly, Shelley-Marie picked up her overnight wheelie bag and swished out of the coffee shop.

'She was staring right at you,' said Simon. 'I was afraid there'd be a cat fight.'

'Most definitely not,' replied Daisy, smiling up at him. 'Just let her go.'

'Thank God for that. The size of her? She'd have beaten seven kinds of shit out of me.'

As for Andrew, he was as good as his word. He went back to New York, finished the Globex case and then, much to everyone's surprise, turned down Macmillan Burke's incredibly generous offer to stay on in New York on the grounds that his wife was pregnant and his place was with her. In Davenport Hall. More precisely, in the gate lodge, where he's now living, whilst Portia has temporarily moved back into the Hall proper. The official reason is that, now that she's big and blooming, it's better for her and the baby to rest up in the Mauve Suite, being pampered and waited on by Tim and Molly and all the staff. Only what she deserves, having worked so hard for so long, everyone says.

And if there were a few raised eyebrows at her living separately from her husband, Portia didn't care.

'If I didn't know better, madam,' Molly often remarks to her, 'I'd say that you and Andrew are more like boyfriend and girlfriend than husband and wife. Another dinner date again tonight! It's like he's courting you all over again.'

Portia smiled.

'And do you think you'll move back into the gate lodge then, madam? After the baby's born, I mean?'

'We'll just have to see, Molly. Just wait and see.'

THE END

REMIND ME AGAIN WHY I NEED A MAN?
By Claudia Carroll

Ever since she was a little girl, all Amelia Lockwood has ever wanted is to get married. The Tiffany ring, the Vera Wang dress, the Jordan-style tiara . . . the whole shebang. The car, the gorgeous flat and three fabulous friends only go so far in consoling her now that she's thirty-seven and still not married.

So when Amelia hears about a course that promises she'll be saying 'I do' before the year is out, she jumps at the chance to enrol.

What Amelia doesn't realize is that a fundamental principle of the course is that you need to revisit all your past relationships to work out where you went wrong. In single-minded pursuit of her ultimate goal Amelia gets in touch with every ex-boyfriend she's ever had – right back to age sixteen – with some surprising results!

059305539X

COMING IN SEPTEMBER FROM BANTAM PRESS

BANTAM PRESS

HE LOVES ME NOT . . . HE LOVES ME
By Claudia Carroll

In the heart of County Kildare is Davenport Hall –
a crumbling eighteenth-century mansion house, ancestral
home to Portia Davenport, her beautiful younger sister Daisy
and their dotty, eccentric mother, Lucasta. Disaster strikes
when their father abandons the family, cleaning them out of
the little cash they had managed to hold on to. But a ray of
hope appears when Steve Sullivan, an old family friend and
confirmed bachelor, suggests that they allow the hall to be
used as the location for a major new movie.

So Davenport Hall is taken over by the *crème de la crème*,
including the self-centred Montana Jones, fresh out of rehab
and anxious to kick-start her career, and Guy van der Post,
a major sex symbol with an eye for Daisy. Throw in Ella
Hepburn, Hollywood royalty and living legend, and soon
there's more sex and drama off-camera than on!

'IT BUBBLES AND SPARKLES LIKE PINK
CHAMPAGNE. A HUGELY ENTERTAINING READ'
Patricia Scanlan

'HEARTWARMING AND WITTY. A WONDERFUL
DEBUT FROM IRELAND'S NEW ANSWER
TO JILLY COOPER'
Morag Prunty

'IT MADE ME LAUGH OUT LOUD'
Anita Notaro

'FABULOUS FUN – A SPARKLING DEBUT'
Kate Thompson

0553816640

BANTAM BOOKS

THE WWW CLUB
By Anita Notaro

THE WOMEN WATCHING WEIGHT CLUB

Luckily, you're not literally what you eat because otherwise Pam would be a hamburger, Ellie a sausage, Maggie a doughnut and Toni a sushi roll. Together they form the WWW Club.

Every woman needs a WWW club in her life – how else would you get to moan about men, absorb the nasty details of detoxing or hear how your latest accessory has, in fact, just gone out of fashion. All while scoffing chicken korma and drinking beer without the slightest trace of guilt, fully intending DEFINITELY to start again tomorrow.

The WWW Club – a tale of calories, gossip, laughter, a little romance . . . and the enduring power of female friendship.

'FULL OF GIRLIE FUN . . . KEEP THE TISSUES AT THE READY'
Company 'Must-buy book'

0553816845

BANTAM BOOKS

A SELECTED LIST OF FINE NOVELS
AVAILABLE FROM BANTAM BOOKS

81400 1	THE HOUSE OF FLOWERS	Charlotte Bingham	£6.99
81592 X	THE MAGIC HOUR	Charlotte Bingham	£6.99
40615 9	PASSIONATE TIMES	Emma Blair	£5.99
40373 7	THE SWEETEST THING	Emma Blair	£5.99
81664 0	HE LOVES ME NOT . . . HE LOVES ME	Claudia Carroll	£6.99
81394 3	MIRACLE WOMAN	Marita Conlon-McKenna	£5.99
81368 4	THE STONE HOUSE	Marita Conlon-McKenna	£6.99
81396 X	SUMMER ISLAND	Kristin Hannah	£5.99
81397 8	DISTANT SHORES	Kristin Hannah	£5.99
81625 X	DIARY OF A C-LIST CELEB	Paul Hendy	£6.99
81726 4	WILD ABOUT HARRY	Daisy Jordan	£6.99
50486 X	MIRAGE	Soheir Khashoggi	£6.99
81186 X	NADIA'S SONG	Soheir Khashoggi	£6.99
40730 9	LOVERS	Judith Krantz	£5.99
17505 X	SCRUPLES TWO	Judith Krantz	£5.99
81641 1	ANGY HOUSEWIVES EATING BON BONS	Lorna Landvik	£6.99
81731 0	WELCOME TO THE GREAT MYSTERIOUS	Lorna Landvik	£6.99
81337 4	THE ICE CHILD	Elizabeth McGregor	£5.99
81604 7	LEARNING BY HEART	Elizabeth McGregor	£6.99
81251 3	SWAN	Frances Mayes	£6.99
81477 X	BACK AFTER THE BREAK	Anita Notaro	£5.99
81684 5	THE WWW CLUB	Anita Notaro	£6.99
81391 9	TWO FOR JOY	Patricia Scanlan	£6.99
81401 X	DOUBLE WEDDING	Patricia Scanlan	£6.99
81577 6	A PERFECT LIFE	Kate Thompson	£5.99
81578 4	LIVING THE DREAM	Kate Thompson	£6.99
81372 2	RAISING THE ROOF	Jane Wenham-Jones	£6.99

All Transworld titles are available by post from:
Bookpost, PO Box 29, Douglas, Isle of Man, IM99 1BQ
Credit cards accepted. Please telephone +44 (0)1624 677237,
fax +44 (0)1624 670923, Internet http://www.bookpost.co.uk
or e-mail: bookshop@enterprise.net for details.
Free postage and packing in the UK. Overseas customers: allow
£2 per book (paperbacks) and £3 per book (hardbacks).